LUKE
TAYLOR

Vault of Dreams
First edition
Copyright © 2016 by Luke Taylor
Cover by Rena Hoberman
All Rights Reserved
ISBN 10 0-9906249-5-1
ISBN 13 978-0-9906249-5-0

Other works by Luke Taylor
Evening Wolves
The Quiet Kill
Shatterpoint Alpha
The Muiread

What is life? An illusion, a shadow, a story, and the greatest good is little enough: for all of life is a dream, and dreams themselves are only dreams.

-Pedro Calderon de la Barca

We all have our time machines, don't we. Those that take us back are memories...And those that carry us forward, are dreams.

-H.G. Wells

To Mom, who read fantasy stories to me as a child

And to Katerina, who inspired me to write this one

VAULT OF DREAMS

AERLYN

CHAPTER 1

If there was a world within a world, it was the dream of distant lands that slept inside a young girl's mind, gilt by the passion of a heart that would be forever bigger than the body that held it.

Every night, counting the rocks on the seashore as the sea swallowed the sun, Aerlyn was that young girl, until the sunsets washed away every hope of leaving Nochgull and the dead eddies of Elgan Firth.

Years bobbled like broken fishing boats as Aerlyn grew, tottering through the tides of time, with only the wind and the sea and the rocky paths of the little stone houses dotting the hillside to whittle away that undying dream.

And though the band of freckles stayed put across her face, the short shock of red hair blossomed into sheets of dark auburn, and wide sky-blue eyes that brightly hoped in the good of the world narrowed to dusky paint-brush flicks of midnight. Rosy cheeks too often pinched by the village matriarchs had hardened to smooth alabaster stone. Clumsy legs and limbs had leaned to lithe willows and reeds.

Even the name, Aerlyn, spoken with the warmth of great promise on the lips of the Elders, had all but vanished with the whistling summer wind its lyrical speaking summoned.

Because Aerlyn O'Rye, only daughter of the Mason before Plague took his wife and his two sons, was no longer the summer rose and beloved darling of Nochgull's small and complacent embrace.

The bitter highland winds, colliding with the hopeless neverend of the sea, had stripped soft petals in bloom.

And a Thistle had grown in its place.

The street, twisting through the broad town of Brachin, so named for the boggy spider's web of brambles and thorns stretching around its timber walls for miles, hummed with all the livery and chaos of the Summer Solstice. Days from its celebration, the timbers were swollen to the rafters with the great ingathering of wanderers and surrounding farmers and laborers alike, all eager to revel till they fell where they stood. Travelling salesman hawked their wares, shouting themselves hoarse, and the aromas of every sort of food under the sun snagged the hungry and thirsty as they drifted through, but a small temptation to the promise of much more if lodging was secured at their respective inn by two clinks of silver.

Aerlyn, eating a somewhat flavorless apple, watched the colorful procession of foolishness with a hawk's gaze from her perch along the parapet of the timber wall. Dragging around the town of Brachin like some misshapen circle, the wall had its moments of shadow and shade, and Aerlyn's perch was hidden from the merchant guards and the strongmen of the rich by the dark angles of the shanties, stacked on top of each other as if they were about to fall.

Picking a pithy bit of apple from her teeth and mashing it between her fingers before flicking the hard green skin over the wall with her thumb, Aerlyn weighed the prospects of her perch, and its safety concerning her business in Brachin.

The Thistle was not in town for the Solstice.

Aerlyn's cold blue gaze drifted up to the sky and the heat of the sun, trickling sweat down the back of her long neck as she stood in the shadows in her brown cloak.

In a collection of uncloaked denizens, sleeves rolled up, faces bright and eager in the high heat, surely she would stand out to a pair of prying eyes eager for a copper penny, and the shanties, with their peepholes and slivered windows, were full of such wide eyes and empty hands.

But Brachin was no different than Kirkcade or Benyllyn, Picwith or Fordair.

Barraburr, Störhaven, Nairnsmoor.

They were all towns, and in towns there were faces, like fish in the sea, swimming and swimming and slapping up against one another in the frenzied haze of their own self-worth.

And The Thistle knew that worth.

To the penny.

For in all the towns there were pockets and pouches, strongboxes and chests so heavy it took four thick-shouldered men and long poles of oak just to move them an inch.

And faces washed wan and cold when they realized it was The Thistle that had emptied them all.

Night fell slowly, agitating Aerlyn O'Rye with shades of violet, and not the deep black her dark art craved. On the shores of the sea, Aerlyn had learned to embrace the black of night, the cold loneliness of it, tripping and falling on the rocks with no one to hear her cry, and no one to pick her up and staunch the bleeding of elbows, hands and knees.

And then, in the highlands, unbroken and unbound, the black of night had been a howling mad sea of its own sort, not giving a damn about her as she clawed an existence from its emerald shoulders and broom-swept fists.

Scraping the dirt from her nails, she counted the paces of the merchant guards once again, though the number hadn't changed since the last time.

Former soldiers, she thought, jaw clenched tight as the light of the moon kissed her alabaster skin with an eerie glow. *Proper soldiers, not fat militiamen that march for malt ale and a loaf of bread.*

A shiver skittered along her left arm and she rubbed it out, her grip pausing softly on the sour bruise that still colored the back of her arm shades of the night sky above.

A small reminder of Murnamoor, not two days ago.

And though no wind stirred the breadth of Brachin, the shiver slipped up her shoulder and around her neck, like a Highborn's unwanted shackle of lace in a pre-arranged marriage.

Some towns were easier to forget than others.

The high whinny of a horse ripped her from painful reminiscence and snapped her vision to the left. And not a moment too soon. Aerlyn stepped back into the narrow alley as a group of merchant guards trampled forth with lanterns and pikes. Light glinted off steel and the hard lumps of cheeks, chins and fists.

And boots. Dirty boots. Dirty boots that wanted to grind their hardness into the small of her back and press the quick freedom of her wrists to the ground.

The Thistle dropped to a knee, midnight eyes keen to watch the shape of a man on a white and gray dappled horse, tall and stoic in the saddle, his own eyes peeled sharp and wide, though buried in the folds of a cloak somehow made elegant by his posture, and the beautiful horse upon which he sat.

"Two of you over there, by the blacksmith." He said, his voice just on the edge of hearing. "And one in that alley that runs between the whorehouses."

The Thistle rose to her feet, the bruise on the back of her left arm beginning to ache. She may've heard just the edge of the man's voice but she hadn't so soon forgotten it.

And the blasphemous oath it had spit upon the wind as she escaped with but the nasty bruise to her name.

So we meet again, faceless one. Aerlyn thought, dissolving into the shadows. *May it be the last time.*

And then, the only wind in the night was a heavy sigh, spilling across the garnet slash of her lips, lost in the swish of a brown cloak swaying in darkness.

CHAPTER 2

Making her way through the musty-smelling and half-emptied stables of *The King's Cloud*, Aerlyn sawed the distance between the blacksmith and the tangled knot of whorehouses in half by vaulting the broken crumble of an unmended wall and skipping across a graveyard of empty barrels. Their rims tottered and creaked to take her graceful weight and height, threatening to spill at the slightest mistake with a thundering crash.

Free of the acrobatic gamble, she advanced through a twisting side-street and stretched out her senses to hear the muffled smacks of boots in mud. Near to crossing Brachin's prime thoroughfare, the danger of being spotted had already put her heart to thumping. The zip of lightning in the sky was already in her blood, the want of the take tingling her fingertips. It wasn't so much the footmen she was worried about. No, their flat-fronted minds were on their own stomachs more than what darted in the darkness two feet from their very noses.

It was the man on the horse. He was dread on shod hooves, a skilled bountyman who could smell greed on the wind.

Wherever he'd gone to.

Just outside *The King's Cloud*, Aerlyn O'Rye *was* that darkness, passing through the breadth of the wide thoroughfare as nothing more than a sniffle or a cough, causing one merchant guard to look at the other with the wry confusion Aerlyn savored in a smile all her own as the darkness swallowed her once again. Re-adjusting their shiny helms and pointing their pikes to the sky, the pair trundled off toward the city gates, where more lanterns were being lit, as if sealing the town from Plague.

The rot-stench quarry stone and plaster walls of the tannery beckoned Aerlyn O'Rye further from the roving net spread to capture her once and for all, and within minutes, she was free of the danger of the street, having woven a path impossible to follow.

Alone in a dead end, The Thistle cracked her knuckles, one at a time, midnight blue eyes casting a wary glance to the alley behind her and its loose trickle of clinks and clanks, indicators of noise lost in confusion.

Laughable, it was.

If the whole city wasn't fast asleep in the arms of revelry's mind-numbing rest, they'd feel it too. The agitation. The unease. The possessive need to wrap her in shackles and chains.

The dire hunger of the hunters released to hunt a rare and wild breed of game.

All hanging low and thick in the heavy summer air, spread across Brachin like a blanket.

But with such clumsy arms casting the net, it would be a breeze. The footmen, their stomachs rumbling, Solstice-only ale breath huffing and puffing to announce their presence a mile away if the racket of their plodding steps weren't enough. And the merchant guards, those housebred louses, standing too close to their lanterns to see anything in the dark.

Laughable!

And Aerlyn did laugh, if just in the narrowing of her eyes and the puff of her lips as she began to run down the dead end of the alley, deep into its darkest corner.

The sound of her leaping from the mud was nothing more than a slick squelch. Brickwork dug into the palms of her hands, already made rough by her lonely life in the highlands. The laws of the earth defied her leaping, her clinging and climbing, and she defied the laws of the earth right back with the grind of her teeth and the strain of her lithe arms. Soon the ground faded, steeply sloped rooftops taking their place, as did the itinerant sounds of the search for The Thistle.

It was at the first chimney in sight Aerlyn caught her breath from the strain of the climb, taking the time to re-examine what she could see of the merchant guard's patrol pattern along the triple-decked woodwork shoulders of the governor's house. If the moonlight could see her, it would've caught the unfiltered glee of the sun, passing through her smile at the nightmare maze of the governor's house.

After all, to The Thistle, there was no such thing as *architecture*.

Places to jab her hands and feet, to climb, to leap from, to skip and skirt.

Places to hide.

The man on the horse was Aerlyn's only concern, and the thought of hearing his voice again made her want to draw her knife. But up above it all, swift as Plague, Aerlyn could not sense his presence. It was as if he'd left the town. Rooftops faded underfoot, slopes melding and mixing into one another like a deck of gambler's cards spilled across the table.

Probably running circuits around the town, trying to flush me out. Aerlyn thought of the horseman, casting a glance over the wall. *Probably out there in the muck trying to set up traps like I'm a rabbit to the snares. Maybe he's even spent some of the reward money he thinks he'll get for capturing me by hiring extra watchers along the road, two steps ahead this time. Two towns ahead.*

Moonlight caught in small pools of stagnant wet around the thorns and brambles for what seemed like forever, until the dark lumps of the foothills swelled up to staunch the poisoned spread of fallow ground.

If it is that we meet again, should Destiny have it, he won't be the one to hurt me.

Because no man shall ever hurt Aerlyn O'Rye again. As long as The Thistle draws breath, no man shall touch her without thorns drawing blood.

But the promise slid down the dark well of Aerlyn's soul, for the roofline to the governor's house stood within arm's reach, and no divisive thoughts could be in her mind as she became silence itself.

Even though the promises of Aerlyn O'Rye were as good as the King's gold, and stronger than the steel of a thousand swords.

No small contortion maneuvered Aerlyn into the attic space of the governor's house by removing a lump of thatch and two boards. She'd been quick with the nails fastening the wood to the frame, removing them with the palm-sized crowbar from the canvas pouch at the small of her back, careful enough to protect her invaluable fingers from catching one of the rusty nails in the dark.

Once in the attic, she re-worked the sweeping folds of her cloak tightly around herself, becoming nothing more than a thin dark shape in form-fitting breeches and boots. Her auburn hair, pinned up in a bun, kept the hood of her cloak peaked to brim and shade her features to the middle of her nose with the anonymity that'd since made her the richest of thieves.

Navigating dusty lumps of overstock in the dark was never a perfect science, but Aerlyn managed to avoid any form of noise, feeling which floorboards were creaky and soft, and at times, slithered and slipped across sacks of seed grain withheld from royal tribute and legal parchments stating exactly the opposite.

Next to the trapdoor, Aerlyn listened for a short eternity before swinging it down, and sliding through the opening upside down to catch the pull rope with a pinch of her feet and close it behind her.

Tumbling to the floor planks with a thud that could've been mistaken for merchant guards on the prowl, Aerlyn somersaulted and stuffed herself in the south corner of the house's third floor.

Both halls were empty and unlit.

Aerlyn bunched forward, easing into full height as she broke into an easy lope.

Within seconds, two lefts and a right opened to an expansive landing; a set of concentric squares connected by steep staircases. Light from the ground floor at the base of the hollowed landing cast odd shadows up through slats of wood, stairs and railing, all twisted with scrollwork embellishment, and Aerlyn slowed upon reaching the railing. Four guards milled lazily on the ground floor, swords heavy in their scabbards, and on the second floor, two guards mumbled in conversation.

Across the landing from her, the governor's room awaited in the darkness of an elbow joint, and Aerlyn advanced slowly around the exposed corners of the square landing, gambling on the chance that no guard stood watch over the governor's room this night.

Revelry was in the air, the kind of the Solstice, and Aerlyn knew better than most the shackles of rich and powerful men were so often set with a woman's touch.

Even if that women was in chains herself.

And though Aerlyn O'Rye's heart pounded the dance of war drums set for battle along the mouth of the forest to fight thoughts of what capture this night of all nights with this mark of all marks would mean to her well being, Aerlyn reached the door to the governor's room undetected.

There, The Thistle swallowed all senses of excitement and dread, her face of alabaster cold and unfeeling as she knelt to pick the lock.

CHAPTER 3

The governor of Brachin was a fat man who could only sleep on his back, and the great mound of his stomach pulled a sibilant hiss from Aerlyn's mouth as she entered the room and shut the door.

Rise and fall, rise and fall, fools one and all, she thought, the mound under his unfortunately thin nightshirt working like some slow billows to a great furnace.

He was a disgusting creature, as they all were.

Rise and fall.

And fall.

FALL!!!

She dismissed the desire to plunge her knife into his heart and be done with it.

That was not her way.

So easy it would be, though, with the spring-loaded trigger mechanism up her left sleeve, the knife would only flick out with a twist and a swift nick across his neck would do the trick.

But Aerlyn denied the hatred, as always. It was the hatred that kept her silent, kept her senses as sharp as the blade stuffed up her left sleeve.

No matter *what* the rich and powerful of the realm did to their women, and the list of sins were great, Aerlyn would never take to killing them where they slept, like a butcher of hogs.

She was not a killer.

She was a thief.

And, there were punishments far worse than death. The toppling of their tall towers and the emptying of their gluttonous feasting tables. Like the slow onset of winter, their lives would shrivel and shrink till madness beset their bones. The drying of their wells and the fraying of their clothes. The loss of their companies of servicemen and the desertion of their armored guards.

And finally, the inevitable release of *their* women, their prisoners, their property.

All debasements of honor given where it should've been earned, and bought where it should've never been sold. Aerlyn knew that by removing their wealth, she was chopping their legs off so they wouldn't stand so tall, so proud.

They wouldn't stand on the backs of so many bodies.

For so many men in the land, title and prestige, if even a smattering of it, swelled the head like sea wind to the mizzenmast. Just as dogs with scraps and bones, the most vicious of them all, whether with tongue or fist, took charge of the weak-willed and yellow-bellied.

King of Fools, King of Snakes. Ruler of frozen winter and all its glittering snowflakes.

But in the end, the trickling down of this evil river led to the spineless governing the broken, and the hurting falling under the harsh hand of tribute.

It was the poor who were stolen from.

And so Aerlyn O'Rye, The Thistle of High Inverloch, was not a balancing weight upon the scales, not tipping them, not righting them, but savagely lifting her foot and kicking them over.

And not two steps in the room, the jingle of chains startled The Thistle, and reached out with a pair of eyes red from crying baleful tears, streaked with moonlight.

Aerlyn put a finger to her lips to shush but it was a trembling one, and dropped it down at her side as she advanced, cautiously, toward the fat man's bed and the heaving mound of a body caught in deepest sleep.

Next to the governor, chained to iron rings in the floor, five women sat in clasps around the hands and ankles.

Barely clothed and underfed, Aerlyn stared at them with a poisoned mix of emotion, black and bubbling like oil spit upon storm sea.

The buzz of her thieving wanted to twitch the knife loose and carve every woman's name in the fat man's forehead, but Aerlyn quickly crossed the room, now ten eyes on her, all of them stabbing icicles of ache and regret in her heart, to grab the keys for the girls, only to find it was the same key for the chest.

Property was, after all, property.

It took everything within her not to mutter, or curse, but to stay as silent as she would've been if her and the governor were the only two in the room.

And she crossed the end of the giant's bed, passing moonshadow. Still the heaving fatness, not so much as a stir.

Stay that way you beached walrus.

Soon she was at the chest, a great big beautiful oaken wonder of deepsea pearls and whorlshells, see-through quartz and pink peridine. Nørd amber of spiders and beetles and blood rubies that beat like a bird's heart with the heat of your hand, said to spell the future in the hands of the Faer.

Aerlyn worked quick and quiet with the key and the oaken chest before passing it to the nearest woman, not two feet away. They eyed her with the same amazement she eyed the chest as she opened it, colors gleaming urgent and needy for her touch, and she could feel their wishing they were her. That and the knowledge that she *was* The Thistle, come to life, not the cold witch of the barman's fables but someone as real as the newborn dawn. A woman, like them.

A woman who knew exactly what they felt.

Chest open, she found she couldn't take anything. Not with all the eyes staring at her.

And they did that, gazing with the sorrow of their life's curse, their hopeless bonds still sealed around their hearts, though iron no longer held them down.

Run! She wanted to scream, but to where would they run? Where were they from? Brachin itself? The shores of other lands? Imports, brought bound and broken in the bowels of bloody great ships?

Curse you riches, curse you golden devils and silver daemons!

Did their families even know they were alive? Did they even speak the common tongue of Albanland?

Run, like I did! Run until your feet bleed and the wind strips you naked! Sleep day and night in highland hovels with the howl of winter sharpening your hatred into a cold steel knife!

And the riches, she'd have no trouble passing them evenly amongst the girls. Curses, she would even resign to taking nothing away from Brachin but the pleasure of freeing them, but what trouble would come of such crippled souls handling the hot loot of the governor?

He would know, if even, in a million miracles, Aerlyn could get them *all* out of the house *and* the city, out from under the blurry gazes of thirty odd footmen and guards. The governor would know they had his precious treasures.

And it would only be a matter of time.

Especially with the bountyman on the gray and white horse in the governor's employ. Or even in the dangerous bountyman's *own* employ, clip-clopping the High Street from town to town, working for his own pleasure to hunt and capture and collect the reward. Surely he or one just like him would wrangle the girls up one by one. Heavens knew what dark tangles awaited their feet.

It would all come to naught.

But with those ten sad eyes staring back at her, as silent and sorrowful as stone-carved saints, Aerlyn turned her attention to the heavy oaken chest.

What the girls did was their own business.

The rubies whispered her name.

CHAPTER 4

Whether the shriek preceded or followed the falling of the knife, and the sound of flesh and blood giving way to steel, Aerlyn would never know.

Halfway done with the bird's heart rubies, stunned by what exquisite specimens they were, the room snapped into chaos as if all the winds of the Four Storms had rushed into the room.

Moonlight just wasn't enough to see clearly, and the five women, who were all roughly the same size, scattered about like dead leaves. Some spun in eddies, lost, others clung to the corners of the room, and one, her bravery fully spent, all but crumbled on top of the governor and the knife, as if holding onto to the twisted black knot of a winter-stripped tree root.

Aerlyn didn't know where it came from, probably his belt, tossed casually on the other side of the massive bed, but it was done, and Aerlyn cursed as she rounded up the girls and shoved them toward the window.

The window held great danger, yes, but danger was only a jaw to clamp the weak and slow in its teeth.

To the able-bodied, it was more of a game of chance. A blood-boiling race, like horses in full stride.

She felt their shivering cold and their confusion as she wrangled them and shoved them into the night, trying to cover their eyes from the spill of blood and the stain of white sheets.

Run, she told them, *down the deck and make a jump for the next roof.* She told them as if she was their war leader and they were her fearless soldiers unafraid to die. She thrust them out into the gross heat of the night, already clammy in the lungs, and trusted they would do it, like she'd done it when her chance came.

Footmen rumbled up the stairs, no small thunder scraping swords from scabbards and shouting enough curses to last a year. Aerlyn loathed facing them, but she counted the seconds. Chance was good on her as of late, bad with the violet-sky bruise now throbbing her left arm to death, but more good than bad, and she told herself she was ready to deal with a nasty streak of bad chance, no matter who was on the other end of it.

Even if it was the bountyman and his words of acid, his promises of keyless shackles, and his blasphemies of every god that had a name.

The bountyman, with his touch that sent shivers down her shoes.

Aerlyn finally spoke with what scant softness she could muster, approaching the girl who'd plunged the governor's own knife into his heart.

"You have to go now."

The girl only looked at Aerlyn, alabaster-faced Aerlyn O'Rye, The Thistle of High Inverloch, as if she'd seen a ghost. As if *she* was a ghost.

She couldn't have been older than fifteen.

"Please." Aerlyn added grit in her voice. Her bruise throbbed.

The girl swallowed, eyes stretching wider and wider till Aerlyn thought they would explode.

But they didn't. Scared out of her soul, the girl ran for the window.

Aerlyn knew she needed a quick distraction. In the moonlight, nothing stood out. Something, *anything* to take the frenzy from the girls escape.

Wondering if she could wedge it in the bottom of the door, Aerlyn took the knife from the governor.

It was then the footmen smacked through the door, lanterns casting murder across the room.

CHAPTER 5

The uneasy silence of three heartbeats held the distance between Aerlyn and her captors, bunched and coiled in the landing, the elbow, the doorway, the room. The lantern's hard angles split their faces with rage and punishments far from legal and Aerlyn took one look at the governor's own knife, its blade slick and red, stuck in her hand as if the whole thing had been her idea.

The knife clattered to the floor.

Shouts blurred in darkness, hands and swords swiping in vain. Lanterns spun to the floor with a shatter of glass and a splash of fire.

Aerlyn leapt through the window, bracing a foot on the multi-leveled deck that ran around the governor's house as she twisted and thrust every fiber of haste and strength into her leap and grabbed the lip of the roof.

Her feet disappeared just as two merchant guards spilled from the window, jabbing lanterns into the dense wash of the night. Muffled shouts died further on down inside the house.

Chaos was on the loose, unleashed like starving wolves in the wind.

Aerlyn was in full sprint, up and down the slope of the roof to skid its last two or three feet and fall into the arms the stable.

Hay bales breaking her fall, Aerlyn stuffed a scream back down her throat as her twisting had been to the left and not the right. Her arm jerked toward her ribs, her entire body stiffening up under the pain, constricting.

In that small moment, her feet didn't want to run anymore, and the thought of the pain that was in her arm making its way to other parts of her body just about convinced her to throw herself deep in the scratchy blonde bales and hide.

Must've used up all my good chance last year.

Rubbing the violet sore did no good as it was and Aerlyn bounced from the hay bales to work her way across the stables, though the broad expanse of the street not ten feet away urged her to grab an unsaddled horse and fly.

Senses stretched, The Thistle dodged down a pair of alleys, stopping ever so often to wonder which way the net was drifting, where the bountyman had gone to, and if the women made it out or not.

It was all madness. Surely the shouts of the guards had awoken every pair of prying eyes in the town.

How would the women get out now?

Four Storms send crows to pick clean my bones, The Thistle cursed, hasted possessing her feet.

Surely there was no way out this time.

And where was the bountyman and his gray white horse made of stone and fog? Of all the hands to grab her for good, his were the ones she dreaded.

Aerlyn bounded into a side street connecting common houses and inns with the more negligent of the merchant houses only to find her answer in spades.

Frozen by the clouds of white puffing from the hooded cloak, Aerlyn stared up into the darkness of the man's face and swore she saw him flinch as their gazes met.

By chance.

Damn *bad* chance.

Aerlyn crashed off down the street, feet barely touching the mud as the gray and white horse reared, its whinny piercing the night. It would be on her in seconds. Aerlyn was no horse. She was a human being. A twenty-year-old girl who'd run away from home. *Someday,* she knew. *Someday,* she always told herself, whether staring at her reflection in a rock pool of rain water or gazing longingly up into the sky as if it were longing itself that made one fly.

Someday it'll all catch up to you.

Already cursed by her knowledge of the town, Aerlyn weighed her chance in a flurry of arms and gluey lungs.

There *was* a way out.

But it would not be easy.

It was when the horse was so close to her Aerlyn thought the damn thing was going to trample her like a patch of broom along the highway that Aerlyn took the costly rubies from her cloak and scattered them in the air.

Distracted for the slightest second at the dazzling display, the bountyman pulled up on the reins, and his steely ghost of a horse reared in shrieking anger.

Fighting to stay in the saddle, the bountyman didn't expect to see the flash of steel slash through the corner of his gaze as his horse settled back to all fours. For a moment, his world upended, slipping and sliding across the broad back of the beast, until mud smacked him upside the face with a splat.

Footsteps slapped off to the left, and he pressed himself up to see darkness, near and far, darkness closing around his ears till he threw off his cloak and screamed for the footmen.

But pressed into the shadows at his back, Aerlyn waited in a tight cleft of a masonry, catching her painful breath till footmen stood thick in the street.

"She'll be going for the gate." The bountyman growled, rubbing the side of his face.

"She?" One of the guards questioned.

Aerlyn heard the slap of gauntlet on skin.

"Yes, she!" The bountyman snarled. "The Thistle's *not* a man, who gives a damn! Get to the gate, you dairy cow! Or I'll cut off your ears and feed them to you one at a time!"

The man ran off with a pair of guards in tow, and Aerlyn stilled herself to listen, as the bountyman gained composure, mastering his pain.

"Who was it?" He asked the three that remained. "She empty the Fränkish carver of his Madonnas? Or was it the Nørd traitor's cache of ambers?"

"N-No, Sir!" One of the chubby footmen stammered, not wanting to be slapped for being the bearer of bad news. Of deadly news. She could see him, huffing and heaving, ill-fitting helmet cocked to the side. "It was the governor! She killed him!"

Aerlyn could nearly feel the bountyman give the man a double-take and a squint that could kill. She swallowed, loudly in her own ears, her guts knotting together like the all the twisted ropes of a sea-bound caravel.

"What?"

"Yes Sir, saw it with me own eyes! The man's very own knife in his heart."

"She killed the governor?" Aerlyn's heart thumped through the pause, and her features soured at the nastiness streaking the man's voice. "Then her reward'll buy me Loch Darvin cast..."

But the bountyman never got to finish his statement.

For The Thistle had sprung out from the darkness, the cold steel of her knife pressed against his throat.

Something feral bubbled in the back of the bountyman's mind and just before he acted on it, Aerlyn's right hand snaked around to the front of his body and grabbed his manhood.

A peep squished from his cheeks, and the bountyman twisted in her grip, poking the knife into his own neck to draw the thinnest stream of blood before he froze completely, eyes wider than the full moon of Solstice.

"You want to live?" Aerlyn used her rough voice, the kind that sounded like mason stones sliding atop one another, the kind of voice she'd earned by screaming obscenities into the wind, learning the wind didn't give a damn.

Till the wind became her.

Nothing but more peeps and squeals. Airlessness possessed his lungs and whitened his sun-darkened face. Aerlyn squeezed harder.

"I asked you a question."

Across from him, the three remaining guards only stared, holding their pikes unevenly, as if stuck in a nightmare. One man even covered himself, face contorted to witness the white-knuckled pain. Behind Aerlyn the gray and white horse chuffed and clopped in a small circle, glad to be free of the saddle and the evil man who sat in it.

Quickly, taking the last of his composure to do so before he passed out and lumped to the mud, the bountyman nodded. Aerlyn's smile was a snarl, the bottom half of her face lit in moonlight and orange lantern wash.

She forced the man down to one knee and switched grips in a flash, catching the clasp of his sword belt and dropping it to the mud, laughing to herself that she shouldn't have. The bountyman who'd bruised her and hunted her for months before he'd come within the rough grasp of capturing her for good would be quite the unforgettable sight, walking all the way to the gate with his manhood viced in hands made strong by climbing and living life in the wild.

Aerlyn forced the man back to his feet, feeling sweat trickle down his skin.

He'd have to walk her out, as dangerous as that was, with size and numbers on his side, using him as a shield would be her only way to level the field.

So with her right hand completely choked around his neck, the knife switched to the base of his spine, where certainly, the threat of death tingled hot and sticky.

And though she hated to say it, she had to use what'd happened to her advantage.

Though it would damn her to hell.

"Walk me through that gate if you don't want to go the way of the governor."

"So…rubies weren't enough for you this time, *thief?*" The bountyman nearly whispered, pain having stolen his bravado, though his words were edged with the malice of class distinction. To him, Aerlyn was dirt. Brown ugly filth on the bottom of his boot. He wanted nothing more than to scrape her across a flat stone and be done with her.

You wouldn't believe the truth. Aerlyn's breathing tightened. *No one could. No one ever will.*

"Nothing to say for yourself now, *thief?*"

Aerlyn O'Rye only forced the brutal bountyman forward into the mud, shuffling the three footmen off to the side with the flick of her alabaster chin.

Knife-point pressed taut into his back, the promise of the bountyman's own death at her hand was as good as a confession.

Better than a confession.

And with the desperation of escape stretching before her like a sea storm shockwave, she couldn't think how hopeless the silence that had always been her friend now made her feel.

CHAPTER 6

It didn't matter how well Aerlyn knew the streets of Brachin because the gate was double barred with planks and chains and somehow, mystery of miracles, nearly twenty footmen and merchant guards had managed to stand dumbly in front of it as if the whole thing had been their idea.

Aerlyn swallowed, stepping slowly through the mud, knife-hand sticky with sweat.

"It's over." The bountyman said, having regained some of the thick timbre in his voice. "Give up now and I'll go easy on you."

What does that mean? You'll kill me?

"The moment I trust you is the moment the sea falls from the sky." Aerlyn only growled the ancient oath.

The bountyman chuckled, their steps all but stopping as more and more men gathered around the breadth of the street. From the left, the right. Even behind. Like bees come back to the hive, they were all staring at the queen stuck in the wrong pot of honey.

"You don't give up," The bountyman stopped, an oak taken root in the middle of the street. "And that bruise on your left arm'll be spit next to the one I'll put around your throat."

Aerlyn met the threat with a thud, and the man crumpled with a howl, only to shoot straight up again, his manhood bulging his eyes wide with agony.

"Open the gate or you'll be picking this man's eyes out of your teeth!" Aerlyn hollered in her rough highland swirl, catching a few of the men off guard. Perhaps the more savage of The Thistle's legends were on their mind, trumped up by the revelry of Solstice in which they'd had far more drinks than they should've, waddling on duty as if the evening guard was but an extension of their allotted nap time.

"Faster!" Aerlyn shouted, moving forward. She tried to sound in control but she wasn't, and one slip from the bountyman and some glory seeker would try to skewer her on a pike. Then they'd all but spit roast her over an open fire, taking turns with what damnable desires festered their black hearts.

And seeing the coals of hatred in their eyes fanned the flame of murder in hers. To be in the midst of the guards and footmen, closing in and around her like the fall of night upon the sea, broke some long-standing anger within her and she wished she could've burned the whole place to the ground.

But it was the land she had the problem with, the way of things. The injustice of it all.

To be born a woman was a curse.

But killing them all would do no good. Their poison would remain, swilled in the dark waters of the deepest aquifer.

Aerlyn moved the bountyman forward and spat, stopping just shy of the gate.

And feeling the heat of their many gazes, the desire to take her and break her like some wild horse, Aerlyn made a promise in the very bottom of her chasm-split soul, that if she made out of Brachin alive she would stop her thieving and do whatever she could to better the lives of the women of Albanland. For far too many of them lie bruised in ditches this very night, and too many more bearing children they had no say in conceiving.

Aerlyn wanted to cry at her own selfishness, that which stole from those who took souls and shamed destinies. She wanted to cry that she had only sought to take, but never give. She'd stolen because she'd been stolen from, an eye for an eye, but she'd never once thought she could find away to flip the whole curse upon its head.

And as she thought a great many thoughts, the gates opened wide before her, pikes glinting silver murder and steel swords shaking in trembling fists as she passed through. Lanterns, once bright and full of accusation, dimmed and receded like the sun in the sea, and the little girl who once dreamed great dreams and things so grand the sky itself could not contain her vivid hopes stood to face Brachin, mixing it with every other town scattered across Albanland, where lawlessness ruled with an iron fist.

But somewhere, inside, that little girl and her dreams had not died.

Aerlyn released the bountyman and forced him to his knees, but pain on top of days in the saddle had exasperated him and he fell to his hands, panting.

Still, evil promises found their way from his throat.

"If I ever see you again..."

A thump shot ache through his skull and he fell splat into the mud. The filth of the highway filled his mouth, grinding in his teeth and coloring his gums brown and bitter.

It took no small eternity to press himself up and fight the clumsy hands that tried to help, footmen's faces blank and merchant guards stunned silent.

For The Thistle had once again slipped into the wind.

Wordlessly, the bountyman limped back into Brachin to retrieve his belt, his saddle, and his horse.

He swore something vile when he realized his heavy pouch of gold was missing.

ULTAN

CHAPTER 7

The battlefield was an uneven sprawl of tufted grass and rough heather, sloping ever so gently from a broad plateau. Far in the distance, the dragon-boats of the Nørds bobbed in the rough gray waters of Curran Firth, curling around the Mull of Montree. The small fishing town had been taken, its weak wooden walls filling fuller day by day with Nørds, making the twisting limb of rocky land upon which it sat nothing more than an obscene gesture. A provocation. A constant reminder of the inevitable, should the semblance of strength slip from Alban hands. It'd been strategically vacated before the Nørds took it, and no Alban blood shed in its taking. But it was still a foothold on sovereign land within eyesight of the Seat of the Throne.

Such a gesture was madness, but bold enough to be carefully conceived from a rival dynasty hundreds of miles across the water.

Because after hundreds of years of raid and ruin, the Nørds had finally split the waves in search of a Crown.

Casting its shadow across the sprawl of tufted grass and the coming battle, the Tower of Ullraye stood guard over its own sons. The Warband of Albanland, arrayed in their Clan finery under banded white clouds and ice blue skies, were ready for war.

Ultan, Champion of Albanland and Guardian of the Crown, peered back at the smoke-black Tower Fortress one last time, nearly feeling the silent study of a watchful gaze cool the back of his neck. The summer sun had already made his skin sticky, and every time a stray breeze tousled a lock of his curly shoulder-length strawberry blonde hair and cupped his chin, sliding around the back of his neck with the scent of distant sage and rose petals, he thought of those eyes.

Eyes that missed nothing, perched high up in the smoke black Tower of Ullraye.

The eyes of a dream, whispering secrets to the wind.

Raucous laughter tore through the line of Nørds, hundreds of feet below across the distance of the slight slope, looking savage and fearsome in their wolven furs and horned helms. Cruel and lusty dragons of blood red and sea blue set their round wooden shields and dull silver bosses, and each of them were built like the boats that brought them. Long and wooden-limbed, knotted with pale hair that looked like sea-salted rope and smelling of fish.

"Are you going to sun yourself all day, Skölhammer?" One of their own band leaders howled, his barrel chest bellowing with the Nørd lilt.

"He has the hair of a woman!"

"And with skin so fine he'll burn in the sun!"

Ultan only licked his lips, staring into the staggered line of them. It wasn't his first battle, and it wouldn't be his last. And though he wasn't afraid of their hefty axes and their drug-induced battle rage, their words had pierced him deep.

With skin so fine he'll burn in the sun.

His pale skin and heather green eyes were Alban, but his chiseled shoulders and strawberry blonde hair were Nørd.

The beautiful hair of his mother.

At times an odd lilt caught his tongue and he knew he could never sound like the highlanders that served with him, so strong in the kilts of their kin, swaddled in proud woolen colors the moment they came from the womb.

As had not happened with his birth.

For his kin was mixed.

And yet he led them against the Nørds just as he did the stoop shouldered monarchs of the South, wasting all the riches of

Angle for a traipse into a land they would never conquer though they tried again the moment they forgot their last defeat.

But to kill an Angle was to swat a fly. To kill a Nørd was to kill a part of himself. Not only in physical resemblance, but in thought and deed.

Ultan was the Champion of Albanland, Guardian of the Crown, but the Nørds knew him only as Skölhammer, the name by which they bestowed heartrending affection and honor.

They were saying he was one of them.

And he knew that because he thought like them.

Because he fought like them.

Because he *was* one of them.

"Don't keep us waiting Skölhammer!"

"Show us your shiny sword!"

"Come and fight us and we will all dine tonight with our fathers!"

Your fathers! Yes, your fathers! Go to your fathers! Leave me in peace! Leave our land alone and never come back! Ultan wanted to scream, but kept his face as hard as the smoke black Tower of Ullraye that rose at his back, keeping watch over his every move.

My father was of Skyeshire, like his father before him, and his father before him.

"Come Skölhammer! Let us show you what fine weapons we've looted from your town!"

"Come see how well you've been feeding us!"

"Yes! Come dine with your brothers tonight in the halls of the stars!"

Fury built within Ultan and he turned to face the staggered line of his own troops. His teeth were bare, as if he'd become a pale wolf. Brothers, he'd called his Alban warriors, many a time, through blood and smoke, though the barbarian Nørds across the field bore more common blood than any of the Albans behind him, as he was the last of the Skyeshire line and without wife or heir. Even to look upon him, set against the kilted midst of Albans, was to see a man standing with his feet split upon two separate lands, two fractious bloods forever locked in a duel.

The eyes of the Warband of Albanland swelled to see the sight, color flushing from his already pale face as the wicked winds of Inverloch and Curran Firth swirled inside his soul and made them all feel the cold in the aura of his presence. Hardness became his bones, stones of the highest mountains of frozen Nørd, this half-breed of war and blood. His green eyes transmuted, like magic, into the indomitable fists of the highlands, and his strawberry-blonde hair danced like strokes of hearth fire. His fury burned raw in his throat, ripping forth with an animal howl and sunlight glistened sweat-glazed arms thick with muscle, bare and pale, save the gold torcs that shimmered and shone around his biceps.

It was then he unsheathed the Blade of the Champion, steel milk white in the sun. In the black kilt of his fathers and the snow white fox pelt cape of the Crown he was both of them, Nørd and Alban. One and the same, like storm rain spilled upon the sea.

"Sons of War!" Ultan roared, with the savage snarl of a Nørd, and the lyrical passion of an Alban. "Today we cut down the tree of woe! Today we seize the dragon of the Nørd and spit upon his grave!"

A roar of one resounded in his ranks, and no one could see the wince of pain flash through Ultan's eyes. No one save the eyes watching him from above, from the Tower of Ullraye, stuck between the ocean and the land as he was the tree fallen and broken between two peoples.

"Today we free the souls of our brothers, and reclaim the honor of our sisters! Today we avenge our fathers! Today we seek retribution for our mothers!"

The roar of one was laced with the passion of tear-stained winters, bitter curses swallowed over all that had been stolen in the skirmishes and burning night raids of a hundred cruel years.

"Today we push the dragon into the sea! Today we slay the Nørd!"

And with the shouts of the Warband of Albanland rising like the Four Storms in his ears, and the clatter of axe on shield a deafening thunder across the expanse of sloping grass, Ultan Skölhammer unleashed his fury and charged down the hill.

Above, the eyes of the Crown watched him with dread, as he ran, with reckless abandon, to his death.

CHAPTER 8

In seeking death Ultan Skölhammer became it, a boiling cauldron of blood and foam. Steel crashed upon wood and skin, and bone cracked and broke like oaken trees to winter's spell. Blood splashed the tufted grass. Death rolled across the field like the endless flood tides of the sea.

Hacking and hewing, dashing and spinning, the milk white Blade of the Champion hummed as if it were alive in his hand, the mystic weapon of some foolish child's dream.

Of his own.

For in his youth, battle had been born into his blood, and folly had longed for it far too soon, aching for a taste of the baird's hero sagas till it reared its ugly head and spit in his face.

And now, after four years of it, he had nothing to spit back but the vain hope that death would find him and spear him right through the heart so that he wouldn't have to hate the Nørds any longer.

So that he wouldn't have to hate himself.

But he did. He hated them for being a half of himself, a dark and animal half that kept him warm at night and spoke to him of the end of the seas and the colors of the dawn. It was the very same half he drew upon to kill them with and that half was fed to grow into an uncontrollable monster by doing so.

And they fell before him, and around him, rolling oaths lost in gargles and shouts. They fell atop his own Alban warriors as pike and axe splintered and bent.

Alone, the milk white Blade seemed to seek the necks it wanted, sweeping a swathe of destruction his own kilted brothers stayed clear of. Its whistling howl struck fear in the heart of the fearless berserkers, and some sought to drop their axes and run from his fury.

Ultan became a pillar of fire, streaked with mud and gold, and to see him in the arms of wrath was to feel oneself tremble deep inside. Alban and Nørd alike fell to mortal wounds and searing gashes, but not a hint of steel could touch the sworn Guardian of the Crown.

It was as if he was clothed in magic.

Ferocious, terrible magic.

Above, the eyes watched, guarded in the Tower of Ullraye.

But the battle shifted when the shores rumbled with the clatter of shield and spear. Hundreds if not an odd thousand more Nørds rushed up from their hiding places among the rocks of the beach, wild eyes ready for war, their ambush complete.

Ultan saw them in a squint, running in full stride though two miles from his schiltrons of pikes.

"House of Cavan! To me!"

His roar was met with a cheer, and pikes folded tall as the line of Nørds crumbled away and re-grouped. Foolishly, the Nørds had split their forces in two, but if they could galvanize, and the smaller group hold as they awaited the larger, they'd become a hammer and anvil, and crush the defensive line of Alban sons in a brutal vice grip ever squeezing tighter and tighter.

Chaos still flurried around him, their Champion and leader, and he seized an opportunity to break the battle in half and snap it like a twig.

He rushed forward as his men held a strong and defensive knot, waiting to receive the surge of the sprinting reinforcements, keeping the Nørd's wild berserkers separated and howling orders to re-group and charge.

But the tactic spread a stark imbalance across the field, and one could almost feel the Nørds bristle with the coming victory. A little over a hundred berserkers awaited the House of Cavan.

And him.

But Ultan Skölhammer didn't wait for the House of Cavan to fall in stride with him, launching himself into the jaws of their shiny axes and horned helms with a shout. All one hundred and so of them, eager to meet him and him alone.

And far above, in the Tower of the Crown, the jaw of a young woman tightened, and a single tear fell from her eye.

CHAPTER 9

It was a song he heard before he woke, as if he was floating just under the surface of Loch Darvin, like the time he nearly drowned in its cold arms when he was a child.

Light snaked through the murky haze, skipping dove wings just beyond the surface. The song danced a beautiful golden circle around his eyes, barely open and glazed over with the sweat of death. The song pulled him up in a dizzying spiral.

From his dreams of death? Of life?

No, caught somewhere in the middle, torn in half by two worlds, greedy for his soul.

Below him, whispers in darkness, the voices of the slain called him back. Faces were down there, kept in the deep black of fallen night and sea floor caves, faces frozen in death's sting.

They wanted him to join them; spirit, soul and body.

But the song, airy and pure, spread warmth all around him, lifting him higher and higher and his eyes fluttered open as the shape of a woman materialized before him, pulled into clarity, spinning and spinning and spinning till his head spun no more.

"Ultan, my brave One. Once again you cheat the hounds of hell."

His throat was dry, stricken with drought, and he opened his mouth to speak but the woman sat gently beside him and tipped a cup of cool, refreshing water to his lips. She watched, tenderly, as the water spilled down his chin and dripped upon the broad muscles of his bare chest.

Thirst quenched, Ultan sat back on the makeshift bed and stared holes in the hastily pitched tent.

He said nothing, though the realization of living through another battle he most definitely shouldn't have sent a pang of regret through him, and the heather green of his eyes darkened in their sockets.

The woman bent over him, her lips just above his forehead, stroking his hair with the softest touch. In her nearness, he wanted to fall asleep again, and felt like she could whisper him to a place of sweet safety. To a dreamy place, where everything was right in the world.

But it was a lie. Nothing was right in the land, nothing ever *would* be right in the land. The honey of her lips was but the indulgence of temptation. Lies to say, in this moment, ignorance was bliss.

Ultan set his eyes upon her and fought blush. She was a delicate beauty, fragile-boned and exquisite. She was from another time, another place. Every bit the grace of royalty incarnate.

Light seemed to emanate from her, either that or she captured it all around her and sucked it inside her skin and bones. Ultan would never know which was true.

"Once again, you save me from the grave."

Only the slightest murmur of pleasure curled ruby lips, and Ultan stared deep into the eyes he felt upon him everywhere he went.

The eyes of Morgance, Faer Princess of the Night.

Whether fighting the sea spray to chase dragon-ships back to their own shores, or shaking the forest loose of rebels and fat Angles along the border come for a beating, the eyes of Morgance never left him, sitting full and heavy in his heart.

They were green, he once thought, but so light, like the sun shining through blades of summer grass. So much so they appeared nearly yellow. Her hair, too, pinned and falling in ringlets to frame those yellow-green eyes of glass beads and sparkling peridine gems, was washed of color that would've made it either brown or blonde, and in the end it just shined with the gloss of sunlight bound to the skin of water.

Ultan swallowed, thick and uneasy as her hand slid down his body, catching his rock-hard stomach across the middle and making him wince.

"I cannot save you if you keep getting nasty cuts like this one."

He could feel it, still puffy, despite her miraculous abilities to heal.

Ultan shrugged, seeing her eyes shimmer with tears.

But she held them back, standing tall and giving him the cup of water as she refilled it.

"What happened out there?" Her soft and airy voice gained a bit of backbone. Did she know he found it endlessly endearing when she did that? One minute she was ready to fall apart that he might die, the next she was acting like she wanted to hear about the tactics and politics of the Nørd war.

When all she wanted was to be with him.

Of that, he was certain.

In so many words or less, she had spoken whispers to the wind as he tossed himself sleepless in the moonlit loneliness of his bed, and her promises had stalked his soul as he walked the cold hills of the highlands like an alpha wolf searching for the threat of rivals.

For he controlled the Warband, and she the Crown.

She was unmarried and childless, young and unreasonably beautiful, and so was he, only his beauty was bound to the battlefield, a living flame of the baird's hero sagas come to life.

Ultan sat up, wincing. Stiffness was everywhere, in every muscle and joint, and he attempted to turn on his side but flopped back in the comfort of the makeshift bed, staring up at the rippling folds of the tent.

"Morgance, you should've let me go this time."

The Princess spun to face him, ringlets bouncing. Pain stretched across her delicate face and she threw the pitcher of water to the ground.

"Damn you and your grief, Ultan of Skyeshire!" She said, her soft voice stretched and thin. "If you die, what becomes of Albanland?" The gloss was back in her eyes, wet and ready to rain sorrow to the ground.

"What becomes of me?"

Ultan thought for a moment and snarled as he pressed himself up. Morgance watched him lurch and find his balance, his head still swirling as if it hadn't been attached to his shoulders for days.

Like it'd been somewhere else, dark and cold.

"We all have to die sometime." He muttered, finding the Blade of the Champion had been cleaned and sheathed and he strapped it to his waist.

"Not you, Ultan of Skyeshire." Her soft voice echoed the melody of whatever song she'd sung over him as she brought him up from the pit of death once more. "Your name can live on for eternity."

Ultan inhaled slowly, his stomach burning with the sting of a dirty Nørd axe. He eyed Morgance with the cold cunning she deserved, since she was *not* only speaking about his legacy as a warrior, but as a King, and a father of Kings.

As *her* King, the anointed Champion of a land split by war and turmoil and rebellion on every side.

Yes, he read in those yellow-green eyes of summer promises. *I am the key to making Albanland one.*

Ultan swallowed again, squinting into her eyes, as if it would stop the gentle voice from skipping through his mind, and the fire it pledged.

Am I that undesirable, Ultan of Skyeshire? Am I so unworthy of your love?

But Ultan grabbed his snow fox cape and left the tent, walking past the cleaved and the healing to the lonely smoke black Tower of Ullraye.

For far stronger than the struggle of his blood, Nørd and Alban, was the conundrum of Morgance, Faer Princess of the Night, Crown Ruler of Albanland, and how she craved to be his love when his heart was still foolishly pledged to another.

Given to a girl, once long ago, before his heart became as hard as the stone of the cloven Throne.

A beautiful little girl who still slept in a dream.

MORGANCE

CHAPTER 10

Day faded along the rim of the earth, losing its will to shine. Summer heat vanished, giving in to the unrelenting grip of night and the ice of the sea. Coral sunlight burrowed into a fringe of trees far beyond the plateau where the black Tower of Ullraye stood still and unflinching, as if the afternoon's brutality had never happened.

And how many battles had Ullraye seen? Surely it was now blind to the sight of steel. Its black stone was the spine of Albanland, cursed by defiance. Inhospitable but forever indomitable.

Unbroken and unbowed.

The scent in the air mixed sea salt with blood, sweat and mud, and it wrinkled the Princess' brow to walk amongst the Sons of Albanland and feel their hurts so strongly in her own soul.

For they had given, while she stood still, stoic as the black Tower of Ullraye up above it all. They had given life and limb as she had watched with full focus on but one of them.

For thousands could fall, but not him.

Never him.

Morgance fingered the pendant hanging around her neck, a simple stone, captured in a silken web of silver.

In her grip it seemed to glow, the peach tones of the sunset sucked into the fractals of its crystal.

Holding it, as if it captured thought, Morgance walked and walked, away from the battlefield, up the plateau and to the edge of the low stone walls of the Fortress. Guardsmen clattered lanterns and changed the watch, settling in for a long night of vigilance.

Morgance didn't notice the guards drifting nearer, beckoning her back to the safety of the Tower where she felt locked up, a prisoner, and rubbing the necklace between her thumb and forefinger she closed her eyes for a moment, feeling the earth stretch its arms wide as day was exchanged for night.

Flowers for blood. Fruit for bones.

Summer for war.

Morgance had worn the necklace since she was a young girl, a tiny little blossom of a soul who dreamt of one day becoming Queen.

But the sea dimmed in the sight of her gaze, dragon-boats still holding their positions out beyond the Mull of Montree.

Somehow, she thought, *somehow I'll make this all better.*

For though she had taken the Throne of Albanland by silken force and soft words, usurping the rightful heir with a tangle of lies spun long ago, enough of them to now smother the truth a thousand times over, Morgance had it in her to reign.

If only she could get over Ultan.

For to reign was to sacrifice. To lead was to bleed. To give. And selfishness constantly plagued her thoughts, all in concert dancing around his shoulders and the touch of his hands. The urgent need of it, so hungry that but a drop of his gaze was a tear of rain upon the parch of drought. Any excuse to be near him was excuse enough, and with the war, well…Albanland had more of a place in his heart than she ever could.

Or so she told herself. That he was in love with the hills and the soil and Sons that fought to keep it safe. She told herself he was pledged Champion of Albanland *before* he was Guardian of the Crown. Guardian of her heart. There couldn't be another, there just couldn't. And she wouldn't dare ask him, though he remained as stoic to her advances as the Tower of Ullraye.

But there was a time, Morgance knew, and that time was drawing fast upon her, upon them all.

A time when Morgance would be forced to wed or abdicate.

Guardsmen came to collect her and bring her back to the Chamber of Lords. Her presence was needed urgently.

And Morgance nodded dutifully, a single tear slipping off to a puff of sea wind, its cold finger sealing her ache in stone.

For she needed him, urgently, but once again she would stand strong in the face of dearth as the Princess of a land that knew nothing but.

CHAPTER 11

Dinner would've settled better in her stomach had not the tangible hunger of desire tainted it.

And though a pair of gazes locked on the dream of her impossibly beautiful face, Morgance did her best to hide the agitating roil of it all as she buttered a piece of brown bread.

Arturo's hand was quick in grabbing the blackberry jam from the middle of the table, receiving a stern glance from Bandon, directly across from him. It was as if they'd both been waiting and Arturo had lulled Bandon into a place of debate just to distract him.

Morgance sighed to herself. They were not the only ones at the table after all. Ten other Lords and Ladies, all of them trapped in their own thoughts about the nearby dragon-boats, sat and ate their meals quietly. But Arturo and Bandon couldn't do that.

They were like children.

Handsome and powerful children. Hot-blooded heraldic land owners, Sons of Albanland who daily pledged their life to *her* Crown, though their eyes grasped for much more behind their winsome and wayward smiles.

Bandon glowered at Arturo, the older Lord by two months, who stood and stretched to place the claypot of jam next to Morgance' plate. Perhaps it was a small gesture, but the Princess had once claimed a fondness for blackberries in an offhanded manner and every time the sticky jam found its way to the table the young Lords competed for the courtesy of offering it to her.

Bandon's glower melted as he plotted for his next small victory and knived slices of roasted pheasant, more than likely imagining Arturo's sunny face on the sharp end of his eating utensils.

Arturo took his time sitting down, receiving a kind smile from Morgance. If there were a dozen candles in the room, none were as bright as her delicate face and its glittering twinkles of yellow-green. Clothed in black velvet and lace, she looked as if she'd descended from another land, high above the stars.

"I do believe they're Fordair." Arturo said, his voice a low rumble. With his brown beard and hair of the same rich color, his sunny skin and white teeth made him the first gossip of all the eligible Ladies of the Clans.

Though his eyes were only for Morgance.

And the Crown.

"What?" Bandon mumbled, mouth packed with pheasant, dripping in gravy. Arturo only stared at him, leaning back in his seat. His rich murmur was degrading, as usual.

"The blackberries."

Bandon frowned and then began sawing again at his pheasant. Morgance had noticed it was overcooked, even though she didn't eat meat.

"They are not." The younger Lord shook his head, stabbing a slice of pheasant with more force than necessary. "Any country bumpkin knows there are no blackberries in Fordair. All the bloody Angles have picked the bushes clean."

Morgance sighed to herself again, not wanting to spoon the contentious stickiness on her buttered bread, even though her mouth watered at the thought of it.

Or was that the thought of Ultan? His chin between her fingers, lips brushing close?

Hot under the skin, Morgance cooled herself with a sip of water. A foolish dream it was to keep meditating on such a thing, despite it being the only solution her heart wanted. Though two years older than Arturo and Bandon, Ultan was a man amongst mere boys. An oak to take shade under as the saplings shuddered in the wind of the Four Storms.

Her glittering eyes fell to the seat at her right hand. Empty. She could just see him in his room, now, recovering in the hands of fitful rest. Thrashing awake with nightmares of blood and Nørds and no one to hold him till the shivers left his soul.

How she wanted to comfort him.

"Aren't they, your Highness?" A voice drew her back from thought, and it took a moment for her to realize which one.

Morgance folded her hands across her lap.

"Blackberries are a wild vine, Lord Arturo of Pallantyne. It's no knowledge of mine where they grow and where they do not. It is my only wish that such small bones of contention do not distract my Lords from what *other* wild vines seek to choke out all the good flowers of this fair land."

Bandon of Tavish shot Arturo a sneer and returned to sawing his pheasant. *Lost that one, Art,* she could nearly hear the impetuous youngster say under his breath. They were actually distant cousins through their mothers, the Houses of Tavish and Pallantyne, and their only living representatives in Lordship were two very different souls, always at odds with each other.

For love, for the Crown.

Morgance watched as Arturo slicked his brown hair back and let a smile unwind across his face. The heavy gold signet of Pallantyne smoldered on the middle finger of his right hand and Morgance was sure one punch could break the long dining table in half, though she'd never seen Arturo fight save his expert displays in the Swordsman's Circle.

"I understand, your Highness. It is not my nature to waste time with bones, contentious or otherwise."

Bandon, trying to get every last scrap of pheasant from the bone, stopped his sawing and stared across the table at Arturo, who sat smugly fingering the pewter stem of a wine goblet. His skin took to jewels and finery as if he had the grace of a woman, and Morgance watched helplessly as Bandon's splotchy skin reddened and he settled to tearing a hunk of brown bread from the loaf to send his own message.

It was not that Morgance favored Bandon in any way, but Bandon was constantly outclassed by Arturo at every turn. Morgance felt the envy of every eligible Lady slap her way like wind and rain to think that such a physically handsome and rich man like Arturo could be all hers, and what ardent affections the vague winks of his velveteen brown eyes promised as candlelight passed across them.

Conversely, Bandon was the son of one of Albanland's greatest warriors, but had grown up in the shadow of such a great man and an even greater brother, till both were killed by Nørds in a bloody night raid. Rumors were that Bandon ran and hid, while fewer tongues claimed he fought the raiding party off his Clan's estate with nothing but a burning stick from the hearthplace and a rusty quarry pick. Either way, Bandon spent most of his time growling around his estates near the highlands, raising his hunting dogs, and feeling impotent and unwanted as his lands withered in drought. Morgance felt the awkward nature of his affection toward her, since they'd grown up together, though Morgance had grown up with a great many Lords and Ladies. She even sensed a misshapen streak of ambition, clouded by the itching need for greatness yet to be achieved, as if the celebrated memories of his ancestors accused his inadequacies every morning with the rise of the sun.

But Morgance doubted his ability to deliver on any of it just as much as she doubted Arturo and his overselling of the opposite. Confidence oozed from Arturo's every square inch and while he wasn't as large as Ultan or had half as much battle experience, he was just about the closest thing to Ultan there ever would be.

But something about him made her want to run away. Was it ancient Angle blood, causing him to think he was naturally better than every other Alban he laid eyes on?

Or was it a lusty fire, burning within, promising a thousand wonders if only she would give in.

But once.

Morgance lifted her gaze from her hands to see his brown eyes full and round upon her. Pressing ruby lips together in a firm line, Morgance' sight dropped to her cup of water, near empty, and the sad reflection that sat upon its glassy surface.

CHAPTER 12

The thought of walking to Ultan's room tempted her with a cord of fire, snaking from her throat to the top of her legs, so she kept those legs moving, slipping past the vigilant guards, into the night.

The summer cool refreshed and the sea breeze tousled her pale ringlets, shining only in the moonlight when the rampant swells of clouds split to let Luna spread a white hush across the plateau.

Morgance looked back as she walked, the beating in her heart subsiding since thoughts of tempting Ultan with her softest words had become muddled with the rush of slipping past Albanland's best guards. Against the night, the black Tower of Ullraye stood like a painful knife wound slashed up into the sky. It was blacker than night. Dead and rigid against the living backdrop of a world asleep.

An ill omen of the future to her Faer eyes.

Morgance' pace lingered and dawdled, entering a grove of trees. Wisdom would say there were Nørds ready to steal her away into their dragon-boats for ransom, but aside from smelling them a mile away, she trusted what Ultan had said in the Chamber of Lords about them being too hurt for any sort of night raid.

Yes, it had been through the most excruciating of winces, as if poison was slowly working its way up his legs from the floor. Every time he shifted positions to address one of the questions of a contentious Lord or a worrisome Lady, the veins of his arms thumped and squeezed and his back stiffened as if his neck were made of ice.

He'd given every last drop of strength and retired before dinner, limping up the heights of the Tower to fall into his bed, too exhausted to be hungry.

To think of him alone made Morgance want to cry all over again.

They were both alone.

What was the point? Neither of them were getting any younger, though twenty-four was half the age of most of the Lords and Ladies in Albanland as so many of her generation had fallen to the sword. And Ultan's apparent need to run and die the first moment he heard a Nørd battle cry was killing her inside, like a drop of water forever dripping on a stone.

Eventually, the water would kill the stone, faithfully beating it into nothing.

Eroding its will to be what it was created to be.

One of these days, Morgance thought, as her steps took her through a copse of trees. *One of these days I'm going to make you an offer with a dagger in my hand. Either kill me now or I'll do it myself. Not having you is killing me any way, like Plague rotting my bones from within. What would I do if the next battle claimed your soul? Or some fat and cowardly Angle paid a rogue to sneak up here poison you? I would be but a shadow of what I am now, and even now I am not what I could be with you by my side.*

But Princess, he would say, *I am by your side.*

And she would throw up her hands. Impossible to reason with, always. Always right in that his duty to protect the land came first, before anything.

Before her.

But Albanland crumbles around us! Even now, we can't wake up in the morning without seeing Nørds and those ugly boats of their sitting in the sea like driftwood! Just beyond our reach they hold an empty town that used to thrum with the hope of every new dawn! And now it sits in silence! Looted! Ransacked! Ruined!

So then he would grab her by the wrists, the softest of shackles, and hands that could crush bones would send gentle sunlight along her spine.

I am doing everything I can Princess, but I cannot do what you want me to.

I cannot.

Or so Morgance dreamed, as she had dreamed before, running the scene over in her mind as if it had already happened.

Even though it never would.

The Faer Princess of the Night threw one last glance back at the ugly scar of the Tower of Ullraye before the crack of deadfall stopped her cold.

Every bit of her small body flushed with shivers and heat, and she looked around the lush twists of the trees for what had been responsible.

Friend or foe.

Nørd?

Yellow-green eyes panning, Morgance inhaled sharply when a pair of pale golden eyes, slim rings set in black and white, met her searching gaze with hungry defiance.

The eyes of a wolf.

Low and bubbling, a growl spun from the wolf's throat as he lowered his head and his shoulders bunched thick and lithe in the selfsame shift of shadow, approaching.

Morgance straightened and gathered her skirts as if to run. The wolf, stalking, was but six feet from her when she spread her arms wide and pursed her lips.

The sound was but a shiver on the wind, quickly ascending in pitch. At first the wolf stopped, frozen, as if reaching the edge of a cliff. Then the fearsome creature twisted its head and began to wrinkle its nose, before succumbing to two heavy blinks, and then three, and then the wolf's muzzle began to dip ever so slowly toward the grass.

Morgance whistled the nearly inaudible sound till her lungs were emptied of their wind and the wild wolf was all but asleep, allowing her next inhale be more of a sigh of relief than anything else.

But the flash of a sword preceded a swish of cloth and a tangle of limbs and leaves. Morgance jumped at the dull thwack of steel and the whimper of one predator dying under the cruel gaze of another.

The dark shape of a man had been stalking her and Morgance stood, caught between wanting to gather her skirts and run and wanting to spin the man around and ask him why he'd done such a thing when the wolf had been rendered harmless by her Faer skills.

She didn't have a chance to do either.

The tall man turned to her, sword low in his hand.

Dripping with sticky red wolven blood.

CHAPTER 13

The tall figure blurred with streaks of moonlight and twisted branches, approaching ever so slowly till the handsome profile she saw so often at her dinner table became clear.

"Arturo? What are you doing out here?"

Sword still dripping, Morgance could see his chest and shoulders heave in the slightest, Pallantyne colors of purple, gold, and green draped about his figure jeweled and rich.

"I could ask you the same question, your Highness."

A quick response flared within and she smothered it. Did he know she had all but escaped from the Fortress? Ultan's final order before retiring to agony had been to lock the place up tighter than an Angle's strongbox. Had he followed her? And for what purpose?

She couldn't tell him why she had left, and what her destination was, though it wasn't far, and his round brown eyes, spiced with moonlight and summer wind, claimed to know all the same as he drew near, sword still low and dripping.

"Did you follow me?" She asked, flatly.

Arturo only stared at her and then cast his eyes to the sword as he held it up from his waist, cocked to the side, watching the wolven blood slide down the blade.

"You know, I can protect you from the many predators of Albanland…" With his free hand Arturo produced a kerchief and wiped the blade clean. "But there are more to worry about than just wolves."

"The creature was no harm to you." Morgance sighed and Arturo glared at her softness.

"Maybe not, but a will a Faer whistle stop a surge of Angle barrons searching for slaves?"

Morgance' tiny nostrils flared and her brow wrinkled. The problem of slavery was spreading along the southern border like Plague. In fact, it was a new form of Plague, and with Nørd oppression at her very doorstep, it was a crippling curse she could do nothing about.

To think, Angles stealing Alban girls from their beds. Soon, Albans would be bred from the land. Gone. Vanished in a matter of generations.

A bloom of hatred swirled within her. If they weren't so busying fighting the Nørds, Morgance would demand her Champion to rid the south of its evil Angle bloodlines.

"We both know how corrupted the southern Clans are." Arturo muttered, sheathing his sword, about half the size of Ultan's. "They might as well all be Angles, fed and fattened by the decadence of good living while their own people starve."

Morgance shivered to think of such a thing, yet she had not been in the south since she was seventeen years old. So much had changed, Angles infecting the very land with illegitimate children and throwing money around to taint town governors and Clan leaders, Clans of which no longer bothered to send representatives to Ullraye, thus, rightly removing themselves from Alban rule.

Arturo stepped closer, shadowing her with his form. He smelled sweet, like honey and wildflowers, and his brown hair and beard framed his sunny face like a ring of velvet.

"I know the plight all too well. You forget how close my holdings are to the southern border. So many times I feel locked in no man's land. With such decadence cursing the dawn before me, and Nørd mayhem cursing the dusk behind me, I sit around all noon on my hands and knees waiting to bring about the change this land needs. But I can't."

Yellow-green eyes shot to meet his gaze as his arms rose from his sides and broad hands clasped her shoulders.

I know what you want, Arturo of Pallantyne. You want me and you want the Crown. You lust for both but the Crown most of all.

Fear wrapped its tendrils about Morgance' small feet. A puff of salty sea breeze rustled the trees and the sweet smell of his nearness echoed in the heat of his hands. Arturo was the kind of man that took what he wanted, and he held Morgance still where she stood.

"Which is why..." He said, mouth stretching wide as his eyes dropped before finding hers again. "I have a plan I wouldn't dare utter in the Chamber of Lords."

Morgance lifted her chin, eyes narrowing. It was almost as if the thought of him seducing her in the trees had been her own, not his. To look deep into his brown eyes was to see turmoil and pressure, despite what shine and polish he projected to the world around him.

"Speak, Lord of Pallantyne."

Arturo's hands left her and clasped behind his back. He walked in a small circle, biting his lip.

"I...I want to strike a deal with the Angles."

Horror melted across Morgance' face.

Because she knew he was right.

His touch found her shoulders again, far stronger than the last time, and he bent closer to her, need underscoring his low voice.

"We're locked in a war of attrition, your Highness. Nørds kill us and Angles buy us off or convert...or *pervert*, however the case may be, and we have to begin to consider the less of two evils." Arturo straightened, a chill in his voice. "Or we may not last the winter."

Morgance held herself, feeling the night chill. By now, she would've well reached her destination, just beyond the trees and down into a hidden glen not a mile away.

"What lands did you have in mind?" Morgance asked, eyes watching blades of grass shiver and shake in the breeze.

Arturo had moved to lean against a tree, his back to her.

"My own."

Morgance' posture fell as if her lungs were void of air and she rushed to him, grabbing his arm.

"No, I forbid it. You are strong and I must have strength in the south!"

Arturo pulled his arm away from her with a sneer dark across his lips.

"Not strong enough."

Morgance watched him take a step and then turn to her, passion curling around the edge of his eyes.

"Don't you see it? Your love of that monster is what's costing us this war."

Ruby lips falling, a tremor rushed through her brow. Her high-pitched voice was weak, nearly lost in the wind.

"Ultan is our Champion."

"He's half *bloody* Nørd." Arturo said each word slowly, grinding his teeth together as his hands went to his hips.

One above his gold pouch, the other above his sword.

"Please." Morgance felt her heart fluttering with sickness' heat. "Please, be careful what you say."

"I say the truth!" Arturo nearly spat, walking a tight circle then standing before her again, wanting to lay a pleading hand to her shoulder. But his blood was too hot, the path of the caged animal he'd been forced to walk catching him equidistant between two very different conflicts.

And the time spent doing so had burned the quagmire to one solution in his mind.

Morgance shuddered as his arms wrapped around her thinness, and she felt his desire seep through her skin like a spring river, rushing foam over soil and stone.

"Marry me, Faer Princess of the Night. Take me to be the one to rule with you. I'm not the one you want. But I *am* the one you need." She tried to twist away but her spine was weak against the heat of his hands, and his nearness was so sweet in her nose. Her skin tingled along with the brushing of leaves as she realized how…*easy* it would all be.

Just to say one *simple* word.

Yes.

Her heart shuddered in her lungs, a captive bird in a cage of bone. He crushed her to himself as her lips spread to speak and his kiss was a hard promise.

If Ultan was pain then Arturo was pleasure.

Morgance pushed him away in the same moment he let her go. He stood strong and firm, a tower of flesh and fabric and riches amongst the trees, staring down at her with the same eyes that'd slain the wild wolf. He watched her wordlessly wipe her lips and take a step back from him.

"I am not a patient man, your Highness." His low voice rumbled. "I will not take no for an answer."

Morgance took another step back. But still he did not move. The threat in his low rumble was enough.

He was enjoying himself, enjoying the power he held in the grip of such an offer. For as much as Morgance was the keeper of the Crown, her authority was but a vessel of sand with a hole in the bottom of it.

Forever slipping into darkness.

"Or what?" Morgance managed to squeak.

Arturo rested a hand on his sword.

"Or what?" He echoed, turning the words over in his mind, finding a small laugh the only suitable response as he turned his back on her and walked back toward the indomitable black Tower of Ullraye.

CHAPTER 14

The night burned violet at the borders of the earth.

By the time the old ruins rose from the ground before her, Morgance was ready to fall to her knees. She had run from Arturo, run from the copse of trees, and hot tears had been her only companion for the mile journey down from the plateau into the hidden glen.

With each passing step the force of his lips had lingered across hers, like boots leaving an imprint in mud. The thought of giving into his request skipped more than one tremor through her heart for more than one reason, and running from it couldn't change the fact that the mire of it all would be ready for her the moment she returned to the Fortress to sit the Throne.

Damn you for being so easy, Arturo of Pallantyne, so damnably tempting.

Damn you for making sense.

Arturo would give up his lands in the south and use his riches to seal off the slow bleed of the Angle ascendency. In essence, the wound would be healed and mend over time. But in exchange he would sit the Throne. With her? No, next to her, as she was bumped sideways for a smaller chair and a quieter voice in the ways of rulership.

Her job would be a simple thing, another sort of prison.

To bear him a male child.

Yes, he would galvanize the land against Nørd oppression, but would Ultan live to see it? Arturo hated Ultan in every way. He hated his near mystical heroism on the battlefield and his half blood.

And he all but seethed himself into Plague sweats at the thought of another man having what he could not.

Her. Faer Princess of the Night. Illumanser Adept. Dominae Tenebris. A rare and delicate beauty no man had ever laid his hands on.

On top of that, Ultan was in position to take, as Arturo had been born to do, take and take and take till there was nothing left. Only Ultan stood in that position ready to take and sought to give.

Damn you Arturo for being so unlike him, so opposite in all ways.

If I could place but one part of you in him, it would be the part that wanted me.

Morgance wiped her eyes and sighed her troubles away the best she could, embracing the quiet murmur of energy she felt as she approached the edge of the old ruins.

Heat flushed her skin and kissed pale hair as she released its length from its pins. Wavy tresses spilled past the small of her back, swaying with the swish of her black velvet skirts like a river willow.

Here she felt different.

Here she felt free.

No one really knew how old the ruins were. *Old* merely denoted an Age, long lost into the dark mists of a thousand stars. Especially since the Faer were all but gone from the earth, and even *they* were only rumored to have tapped a fragment of the power that those who built the ruins had billowed with, like full sails in the wind of the sea.

Forever alive. Forever asleep. She thought, the incantation wispy in her mind.

Forever Faer. Forever Free.

Forever alive. Forever asleep.

Forever I see. Forever I dream.

Morgance continued down the slope of the plateau till she reached the hidden glen, the geography of which captured the wind and whipped it around in a bowl, heating and cooling at the same time. Heavy blocks of milky white stone, cast to their side, sat in a loose circle around the slow rise of a giant mound of earth. Soft emerald green grass carpeted the mound, yet no plants grew upon its richly textured surface. To look upon it was to be confronted by something both mysterious and ancient, a place that defied both reason and logic.

Pure and undiluted power.

Having walked the path to the ruins so many times, Morgance let her eyes flutter closed as the pull to the mound and the circle of fallen white stones became too strong. With the earth in Summer Solstice, she could feel the freedom of the currents overtaking her bones, and walked to the entrance of the mound as if in a trance, feet barely touching the ground, eyelids twitching.

For the mound was an azimuthal circle, and the rocks were magnetic anomalies, a giant spinning centrifuge of polar energies, alternating with the seamless symmetry of opposites.

But the Faer had another name for it.

Hafnröth.

A word from the Haunted Tongue, *Hafnröth* was a place of transcendency, where one trained in the ways of the Faer could reach beyond the black ink of the sky and the eternal stars to the deepest pits of space. There, destinies swirled through a spiral of colorless existence, forever ascending and descending as time worked its wonders of magnetism and gravity, life and death. Kingdoms rose and fell to the splash of blood and the whispered voices of the masses and the brooding silence of the infinite beyond sat heavy and ageless above it all.

But locked in that deepest pit of space where the cords that connected heaven and earth held both root and branch, all the secrets of the past, present, and future lie bound and woven in dark veins.

And at its shadowed mouth, Morgance felt a thousand faces swim past, their voices a muted murmur against the wind.

Somewhere, sleeping along that invisible cord of rope that ran from the mound way out into the furthest pit of space, the answer to all her troubles sat swaddled like a child.

If only she could find it.

But Morgance could only fall to her knees, bludgeoned by the great power of the magnetic polarities alive in Summer Solstice. She could only crash to the ground and crawl, unable to fight that daft and giddy sensation of spinning, making her body think it was going to float on up into the sky and never come down.

Like a storm in a bottle half filled with water, constantly swirling and sloshed around, her mind seemed to separate from organ and bone. Flesh and skin fell away in consciousness as numbness invaded her muscles.

She could only crawl, fingers and joints of dark honey and glue, yellow-green eyes rolled back in their sockets.

And crawl she did, one inch at a time, until the mouth of the mound had swallowed her in its infinite darkness, where her head became too heavy to carry and lolled to the soft carpet of grass.

There, sleep took her captive.

Captive, inside *Hafnröth*, Vault of Dreams.

NEVAN & NILES

CHAPTER 15

The noise was distracting to Nevan but not Niles. The younger brother thrived under the riptide of voices, desperate and drunk and standing to lose a lot of money if his darts were on target.

Brown-haired Nevan's blood bubbled in his veins, anticipating the explosion of the crowd when their money was ripped from their hands, but blonde-haired Niles' face was a carving of stone. Smiling stone, hard and unfeeling to the animosity slapping his way from the upper deck of the giant common room.

In fact, he enjoyed it all.

Us against them. Just like always.

Niles passed a look to Nevan as the dartist before them missed his final toss, writing him out of the victory. It was all but sewn up, now. Niles would have to miss the board completely if he wanted to lose.

And that just *wasn't* going to happen.

The public house, named *The Crook and Crown*, was known on the gambler's circuit as the pinnacle of all darts tournaments during the week of Solstice. And as it stood, both Nevan and Niles were ready to walk from the final game with so much gold they could barely carry it between them their spindly sixteen and seventeen-year old arms. Who would've thought a scruffy pair of upstarts could've bested the legends of the gambler's circuit?

Halfeye Fraser and The Twist of Dundy. Swifty Grant and Mallan Meadbeard. Lefty O'Connal all the way from the shores of Eire and the big ugly Angle known only as Flax, who downed a pint of bitter in between each toss as if dying of thirst and threw his darts so hard they jiggled the board on the wall.

All of them, despite their legends and their many victories, down two perfect tosses to scruffy-chinned and toe-head Niles and his poky ears, too young for a decent nickname.

Us against them. Just like we like it.

Music and laughter buffeted the background, fists dripping with coins, stretching to place new bets. Nevan caught his brother's arm as Niles moved to toe the line. Taller Niles tipped his chin down to Nevan, who was always using his one-year age advantage to pass younger Niles nuggets of wisdom.

Even though all of their experiences had been together, like a rowboat and its oars lost in storm.

They were a team.

"Maybe you should miss." Nevan said at normal speaking volume, considering the mindless noise consuming *The Crook and Crown*. The wooden walls all but shook with cheers and shouts. Ale-soaked curses and oaths so dark and blasphemous neither teenager even knew what they meant.

"But why?" Niles' smile spread, crooked white teeth impossibly charming.

"Because I'd like my head to stay on my neck, thank you very much."

Niles only squinted. If anything, they shared the same brown eyes. Other than that, one would have a hard time believing they were brothers. Different body types, different voices, different attitudes.

But their brown eyes were the same, bound to the same horrors, the same diseases, the same tears.

The same promises.

The same dreams.

Niles paused, looking at the pair of darts in his hand. They were simple little things, who knew they could do so much damage? Just like him and Nevan, two insignificant scraps of humanity, flying through life, messing up anything and everything they came in contact with.

Troubleseekers? Troublemakers?

No, trouble magnets. Moths to flame.

Sixteen and seventeen-year old cyclones of vinegar and soda.

Niles sighed and flipped the darts around in his hand as the chants grew. Ale splashed and faces spit red and ugly, venom on their lips.

"You really think so, Nev?"

Nevan's thin lips wrinkled, looking around. They were surrounded, buried in a den of drunkenness. He merely shrugged and let the impending riot speak for him.

It was then Niles' smile was all sorts of devious.

"Hey, maybe one of those pretty highland girls bet on *us* to win. I wouldn't mind a black eye if there were someone to kiss away all the trouble I went through to get it."

"Ni..." Nevan reached out but Niles had already moved to toe the line, brown eyes glazed by the perfection of focus he found only in the heart of the storm.

The worse it was, the better he did.

It was idle time that was the curse. Not action, not chaos. Boredom.

One could say he dreamed of it, the fury of the moment, like a beggar longing for a hot meal and a place to stay. The very opposite drained him of his sanity with all the symptoms of Plague. Slowly stalking his sleep and robbing it with dreams of excitement and adventure.

In that, he was alone, and Nevan all but started to eat his own hand as Niles cast his first dart with a meaty thwack into the center of the board.

He never got to throw the second dart.

High Street mud tasted the same in every town, and it took the walk to the next one to remove the taste of it from the mouth.

Nevan splashed to the ground three seconds behind Niles, his bumps and bruises not as bad as the champion dartist. Nothing short of mayhem swirled about *The Crook and Crown*, happy to rid themselves of the impetuous youths who dared lose them all so much money. In that regard, a crime of hundreds had been committed against the brothers, but as the darting was illegal to begin with, and many of the town's authorities standing to lose monies themselves, the whole thing was an extravagant waste of time, save the unbelievable story their bodies now bore the witness of.

Honor amongst thieves and all that.

Niles could see it now, them as bent old gray-bearded men, toothless and blind from a life of wild escapades.

Remember that one darts tournament?

Which one?

Solstice, of course!

Which Solstice? The one in Fordair?

Yeah! Tournament of Champions! Biggest purse ever to grace The Crook and Crown.

Curses, Nev, that's the one where I got our teeth kicked in for tossing six triple rings in a row.

Yeah! And I told you to throw the game but you were being your usual donkey-headed self.

That's me. Donkey-head Niles.

"I..." Niles went to speak, rising to his hands and knees before the feeling of being a winter gourd trampled under the feet of a dozen wild horses rippled through his stomach. He wretched, but nothing came out, and in the end he splashed back to the mud till his tougher older brother came and hoisted him up.

Nevan never said, *I told you so.* No matter what the outcome, he *never* said that. Even if it were the truth.

Because they were in it together.

Instead, he only patted Niles' bruised ego on the top of the head and let the taller young man lean on him as they tripped their way to the town gate. Even the footmen manning the gate cast them pity, not even bothering with the how or why of their plight.

Once they were on the road, Nevan looked back at the town and spit, wiping his mouth on his sleeve and cringing at the sight of his own blood.

Niles was a lump of moans, holding his head. Crusted in now dry mud and filth, he looked scruffier than ever and smelt twice as bad. His blonde hair was almost as dark as Nevan's brown hair with his time in the dirt.

"I can't believe they tried to drown you in a vat of ale before they beat the pudding out of you." Nevan mumbled, fighting to keep them both staggering down the road in the darkness. Highwaymen were not the issue now, they had nothing but the clothes on their backs and the laughable stories of a hundred town shanties and a thousand more feathers ruffled. Grass ruffled alongside the road with a pleasant murmur, wind urging them east, along the southern border.

"I know…" Niles groaned. "Perfectly good stuff to waste. Very nutty. And smooth! Oh, ouch…yes, nice and smooth. Like my tosses."

"Well, I never did see that highland lass you were looking for." Nevan chuckled. "Maybe I would've if I wasn't so caught up in running for my life."

"Yeah…" Niles eased on to his own two feet, taking his own weight. "Sorry about that."

"At least we got in a good meal." Nevan said, dabbing his thin lips with the back of his wrist as his smile faded. "Wait, you didn't eat, did you?"

"I *always* toss better on an empty stomach."

Nevan rolled his eyes. Yet another worry the future would hold. Niles may've tossed darts better on an empty stomach, but tossing was done while standing, and Niles couldn't *walk* a pace and a half without complaining if they'd skipped a meal.

"Shoulda stuffed your ruddy little face with as many meat pies as I could get my hands on." Nevan sighed, staring at the darkness before them both.

Dawn was closer than the next town.

"Well," Nevan squeezed his brother's shoulder. "You're a winner in my book."

Niles' crookedly charming smile was too painful to flash, but it was there all the same.

AERLYN

CHAPTER 16

Night had a way of frightening so many as it stood dark and thick till Solara found the strength to replace Luna. And with the murder of Brachin's governor still up in the air, The Thistle could feel the fears of many spill from the walls of the dwellings she passed on by with the feet of the wind.

Running all night.

Sad, Aerlyn thought, catching the scent of pine as the forest sat low before her, and beyond it, the toothy snarl of untamed land known only as the highlands. *Night is a blessing, not a curse. And failing to look something you're afraid of in the eyes only makes it worse.*

But looking her path in the eye as she finally slowed to a walk didn't make it any better. Dawn rose pained and slow around her, threatening her with fewer choices than she liked. By now, a dozen towns would've heard of her crime, her *murder* of the governor of Brachin, and the roads would be unsafe. And after all the trouble she went through for Solstice, her excursion south along the border had been met with twenty poor strings of saltwater pearls, a nasty bruise, and nothing short of the closest call she'd ever had since becoming The Thistle.

But the thought of murder was an affront to her very nature, a crime she felt herself incapable of committing, despite her own wretched history.

It was enough to make her sick, but there was no changing it now. Only running and running and running. And as if it'd never happened, Aerlyn greeted the dawn as always, on her own two feet. With the wind nipping at her long and hooded brown cloak, and an apple in her hand, freedom again was hers.

Smiling to herself, Aerlyn chose her path with the twisting of the apple stem. She had no map of the south or the east, didn't need one, and when the stem popped off in her fingers, she stared a hole in the thick velvet fringe of the forest and set off for its safety.

And by the time she reached its grace, the highway far behind her rippled with the trail of fifteen horses in full gallop.

Blending in with terrain was something Aerlyn had learned to do at a young age, and her time in the highlands had only brought that skill to nearly inhuman levels. But in the forest, Aerlyn always felt lost and alone, in the best of ways, as if she were travelling aimlessly through someone else's dream.

So many places for the eye to dart, so many creatures and scents, like a town of nature, or hundreds of them, each little leaf and fallen log a street or an alley all to itself; each and every tree a mansion of creeping things and hiding places.

Hearing the cry of a hawk eager for a rabbit pricked her ears and Aerlyn saw a flash of wings up above some thirty feet away, though the dense texture of the greenery swallowed the hawk as if it'd never been.

And its cry.

Strange, Aerlyn thought as she paused, her tread light and soft across the earth. *That's not possible.*

The image of the gray flutter of movement, yes, but the sound wouldn't just disappear as if she'd never heard it. Sounds carried. Didn't they? They didn't just stop.

Listening carefully for an echo, the flutter of wings or the snap of the rabbit's neck, she heard nothing in the end, save that low hum of the earth.

Alive.

Peering through the undergrowth and listening, Aerlyn straightened when she realized she *hadn't* seen a hawk, but something else entirely.

Not that she was sure of that either.

And since she was on the run she didn't have to be sure to keep moving. Life had already spilled over and there was no cleaning it up.

Not that running in the forest did anyone any good. A forest was a confusing thing by nature. Even the forest itself had no consciousness of what grew and when, why it grew or how.

Just that it did.

And the forest didn't care who took residence in its many darknesses. The unwritten law of it all was just to stay clear of a forest unless one knew what they were doing, which Aerlyn certainly did, though she wasn't quite sure who or what was in the forest with her.

Just that she was *not* alone, lost in someone else's dream.

And as it stood, The Thistle pinched her hood down a bit lower, walked a pace slower, and felt a tingle ride down the length of her left arm where the burning bruise and the safety of her spring-loaded knife slept in perfect harmony.

With every crack of undergrowth and deadfall, no matter how near or distant, Aerlyn's spine shivered and sent a foamy buzz all the way up to her ears, pricking them with heat. In the folds of her hood, her senses were amplified, and Aerlyn barely made a sound as she passed across the softness underfoot, though the forest was every kind of folly.

Muscles taut and sight sensitive to the periphery, Aerlyn continued on the meandering path of the forest till she could take no more of the tension worming its way up the back of her legs.

Aerlyn spun in a slow circle before squatting next to a very large spruce and a tangle of holly shrubs and ferns.

Come out, come out, whomever you are...

It was as if whomever...or *whatever* was in the forest with her was tracking her, not *hunting* her.

A small comfort? No. Aerlyn was skilled in dealing with animals of all kinds, especially the ones that wore the face of a man, the skin and bones of a man, but had the minds of the savage wolverine or the hungry bear.

The mind of the stray dog.

But the watcher *tracking* her was mirroring her movements more in study than anything else. Moving when she moved. Using the noise of her own movements to hide its own. And because of it, the disease of ignorance burned hot down The Thistle's back. Not the peril of Brachin or the days behind its misfortune, but sometimes not knowing was the worst danger of all.

It was just when The Thistle was about to stand that she smelled it the same time she heard it.

A whistle of nostrils and a scent of rosemary.

A human.

Aerlyn froze, heart thumping, and tipped her alabaster chin to the wind to before finally *feeling* what was haunting her sit but a foot away. The Thistle turned ever so slowly until blush colored her cheeks and chin rose petal pink to see a pair of exotic almond-shaped eyes hued reddish brown and marbled with pale green and gray stare back at her.

Forever watching, unblinking.

Voice caught in her throat, Aerlyn locked gazes with the forest eyes for the quickest moment, pupil to pupil, wondering *how on earth* someone could possibly sneak up on her. But the eyes blinked and disappeared from the small space they'd carved out of the bushes.

Spooked, Aerlyn spun, seeking the path back to the flat roads east before she felt two more eyes on her.

Then a dozen.

And then she lost count.

Knowing nothing good would come of running, though she hated relying on her mouth to get her out of a bad situation as it was nearly guaranteed to do the opposite, Aerlyn stopped, sighed, and spun.

Before her stood the eyes of a woman who'd made the forest her home. Around her the forest bent as if her guardian, dark green clothing meshing with the living tapestry of trees and wildlife.

Even though her true home was in Ullraye and the safety of its strong black Tower.

Aerlyn swallowed hard and removed her hood with what reverence she could, spiced with fear.

Wild misery streaked through those stunningly-colored irises, unblinking and resolute. They were eyes far from where they belonged, long forgotten but in the hearts of a faithful few.

Eyes of promises and dreams.

Aerlyn managed a small bow, which was something of a miracle, because Aerlyn O'Rye bowed to nothing and no one.

But the woman was hardly nothing and *far* from no one.

She was the only child of King Brom the Chosen and his wife Kathron Caelie, Lady of a Thousand Lochs.

She was Princess of the Throne, Heir to the Crown of Albanland.

Her name was Rhoswen.

And she was not alone.

CHAPTER 17

Rhoswen held the much taller Aerlyn in her captivating gaze as the near and distant forms of men and women, her forest companions, joined from the undergrowth.

The place was literally *crawling* with them.

"The forest welcomes you, traveller." Aerlyn detected a hint of suspicion. "*If* you come in peace."

Their weapons weren't out, but they were everywhere. Bows, swords, daggers. Visible but not drawn and ready for first flinch. Rhoswen herself was the match to the flame waiting to alight the forest with her fire. It burned in the brown of her eyes, wisely tempered with green and gray.

Ready for war. But waiting.

Toughness framed a soft face of pink skin, crowned by a rich mass of brown curls so dark they were nearly black. The strength of her short and compact frame was a clear contrast to lithe Aerlyn, and her cloak was the shade of tree shadows and shrubs.

Aerlyn's bruise was throbbing and she didn't think the Crown Heir would just run a blade through her without a reason, but she sure as hell didn't want to give any of the stone cutters and hunters behind her a reason to get all grabby. Especially her bruised arm, not to mention any other part of her.

Aerlyn folded her hands together and tried to soften her voice, though it was a rough thing anyway, like sea-faring rope and gnarled tree roots.

"A fugitive finds no peace these days, your Highness. Even in the forest."

Something flashed across Rhoswen's features at the words, and her almond eyes narrowed as she took a step toward Aerlyn. Aerlyn spent the moment in contemplation, but thoughts were sometimes themselves more of a curse than any of the salty oaths she could spit with the best of them.

"A fugitive, you say?"

"Would you prefer…skilled vagabond?"

Rhoswen advanced till she was but a foot from Aerlyn, which Aerlyn noticed drew some form of concern from the wiry pack of lieutenants at her back. She could all but taste the ferocity of the small woman, thinking in that moment that she could stand before an eighty foot swell and be unafraid.

"And Brachin? Was that a display of your…*skill?*"

Aerlyn crossed her arms.

"Does the forest gossip as much as the Chamber of Lords?"

The lids of Rhoswen's peculiar eyes dropped and her pink lips flattened across her face.

"Does The Thistle still grow in the highlands? Or has drought moved it south?"

"Has an Angle garden ever welcomed such a weed?"

"No, but the Nørds are in desperate need of a thorn in their side."

Aerlyn bit the sour slash of her bottom lip before a smile slid across it.

"How do you know I am The Thistle?"

"How do you know I am the Crown Heir?"

"My life alone has made me perceptive."

"But not enough." Rhoswen straightened. "It is unwise to walk alone in the forest. You never know who you'll run into."

"But this forest is said to be protected by the spirit of Brom, is it not? King Brom the Chosen was not only known to have romanced the most beautiful woman in all of Albanland, such they called her the Lady of a Thousand Lochs, for so rare was her beauty. The good King was also known to have a daughter, his only child, whom he loved without condition, and raised with all vigilance to one day take the Throne in his place."

Rhoswen clasped a fist to her chest in honor. Far too many years ago, his laugh was rich in her ears, and his own huge hands engulfing hers to teach her the sword.

"Truth and Faery tales."

Aerlyn nodded slowly, not knowing which part of the legend was truth, and which part the Faer had corrupted with their cloven tongues.

But Aerlyn blitzed on.

"Well then *you* would be the reason why the strength of King Brom the Chosen, heaven hold his soul eternal, still lingers in Albanland. You are his only child, Rhoswen of Kathron Caelie. And if you are not, then I am not Aerlyn O'Rye, The Thistle of High Inverloch. I have also been called 'a hand without shadow in a land without sun'...is there another title I should know *you* by, your Highness?"

Pain knifed through the Crown Heir, and her pink skin paled, though still rosy compared to Aerlyn's alabaster complexion.

"The Queen."

Aerlyn took to one knee and bowed her head.

"My life is yours, good Princess of Exile. I will serve you and your Crown, long may you reign, so long as you believe me when I say have killed no man and never will."

Rhoswen removed her right hand from a fold in her cloak for Aerlyn to kiss as was the custom and a sliver of shock zipped through the thief as her graceful and nimble grip held the hand of the rightful ruler of the land.

For the third finger, where the Ring of Rule was to be placed, was completely gone.

Cut off from the joint.

Gone.

Aerlyn gasped and her midnight blue eyes shot up to meet the gaze of her monarch.

"Be careful what you promise, Aerlyn O'Rye, for there are only two kinds of people in Albanland. The ones you will kill and the ones you will kill for."

Aerlyn fought her hand from shaking. The trembling ran down her spine instead.

"And you're about to find out which kind of person I am."

CHAPTER 18

Crown Heir Rhoswen stayed silent despite the many questions forming in the mind of the notorious thief and Aerlyn knew it would only be a matter of time before they had some form of heart to heart about how rotten life had been to the both of them.

To Albanland.

Her midnight blue gaze stole peeks at Heir Rhoswen's right hand as they walked and walked. The forest soothed and shushed and Aerlyn fell into a trance, walking.

Watching that three-fingered hand dangle near the hilt of a mean-looking sword.

Aerlyn's own body had seen its share of terrors, but her fingers were all still attached, beautifully graceful and pale white at that, like the rest of her moonlight skin. Just to think about it, Aerlyn could only imagine what damage the disfiguring had caused the Heir's soul, and how the roots of the tragedy had burrowed deep into her mind.

Such a thing must've twisted her development as a woman both born and bred for and from equal portions of grace and strength.

It was worse than blindness in a way, worse than being barren. Because it was both, in a custom Aerlyn didn't quite understand yet still felt the crushing weight of.

For the ruler of Albanland had worn the Ring of Rule on the third finger of their right hand since the Ring's casting and anointing in a time long buried in myth and lore. To wear it was to link the past and the future. Whomever had removed Rhoswen's finger had done a cruel thing indeed.

A crippling thing.

And who had done it to her? Who had so heartlessly put the knife to her joint and separated her right to the Throne with more than just a symbolic act of defiance? For to kill would've been greedy, but to maim was vengeance born of jealousy, hideous and bent. Whose hate ran so deep that the tearing of skin and cracking of bone, bending to the will of frozen silver steel, had been the only solution?

Aerlyn had only one name in mind, though she dare not utter it.

Yet.

Aerlyn noticed Rhoswen studying her as they walked the dizzying path into the heart of the woods. Questions were curved into her lips, sitting silent just beneath her slender nose.

Aerlyn was all but dead on her feet after running all night.

"Speak and I will answer, if I can." The Princess said. Aerlyn nodded, smelling the scent of rosemary again, at her nearness. A gleam in Rhoswen's lovely eyes favored her, for sure. The Thistle didn't know to what extent, but she'd seen enough hatred to know the very opposite of it at first sight.

Aerlyn only watched their feet tread the dirt and mats of turf. Nearly in step with each other. Sisters of the same land, the same blood, the same fate. Distant, yet One, daughters of a cloven Throne, a broken Crown, a dream of life, beaten and bruised.

But still so alive, like the forest stretching around them.

"I'm sorry…about that." Aerlyn only said, rubbing the injury on her left arm. It was nothing compared to Rhoswen's right hand, and Rhoswen knew the pity, for she'd seen it on every face sympathetic to her cause. And how many years old was the injury? How long had she lived with the reminder of what had been stolen from her?

The Heir simply held her right hand out before her as if she were a bride to be inspecting the size of the diamond on her finger. The gap in her hand was like an eclipse in the sky, something that stole breath from the lungs.

But yet, Rhoswen wore it like a badge of honor. She had earned it. By birth and by conflict. By destiny's twisted blade.

If the Crown was to be hers, it would also be earned in the same manner.

In blood.

"*I'm* not sorry." Rhoswen said, following the snaking line of green-cloaked woodsmen before her, her hidden army of men and women. And though it blessed Aerlyn to see women walk alongside men, both bearing the same weapons and the same burden, it reminded her of the horrid contrast of Brachin and all the fattened towns of the south strung out along the border roads. There, women could only dream of death to free them from the curse of their life. The Plague of slavery had become something of a tidal wave, consuming all in its daemonic wake.

Perhaps it would wash all the way to the forest. So many brave souls yet to free from their chains. Certainly Rhoswen could reach a hand, if even a maimed one, out to them and save them by giving them a hope and a purpose.

By giving them a *united* kingdom.

"Royal birth has its difficulties." Rhoswen continued as the dense thickets of trees and bushes made way for a small clearing conjoined to a much larger one by a babbling creek. "And this," She spread her arms wide. "*This* has made me the Queen I was always supposed to be."

Aerlyn watched the true Queen of Albanland gaze across the co-joined clearings, separated by gender. They were alive with the vibrant thrum of life and laughter.

All around, the dark mazes of the forest kept them tucked away from the prying eyes of their enemies, and Aerlyn began to study the scene alive around her, but Rhoswen continued, drawing the eyes of midnight back to her own magnetic charisma.

"There are some things you just can't learn in the Chamber of Lords or the Tower of Ullraye. One in a hundred Albans are of

High blood. That leaves ninety-nine to fight for the scraps of a hard land like a pack of wild wolves. With my ring finger gone, my soul was given to those ninety-nine, and I became one of them. And with those ninety-nine I will rise up one day and take back the Throne that is not mine, not my late father's, but *ours*."

Rhoswen tipped her chin to the waiting warband ahead of them, almond eyes of brown fire glinting gray with the steel and stone of her quest, yet still kissed by the eternal hues of the forest, and the ancient lifeblood of Albanland's wild and untamable emerald green purity.

"And mark my words, thief, that day *is* near."

The women's camp was smaller than the men's due to the two to one ratio of Princess Rhoswen's army in exile. Aerlyn was keen to notice the system of administration Rhoswen employed, where one leader was in charge of no more than ten of the rank below them, on down the line, so that a lieutenant was in charge of ten sergeants, and each of those sergeants were in charge of ten warriors.

There were no more clans, simply memories woven in the colors they wore. Surnames and past disputes had been abolished. What clothing they'd taken with them, severing themselves from class and clan had blended into the whole, as all wore variants Rhoswen's green and brown.

And just like her eyes, those flashes of gray were swords or knives at their sides, and defiance in their hearts.

They were One.

Unlike Albanland's Warband, stuck up north under the watchful gaze of Faer Princess Morgance, Rhoswen's Army was one in thought and deed, and not name only.

No matter what the task or the skill, each warrior was held accountable to know how to do it, and though the impoverished sleeping quarters were clearly divided by the babbling brook that ran through the two clearings, the fresh sunshine of noon saw both men and women, elbow to elbow, engaged in the many activities needed to sustain life in the forest.

Aerlyn smiled as they wove through the bustling activity of the women's camp and reached the brook. Outside of the forest's outstretched arms, factions warred for scraps of power, distorting the authority given to them, lost in a nightmarish swamp of never ending curses.

But here, in the forest, order walked hand in hand with freedom.

Balance.

Not the perfect freedom of the highlands and the various towns and villages born into the blood of Rhoswen's diverse warband, but a sense of belonging. Undivided loyalty. An unshakeable identity that was theirs and theirs alone.

Aerlyn inhaled the scent of the pine and the heat of the sun along with the vibrant thrum of unity, hushed by the thickness of the forest.

Her time alone had made the feeling a crippling hunger pang, and to be in the fullness of its fruit nearly made her light-headed.

It was beautiful.

"If this is not the fruit of Albanland's true leader, then what is?"

Small Rhoswen took it all in a subtle smile that twisted the edge of her eyelids. Arms crossed she nudged her shoulder to the men's camp across the creek.

"You must understand I have a very strict policy concerning...fraternization. Even though my taste in men is Princely, I must admit there is a handsome man or two or ten over there. Strong, too. But most of the strong ones are ugly. You know, smashed noses and the like."

The smirk working across the garnet slash of Aerlyn's mouth brought a smile to Rhoswen's lips.

"I thought as much, thief."

"I said nothing!" Aerlyn turned from the brook and the mystery of the wooden huts and wool-topped fabric tents. She didn't know why the Princess was so happy with herself. All of the legends concerning The Thistle said that she hated men and was hated by them, with the robberies to prove it.

"Your face says much, thief. Trust me, I'm the one who's looking at it."

Aerlyn's rough voice was laced with sarcasm.

"Yes, your Highness."

Rhoswen laughed a small chuckle and reached down to rinse her hands in the cool brook and splash refreshing water on the back of her neck to free herself from the heat.

"Obviously we are the stewards of the next generation, and we fight for those children yet to be named. We'll fill up the walls of empty towns. Hell, we'll build new ones that make this whole thing look like a joke." Rhoswen looked to the sun in a squint, staring up from her spot near the sparkling creek. "But now is not the time for them. Now is the time for patience. We draw our strength from patience, and from each other. To wait is to want." The squint fell to lithe Aerlyn. "But don't worry. We won't live in the forest forever. Some day this moment will be forgotten. But you and I will remember." The Heir's laugh stretched, the thought crazy to her ears as she spoke. "To think Albanland was reclaimed by two-thousand outlaws! Two-thousand! Ha!"

Aerlyn's smirk wound its way back to the men's camp, wondering why the trees shadowed its huts and tents in such mystery.

And why are you so interested in what kind of men are here, Aerlyn O'Rye? Afraid for your life?

No. Afraid of your selfish heart finally being wrong for once, holding every hurt so close to make them all the wind of the Four Storms in your sails.

Somewhere out there there has to be a good man. There has to be. If there isn't, just leave right now. She'll understand. After all, how can you be her free servant if she won't let you go? Is anybody here because they have to be? Is this a prison? A last resort, maybe, but there are no women in chains here, Aerlyn O'Rye, and no fat men waiting to die from their own daggers.

No, this is as close to heaven as you've ever dreamt it, and this is only the beginning of it all if you fill your heart with as much hope as you've been filling your hands with jewels.

It was then The Thistle removed her brown cloak to wet her own hands and slake her thirst, because maybe, now, The Thistle had finally found good soil and sweet water.

And plenty of sun.

Make that two-thousand and one your Highness.

Above her Solara baked, and Aerlyn splashed water on the back of her neck and let her rich auburn hair fall free.

Yes, good soil and good water to take root, but was there enough sun to peek into the shadows of the huts and tents of the men's camp across the trickling blue diamonds of the cool creek?

A whistle pricked her ears and she turned to see a tall man staring down at her, his arms laden with firewood.

"That's quite nasty."

Aerlyn looked down at her left arm and the spring-loaded harness that could twitch her knife into her hand as if she was a practitioner of Faer magic.

Or was he talking about her bruise?

Aerlyn stood tall and did nothing, not knowing *what* to do, because the welcoming arms of Rhoswen's chosen saviors had so quickly stripped away everything she'd used to survive her life alone in the wild, and her need to carve through a busy crowd as if everyone was out to get her or her skill of climbing stone walls in the dead of night had all but left her mind like a bad dream.

"Well..." The man nodded, politely, if a bit awkwardly. "I don't expect you to courtesy, but my name's Quill and I hope you feel welcome here."

Aerlyn opened her mouth to speak but the man's duties carried him swiftly across the creek and off into the shadows of the men's camp.

Suddenly feeling alone in a brand new world, Aerlyn turned, expecting to find the Crown Heir laughing behind her, sun kissing her almond eyes with glory.

But Rhoswen was nowhere to be seen.

She had a war to plan.

ULTAN

CHAPTER 19

True sleep lay before Ultan like a rope in the darkness, too slick to grab a hold of. Tossing and turning in his bed, his body ached with the many pains of battle. Groans echoed throughout the stone of his chambers, howls of agony muffled in blankets and furs.

In the end, the Champion of Albanland resorted to drowning himself in an old friend whose lies he'd grown accustomed to believing, despite the warmth and numbness that always made him feel his sense of control slip away and leave him helplessly swallowed in a dark pit.

And when dawn finally came, Ultan could barely open his eyes, sprawled half-naked and bruised upon the mat of his furs and woolen blankets.

Prisoner.

But even in the cruel embrace of that whiskey-soaked sleep, Ultan ran. There was no safety in sleep, no rest from the weariness of guilt.

No rest from his dreams.

And in his dreams, the most fearsome warrior of the land turned his back and ran from those eyes that wouldn't leave him alone.

Eyes that would never die, despite what he'd done to them so many years ago.

Ultan roared awake with the hand shaking his massive shoulder and he blinked the blurs away to see the perfectly trimmed beard and slicked-back brown hair of Lord Arturo of Pallantyne.

Mind still dizzy and reeling too much to put a thought together, Ultan only sat and stared at the younger Lord, clothed for combat, though his polished riding boots and broach-fastened cloak spoke more of a civic appearance.

The kind of thing Ultan despised.

When was the last time Arturo had seen the field of battle anyway?

Oh, that's right, Lord Beautiful, you only play at soldiering in the Swordsman's Circle. I hear you're very good, but I never have time to see you because I'm too busy SAVING THE KINGDOM FROM NØRDS!

"Sorry to wake you," Arturo's rich voice rumbled. "But I just wanted you to know that I'm headed south for awhile and I haven't seen the Princess since last night."

Ultan pawed at his face, digging grooves into his skin as if to strip away a mask that'd formed across his strong features like glue. His deep-set heather green eyes stared down at the bridge of his broken nose, as if it didn't belong on his own face.

Such was the way of whiskey, sometimes.

"Princess…what?"

"I haven't seen Faer Princess Morgance since last night." Arturo spoke slowly, never a patient man to begin with.

"After…dinner?"

Arturo hid his lie in the act of sitting down on the edge of Ultan's giant bed. It was then he noticed the broken bottle glittering in the corner of the room and the sweet and smoky smell of fermented grain.

His sun-kissed face gleamed uncomfortably handsome against a flash of white teeth.

"Yes, that's right."

"But my orders? What about the guardsmen? I'll have the lot of them flogged."

Arturo waved a hand, signet ring heavy and catching the light cutting slits through the stone keyholes.

"She is…a tormented woman. A woman with her…" Arturo rubbed his fingertips together as he thought. "…*gifts* needs some space. Some time alone. I'm sure she'll come back here. Back to you."

The last words Arturo had spoken had been nearly too soft to hear.

Ultan sat up and walked to the bath as if he hadn't heard *any* of the words the younger Lord had said. There, he stripped and splashed in the cold water, leaning his head back to hug the shivers away.

Arturo's shifty gaze narrowed and he sighed. Even in bathing Ultan was stronger, sitting in the frigid water as if locked in some deep meditation that made him invincible. Arturo still smelled of the warm rose-petal spring water he'd bathed in last night, and his scent was as sweet as always.

"So, you don't care, then?" He asked.

"About her location or her feelings?"

Arturo looked at his glossy nails, so well trimmed and nearly elegant.

"How long will you deny her?"

"How long will you bug me about it?"

"How long will you pretend you don't want her? Sleeping alone in this drafty old room with your damned whiskey and the many pelts of your hunts."

"I'm not losing sleep over it."

Arturo stood, storming over to the bath.

"And the Crown? Surely you want the Crown? You can't be so stonehearted as to deny two lusts when every man on this cursed rock would seize either one or the other without a second thought! And you have the Warband in the palm of your blood-stained hands! All you need is Morgance and she will make you the most powerful man Albanland has had in ten generations!"

Ultan's head only lolled over, strawberry blonde curls drifting in the water like the tendrils of a jellyfish. His eyes were barely open, bits of highland heather set against the pale and nearly bluish tint of his cold skin. Soaking in the frosty tub, he looked nearly dead, or dead tired, or tired of making others dead, either way.

His brows and cheekbones protruded like fists, hard and unyielding, but his shadowed eyes were soft and green and aching to slip under the icy wetness and forget it all.

Forever.

"And do I invite the Nørds to this wedding you're planning? I hear they like a good party."

"Very funny, *Skölhammer.*" Arturo nearly sneered, hiding his disgust as he began to pace.

"There are only so many weeks of summer left." Ultan continued his joke. "What am I sitting in here for? Shall I wear the Skyeshire colors or something a bit more ornamental?"

"Don't be a fool. It does not become you."

"No? But haven't I become one already? I fight an enemy without end while my Lords play match-maker."

Arturo bit his lip.

Not only was Ultan quick with a sword, but his tongue was quick, too. Perhaps it had formed in him the toughness that kept Albanland from falling apart.

How many fights had the youth started with his tongue? How many more had he finished with his fists?

Now sat before him a fight started long before his fists had been forged in the blood of others, but all could be made right with his tongue and the utterance of one simple word.

Yes.

"You're ruining this Kingdom." Arturo said, slicking his hair back and pointing an accusing finger at the Champion. "Your ghosts will one day take you to the grave a lonely old cripple when you could've had the love of the most beautiful woman I've ever seen. Are you so blind to not see how much she loves you? How she thinks of you? How she wants you? Are you so hard to deny her what *she* wants?"

Eyes closed, nostrils flared, a frown stretched across the Champion's face.

100

Arturo is a fancy man, hungry for the touch of a woman like a dog for the crumbs from the table. But he does have a point, and it's painfully obvious.

If not you, then who?

If not now, then when?

Didn't you once promise the Four Storms on your father's honor that if you could drive the Nørds from the land you'd finally give in to her? The land would finally be stable, and you'd be able to rebuild what's been stolen, what's been lost and destroyed.

And why are you waiting again?

Oh, that's right. Her.

Those eyes of your dreams.

Well, Ultan Skölhammer, you had your chance with her and you blew it.

You might as well just forget about her. For the sake of the Kingdom. Fall in and forget. Let it wash over your skin and sooth your soul.

If Faer Morgance can't make you forget, then you are a hopeless cause, cursed by your own memories.

You know her lips are sweeter than the juice of fresh mountain blackberries, and her touch softer than the airy song of Luna that she whispers to the wind.

You are a fool, Ultan Skölhammer, if you believe your dream makes more sense than this reality.

Arturo watched blankly as Ultan ducked his head under the water, held it for nearly a minute, and splashed from the surface, his heather-green eyes clear and clean.

Free from the grit of battle, the guilt of the night, and the sticky embrace of whiskey.

"Off with you, Lord Arturo." Ultan said, removing himself from the bath, with little diamonds of liquid ice dripping from thick cords of muscles and scars. "May your business in the south be expedient and prosperous. And may the Four Storms be at your back. I'll need every able man on my side to save this land from the Nørds and I expect you back here within a week for my final assault."

A shadow passed across Arturo's greedy gaze. Ultan pretended *not* to see it, heather green eyes shaded by a sheet of strawberry-blonde curls.

Arturo's bow was quick and tense, as if pre-planned. "Yes, My Champion."

And as Arturo left with a flourish of his proud Pallantyne colors, taking his headache-inducing sweet savor with him, Ultan dressed himself quickly, grabbing the milky white Blade of the Champion.

He was going to need it.

CHAPTER 20

Even though Ultan knew where to look, it didn't change the horror of what he saw.

"Morgance!" He shouted, but she did not move.

She was locked in one of her trances, more addictive than Ultan's whiskey. Even from a hundred feet away, entering the hidden glen, Ultan could see her eyes tremble behind the lids.

The wind whipped his long and curly hair across the face, trying to tear the white fox cape from his shoulders, yet the bejeweled dagger hanging above Faer Morgance' head would not move.

It was as if it was suspended, hovering.

By magic.

Ultan ran up the emerald green mound of *Hafnröth* as fast as his strong legs would carry him and snatched the dagger from the space of air and threw it on down the mound.

Eyes fluttering, Morgance' head tottered on her shoulders before she fell back to the warm grass, in between two of the large and ominous white stones that lined the circle like otherworldly sentinels.

Ultan took her in his arms quickly, his firm grip rubbing blood into limbs that had gone limp, as if fallen asleep.

"Morgance." He took her by the chin, as gently as possible, though his own pale skin was flushed a furious red.

How many times have I told you not to come here?

And in his mind, he swore he could've heard her response.

You forced me here, noble Champion.

This is your doing.

"Morgance, wake up." Ultan shook her softly and stroked her cheek.

Slowly, he watched life leak into her. Had it all been stolen in her trance, cast to the wind?

I curse your bloody Faer rituals. Though I don't understand the half of them, they anger me so.

And though her body was shadowed by Ultan's broad-shouldered physique, a living stone himself in between two of the white markers lining *Hafnröth*, her eyes were alive with the sun, capturing the fullness of the wind-whipped summer grass and its many promises of freedom.

She truly was the most beautiful woman in all the earth. Her hair was light itself, her eyes like glass. Lips of pure ruby, glistening.

Something inside wanted to kiss her for not dying, for not floating away in some forsaken Faer dream, but to hold her so close and look into her eyes was to once again taste the conflict they both knew was coming to an end.

"Name her." Morgance said.

"What?"

"The one you love so much." The Princess' graceful touch snaked around Ultan's neck and traced the hard line of his chin before falling to his chest. "The one who you won't let go of."

Ultan swallowed and fought the urge to drop Morgance on the ground and run off to what horrid plan his love of whiskey had formed in his mind, tossing and turning in his bed.

"I...I don't even know if she's still alive."

"Then all the more reason." The Princess whispered, her high-pitched voice one with the wind, swirling all around Ultan.

Maybe it was the rotten prison of the night and the battle of the day before, nothing in his stomach but whiskey and old wounds, but Morgance was simply irresistible in his arms, tempting him one last time to forget.

If ever there was a moment, it was now. With her in his arms, *he* felt vulnerable, like she was looking through his eyes into the shadows that sat behind them.

"I can't."

"You can't love me and you can't love her. What can you do, noble Champion, but die?"

Ultan nodded once faintly and then again.

"And that is what I intend to do."

"We've talked about this, Ultan. It's *not* the way."

Ultan sighed. She was a feather in his arms. He could carry her all the way up to her chambers in the top of the Tower of Ullraye and be done with it.

But the sun would shine from her eyes alone, and his heart would curse him from within, turning his blood to vinegar in his veins.

"It is the *only* way."

"Are you so confident in your abilities as a swordsman? Or are you so afraid of my love? So afraid you will love me more than you could ever love her, whoever she is." Her hand was to his chin again, and up around his neck. Touch paralytic, Ultan leaned back against the nearest stone as she laid her head to his chest.

"I'm not afraid of death. I'm afraid of meeting her face to face and looking her in the eye."

"Then name her to me." Morgance whispered. "I will pardon her if she has committed a crime."

Ultan stared up into the sky, free of clouds. Heaven was near them both, its fragrance full of dew-kissed grass and sea salt.

"Is she a thief? Is she a murderer? Or is she both? You know *I* hold the power to absolve. Speak her name and it will be done. She will be free and then *you* will be free to love me. And I will make you forget her name. Then, *my* name alone will be on your lips forever."

He would never forget.

Not her name.

Not her eyes.

Never.

"You cannot pardon her crime, for she did none, save that she was born. It was you, Faer Morgance, who did evil, and I have *not* forgotten."

Repulsion spilled across the delicate features of the Princess like ink soaking through cloth. It spread its liquid black blood till it tainted the whole of her body, burning her bones to ash.

"Her?"

Ultan didn't stop her as she peeled herself from him. Nostrils flared, her shoulders began to heave.

"You love...HER?"

Ultan pressed himself up slowly, as if the dragon of an ancient saga had fallen from the sky and was waiting to swathe him in flames and crisp his skin to charcoal. Her eyes were not her own, drowned in madness so hot Ultan wondered if the fires of hell could hold a candle to them.

"HEEERRRRRR???"

And in that moment, pressed between the hard white stone and the fomenting wrath of Dominae Tenebris, Faer Princess of the Night, Ultan remembered the moment when fate walked the woods with him and showed him something that would forever change his life.

The moment when two young girls in love had run into the forest. Both in love with the same boy. But only one could have the boy. He'd followed them. He remembered when they talked. When the talking became fighting. When the fighting produced a blade. When the blade stole the finger of one destined to sit the Throne.

"Yes Morgance, *her*." His mouth said though his own voice sounded foreign in his ears as he thought of that moment when he saw and had said nothing, and when the young girl he had pledged his heart to as only a young boy could screamed and cried, clutching a maimed hand, soaked with royal blood. "She's the one I love, the one I've always loved, the one who has been with me all these years."

"Rhoswen of Kathron Caelie. The Crown Heir." Morgance sneered, revulsion pulling her skin taut, holding her bones rigid. With her hatred stoked, she looked powerful. Fearsome, even.

Ready to howl the Haunted Tongue to the wind and summon the Four Storms to rain fire upon the highlands.

Her high pitched voice became a low moan in the back of her throat.

"I should have known."

Pressing himself from the stone, Ultan stepped toward her and she stepped back, the hatred nearly slipping from her skin in a flash, as if it'd come upon her in a fit, without her knowing. Her eyes bulged in their sockets like Ultan was a Nørd, come to slay her.

Once fearsome, now deathly afraid.

"I know what you did to her, Morgance, and I have forgiven. But I haven't forgotten. One day this land will be free of war, and we will be together. I don't know what will happen to you, but when I have the time to find her, I will marry her, Crown or no Crown."

Morgance shuddered, breathless as Ultan's crushing grip fell ever so softly upon her shoulders. Her wrath had been sucked from her like a whirlpool in the sea and left her frail and weak, tormented by a hate that felt so ancient even though it had only been a decade ago. In its wake, she was scared, as if something terrible and ferocious had overtaken a soul as finely-boned as a summer wildflower.

"My only hope is that she can forgive me for being a coward on that day, and forgive me for saying nothing about what you did to her. For letting her run away and plunge this Kingdom into the madness we have come to accept as a normal way of life."

Breath came to Morgance in sputters, her delicate features twisted in agony.

"Don't go." She squeaked.

"I must."

"You can't leave me here like this."

"I'll be back."

"…You…you really think you'll just sail into the Nørds' stronghold and win this war? By yourself? In a duel?"

Ultan hugged Morgance to him, squeezing her in pity more than anything.

She wasn't a villain.

Just a troubled young girl who'd made a bad choice, a truly *terrible* choice, and had watched an entire Kingdom suffer because of it.

"It's an ancient way, Morgance. I'll challenge their champion to a duel for the Crown. If I win, they'll stop this war. I'll even let them have the Orken Islands. They're too far away for us to govern anyway. Trust me, they respect strength. I know their ways. But if they win, then I'm only bringing about the inevitable sooner than later. A swift end to this one-hundred year old evil."

Ultan held Morgance at arm's length. She, like him, was a creature of guilt, loving someone she couldn't, thrust into a cauldron of responsibility she never truly wanted, though she dreamed so desperately for the name that such duties were attached to.

"I will win, Morgance. I will not die. I will return to you and I will help you through this."

Morgance laughed, her body lost in its own duel between the half that detested Rhoswen and embraced the ancient rites of the Faer and the half that had stared at her tiny hands and the knife they held, shocked beyond belief that such a thing had happened, as if she'd been possessed to do something she didn't even understand.

In some ways, Morgance was two different people, since that moment when she had lashed out in anger and taken Rhoswen's finger, the finger upon which the Ring of Rule was to one day be placed. Her soul had been cut to pieces by the same knife, and two gardens had grown in a heart once as soft as the emerald green grass of *Hafnröth*.

But like the mound and its white marker stones, dark forces had captured her, feeding her thoughts of jealousy and rejection, till the moment of destiny had looked her in the eye, and caught her in her weakness.

With a knife in her hand.

The laugher continued, distant, as Morgance' face was twisted with emotion.

"Such a Faery tale. But how will she reign if she has no finger upon which to wear the Ring of Rule?"

Ultan sighed.

"It is high time some of the old ways died, Morgance."

The laugh straightened, eerie and mocking, though the face it spilled from did not belong to it.

And in her eyes, Ultan saw a reflection of the future, his own future.

Two souls locked in a fight, forever battling.

"You're the one embracing the oldest way there is," her tone mocked him, "*noble* Champion."

Ultan nodded, turning to leave Morgance to her struggles. He truly pitied her, but didn't know what to do about it, just like he didn't know what to do when he'd seen her cut off Rhoswen's finger in the forest.

"Some ways never die, Princess."

And as Ultan headed back to the Tower of Ullraye to gather his things for his duel with the Champion of the Nørds, all he could hear a woman's laughter.

And behind it, whispers on the wind.

A plea, a prayer.

The desperate song of hope, though Morgance was herself a prisoner, held captive in the arms of her choices.

Maybe, Ultan wondered as he walked, seeing the fleet of Nørds and their dragon-boats hover in the glassy waters off the Mull of Montree, *maybe the truth will set her free.*

At least I feel better now. I feel ready to fight. Ready to win back the Crown.

Even though I have to sail straight into the mouth of hell to do it.

NEVAN & NILES

CHAPTER 21

Nevan was practically propping his younger and much taller brother up as they walked the southern highway, and when the heat of midday threatened to dump Niles in the ditch from exhaustion, Nevan waited till they reached a signpost to take a rest.

Niles all but collapsed against the wood post, skin glazed with sweat, and Nevan peered toward the nearby towns.

In the end, the decisions were always his, but Nevan never made them alone.

"Well brother, Nairnsmoor or Baraburr?"

"I can't decide…" Niles' smile was weak, his lips cracked and peeling. "I'm too busy dying."

Nevan shook his head as his brother slid down the post as if there were no bones in his body, till his head was cocked away from the hot sun, legs crossed low at the ankles as if he were simply goldbricking from hard labor. His crooked smile was seared on his face, as if he was content to spend the day there.

"You just sit there and dream of lamb stew. Or sausage and mash. Or vension! Yes, good venison with blackberry sauce and milkbread."

"All of the above, and a pretty lass to serve it to me?"

"Whatever you want." Nevan muttered, mopping his forehead with a sleeve. "I'll dream of the coin to pay for it all and a bloody cool breeze to go along with it."

Nevan squinted across flat and fallow fields cut by wild bands of thorns and weeds. Baraburr was a quaint little town, not much more than a street or two built up from the highway, lined for lodgers and the business of wayfaring, overshadowed in every way by distant Brachin and its high wooden walls. One could say those not rich enough to live in Brachin settled for Baraburr, like a human drainage ditch, though Brachin had one of the largest shanty districts in the south, as if those living in it didn't know they'd chosen the squalor of affluence over the unambitious peace of modesty. Nairnsmoor, across a gigantic pond wet with reeds and kingfishers darting and diving for supper, was a town known for its mostly gypsy population, and it felt vacant with the Summer Solstice celebrations stretching across the south, as the exoticism of gypsies spiced celebrations like Solstice with their fire-breathing, fortune-telling, and flashes of colorful clothing.

"Better food in Nairnsmoor." Nevan said, thinking aloud.

"You always were a sucker for a dumpling."

"It's not the dumpling, Ni. It's the sauce."

"Right. So cultured you are."

Nevan stood straighter in agreement.

"Well I'm scared of gypsies." Niles pinched his eyes and pressed himself up. "They can read minds, you know. All of their girls'll run the other direction the moment they lay those shiny black olive eyes on me and their mothers'll reach for their wooden spoons and knock my lights out. I just can't take another beating."

"I got a beating. *You* got a walloping."

"Gallows, Nev! It'd be easier for me to see the difference between them if I could open my left eye."

Nevan pulled him by the shirt as they walked toward Baraburr. There were shades of purple setting in, but his left eye was far from shut.

Niles liked to gripe, but he was as tough as they came. But one would never know it just listening to him speak.

"I'm not scared of them." Nevan grinned. His own smile was always a closed-mouth affair, a wise quirk of contentment rather than the devil-may-care twinkling of his younger brother.

"Why not?" Niles rolled his tossing shoulder, wishing he'd thrown the darts game after the flurry of fists he'd taken. Hungry, thirsty, battered, and ready to sleep through the rest of the year and well into the next, some young gypsy girl reading his mind was the last of his worries.

"Because they believe in destiny."

It was then Niles laughed loud enough for both towns to hear, grabbing his brother by the ear and giving it a tug.

"Always the philosopher, Nev, always the philosopher."

Baraburr sat unevenly in the earth, its scattered displacement of wood and mud structures sagging from the weight of age and the many curses of the working-class families that called Baraburr home. Like the brothers that staggered into its borderless confines, it was in desperate need of repair.

Nevan squinted across the broad splat of the main street, ruffling his brown hair.

"So, what do you think? Mucking out stables? Chopping wood for the blacksmith? Lugging empty ale barrels for the brewer?"

"Anything but the tanner." Niles belched, the back of his hand covering his mouth. With the lack of food in his stomach, the stench of leather-making was spiraling him to sickness.

"Fine by me." Nevan said, spotting a humble common house with a covered deck. "Let's see if we can get a sip or two of water over here and we'll ask around."

Niles nodded his brother on ahead with a finger begging a pause as he doubled over and concentrated on his breathing.

Slowly, Ni, slowly. Nevan thought as he eased himself into the creaky chair and sunk into the meandering pace of life consuming Baraburr with quiet mumbles.

Maybe we can take a break from adventure for a while.
A long while.

"Can I help you?" A musical voice lilted above Nevan's shoulder and he twisted to see a young woman with a heart-shaped face nearly buried in hair as black as shiny boot leather and skin the color of cane sugar burnt to caramel.

Niles mouth sagged open, jarred by his brother clomping up the steps.

"Two pitchers of your most refreshing spring water, Mi'lady." Niles smirked. Nevan hid his displeasure.

Thanks Ni. I was about to have a quiet moment without your gab.

"No springs within miles of here, Sir. Only water we have comes from the pond and that we have to boil just to use for washing, with the sulfur and all."

Niles mouth twitched at the corners to think of dysentery on top of how bad he felt now, and he just faded against the corner of the deck, managing to find the smallest of shadows in the hot sun above. Nevan watched him for an extra second, keen that he'd switched off.

"Don't mind him." Nevan nearly whispered and the lovely young woman bent forward to hear him. "We've travelled a long way and we're very hungry. We'd be glad to work for our meal and we need some coin for our journey."

"North?"

"…Yes." Nevan frowned. "North."

The woman clasped her hands together as if praying and smiled. Nevan felt his spine bubble to see such beautiful white teeth shine out of that soft and mysterious skin. In her eyes, black like pits of the sky in which the brightest stars alone could shine, the mystery spread, as did the warmth alive in Nevan's body.

"Rest easy." The young woman said. "I'll be right back."

Nevan's smile was broad and his brown eyes were pinched with happiness, scanning the street until he felt his brother twitch next to him.

"Is she gone?" He whispered.

"What?"

"The gyspsy, is she gone?"

"Yes…why?"

Niles didn't answer as he sat up, creaking the chair as he did so. His eyes were on the tanner just across the street, and green and blue tinged the edges of his face like pastel shades of the sunset on the sea. Thankfully, they were upwind of the stench, but Niles looked like he wanted to find a quiet hole in the forest and die.

"She was about to read my mind and I didn't want her to know I was about to puke all over this less than perfect deck."

"Ni," Nevan bent forward over the small table and it creaked, so he backed off and resulted to scootching his chair closer to his brother with a series of small scrapes. "*All* gypsies can't read minds."

"We can't?" The musical voice startled him and he turned to see two cups of hot tea falling from her smile, the shine of those black eyes lost in steam.

She left before Nevan could say anything.

He turned to see Niles staring at him, cup already in hand, sipping gingerly. His brown eyes held the twinkling that Nevan's never could, and one eyebrow was raised, as if laughing would be too painful for his sore body so he was forced to let the one eyebrow speak for him.

"You know that rule we have about not pushing it in the other's face when one of us is right?"

Nevan's mouth squashed itself into a line.

"Don't go there, Ni."

Niles' wayward smile was as free as could be.

"Then tell me how she knew you like to drink hot tea in the middle of the day? I mean, really, I'm the only person in the world that knows how strange you are."

"I'm not strange." Nevan sat up straighter. "I'm sophisticated."

"That's right." His sixteen-year old brother pretended to bow at the waist with a swooping flourish of his hand. His mocking accent was nasal. "My brother the sophisticated philosopher. Life is but a road from one small trouble to the next. It's not what you make of these troubles, but what they make of you."

Nevan frowned, head shaking.

"Rubbish! I wouldn't say that. It doesn't even make sense."

"You should hear yourself when you're drunk."

"I don't get drunk."

"You should. It'd do wonders to your philosophy. Then you could listen to yourself. Or maybe have an argument with yourself. Imagine the possibilities."

Nevan considered it for a moment but the mouth-watering scent of food stole the idea from him as two cutterboards of fresh bread, cold butter, sharp cheese and fat red grapes so swollen with juice beads of it were tearing up near the stems.

"Heaven bless you abundant!" Niles said, pulling in his chair.

Nevan's face was flushed pale.

"But...I can't pay for this."

"Don't worry." The young woman said, brushing her praying hands together and leaning against the railing of the deck. "I had a premonition of your coming."

Niles was in the middle of a sip of tea and choked, spraying it on the wall of the common house.

Nevan's eyes were wide, speaking for the both of them. "You...*did?*"

"Sure. You're Niles." She pointed, her eyebrows arched flirtatiously across her caramel skin. "Or Nevan? Which one's which?"

The brothers only looked at each other, as if they were sitting in front of an exotic and lovely young Faery tale.

"My name's Finleigh, by the way." She crossed her arms and pulled up her leg to lean on the rail. The skin of her knee popped from the fringe of her yellow skirt and her eyes brimmed with all the confidence in the world. When the brothers looked like they'd lost their appetite, she leaned over and plucked a grape from the stem.

"Well don't just sit there. Tuck in! We've got a lot to talk about."

Niles released his wayward grin and followed the young woman's orders. He was in over his head, but what was new?

Nevan, however, had lost his appetite, now afraid of gypsies and the fact that one so pretty was standing right next to him and seemed to be quite pleased with herself because of it.

CHAPTER 22

Niles ate as if with child, but Nevan only picked at the grapes and sipped his tea.

And there was that one time when both Nevan and Finleigh had reached for the same cluster of grapes and the touch of their skin had fuzzed the back of Nevan's neck but Finleigh took the grape and tossed it in her mouth like it never happened.

But when Nevan stole a peek at her, her night black eyes shimmered, set between the frame of her shiny boot leather black hair and Nevan wondered where the hell that cool breeze he wanted so bad had run off to, because the warm fuzz on the back of his neck had transformed to itchy heat, the kind reserved for that feeling when him and his brother were both about to get beat up.

As a result, Niles did most of the talking, which was usually a bad idea.

"So how do these premonition things work?"

"I don't know." Finleigh shrugged, picking grape-skin from her teeth and finding a way to be graceful about it. She took to sitting on the railing of the deck, and her legs kicked freely as if on the edge of a dock. "They just...do. They're dreams, really. But I'm not sleeping. That make sense?"

"Only to Nev." Niles winked his cheeky grin. "He's the brains."

"Oh and you're the brawn?" Finleigh's naturally arched eyebrows wriggled. "It's hard to judge brain but I've seen much better examples of brawn." Finleigh made a flexing motion with her arms. She wasn't large by any means of the word, but in personality alone, as if the world around her shrunk when she entered it. That said, her darker skin and the slender build of her body was the sign of a gypsy from Espaiña, and not Romany, as Romany seemed to sleep so far off the horizon that it was the stuff of fables and legends. Plenty of Angle sailors had stories of Espaiña, or at least its many ports, even if the stories were a bit exaggerated, they were common enough.

But her name, *Finleigh*, did not sound like a name from Espaiña, a land with a very different language than the common tongue of Albanland and Angle. Perhaps she was born in Albanland to parents immigrated from Espaiña.

"Now who's bragging?" Niles kicked back, his boots finding themselves crossed not two feet where she was seated on the railing.

Nevan picked at the grapes, their taste bittersweet.

She's not like every other girl you seem so content on charming into a laugh or a giggle in hopes of a stolen kiss, Ni. Can't you see she's different? Why do you have to treat her like every other girl?

Sometimes you disgust me.

But I'm not the one that thinks I can do everything I put my mind to. I know I have limits. I know I'm not that good looking, or even that smart. But I always find a way, and I always manage to smooth over what you've screwed up.

And I don't know that much about women but I know that they shouldn't all be treated the same bloody way.

So just shut up for once.

Nevan turned to see Finleigh's eyes on him again, and this time he stared back dumbly as if she'd heard each one of his thoughts.

She was about to say something but Niles interrupted.

"I'm sure we don't smell all that great."

Finleigh waved a dismissive hand.

"Save it. You have to hear me out first."

"Will this be a long story? I have an ode to write. I've just met the most wonderful girl and..."

"Ni! Be quiet."

Finleigh's eyes danced around the floorboards as she tried not to smile. When angered looks had passed between the brothers her hands clasped together, praying, and she cleared her throat.

"So, I've had the same dream four times already, always at Solstice. So this is the fourth year in a row." Finleigh shrugged and one eye twitched a blink but the other did not and her right hand curled her black hair. "Fifth? No, fourth? Yeah, fourth. I have no idea why, but it always happens this way. And so in the dream...well, it's *like* a dream, but it's like I'm really there. I'm not asleep. Anyway, there's this great big mound with white rocks all around it. Somewhere in the north, I think. Near the ocean. It's cold and windy and dark and there are two women staring at each other."

"Are they Princesses?" Niles ripped a hunk of bread for himself. "Or just a pair of girls from Sailor's Row?"

"I don't know, but there's a very tall man that stands off to the side of them. Watching. He scares me, the way he stands like he's one of the rocks, holding this giant sword stuck in the ground. And he's big, but it's like there's a giant black tower at his back. The whole thing gives me the creeps, like someone's about to die. You know that feeling. That horrible feeling, turning your stomach rancid and sending shivers up and down your spine."

"Fascinating." Nevan said, finishing the last of his tea, so only the leaves were left stuck to the bottom of the cup.

Finleigh noticed and continued.

"The next part is hazy, but there's a giant battle under the sun, and it's like the sun doesn't move. People everywhere killing each other. Just...madness. Pennants, spears, horses, blood. All of it. And then there's us, just walking along the road."

Finleigh crossed her arms and Niles' mouth fell open a bit, a wodge of bread stuffed in his cheeks.

"Woah, all that, and then the three of us?" His face reddened but he reached out across the table and tapped his brother's shoulder. Nevan looked like he was in a trance of his own.

That of the thinker. "Hear that, Nev. We've reached the big time. Pissed-off royal Ladies and guys on horseback chopping each other's heads off." Niles turned to Finleigh with his mock bow. "I must say you are the most creative Solstice entertainment I've ever even heard of."

Suddenly Finleigh's beautiful skin became chalky and her lilting voice became a near-whistle through clenched teeth.

"You think I'm...*entertaining* you? You think this is the part where I read your tea leaves and ask for money?" A feral snarl tore across Finleigh's mouth as she pointed toward Baraburr, and she managed to calm herself down, though her voice quavered with rage. "I'm not like them, okay. That's why they kicked me out of their little community. That's why I'm over *here* where I'm the only one of me, mind you! Just me and my crazy dreams and no one to ever believe a word I say! I'm over here because I can see what they *claim* they can see, what they make a profit off lying about to every fool who wants a fortune! They're all afraid of me because I can actually *see* the future!" Finleigh gripped her forehead, fingers stretched, as if to scrape her long fingernails down her lovely young face but stuffed them in her armpits, tightly, as if they would fly out and grab something at random and throw it across the muddy street. "You have *no* idea what it's like to see something and not know what to do about it. It's bloody agony."

She was about to continue and decided against it, figuring it best to leave and sob her confusion away inside the common house when Nevan caught her wrist as she passed, halting her.

"What do you want to stop?" He asked, voice level-headed as always. "A duel? A war? Or the three of us actually becoming good friends?"

Finleigh's shiny black eyes nicked a glance at her wrist and Nevan released his grip, but instead of storming off, Finleigh fidgeted with the cuff of her blouse and combed her hair behind her ear.

"I wouldn't know where to begin." She said, softly, just to him, as if Niles wasn't there, and she couldn't *feel* him roll his eyes, even though she did.

"Well, how about the fact that you knew we were headed north?"

"You came from the south."

"No, we came from the east. This whole area is the south. All the towns along here are the south. We were just trying to find one where we could get enough money to journey north."

Niles remembered to chew the bread stuffed in his mouth and did so thoughtfully, as if watching his older brother negotiate a deal.

Nevan was good at that.

"What about our names? Did you hear our names in your premonition?"

Finleigh's lips went flat.

"...No."

"Then how'd you know them?"

"You two are kind of famous for making trouble along the highway."

"Really?" Niles piped up. Nevan swatted a hand.

"And in your premonition, did you see our faces? Or did you see us from the back?"

"From the...side?"

"But you're sure it was us?"

Finleigh shrugged, her hands falling at her sides. Perhaps it was her exoticism that made Nevan think she was older but it dawned on him that she was all of sixteen or seventeen, just like them.

"I think so? I don't know."

"But you want to stop people from dying, right?"

Finleigh started to bite her thumbnail and threw her hands up in the air.

"How can *I* stop something like that? Seeing something in a dream doesn't make it true."

Niles frowned at an odd smile on Nevan's face.

"Not yet, anyway."

Finleigh's chin dropped, her bird's wing brows naturally inquisitive but looking even more so.

"So you believe me?"

"If you believe that I'll do everything I can to help you."

"You will?"

Nevan held out a hand.

"And if you'll believe that my brother's a much better person once you get to know him."

Finleigh smiled quickly at Nevan and then the smile faded but she managed to shrug at Niles who more than returned the gesture with a tip of his tea cup.

Which was empty.

"Well then we should leave as soon as we can." Finleigh said, her shoulders nearly to her ears as she held her hands tightly together in front of her.

"Absolutely." Niles stood up with a spring in his step as if he'd never been beaten up in his life; like the idea of being sick only an hour ago was something of a joke. "But first, if you'd be so kind as to read these mysterious tea leaves for me, you could do me the great service of making fun of every one of your less than gifted kin when I ask them to do the same this Solstice and see the look on their face when I tell them they have absolutely no idea what they're talking about."

Finleigh only stared at him before casting a look to Nevan, who splayed his palms wide as to reinforce his statement of Niles being an acquired taste like Angle blue rot cheese or Nørd pickle fish.

The gypsy from Espaiña sighed, picked up his cup and gave it no more than a second glance before saying one word, emotionlessly.

"Larlaith."

CHAPTER 23

Brachin was so thick with bodies the day of Solstice, one could barely move without stepping on the toes of someone else, not that it mattered much in the drunken state of so many partygoers.

Games were aplenty, rife with skill and folly in equal measures. The colorful gypsies of Nairnsmoor and beyond mingled through the square in their bold hues, beckoning the shiny-faced and open-palmed off to the spicy-smelling side streets where their carts served salty flatbreads and skewered lamb dripping with thick red and green sauces and flamboyantly painted booths promised mystery and fortune in folds of darkness.

Highland drums, pipes, lutes and lyres competed for copper pennies and dancers hopped and spun over swords, Clan colors whipped around their waists at the flick and flourish of intricate steps.

But the murder of the governor had cast a heavy cloud across the proceedings, the noose still empty as the gallows awaited their own spectacle on the edge of the town square. An increased presence of merchant guards and footmen only added to the staggering totter of the High Street drifters and back-alley gawkers, and the hot sun mercilessly baked the spiked wooden walls of Brachin and those trapped within to celebrate Solara Aeterna, the life-giving sun.

Nevan mopped his forehead as they walked the throng. Crowds rolled obnoxiously on an ebbing tide of song and dance, sloshing ale mugs and nibbling jam-glazed beef riblets.

Niles stood on his toes now and then, but Finleigh was knifed between them, carving a path through the mob.

"Where is this bloody Larlaith thing?" Niles grunted, his calves aching from constantly poking up on his tiptoes to see through the flurry of sound and color.

"*What* is this bloody Larlaith thing would be a better question." Nevan mumbled, keen to the fact that Finleigh hadn't said a word since the wooden spikes of Brachin's walls had stretched around them.

Did the presence of so many gypsies hush her lyrical voice? Did she see accusations in their dark eyes the brothers could not?

And what *could* she *really* see, beyond the story of her living dream and its promise of violence and bloodshed. Did life look differently to her?

"Always the questions, my philosopher?" Niles mused, brown eyes lingering on the sway of a Cavan Clan dancer, her flaming red hair in braids down to her waist. Fully absorbed in the cadence of the pipes and drums, she was a symbol of the highland beauty the young southern man had always dreamed of.

Her own eyes raked across his in her poetic dance, leaving him breathless and unaware that Finleigh and Nevan were still walking through the masses.

"He's not the one who had the Larlaith in his tea leaves!" Finleigh laughed, tickled with the suspense she'd placed the brothers in.

Niles fell behind with his gawking at the dancer and pardoned himself through a pair of fat patrons to catch up.

"What's the secret to that whole business, anyway?" He asked, catching only the last of what the gypsy from España had said. *Leaves.*

"With what?" Finleigh asked as if she hadn't heard.

"The leaves?"

Finleigh's arched brows nearly touched and her slender arms hung at her sides.

"I don't know. I can't read them."

Niles was about to protest and then wondered if she was pulling his leg but Nevan grabbed him and whisked him aside.

His face was chalky, and his brown hair looked disheveled, as if he'd ran his hand through it too many times.

"What happened to you? You were just..."

"Shh!" Shorter Nevan burrowed himself closer, his near-whisper impossible to hear until Niles nearly bent in half. "He's here."

"Who?"

"*Him.*"

"Which him?"

"Ewan Ust!"

"The bountyman?"

"No, the flipping chimney cleaner. *Yes,* the bountyman! He's over by the governor's, right across the town square." Niles used his height to sneak a peek but Nevan jerked his brother closer. "*Don't* look. I'd bet every penny I had if I had a penny to my name Ewan Ust hasn't forgotten that ten of clubs you pulled out of your sleeve."

"Ten of..."

Nevan grabbed a fist of his brother's shirt, his voice a hoarse whisper, as if the bountyman had the ears of a stag.

"That night we played Rook's Table at *Donnegan's.*"

Niles shuddered to remember and pulled his neck in between his shoulders before chancing a look behind him. Niles didn't like to cheat, but something about the bountyman made him wish he were better at it so he could cheat the slimy man out of everything he owned.

"...That was a year ago."

"Nine months and fourteen days."

Niles shifted quickly between biting his lip and grimacing, as if tossing between two thoughts.

"How many rogues has he gone after in that time? How many murderers and thieves?"

"He said he never forgets a face."

Niles chuckled with a bit of a blush, recalling the Clan Cavan dancer.

"Well, neither do I, brother, but they sure as spades forget mine!"

Both brothers jumped with a spooked grunt as a determined grip took them by the shoulder.

"Hey." Finleigh tugged them toward her. "I'm trying to stop a war, remember?"

Niles nodded quickly, but Nevan's steady brown gaze forbade him from doing anything foolhardy or brash.

But as Finleigh jerked them off toward the gallows, Nevan had the sinking feeling that the foresight-adept gypsy's way out of the long string of southern towns was just that.

The hawker's voice was the first thing anybody heard, drawing a generous crowd from the drifting mass. Claiming to have in his possession *a prehistoric wonder* was just enough to drag in the most skeptical of Solstice goers, but once those who could crowd around the sunken-in mud pit actually *saw* the thing with their own two eyes, the hawker's claim fell shallow.

Finleigh assessed the semi-circle surrounding the makeshift mud pit arena, shallow and not very safe considering what monster slithered around its shadows.

The Larlaith.

Stepping up to the queue where several teenaged boys were waiting in nothing but their trousers, rolled up to the knee, Finleigh caught the eye of the hawker, but he continued on in his booming voice.

"Watch one and all, a mere copper penny for a try, and rod of the King's own gold for the winner! Where else in all of Albanland this Solstice do you find such a magnificent bargain? Come up and test your strength against the mighty Larlaith!"

Finleigh waved the brothers closer but apprehension had already gripped Nevan in his nethers. Something about the shine in

Finleigh's black eyes made her caramel skin look that much more inviting, set against the many pale faces and dirty shirts of those who had paid a copper penny to wrestle the Larlaith and those who were about to.

Even though the faces of those who watched on in horror were paler.

Nevan and Niles took to the lip of the small arena pit and saw why.

The Larlaith was among other things, a giant wolf eel. Two eyes the size of boulders and just as hard and gray and fatal sat in sallow folds of white flesh above the massive ridge of the creature's skull; a severely rounded triangle that found its grisly end in a horribly wide and disapproving mouth. Nevan bit back bile to gauge the size of the Larlaith's head, perhaps the crown of the skull coming to his own waist, maybe five and a half feet. Dead and scaly gray and white flesh covered the sickly length of the monstrous Larlaith in dappled bands, ghastly colors cut by the deep black of the pit's shadows. Sitting wrapped and bunched upon itself, its length was impossible to determine, and its expression was one of indignant silence and stern disapproval when the giant black maw was sealed shut, possessed anger and outrage when it flew open and yawned hot and sticky shadow into the mud pit and all who watched on.

To see it was to know the horrors of the sea, a patient death that waited to strike all those who passed by its hidden cleft in the rocks and kelp, reaching out as if a living entity of both opposite energies put together-the shaded appearance of stone, but the snaking grace of seaweed, with a tough skin that sat in between the textures of both, repulsively repellant.

Gasps wheezed from the black pit of its throat as if it was sick and it began convulsing, spasms jerking throughout the length of its hideous gray and white skin. Its slimy surface caught handfuls of light as to show the crowd it was nothing but a nightmare of a face attached to a long tube of muscle.

A muscle with a mouth.

A muscle with a hungry stomach.

The hawker nodded to two scrawny youths who emptied pales of water upon the endlessly coiled length of the slithering beast, which merely stayed put in its dark corner of the pit. The hoarse wheezing subsided, but the creature worked the hinge of its mouth in a soundless scissor, as if one thought dominated its mind.

Eat. Eat. Eat. Eat. Eat.

Niles glanced over at Nevan who was biting the knuckle of his pointer finger white. His eyes drifted to Finleigh, who looked as if she were adorning the prow of a sea-bound caravel.

"There she is." The gypsy's teeth flashed flirtatiously. "Our ticket out of here."

CHAPTER 24

The first teen started screaming the moment he set foot in the mud and the Larlaith lurched his direction.

That was all it took. A lurch. A fighter's feint, nothing more than a twitch of its bulk to frighten the young tough back up to the crowd.

"Alright, who's next? Step right up!"

Finleigh put her arm around both Nevan and Niles, leaning awkwardly with the three inch height disparity between them, as she was an inch shorter than not-so-tall Nevan.

"So, who wants to try first?"

Nevan passed brown eyes to Niles who passed his own back and they both fell to the next teen, a farmer, judging from his muscles and his thick frame. Life around animals gave him more of a chance, but in the end, the lidless stone eyes of the giant wolf eel sent him out of the pit empty handed.

"I do believe this is an older brother's privilege." Niles managed to smile, shades of green tempting to tint his own face sick as another hopeful teen dropped down into the pit to get the rod of gold the Larlaith was merely sitting on.

Move the Larlaith and get the gold. That's all there was to it. Yet Nevan couldn't see himself doing that, watching the three that'd gone before. Three different body types, three different plans of attack. The Larlaith was numb to them all.

The heat exhaustion stretched the yawning and toothless mouth wide and wheezed a labored moan from the creature. The final hopeful staggered back before falling on his butt in the mud and making a mess of trying to get out of the pit again.

"Come on." Finleigh shook them, but their faces were flat. "How hard can it be?"

Her dark eyes nicked between both brothers before she released them.

"Aww…five hells and a hairpin…" She muttered, marching off.

Nevan only passed Niles a shocked shake of the head as Finleigh stepped up.

"Umm…" The hawker looked down, a tall man who cast her in shade. "Sorry, young lady. I'm afraid you can't."

"But I have my penny!" Finleigh pressed it in the man's hand. He looked at it and wanted to give it back but couldn't.

"N…no, it's Angle rules."

"We're not in Angle!"

"Well, we might as well be."

"But the thing's got no teeth! It's like four-hundred years old and you've just about given it heat-stroke leaving it out of the water for this long."

The hawker worked his mouth around as if he'd been hit. Some in the crowd straightened, but he gave the penny back, saddened that no more youths wanted to try to wrestle the Larlaith.

"No. I can't take your money. I'm afraid this is a sport for men only."

"Pity." Finleigh cast a glare over her shoulder. "I should have *brought* some with me!"

"Alright." Nevan said, unbuttoning his shirt and walking up to the steps down into the pit. Just as he did, the Larlaith shuddered under a wiggling tremor and belched.

"Nope." He turned around, buttoning his shirt.

Finleigh sighed, knowing what a rod of gold would do. They didn't grow on trees, after all. Cashing out a rod of gold would get them each a pouch of silver for their travels, for room and board and food all the way up to Ullraye, where Faer Princess Morgance sat the Throne.

Believing the dreams of a sixteen year old Espaiña gypsy was another matter entirely, but practical Finleigh knew they had to bloody well get there first.

So she offered the brothers an incentive.

"Whoever gets that gold will get a kiss from me." She said, a singsong temptation.

Nevan stopped and looked up at Niles. A smile framed the younger and taller brother's face, his blonde hair shining in the sun. But the smile was weak.

Sickly.

"A really *really* big kiss."

The smile widened.

"Crows pick my bones clean if that'll ever fail to make me a hero." Niles said, stripping off his shirt.

Niles decided Nevan's absurdly loud two-fingered whistle didn't help as he stepped into the mud and walked the small circle. His stomach was a sticky ball, like sourdough set to the kneading table, and every step he took, barefoot in the muck and mire, was like a baker's palm mushing his stomach down and working it upon itself.

Tighter and tighter.

Relax, Ni, relax. He told himself. After all, wasn't that what made him great when the tension was ready to snap the bowstrings? His ability to slow everything down and *relax*. It was boredom that was his enemy, not the revolving mystery of life and the unknown of the next adventure.

It's why you're good at everything, Ni. You can do anything you want. Anything you want.

But the stern gaze of the Larlaith, and the endless body of its slimy old flesh said otherwise.

Eat. Eat. Eat.

Eat.

Eat.

You.

All bottled up in the wet shadows where it waited for the day to be over in hopes of returning to the water, it was defending its territory, and Niles could only imagine what a natural predator would do when *literally* backed into a corner.

"Come on already!" He heard a voice shout and looked up to see Finleigh's bright countenance, her jet black hair framing the sweet and spicy face he could only wonder what it would be like to kiss.

Even just a peck.

Standing there, with the sun at her back, and Nevan looking so sick and helpless and insignificant next to her, Niles took a moment to ask himself why his eye had only been for highland girls when dear Finleigh was full of fire but of such a different flame.

And that's when the Larlaith charged him.

Niles yelped and leapt across the small arena as the massive eel stretched out its length and smacked the wooden wall of the pit. The ground welcomed him with loose and open arms, weighting him down with muck and filth.

Face full of mud, Niles pressed himself up, disoriented, blood running to foam in his veins with the shouts of the crowd.

Above all rose the lyrical voice of a woman.

A scream, really.

"It's there! It's there! It's there!" Finleigh shouted, and he knew she meant the gold the Larlaith had been covering, but he didn't know where *there* was, and when he turned to his right, the eerie sight of the Larlaith rotating on the ground as its dead eyes searched for him put the spark of Finleigh's scream in his feet.

Niles crossed the arena quickly but it was too small, and the giant skull of the creature came from behind like a battering ram, smashing him into the wooden wall.

Cringing, Niles felt the mouth stretch open behind him and used his height, sending a ripple through the crowd as he leapt to grab the lip of the arena and launch himself just feet away.

The Larlaith turned the opposite direction, slithering and swaying in a lost circle and Niles stopped when he realized the other danger.

There was just too much of the damn thing.

The slimy trunk of muscle thwacked him straight in the lungs and he doubled over as if a thousand arrows were sticking from his back.

The arena bent and blackened, and high above Solara dimmed, but Finleigh ceaselessly screamed her exhortation and the location of the gold, leaping and pointing desperately toward the wet splat of mud where the shadows sat cold and dead.

This ain't worth a kiss, even from Faer Morgance herself. Niles thought, air coming back to him as he staggered free of the sloshing tail of the infernal beast.

But then again, you can't put a price on being the man to have the best story in the bar.

It was then Niles ran forward, following the Larlaith back to its lounging spot, stepping on its tail just as its dead eyes passed into the shadows.

The creature twitched, snapped its mouth open, and recoiled with a blinding twist. Niles guessed and leapt.

Maybe Finleigh was the one to be kissed for the luck she brought. He dove to the right the same time the angered maw of the beast snaked around from the left.

Niles then launched himself up from the mud and felt as if he was some strange middle ground between the fastest wind of the Four Storms and the cruelest splat of a battlefield from hell, running for that one dark spot where he could pick out the dullest shine alighting the mucky brown soup.

Running, yet not fast enough.

He scraped down and snagged a clod of mud the same time force he'd never sensed before silently thundered across the mud and slammed into him. Niles shrieked to see the mouth open in a flash and close around his feet, and he crashed to his knees as the toothless gums gnawed on his legs.

His skin flared with flushes of fear and he brought his free hand down in an arc, watching the mud fly from his hand, revealing the matchless purity of the King's own gold, and realizing that it'd bounced off the Larlaith's slimy skin as if it were the head of a drum.

The creature's jaw worked maddeningly, the endless length of its slimy muscle sucking with dry squelches and Niles floundered in the mud, wondering if his heart would give out from fear before the thing would swallow him whole.

He wriggled, it shook, he scraped and clawed, and it chomped on, till he managed to free himself from its toothless and tired-out hold and roll across the mud.

His breath was a jagged scrape in his own throat, and he staggered to the edge of the pit and leapt up deftly, but only with enough strength to hang precariously scissored at the waist, half of him in, half of him out.

"Hell on fire, will you..." He gasped, unable to finish the plea for help because hands were already pulling him over the wall, dragging him as if he were shipwrecked in an evil sea.

Panting, Niles stayed flat on the ground, head to the side. Cheers and applause rocked his senses, and thoughts of Finleigh's lips somehow mingled with a thirst-quenching draught of summer ale...or was it the sweet and sour squish of a fresh fruit pie? His empty stomach had him near delirious with the promise of the future.

Gold.

Exasperation turned to bewilderment, and before a racking cough of strained laughter came the winsome smile that'd landed him in so much trouble.

As it did now.

For Niles pressed himself to his knees to see Finleigh and Nevan and the smile on his mud-slathered face faded like Solara in winter fog.

Standing behind them both with strong arms crossed was the bountyman, Ewan Ust.

CHAPTER 25

The bountyman didn't give Niles a chance to stand on his own, yanking him to his feet with a gnarled hands. The scent of tobacco was a thick and choking perfume about the man, along with that of sweaty old leathers bound to a life on the road.

"I see the Solstice brought you good fortune."

Nevan's eyes burned hatred as the bountyman ripped the gold rod from Niles' slacked fingers. Finleigh reached out her hand to comfort Nevan, as she stood behind him, but pulled back, seeing the violence storming in the older brother's gaze had been tempered by better judgment than to strike the bountyman.

Ewan Ust spun the rod of gold around in his gauntlet-clad fist. The rod was the length of ten coins.

Lust gleamed gold in Ewan Ust's road-weary eyes.

"As it has now brought to me."

Hot, dead tired, and hungry enough to eat his own shoes despite the tasty nibbles Finleigh had provided hours ago, Niles looked left and right for some sort of savior. He could feel the air leak from the crowd around them, ready to celebrate the young blonde's victory over the Larlaith as if it were there own in the true spirit of Solstice celebration. But the bountyman and his pair of merchant guards, severing them from the crowd, left them to their own thoughts.

It wasn't until they'd crossed the square that the bountyman released his hold on Niles' collar. There was something of a vacancy near the boarded-up entrance to the governor's house, and Ewan Ust took the liberty of throwing Niles to the ground.

Thanks you bleeding wazzock. Niles nearly spit. *That's what I need, another mouthful of mud.*

I'd like the throw you down in the pit with that old sea sausage and see how tough you really are.

Finleigh winced to hear the tearing of a seam, and bit her bottom lip.

Shamed to no end, Niles lifted up his arm and stared at the ruined sleeve.

"So we meet again, card cheat." Ewan Ust growled.

Nevan stepped forward and was about to interject when the bountyman only raised the back of his hand to smack the smooth-talking older brother across the face. Nevan backed down, and Finleigh hooked her arm around his, pulling him aside a step and giving him comfort.

His smile to her was flat, but grateful.

"Ten of…spades, it was?" Ewan Ust flexed his fist, carrying the menace of a falconer's leather gauntlet.

Not that he needed one. *He* was the falcon, that curved nose, that small mouth, and those eyes that saw just about everything and claimed to never forget.

"Maybe there was an extra in the deck." Niles squinted up into the sun.

The bountyman's shadow smothered him.

"Humoring me, now?"

"Oh no, Sir. I'm just a rascal, not a Faer Prince." Niles rolled to his knees. "I can't make someone laugh if they don't have a sense of humor."

"I oughta cut your tongue out!" Strong hands hoisted him up and held him off the ground, making it hard to breath. "I told you I'd never forget. It was a ten of clubs and you cheated me out of ten silver coins. Ten of clubs, ten coins. That's a week's wages, boy!"

Ewan Ust released Niles and he fell unevenly. Finleigh dug her nails into Nevan's arm to see the pain of a twisted ankle stretch across Niles carefree features, but Niles kept his mouth sealed shut.

"What'd you do with that much money, boy?" Ewan Ust growled and then a chuckle passed through him, like a wind through overgrown weeds and bushes. "You certainly didn't buy that cute little gypsy over there. She's worth twenty, at least."

It was then Finleigh strode up to Ewan Ust and kicked him as hard as she could square in his manhood, the bold surprise of the impulsive act striking the trio's escape like fire to a handful of tinder.

Ewan Ust fell to the ground as if the stool for the gallows had been ripped from his feet and the noose had been pulled taut around his neck.

Niles didn't need an exhortation to run. Running was in his blood, his fight or flight response now a well-trained and virtuosic skill. But Nevan, skilled in the way of pausing to assess and reason was always slower to bolt, and found himself smack between two merchant guards. One went for his short sword and the other reached toward him.

Nevan used the smallness he'd been teased about so many times to dart in between them, nearly falling to his hands and knees in a desperate scamper.

And he made it through and sought the safety of the crowd, standing up again.

Until one of them grabbed a tuft of his hair.

Nevan shrieked and nearly lost his balance as he twisted to meet the point of a short sword.

Finleigh appeared out of the side of his vision and kicked the merchant guard with the sword, seeing only one place *to* kick, and shoved him with all her might as he gasped in pain.

The pair of merchant guards toppled like two empty milk pales, falling upon the wincing form of Ewan Ust with the metallic clatter of armor and weapons.

It was then Finleigh ran, feeling the wind tear at her black hair as Nevan ducked and darted, dodged and weaved.

Niles was already long gone, nearly at the wide-open gate.

The crowd had all but swallowed them when Ewan Ust finally stood and hollered his rage into the deaf ears of Solstice. No one listened, no one cared, and no one could do a thing about it.

"You can run you bloody card cheat! But I'll find you someday! I'll find all of you and put you in the stocks till you go gray! Mark my words!"

And like the throng surrounding, neither Nevan nor Niles heard.

They were running. Running like always. Running from town to town with the jaws of trouble nipping at their heels and cursing the dust beneath their feet.

But Finleigh cast sad eyes over her shoulder as Brachin shrunk in their view, thorny bogs surrounding the spikes of its walls like a cursed crown.

They had escaped, yes, but how far would they get without the gold?

FINLEIGH

CHAPTER 26

Several spots caught the eye for hiding along the southern highway that ran east and west through the border towns.

But far too many of them were ruined by the prying eyes of farmers in need of the copper pennies a bountyman like Ewan Ust would offer in exchange for information and once the knowledge of the hunt was his, would walk away without paying the poor farmers, making them feel the fool because of it.

Finleigh cast a somber smolder on each and every little cottage they passed, whether near the highway or tucked far back on the green swell of low and lumpy hills scattered with black and white sheep and the occasional milk cow.

The only thing worse than being poor, she thought, *is being poor and gullible. And that describes just about everybody in the south.*

But I still like the south. It's my home. It always will be.

After hours of hasty and wordless travel, their blood still rippling with the fearful rush of being chased, a shallow hollow crowned by two spindly yews offered the three a cool place to flop down for a rest.

So they did.

"See anything?" Niles asked as Nevan peeked out toward the highway.

"No. We're good."

"We've been good for miles." Finleigh offered, her eyes much different than theirs in every way.

Some people see with their eyes. But I see and hear and feel and taste. I see beyond what is seen.

"This isn't one of your dreams." Nevan nearly whispered, managing to sound respectful where Niles would've sounded derogatory. "You never know who could be watching or why. If you have a special sense to see the future, we have our own unique ability to know if and when we've made a clean getaway or not."

Finleigh closed her eyes, the cool grass soothing with the two yews breaking the boiling heat of the sun.

"So we're good for…how long?" Finleigh sighed, feeling like she could stay in the hollow till nightfall. She was an active girl, working around the common house, but she'd never been so far away from her hometowns of Baraburr and Nairnsmoor.

"Not long enough." Niles said, propping himself up on his elbow. Finleigh could nearly feel the intensity of his needs, a great many of them bordering on desperation, and what'd filled him so buoyantly after conquering the Larlaith had been stolen by the grimy hands of Ewan Ust.

Hope.

Hope was forever the victory just as much as it was the victim. The rope that could hoist someone out of a pit could be the same rope to hang them in the end.

Finleigh squinted at him. One giant mudcake with dirty blonde hair, everything about him brown and sour-smelling, unbearable to be around had she not seen another side of him pop out, like a weed gone to flower.

A kind of charm sat in the idea of blooming petals no one ever talked about, colors no one else saw, a weed that grew wherever the wind carried it and popped up its own beauty where no one expected to look.

For the Niles that'd selfishly eaten what little she could offer as she told them her story on the front porch had been the kind of young man she avoided like Plague; always so sure of himself, despite his crooked teeth and the way his ears poked out of his blonde hair.

Arrogant. Self-involved. Or was it self-absorbed?
More like self-obsessed.

But the young man that'd faced that hideous thing in the pit for his brother, for his country, maybe even for *her*; he was a different sort. Like the weed gone to flower, he was tough and hearty. Resilient. Everything the truest nature of Albanland was. Angles were perverting the idea of what it meant to be Alban, to be rough around the edges, still so captivating and unique. They were flaunting their fineries in promotion of intellectualism and slavery, turning their nose up at the common folk for being backwards and antiquated if they did not see this new way of life as the pinnacle of creation. Not all Albans were the same. Not all sought the false idyllic standard of mindless decadence creeping through the south border towns.

But what could they do to fight it? They were poor and humble people. Rich in song and dance, not coin; lusting for adventure and warfare, not delicate pastries and soft clothing.

Even now, the Crown had lost its grip on the south. Angle was moving in, slowly pulling down an ancient and beautiful willow like an army of creeper vines

South Albanland had become South Angle, even though it was truly Angle's extreme north. The name itself was a part of the grinding of the knife between the Crown's ribs, to say Albanland had been cut away and Angle grafted in its place. Leave the capital *A* and erase the rest to be filled in with a poncy flourish of Angle penmanship. Leave the towns, leave the farms, leave everything just the way they are and let thoughts of something better, something *higher* take over. Leave contentment and take up ambition; trade in your humility for haughtiness and your wool for silk. A hybrid territory of replacement theology, where Clan and Land had been exchanged for self-gratification and the deification of intellectual thought.

Curse me I can't fix all that. Finleigh thought. *But I know I can stop this war that's about to take place.*
It wasn't just Albans and Nords. It was everybody.
Everybody and everything. Fighting and dying.
I love life. And I love it here.

There's got to be a way to break this curse.
And I've got to do it with these two scoundrels. One on each arm.
What could be better?

Silently, Finleigh studied her filthy companion and hoped he would stay sober through their hurried trek up north, away from trouble, though what foresight she possessed was sure the temptation to return to his insufferably cheesy self would be as certain as the hunger and exhaustion holding court in the back of their minds.

Finleigh flipped around and shimmied up the swoop of the hollow to spy on the roads with Nevan, who silently took it all in. The east, the west, the verdant green swirls of land, spiraling off into the curves of the earth, the trees of the forest to the northeast no bigger than the fingernails of an outstretched hand, clouds of clotted cream high up in the big blue sea of the sky.

"Why's your name Finleigh?" Niles asked, catching his breath on his back, staring at the broad blue above. Even the clouds were racing north, tired of the cries of the slaves and the poor caught in forced labor for the rich.

"Pardon?"

"Yeah." Nevan frowned. "You're from across the water somewhere."

"Espaiña." She said with the lyrical bell-curve of her accent.

"But your name…" Niles watched a cloud stretch out to catch another.

"It's Alban." Nevan finished his sentence.

"I know." Finleigh nodded.

"Well?"

"Well what? I like it. Do you think I should change it or something?"

"No." Nevan shook his head. "I like it."

"Me too." Niles piped up.

"But what's your given name?" The young philosopher wondered. "You know, the one you were born with…in your own language."

Finleigh only shrugged, like she had when Niles asked her about the secret to reading tea leaves.

"I don't know. I don't remember."

"Well you're not supposed to remember because you…" Nevan said, working it out and his mouth sealed shut. "Oh…I'm sorry."

Finleigh nodded.

"It's okay. I can't feel bad for losing my mother and father because I didn't even know who they were. I was too young. I don't even know how they died."

Nevan leaned closer.

"No, I'm really sorry. That's rough."

"Yeah," Niles offered. "We still have parents. They're horrible people once you get to know them but we still have them."

Finleigh picked at the grass in front of her, running her fingers through a cool tuft as she scanned the horizon.

"The fine gypsy community of Baraburr never told me. They did tell me not to ask, but they never told me why."

"Sounds like guilt to me." Niles muttered.

"I don't dwell in the past." The gypsy's shiny black eyes glittered. "I dream of the future."

Nevan smiled at her as if he were staring into the sun.

"There's one for your book." Niles chuckled.

"Your book?" Finleigh cocked her head to the side, curling her straight jet back hair behind her eyes. "Are you a storyteller?"

"Umm…no." Nevan scooted further from her, feeling his cheeks flush. Finleigh wondered if he was plotting revenge on Niles for uncovering his secret.

"It's just something I say because he thinks he's so wise." Niles said, both a vague apology and an insult.

Finleigh stared to the horizon again. In a few hours, dusk would take its first yawn and the evening meal would scent every house across the south with its humble flavors of fatty meat and fire-charred parsnips from the hearth. Maybe some plowman's cheese and a handful of wild blackberries.

"My blood's from España but I was born here and I'll die here. I love this place, I love everything about it." Finleigh smiled with flared nostrils, taking in the cool clean of summer clover and warm grass. Farm winds distant enough to smell earthy and rich, and no scent or sight of a town for miles.

A small silence worked between them until muddy Niles stood up from his spot and fell down beside her with a weary sigh.

His chin was turned toward her as he sat on his stomach, arms folded beneath him like a pillow, as if he was as used to sleeping outside like the limb of a fallen tree. To look upon Niles was to see pure and utter exhaustion, and his voice was barely audible as his cracked lips stuck together.

"So, Fins, where do your dreams take us now?"

But even if Finleigh had an answer, Niles was too tired to hear it. His slow and rhythmic breathing sunk him down into the perfect dream of a deep darkness known only as sleep.

Finleigh turned to her left, a smile stretching across her face, seeing that Nevan had succumbed to the weary burden of the same dream.

I guess adventure is a full-time job.

So Finleigh stood, silently, and left the brothers in search of some firewood and a few plants for them to nibble on once they awoke.

Hopefully, by then, she would have a plan.

Because to the brothers, bless their hearts, plans seemed to be something prone to hitting them upside the head.

It was about time their nose for trouble had a woman's touch.

ULTAN

CHAPTER 27

The emissary couldn't return quickly enough, but Ultan knew the answer to the message even before it'd been delivered.

After all, he was half Nørd.

He knew who they were.

Who he was.

Still, he took the wax-sealed parchment from the swift emissary and ordered him back to the boat, telling him he would be along right behind.

His eyes scanned the wild Nørd script, but he did not read what it said. Already he saw the future it spoke of, and the battle that awaited him in enemy territory.

Before Ultan, the cold waters separating their peoples stretched gray and impassable, and the islands of contention hugged the curve of the earth behind the staggered wall of their proud and hand-carved dragon-boats. Since Montree had been vacated and taken, sitting isolated and alone out on its spit of land, the Nørds aggression demanded pitched battles as their hunger for the Crown possessed them with rage.

But the last result, that of Ultan's furious swordcraft single-handedly breaking the aggressive Nørds army apart like clay pots and kindling twigs, had sucked the life from them, forcing them to hold their positions in the sea with nothing more than the stubborn roots of an unwanted wart.

Today is the day of salvation. Ultan pondered, salt wind swirling around him, chilling him with clarity in Skyeshire colors of black and gold. Golden torcs rippled sunfire throughout the muscles of his bare arms and the wind whispered vengeance each time it tore at his strawberry blonde curls and the snow white fox pelt cape of the Crown.

Salvation or damnation.

Either way, today sits between my hands. Today is a blade within me, and it will never be sharper than it is right now. I am the weapon to rend the curse of this land from end to end and watch it bleed.

Or watch my own blood stain the soil of my mother's home with my father's green eyes.

If these two lands are ever to be united, they are in me. And if they are to ever be divided, they are in me.

My blood is the sea that runs between them.

Ultan sighed and began the long walk to the boat. Thinking and walking, the Guardian's companions more than his sword or his subordinates. The last thing he would see would be the black Tower of Ullraye, stretching high above the clefted rocks along the beach, but he would not look upon it, nor think about the unblinking gaze that stared out from its impenetrable safety.

Morgance would be watching, crying the glittering tears of spring sunlight melting winter frost, pleading with all of her Faer knowledge that he'd once more become a wild beast of battle who knew no equal.

And he would push her from his mind just like the wind would push his boat across the sea.

Rhoswen, if you could only see me now. You would see what destiny has carved me up to be, like you, a servant with something hopelessly missing from my soul.

Something taken from me.

Even though it was I who let it be taken. It was I that did nothing to stop you and nothing to save you as you ran away and left a vacant Throne in your wake.

It was I that fought forever after with blind bravery to remove the hatred of my own cowardice, and if I can win this duel for our land, I will find you and make you mine until the end of our days.

I take this day like the sword in my hands to fight for the hope of that day.

And if time has already taken you away from this world, then I will find you in the next.

I have not forgotten you, Rhoswen of Kathron Caelie. Your eyes hold my heart prisoner in chains of hearth fire and whispered promises.

Even if those promises be the lies of my own dreams.

The boat rocked to take his weight and Ultan nodded to the crew to shove off and hoist the sails. It was a somber silence that held him still as stone, cut by the whistle of the wind and the creaking of wood, the lap of waves. The tormented sea was like a slick wall of shale reaching out to the horizon, cursing him for thinking he could simply sail across its flattened caps of sunstroke white and liquid steel to end a hundred-year old struggle by simply flashing the milky white sharpness of his one and only weapon.

The Blade of the Champion.

So much had been promised.

So much would be realized.

And Ultan looked up to the sun above, making its way through its own blue and white sea of sky and cloud. Luna would rise by the time he reached the distant shores of Nørd rule.

Once again he was ready to fight.

Once again he was ready to die.

The drum came to him first, the dull thud of spruce sticks beating tightly stretched deerskin.

Thump...tum tum tum...Thump...tum tum tum...

Ultan straightened at the sound, feeling its primal cadence simmer his blood and thicken his bones. He could all but see the axes and the horned helmets casting daemon shadows in the night, and the scent of berserker's favorite red cap mushrooms and pinefrost mead drifted like a thick fog across the hush of the waves, welcoming him home to the warrior's grand table in Valhöll, where the slain would celebrate the blood they had shed.

Thump...tum tum tum...Thump...tum tum tum...

The shore was little more a flicker of fire licking across the dread of black water, yawning across the sea like a gate to the hottest flames of hell below. Ultan saw the shore long before he reached it, the muscles of his jaw tightening as he stood tall at the prow of the boat. The voyage had been easy, but long, and behind him, though he refused to look, five dragon-boats loaded to the gunwales with archers and axemen boxed in his escape.

He was trapped, bound by honor.

Thump...tum tum tum...Thump...tum tum tum...

And just like the good luck piece carved into a merchant ship's bow, Ultan refused to move during the crossing, staring daggers into the slender curve of infinity, scarcely blinking as he hardened himself deep inside to become the sword unsheathed to divide the world asunder.

CHAPTER 28

He managed to keep his feet dry by leaping from the boat to the scatter of pebbles and stones that formed an uneven beach stinking of rotting kelp and dead fish and followed the two burly warriors who were sent to escort him along a strung-out line of misshapen goat skull torches. The eerie crimson flame spilling from their eye sockets and drooling from their mouths to splash upon the wet rocks, sending up ghosts of steam, reminded Ultan of stories his mother told him when shadowfits would rack his body. She would take him from his bed into her own and hold him, speaking to him with the voice of a lute of the many horrors he would face as a warrior, like his father, whispering strength into his mind through the darkest stories of Nørd legend.

Though I walk the death god's trail, I will not be afraid. The torches lead toward a copse of trees, staring down upon a pavilion of tents as if they were the shapes of Thör and Wøden, hulking against the violet sky and the black water, come to relish a warm summer night of blood-soaked drama.

Though I hear the fallen wail, I will not be afraid.

From the darkness warriors joined one by one, some larger than him, few smaller, all wrapped in the culture of war and the trinkets of their individual glories. Animal skins and teeth, hair-braids of their rivals and ceremonial broaches of amber and pewter. Thick and tangled beards fell from their faces like moss, light-colored eyes of grass and sky reveling in the heat and fire of the goat-skull torches.

Though the death drum calls my name, I will not be afraid.
Thump...tum tum tum...Thump...tum tum tum...
Though my heart burns black with flame, I will not be afraid.
I will climb the hills, I will cross the sea, I will face my fear and I will be set free.

Ultan squinted to see the shapes of several hundred more warriors curved around the mouth of the large pavilion like two tusks of ivory, flesh and metal, large cauldrons of flame behind them throwing blood-orange sparks into the sky. Those on the left held their round wooden shields low in their left hands and hoisted their axes high in salute in their right, mirrored by those stretching off from the entrance of the pavilion across from them.

Thump...tum tum tum...Thump...tum tum tum...

He could see them all as he approached, arrayed across the pragmatic dais of thrones where the Nørds royal dynasty awaited, the drums beating behind him. Arms bearers, chroniclers, bards, and yes, even the children of the royal dynasty.

All come to watch.

Him.

Thump...tum tum tum...Thump...tum tum tum...

Ultan sighed the clammy dread from his skin. The heavy footsteps of a hundred warriors stomped the rocks beneath, mingling hushed thunder with the pounding of the drum. Ultan shunned the feeling of walking into the mouth of hell with the hands of death ready to catch him if he fell.

And with seeds of doubt in his heart, bristling thorns of jagged lightning sent shivers up his spine.

I will face my fear and I will be set free.

He was *not* invincible, despite what the Nørds thought of him, giving him a god's reception, and the urge to cry welled deep within his belly. He could nearly feel their honor cover him like a cloak, an adoration that made him feel loved and treasured, held in the highest esteem.

In that, Morgance was right. Even if he died childless at twenty-four years old, his name would live on.

And on.

And on.

Thump…tum tum tum…Thump…tum tum tum…

And craving that first clash of steel puffed the veins in his arms and hardened the clean-shaven line of his chin as if it were the cold and unfeeling Tower of Ullraye a half-day's sail behind him.

It was then the drums stopped.

The loss of the beat froze the warriors behind him, boxing him in to the rocky space before the pavilion and the cauldrons of sparks and dark flame.

Ultan let the salty air tainted with smoke and Nørd seer herbs fill his lungs and walked forward to meet the King of the their people, a myth of a man known only as Father of the Wolf.

In his youth he was a beast of a man, and in middle age the man became myth, slaying all who stood in his way to unite the far north where the ground never thawed and the sun never set with the fortified towns of the seacoast under one banner. But in the twilight of his years, a mysterious disease had taken root in the base of his spine and withered his proud limbs. Even now, the Father of the Wolf sat the throne with what supremacy his bent shape could afford, the grimace of a scarred mouth equal parts pain and pride amidst a hoary white beard. Blue-gray eyes like fish skin held an unblinking gaze above sunken cheeks of leather and scars. The mouth of a dire wolf opened around him, its head a hood, its sharp fangs just above his eyes, and he wore the giant pelt of the thing like it was a part of his own body.

And Ultan held his gaze for the space of several heartbeats, feeling the man's adoration stretch beyond bones that could barely move. But in the worship there was judgment, the keen eye of a hunter sizing up his prey and reaching for the knife to bury in its back.

And when Father of the Wolf spoke, his voice was low and harsh, yet whistling with the wind of near death, and his tongue of common Alban was heavily accented, foreshadowing what a gnarled old apparition Ultan himself could one day become.

"Welcome home, my son."

Lips set firm in his ruggedly handsome face, Ultan managed a small bow.

"My heart swells with the honor you have given me. But Albanland is my home."

"Your mother, Skölhammer, she is of my blood. A sister of my own nephew. This we all know. You do not?"

Ultan fought the urge to flinch as if a firebrand had been jabbed toward his face.

Lies. He thought. *Father of Lies.*

"I do not wish you to die tonight." The King continued. "Stay with us while we conquer your lands and we will make you Lord Regent over them. One of my many daughters will bear you many sons, and we will fill Valhöll with the glory of our own name."

Ultan stood his tallest, the massive blade strapped to his back glowing under the spell of Luna's violet and silver white light.

Think of the duel, nothing more.

"You have agreed to the terms?"

"Yes, I have."

Ultan released the sword from its simple straps and held it low before him.

"Then give me your Champion and I will give you his head."

Next to the King, his only son and his son's young wife sat on the edge of their seats. The son wasn't much older than Ultan. They could've been brothers, with the same strawberry coloring. The Prince leaned forward and whispered something to his father, sitting back with a guarded gaze, looking crafty and wise in black chain mail.

But unlike his father, he did not wear the skins of the wolf.

But rather, the bear.

The black bear, the smallest and most aggressive of all.

Ultan squinted at this discovery and looked to the man's young wife but the croaking voice of the King demanded his attention.

"You know we love you, Skölhammer, and you have a home with us. You have slain a thousand of our fathers, brothers, and sons if you have slain one, but we know that the gods have made a rare mistake, giving you to Albanland and not Nørd. Your father robbed us of a great warrior worthy to take the head of the table in Valhöll. This," Father of the Wolf wheezed to move himself to a more comfortable position. "This is why we have given you the name *Skölhammer.*"

Ultan's nostrils flared and a streak of fire mingled with blood and darkness in the King's eye.

"Yet you don't know what it means? Have you forgotten your mother tongue, the stories, the legends? Everything we have is passed down, spoken from the elder to the younger, everything from building our boats to the sagas of our great gods. You may cut us off from your lands, Skölhammer, but you will never remove us from your soul unless you take a dagger to your own breast and cut out your own heart. Even then, it would curse you for hating what you know to be as true as the sky above and the sea beneath."

Ultan glanced again at the son, the son that could've been him. Wisdom beyond his years sat in darkened pools, forefinger and thumb rubbed together in contemplation of what mind sat inside the skull of Skölhammer.

You could be me. The Prince's eyes said, darting to his young wife who emanated a cold and elitist sense of beauty, severe and hard-edged compared to soft and vulnerable Faer Morgance.

We could rule together.

Brother.

Ultan's grip flexed around the Blade.

No, I bind that thought and cast it down. My mother is not of Wolf blood, or Bear. She was a Nørd with the voice of an angel, a simple girl of the islands, of a fishing village. Nothing more than another forgotten name. She ran away from the wars of her people. She ran into the arms of my father, Lord of Skyeshire. Whiskey weakened his judgment, yes, but the only wrong he did is that of his own people's prejudice, for he loved my mother with everything in him, and took her to be his own despite losing his seat in the Chamber of Lords because of it. His own people hated him so, making me hate myself, but in her arms I felt what my father felt, like the wars of the world had washed away and love had taken their place.

Ultan's teeth ground together.

Enough was enough.

"I forget but one thing." He said. "The day I promised the Four Storms I would cleave your head from your shoulders and bring it home in a milk bucket."

Shock rippled through the face of the Prince and some of the younger warriors but Father of the Wolf pressed himself up from the throne with a roar.

"Yeeesssss!" He growled against the pain of his own body, feeling his blood rise in anticipation. "Your fire burns as hot as my own. Show me, Skölhammer! Show me your war!"

But Ultan stayed, shoulders just beginning to rise and fall like the tides of the black waters at his back. Whispers hissed through the surrounding wall of warriors and Ultan's ears tingled with prickles of heat.

Father of the Wolf continued, a crazed smile holding him hostage.

"Show me what they speak of, what I have not yet seen with my own eyes! I have heard so much! I must see it before I die! Show me Skölhammer! Show me who you are in battle!" The King spread his arms wide as he took a pace from the throne, spinning to bathe himself in the light of the fire cauldrons and the shadows of ancient holy trees. "Transform for me!"

Ultan's brows nearly slid together in no small horror.

Now he understood.

"Yes," the King growled, aching to see the mastery of combat and the wildfire of fearlessness his soldiers had told so many stories of, finding that their only savior in defeat after defeat was the story of the man that dealt it to them, warming the idle time of the cursed King's imagination with blood-soaked glory.

"Yes what?" Ultan growled back.

"Your name, *Skölhammer*. It is the legacy of the Wolf in you."

No! No! No!

"Sköl is the son of Fenrir, and Fenrir the son of Loki. *Hamrammr* is to be shape-strong, like I was in my youth, and all those who have taken the mantle before me. To transform, Ultan, my son. To *become* the Wolf that howls in your blood. To *become* Sköl, son of Fenrir, seed of Loki."

Nooooooo!

Ultan shouted a savage and wordless snarl, charging the King to bring the Blade of the Champion down upon his head.

Steel flashed white and silver with the spitting sparks of the cauldrons and the rocks clattered unevenly beneath his feet.

For the King's own son, Eyvind Frey, had whipped his own blade into the violet pulse of the night, locking eyes with Ultan to push him back with a heave of bear-like strength.

And as Ultan stumbled back, the adrenaline of the duel for the Crown fell around him like the deluge of the Four Storms in cascading showers. He felt every eye in the world upon him, even the glassy yellow-green prayer of Faer Morgance no small sea away up in the Tower of Ullraye.

He felt her love for him thrum in his heart like an axe stuck in the root of a tree.

And with her eyes, too, were the eyes of Rhoswen, chained to his dreams, forever duelling the shadows between what he couldn't remember and what he would never forget.

CHAPTER 29

The blistering foray of the duel's first few seconds were nothing more than rage and a cold-blooded reaction to it. The Prince of Nørd launched himself with a stretch and Ultan threw his weight into a block, feeling the shock of the blow rattle down to his toes.

The man was not afraid of him. If one thing blackened his gaze, it was a lust for the glory his own father had given Ultan.

Ultan slid his blade down the length of Frey's and twisted, whistling violet air as Frey leapt back to avoid being eviscerated. Frey feinted and wheeled his blade down in a wicked arc, and once again the *thrang* of steel split the eerie silence of the night.

Father of the Wolf roared with laughter, ending in fits of coughing as he bunched back in the throne. Cauldron fire danced in his eyes and his twisted hands gripped the throne with elation. Ultan forced their swords to the rocks on his right side and leaned into a snapping left hook, catching Eyvind Frey on the mouth. The Prince countered with a swift kick to the knee, spitting his own blood down the length of his blade as he hoisted its heft for another strike. He was a smaller man than Ultan. Quicker, too, but not more experienced.

Hungrier.

And somehow stronger.

The duel continued with cagey pauses cut by rattles and smashes, grunts and growls as each warrior focused their will and the legacy of their people into the tips of their blades. Eyvind Frey pushed Ultan around every chance he could, whether in the lock of their two-handed swords near the hilt or in a jostling bump of the shoulder, a slap of the elbow, even a wayward foot seeking Ultan's groin.

Ultan wondered if Frey would wear himself out that way, consumed with violence and not concentrating on victory, but Eyvind Frey was transforming into the bear, somehow looming larger and larger in the firelight and shadows the way his father lusted for Ultan to as the battle raged on.

But to be a warrior was to know discipline and control, not mindlessness.

Even though Ultan knew damn well wild fury was the only thing that poured through him when he fought the Nørds and broke their lines like the floorboards of a rotted fishing boat.

"Bleed for me, *Skölhammer*," Eyvind Frey mocked. "Make my name great amongst my own people with your death."

Ultan's sword answered for him as he thrust the hilt forward with his right hand, sliding the weight up to his left, high overhead to leave his chest exposed for Frey to spear. But the moment before Frey committed to a lunge, Ultan dashed the distance in a stretched pivot and ripped his blade through the air as if to topple an oak with one swing.

Frey fell to the ground, his back throbbing with the knowledge he'd narrowly avoided a cloven spine, and Frey rolled, the whites of his eyes boiling with indignation as Ultan re-gripped his sword and drove the deadly point into the rocks where Frey had been a moment before.

Eyvind Frey pushed himself to his feet and roared forward, stealing the precious second it took Ultan to remove his sword from the rocks that pinched it tight.

Ultan staggered back as two desperate *woops* lusted for the pale skin of his neck, the third right behind when a rock caught his heel.

There was no fighting it, and Ultan clenched his belly to roll back into the damnable fists of the stones thumping his body with dozens of blows.

It was a blink, nothing more, one blink and the Prince's blade sizzled the air as it fell toward him, seeking to split him down the middle like a hunk of sirloin on the butcher block.

Ultan twisted his blade to hold it between the palms of his hands and thrust it against the Prince's assault.

But it didn't stop it.

The Prince was possessed, hacking down thunderous blows upon Ultan's barrier of steel with the heat of hell slicking his skin and burning up the black chain mail and furry bearskin of his *Hamrammr.*

Ultan shimmied and squirmed, his bare arms tingling a thousand red-hot needles.

Clash! Clang! Crash!

He had no defense but desperation itself as the Prince roared his rage, breathing in the wispy smoke of the cauldrons, and Ultan pushed his sword up toward the black fury of the Prince, locking their blades.

In a breath, he stretched his left leg nearly out of its socket and angled it like a hook, smashing Eyvind Frey's ankle with his right foot.

The Prince toppled to the left and yelped as his sword clattered to the ground.

Ultan shot up to height as the Prince whirled, his black bear cloak flaring in his twist.

His right hand was buried in the armpit of his left.

"You wanted blood?" Ultan shouted.

At Father of the Wolf. At the Prince.

At every Nørd who'd ruined his life by taking up axe and arrow.

"I'll give you blood."

The Prince staggered back, crimson rivulets streaming down his arm from the cut to his hand. Fear twisted the rage in his eyes, marking him with the savage desperation of self-preservation, but the fear faded to something else as Ultan took the milk white Blade of the Champion and stuck it in the earth.

"Come on, Prince of Nørd." Ultan tore at his pelt cape, tossing it on the handle of the Blade. "Come bleed like a man."

The Prince snorted and charged.

Ultan dodged his swipe and waited till the Prince faced him again to pop a stiff jab to his nose and then twisted his entire body to rip his right hand across Frey's chin.

Blood splashed from his face but the Prince did not fall. He wobbled his weight toward Ultan and grabbed him around the chest, pinning his arms down and driving him across the rocks.

The only thing Ultan could do as they fell was drive his head into Frey's shoulder. So shameful it would've been for the mighty Skölhammer to hit his head on a rock and die like a man drowning in a sea of nausea.

The rocks stole the air from his lungs and Eyvind Frey roared as he reared back and crashed his fist into Ultan's chin.

Ultan blinked away the blackness, dark spots popping up into the violet sky like stormclouds, there and gone, there and gone with each blink. Frey launched another fist, snapping Ultan's chin to the left, fixing his gaze to his cape, covering his sword like a tent.

Frey's grip was weak and firm at the same time, leaking blood as the Prince attempted to choke the life from Ultan but the cut sapped the strength to do it, and Ultan thrust his own grip to Frey's neck and drove him back, as if slowly pushing a stone uphill, till Ultan could sneak his left leg to his chest.

Frey flew back across the rocks, rolling to a weary heap, groaning to push himself up.

"Had enough, Prince of Nørd? Or are you ready for a family reunion in Valhöll?"

Frey howled his rage and ran blindly forward but Ultan fell to his knee and shot up as the Prince smacked him in the shoulder, flipping the man end over end to thud upon the rocks. Pain hissed through a snarl of teeth and cursed the Prince for contesting the mighty Skölhammer.

"Rocks are no bed for a Prince!" Ultan snarled as Frey moaned through the pain and labored to get himself to his feet again. "And you!" Ultan stared daggers into the Princess, the man's young wife. "Is this what you want?"

Frey rushed Ultan in delirium, a thousand thoughts forming the same dire command.

Ultan caught Frey, and thrust a knee into his manhood so hard that the Prince leapt into the air, face whiter than snow.

Spying a sharp inhale from the Princess and a strong attempt to hide it with a mask of unfeeling stone, Ultan called out to her again.

"If you're not with child Mi'lady, you'll never be now!"

Frey rolled around and pawed to get to his feet again, blood rushing to his face like fire consuming kindling.

"But I'd see no better way to unite our lands." Ultan smiled as she bristled and bit the inside of her mouth. "What do you say, Prince of Nørd? Is she up for grabs, too?"

Eyvind Frey cursed in his own language as he gained his height, breathing as if he'd run all night, and his hand trembled and dripped blood, telling Ultan the gash wasn't in his hand at all, but further up his arm, and the frenzy of their fight was only working to pump the life quicker from his body.

"Come on, Prince." Ultan rolled his shoulders and felt the skin of his arms stretch tight against his golden torcs, blood flooding his muscle instead of staining the earth. "I'm not going anywhere. Pick up your sword."

Frey gaged the Champion of Albanland with the guarded ire of a man who knew he'd been defeated but couldn't escape the inevitable.

Death.

Clarity flickered in the Prince's blue eyes and he passed Ultan a subtle nod of thanks, as he reached down with the trembling fingertips of his soaked hand to retrieve his sword.

Ultan was allowing him one last chance to gain the glory his father had never allowed him to take.

Some shadows were just too dark for the sun to burn through.

Ultan replaced the white fox pelt cape about his shoulders and unstuck his weapon from its wedged spot in the rocks.

The gates of Valhöll were always open to the brave, whether they faced their end willingly or unwillingly. It was only a matter of not being afraid when that moment came, and being the only son of Father of The Wolf, Frey never had a hope in hell to take a place at the table without spilling more blood than the man who'd made the rivers of his own land run red with it.

And heaving his sword high in the air, Eyvind Frey launched his final attack.

But before the *hamrammr* battle-bear reached Ultan, the Champion of Albanland stared down the length of his blade at the man's young wife, a bitter promise glazing his heather green eyes.

CHAPTER 30

Ultan thought about something fancy but met strength with strength, becoming the aggressor.

Unlike Eyvind Frey's wild and savage arcs whooping and slicing the violet air, Ultan's stroke was a deft balance of speed and power, sending the sharpness of death to the left, low, then sliding it up to demand Frey shift his defenses, only to flip his grip and wheel something hard and fast from the other direction. And if Frey saw a pattern, Ultan changed it and charged forward, becoming a windstorm of white steel, pale muscle, and strawberry blonde curls.

To see the Prince was to see a wounded animal grasping for a stone in the river though the current was carrying him to sea. Ultan gradually pushed the pace, their clanging ever increasing in speed and volume, and planned his moves two and three blows ahead.

Each rattle and clash was a stick to the fire, the realization bleeding through the Prince's gaze that Ultan was a living flame come across the waters to consume him.

To fight such a man was madness, for Ultan fought with madness itself, bravery beyond comprehension, the stuff of legends and dreams Frey could only hope to attain through the red cap mushrooms and pinefrost mead the berserkers used to become shape-strong.

On the throne next to Father of The Wolf, the Princess was breaking with each snap of silver and white like the shores of the black waters but two dozen feet away. Each thwack and thrust was a swipe at her own heart, and though Ultan knew how hard Nørd culture could be for a woman, he knew real love and devotion when he saw it.

Father of the Wolf seemed not to notice his son's plight and the jeopardy of his throne, but rather, his gaze sat narrowly between intense focus and being forever half-shut in death. His heart beat with every lick of firelight across their blades and he shook his head at the mastery of Ultan's swordcraft.

From somewhere deep within, for the love of his young wife if not for the fear of his father running his own sword through him, Eyvind Frey put up a hell of a show.

Until Ultan ducked a whistling blow and thwacked him on the back of the thigh, taking a meaty chunk of flesh from him with a labored shout.

The Princess bit her thumb, hushing her scream to but a peep, as her husband's body seized and stiffened. The sword twisted from his hand to clatter on the rocks and his staggers were that of a dark fable risen from the ground under a full moon. His face was waxy, covered in a clammy film, and he lurched around to see Ultan's blade ram his chest hilt first.

Clarity whooshed from his lungs.

He had lost.

But Ultan was not finished, shoving his sword in the rocks as he hoisted the man up only to roar an unearthly sound that shook the ground and the trees that cast shadows behind the pavilion to flatten Frey again with a thunderous fist.

"You want war?" He growled as he pulled Frey to height. "I am war!" He crashed the man down with a right hook. "You want death?" Ultan pulled him up again and stilled a near lifeless face by the chin in his left hand, cocking back the right. "I am death!"

Frey fell like a sack of potatoes, limbs flopping and loose, sprawled across the rocks on his chest.

The Princess couldn't fight it. Her full lips, torn down at the corners, trembled with the same cadence of her husband's weak hand, tears streaking her cheeks like blood.

"You want me to become? To transform?" Ultan roared as he spun, heather green eyes ablaze to the crowd, to the hundreds of armed Nørd warriors caught between dread and wonder. "You want me to *transform???*"

In his eyes lived madness. Pure and unfiltered madness.

"This day I shall become…"

The Princess moaned, a hand clawing at her face as Ultan reached down for Eyvind Frey and gripped him by the hair, lifting his head for all to see as he opened the Prince's mouth and wedged a heavy stone deep against his teeth.

It was then the Princess ran from her throne but Father of The Wolf snatched her arm with a twitch of lightning and pulled her to himself.

It was a duel. A sovereign thing. There were rules. And the King's own seed, his only son, lie prostrate on the ground, a stone between his teeth.

Father of the Wolf held his daughter-in-law tight, stroking her hair as she cried against the breadth of his chest, unable to watch the horror of what Ultan was about to do.

"This day I shall become…"

Ultan stared down upon the barely-living body of the Prince. Sticky saliva dripped from Frey's mouth, pooling around the rock. Ultan raised his foot, ready to smash it down on the back of the Prince's head with every ounce of hatred that burned so hot within him the cauldrons siding the pavilion were like a tear drop in the ocean in comparison.

Ultan held his foot, knowing he held the breath of every warrior and every soul in his grasp.

And it was then, in that moment, the madness of his green eyes fell into his mouth to speak one single word.

"Forgiveness."

Ultan lowered his foot slowly and rolled the Prince on his back, letting his breathing slow as no small murmur rippled through the surrounding barrier of warriors. They exchanged glances and whispers, staring at Ultan Skölhammer with more dread and wonder than ever before.

The Champion pulled his blade from the ground and stared down its fire-catching white length to the throne.

"Heed the voice of victory, Father of The Wolf. If you don't stop sending your sons and brothers to the shores of Albanland to die I will never stop killing them. But today, I offer grace and wisdom. Let us end this feud against one another. Let us become allies in war and trade, and let our great nations exchange the stories of our fathers around the fire."

The sword caught cauldron flame once again Ultan stretched his reach to the black waters of the sea and the bend of the violet horizon.

"And if you want war, let us bring it *together*, to the fat Lords and sour-faced liars of South Angle, who have stolen our lands and infected the hearts of our own with vanity. For even now their fleets steal your fish and their merchants trade with everyone *but* you. Soon, you will be left out in the cold, like a toothless old winter wolf who cannot hunt for his pack, and the only comfort you'll have is the root of one of your sacred trees to curl up and die in."

The murmurs rippled through the crowd of warriors and the King paled to receive the winner's words. In a sense, Ultan was offering something so terribly easy, but knew full well how it went against everything the King had built himself up to be. But if a man could not learn to forgive or even receive forgiveness when his own life had come to its end, when could it possibly be learned?

The King's brow twisted, nearly coming together, and his grip on the Princess slacked, allowing her to gather her skirts and run to her husband.

Upon hearing her muted whimper, Eyvind Frey's head lolled to meet her, life weary in his eyes.

Her hard and stern beauty still struck with horror, she stroked his face and buried her head against his chest before rising and throwing herself at Ultan's feet to kiss them repeatedly, a quivering thanks whispering from her full lips.

"Heaven bless you, sovereign Champion of Albanland. May your name be great amongst your people till the end of days."

Ultan tried to hide the burning sensation taking over his skin and prickling his back. He wasn't his people's King, or even a Lord. His father had lost his Lordship by marrying a common Nørd fishing girl and he'd only gained entrance to the Chamber of Lords by Morgance' appointment as Champion.

That and his skill as Champion, his bloody well saving the nation from slaughter time and again at the ripe old age of twenty-four.

But who better to unite the nations? He thought, as the Princess wept at his feet, her body overcome with sobs that the husband whom she loved with every bone in her body could've been taken from her this night but would live on to tell about it.

She was weeping in gratitude.

Who better to unite the nations that a man of both bloods?

Ultan left her and strode the rocks to face the King. Weathered by war and the Four Storms of sixty some-odd seasons, the man was a breath and a half away from giving his final order any moment.

Ultan sheathed his sword in the straps at his back.

"If you don't, King of Nørd, your grandchildren will be the slaves of Angle. I can't fight them alone, and neither can you. Some day, they'll rule the world, unless people like us would stand up and band together."

The King swallowed laboriously and eyed Ultan up and down once more.

"And you believe this?" He said.

"I do."

"Why?"

Ultan chuckled, glancing at the impressive spread of warriors surrounding the man. Obviously it was impossible for him to see the future, surrounded with such men.

But one could only feel the heat if they sat close to the fire.

"Wealth, King of Nørd. For the simple reason they are the richest of any nation I know, and though I do not know much more than the way of the sword in my years, I still know that riches pave the roads and even roads to hell. It is the want of them that drives men to become twisted trees of bitter fruit, and the lust of them that sets fire in their hearts and turns the rivers to blood. Even now, Albanland's own Lords are plotting to overthrow the Throne. I tell you this, because you could invade our land at our weakest moment, but you'd find yourself face to face against the teeth of a war machine with no shortage of hands to twist its gears. You'd pass through our towns like rainwater, but you'd be crushed and ground to powder by the time you hit the border. The end of your legacy would not be that of dread, but of weakness and foolishness."

Ultan reached out his hand, the mighty hand that held the Blade of the Champion.

"I'm asking you to join me to save both our skins. Let me live to be as old as you. Let me be known not as the one who killed a great many men, but the one who saved his nation from destruction."

Father of The Wolf stared at Ultan's open hand, peered up into the heather green eyes of Albanland's Champion, and let his eyes drift back down to his hand.

And then, with a mighty groan, Father of The Wolf rose to speak to his people.

He had made his decision.

And as he staggered across the scraping rocks to stand next to his son and his daughter in law, Ultan had no idea if the King would agree to his plea or if he was about to release his men to cut Ultan in a thousand pieces and toss him in the ocean.

AERLYN

CHAPTER 31

Even though The Thistle felt most at home when she was alone, she couldn't help but walk through the men's camp like the skulking thief she was in nothing but a simple pair of breeches and a sleeveless tunic to clothe her.

And the darkness, always the darkness.

And moving through their midst, Aerlyn watched them sleep every night, hearing the rise and fall of their lungs, wondering what dreams stretched across their minds. It was said The Thistle hated men and while she might've hated the ones that'd attempted to ruin her in her youth, they were still a mystery to her, a flame she could not look away from.

Chief among the mystery, the many men under Rhoswen's rule, those pledged to the Throne and to the true Crown Heir, sworn to her strict laws of forest conduct and separation, ever preparing for the final battle to seize that which was hers and ultimately theirs as well. They were not like the others she'd met, those disgusting creatures of single-minded purpose, those loathsome beasts of lust.

They were different.

They weren't like the men of the towns and the borderlands where South Albanland had become South Angle, eaten alive and corrupted by the thoughts of women as objects and not equal in the raising of children, the building of a home, the functions of the farm and marketplace.

Not seen as the perfect compliments of two halves to make a whole.

But here, under Rhoswen's thumb, that ideal had been realized, and the balance achieved.

And one man, above them all, had spoken to her without saying a word.

And the thought of what was taking root in her stony heart towards him was scaring her.

At night, Aerlyn liked to slip down to a hidden loch of cold water, cut like a tear in cloth through the dense blankets of the trees. Luna favored the unnamed loch, staring down with slivered smiles of white and silver, rippling its pale colors across the glassy surface to where Aeryln would sit on a rock and dip her toes in the chilly water.

And it was on the third day of doing this Aerlyn heard a crack in the undergrowth.

Immediately the desire to flee tensed her stomach. But to where would she flee? Back into the trees, in the darkness? Running for her life? Running from what?

A man?

She was safe here. Rhoswen promised her she would not have to run. She was a part of them now, there was no going back to being The Thistle, the thorn in the spine of the rich.

Aerlyn knew who it was before she saw the shape. She'd heard the rise and fall of air in his lungs and could distinguish it from the others.

He was a singer.

She watched, on her rock, as he strode down to the loch with a small object in his hand and plopped himself down on the rocky shore. With the light of the moon taking his focus, he did not see her, though she was but ten feet away, behind him.

And Aerlyn listened as he held the object tenderly, cradled in his lap as he hunched over it, plunking the strings a few times to tune the mandolin before he began to strum an easy cadence and stare up into the eyes of the moon.

Aerlyn tipped her chin to watch the man, transfixed by the peace, the stillness, the beauty, so very different from the world she knew to be so horrible and ugly.

Here, in the forest, it *was* another world. It was its own separate kingdom. A hard existence, yes, and not one without Rhoswen's strict rules, but it had its moments when nothing seemed to happen, as if all of life was asleep, and Aerlyn could stretch out her senses and hear the earth's heartbeat beneath her feet.

Aerlyn listened as the man, invested in the soft strums of his song, began to hum, unconscious of her or anyone else for that matter.

And the hum loosened his voice, quiet against the lap of the loch.

Unborn, in ancient days, I resided in you
Land of my fathers, unbeknownst who
Sacrificed the very things
That made them who they were
Upon alters well-traveled
Its name callously, Hope
But all for what, town bathed in blood
Bound in chain and rope
The melodies
Woven in the wind
They bring me right back to you
As if I'd never left, my kin
The unrelenting rhythm
It shakes my brittle bones
I follow its leading
Wherever it may go
The swiftly coursing river,
The gentle ebb and flow
Remember when I met you in the hills

And we stared into the sun
Our eyes burned with white light
And you turned to me and said,
Our journey's just begun

Aerlyn fell to thought as the music stopped and the man set the mandolin in his lap and inhaled deeply, scratching his hair just above the ear as he stared at the moon. The secrets of the man's heart slept in that song, for why else would he sneak out of camp when he was supposed to be sleeping and sing it when no one else was around to hear? And while she felt the rising bubble of excitement run up her spine for once again being invisible, she did not wish the feeling to have stolen his intimate moment curse her in the future. For though she was hidden in darkness and silence, she was not here to steal.

Destiny had provided her with a glimpse of the mystery she could only wonder at from afar, and she would not turn her back on its nearness, or keep her mouth shut to its questions.

And with a smile hidden by the darkness sliding across her face, Aerlyn spoke.

"That's lovely."

The man jumped straight up in the air as if he'd sat on lightning. He almost dropped his mandolin and caught it before it fell into the water.

"I'm...I'm sorry..." He bowed, tightly.

"Why?"

"I didn't know anyone was out here."

"I'm not anyone." Aerlyn said. "I'm The Thistle."

"Oh..." The man straightened a bit and walked over, his feet casually clacking and scraping the rocks. "We met a couple of days ago."

"Yes, I remember. Your name is Quill."

"Well..." The man chuckled, seeking the light of Luna rather than the darkness of Aerlyn's face, wrapped in rich waves of auburn hair. "It's actually Uilleam. Quill's just what everyone ends up calling me."

Uilleam. Aerlyn rolled it over in her mind. *I wonder what it means?*

But I don't even know what my own name means.
How can I get to know you if I hardly even know myself?
"Why do they call you Quill?"

The man stood next to her and watched her dangle her toes in the water. The light of the moon snaked up the ripples of the loch and kissed Aerlyn's alabaster skin.

"It's the same as Tanner, Smith, or Taylor. You know, an occupational name."

Aerlyn studied the man. He'd been carrying stacks of wood the first time she'd laid eyes on him. He had broad shoulders, he was tall, and while not barrel-bodied like many of the woodsmen, he looked to be strong and capable, with a thick neck and a sturdy frame.

"You're not a warrior?"

A murmur spilled from his lips and he looked at his mandolin as if it were a club. A hollow club with feminine carvings and intricate frills inlaid into the alternating maple and cherry panels of its bowl-back design.

Aerlyn had the thought he built the instrument himself.

"Rhoswen tells me there are many kinds of warriors, but no, I don't carry a sword. Just a pen."

"And a mandolin." Aerlyn smiled, nudging him with her shoulder.

It was then Quill took a step back and stared at her.

"You're very nice, you know that? You don't mind if I say that, do you?"

"Should I not?"

"Not mind or not be nice?"

"Both."

"Well…it's just that…"

"Ah," Aerlyn nodded, kicking water across the lake and pulling her hands through her hair, watching the moonlight swim through the ripples as if it were an eel from another dimension. "My reputation."

"Yes."

"What of it?"

"It's a nasty one."

"So they say."

"But you're not a killer."

"No I am not. Just a thief."

"Just?" Quill tipped his chin, eyebrows raised. Aerlyn's question back to him was unspoken. She could see he had blue eyes, like the water. "I'd bet your more than *just* a thief."

Aerlyn's gaze fell to her feet, dangling in the water.

"A good judge of character, are you?"

"No. Not at all."

Aerlyn smiled to herself, fighting a laugh. Her voice hushed.

"What are you good at, then?"

"I'm the opposite of you. I have quite a reputation myself." Quill said, his accent that of a highlander, but subdued, as if he'd spent time travelling.

Aerlyn frowned, not at the statement but at the burden that it was spoken with.

"What do you mean?"

"You may be good at taking things, but I'm only good at giving them. It's all I can do. All I've ever been good at doing. And this…" Quill gestured to the peace and quiet, the gentle sigh of the wind through the needles of the trees. The colors of the drowsy night and a world at rest. "This is what I need for myself. If I can't get a bit of it for myself then I can't give it to everybody else."

Aerlyn pulled up a leg and crossed it, brushing the water from her alabaster skin.

"What is it that you give?"

"Whatever is needed. A song. A story. A smile. A hug, kind words, an extra hand with the firewood. I cook and build and clean and sew. But mostly a song. I'm always ready to give a song that hopefully stays with them for as long as they need it to. And the story of this whole thing, you know, Rhoswen's story. I'm here to mark it down. For history."

"Oh." Aerlyn smiled to herself as her hair curtained her features. "A noble goal indeed. Does this story have a name?"

"Umm…" Quill fiddled with his mandolin, squinting into the trees. If Aerlyn didn't know better she'd think he was blushing.

"I've thought about *The Chronicle of the Crown Heir of Albanland*, but that might be a little long."

"Yes. A little."

"Also, *Rhoswen's Right to Rule*."

"That sounds like a children's game."

"That's what I thought."

It was then they laughed together, Aerlyn's a bubbling of contentment, like water sneaking over the rocks and weeds of a highland brook, and Quill's a great guffaw to fill the dark night of a bonfire and a chorus of raised ale mugs.

And without thinking, Aerlyn shot her hand out and clamped it on Quill's mouth, feeling the soft short hairs of his red beard.

She pulled her hand back as if she'd touched a wild animal and realized, like a slap of cold morning air waking her up from a night of fitful sleep, that wild animal was tame and harmless and just as lonely for companionship in the wild as she.

"Sorry...I just don't want to wake anyone."

"Mmm..." Quill said, staring up into the sky. "Rhoswen's rules?"

"Right."

"She's a firebrand, that one."

"Aye."

"I'd hate to be on the other side of her sword."

"As would I."

Silence fell between them and Quill peered off across the dark glass of the loch and the prickly veins of the spruce trees gone black against the night.

"Well," his voice was hushed as he moved back to the spot where he'd first come to play. "I won't tell her I saw you out here if you promise not to listen to me play."

Aerlyn's lips twisted in a gentle curve and she hugged her legs close to her chest, perched on her rock.

Her agreement unspoken, she marveled at the sweet sound of Quill's mandolin and the way it made her eyelids heavy with sleep.

And though she might've been dreaming, Aerlyn could've sworn just before she fell asleep she didn't fall into the water, but rather, fell upward in the air, toward Luna, to be carried off into the forest like stacks of wood.

CHAPTER 32

No small commotion had shaken the camp when Aerlyn awoke without the foggiest idea of how she'd been placed in a small tent just barely large enough for her tall body, bundled up in a woolen blanket like an insect fit for a meal in a spider's web.

Aerlyn wriggled her body and removed a lithe arm, tearing at the tent flap only to see the full light of the sun sear razors into her midnight blue eyes, and she let the flap fall, rubbing away the sleep and the spots of blindness that came as a result.

She was too tired to hear the voices chattering outside, the chomp of axes in woods, the lashing of rope to logs to build more huts, and the smells of the cook fires preparing the first meal of the day. Whatever was happening in the camp, it was bottled up in raucous laughter, but since she was so far removed from what had sparked the excitement, she would only be an observer after the fact, so there was no reason to rush out and investigate as if she were missing something vitally important. It's not like the fact they were all going to attack an Angle fortress that afternoon or something.

That only left the temptation continue sleeping, and Aerlyn sighed away the stringers of drowsiness begging her to stay in the warm but scratchy embrace of the wool blanket for another hour or two, scented as it was with spruce and lavender and the smoke of bacon fat sizzling in the campfire.

Aerlyn rubbed her forehead in thought. When was the last time she stopped, burrowed down, had a full night's sleep?

No running, no looking over her shoulder as if the noose was an inch from her long and pale neck?

Aerlyn squinted and nestled her head against a second blanket, rolled up for a pillow. Something caught her eye and she turned.

Her boots had been removed, cleaned, shined, and polished, and set neatly together within arms reach.

Who would've done such a thing?

Aerlyn had an idea, and slipped them on, poking her head out of the tent for a breath or two to take it all in before joining the gathering circle around the fire pit that marked the center of the women's camp.

A circle that'd formed around a charismatic young man with blonde hair, a shorter young man with brown hair that could've been his brother if she had to guess, and a caramel-skinned young woman with hair as black as jet.

The blonde's eyes were nearly the shade of Aerlyn's boots and not as shiny. She'd seen a thousand of his type if she'd seen one. A Son of the Four Storms, constantly caught in the blustering flow of the wind like a leaf fallen in the water.

His story about wrestling a Larlaith was proof enough. Only a born renegade would tempt his chance with such foolery.

It was all for a kiss, he'd said. *A kiss!*

His brother, or friend, whichever, was of a more phlegmatic disposition and perhaps more prone to think before speaking, but the tall blonde was the kind to be as quick with a cutting remark as a he was a compliment, stabbing a smile or a jabbing a sneer.

At least that was her first impression.

Aerlyn felt wrong to size him up after the time she'd spent with Quill last night. Before last night's encounter she'd spotted Quill in peeks and glances for going on three days without saying a word to him, other than that first introduction, but she'd always noticed where he was when supper was served and remembered which logging detail he'd been assigned to.

Why he didn't train with the men at arms or their squires.

Why he didn't carry a sword when Rhoswen's army had been built and trained for one thing.

To get the Throne back.

That was what she'd said, right? Men and women, they both fight, no exceptions?

Even though it was brief, her moments with Quill last night reminded her that not all men were created equal.

Neither were all women.

And of the new comers, *she* caught Aerlyn's eye. Portugeça? Espaiña? Certainly a long way for a Romany to travel, but the young girl, what was she, fifteen? Sixteen? She was a gypsy, through and through and there was something different about her. Yes, different from southern girls or highland girls, but even something that set her apart from other gypsies.

A secret hid behind the glossy shine of her dark eyes, and Aerlyn knew she'd learn that secret whether she wanted to or not.

Because the young woman had boldly scanned the crowd, looked Aerlyn straight in the eyes, and smiled as if the sun shone from her face.

Aerlyn wondered if she blushed. In her time alone she hadn't had any reason to, even when she slipped on the riverbank and splashed in the mud on her bum, or when she chased rabbits for her meal and ran into badger's nest. But with her alabaster skin it was impossible to hide. Maybe it could've been explained as the light reflecting her dark auburn hair.

Not that The Thistle had ever had to explain herself to anybody.

But with what space she couldn't fight Quill from carving out inside of the stony veins of her heart, she didn't expect to meet another so soon who could speak to her deep inside, like he had, without even saying a word.

Maybe it was simply the wages of loneliness, and it'd finally caught up to her.

Aerlyn took her lunch at the training ground where Rhoswen took her own lunch and barked out commands now and then to the young men expending the endless energy of their youth while the older men took a break and stretched in the shade of the trees to dab their foreheads with rags cooled in the loch. Lunch wasn't more than a few bites of smoked meat and as many leeks stewed with rosemary and pickled wild mushrooms as one could stomach. Sometimes there were beets and turnips, other times spring onions. Fish was always reserved for dinner, as the loch was brimming with foot-sized trout and something quick and hard to catch and nearly too thin to eat.

Some of the men had been calling it *Thistle Fish*.

Aerlyn studiously watched the young men train, noting their strengths and weaknesses as if they were all castle walls. Every castle wall had a gate, to enter or exit, but gates were always fortified and given far too much attention, allowing the castle to be conquered by some other means to someone with enough wit to figure out the weaknesses. And now four days removed from her ways as The Thistle, she was still seeing life through the eyes of a thief. Everything was a challenge, a puzzle, a race, a mystery, a locked-up box of riches and wonder.

Either something to defeat, or something to be defeated by.

Except Quill. He just was. Content to let her be…who *she* was. Aerlyn sighed in the freedom of that thought, a smile touching her lips as her eyes stared far beyond the small host of young men hard at work learning the art of war.

"Got your eye one of them, do you?" A lilting voice asked, sitting down next to her on the cool grass.

"Pardon?"

"Oh, you heard me alright." The gypsy nearly whispered, popping a mushroom in her mouth. "I can read minds, you know. Ask me about any one of them and I'll let you know if you've got a chance. Or maybe you can offer them a cup of tea and run it back to me after they've finished drinking." Her glossy eyes jumped up and down Aerlyn's features twice before that summer smile returned. "I'm Finleigh, by the way."

"Pleasure to meet you, Finleigh. I'm Aerlyn O'Rye."

"An Eire?"

"In name only. I'm a highlander."

"As if I couldn't tell, your gorgeous red hair and all. You look like a highland rose, lost in a glen for one of these lads to stumble upon and be struck speechless. Hey, can I see your palms?"

Aerlyn swallowed and coughed in a clenched hand before crossing her arms as if she were cold.

"You're aware of the Crown Heir's policy, right?"

"Hey, until she's crowned Queen of Gypsies she has no rights to *my* heart." Finleigh waved a hand, her nose scrunched up. Aerlyn chucked at her obvious sarcasm, though it was a thin veneer to cover the sparkle in her dark eyes. They were made for men to dream about, capturing hearth fire or bonfire or sunlight in the curve of their own shadows. "As one of my uncles used to say, there's too many fish in the sea for me to spend the rest of my life eating vegetables."

Aerlyn hid a smirk in the curtain of her auburn hair as Finleigh sighed, staring at the display with a dreamy gaze. Never had she seen so many young men desperate to defend their land of their birth packed together in one place with their shirts off.

"Don't forget to eat." Aerlyn reminded with a nudge of her elbow. "You'll faint in this heat."

Finleigh nodded and popped another mushroom in her mouth, speaking with it bulging her cheeks.

"Us España take the heat well. It's loneliness that makes us drop like flies."

And as Aerlyn had taken a bite of meat, she nearly choked on it with laughter.

"Well, you've got a friend in me." Aerlyn said, regaining her composure after sipping at a cup of cold loch water. "I'm the loneliest person you'll ever meet."

It was then capricious Finleigh reached for her own cup of water, which Aerlyn assumed for a toast on the subject, and Rhoswen stood up and asked for the training ground's attention. She had an announcement to make.

CHAPTER 33

In even just half of her battle armor, Rhoswen was a fierce young woman. Aerlyn put her at twenty-two or three, just two or three years older than herself. But, whatever had happened to her as a child, whatever had cloven the ring finger from her hand, had planted a seed of steel and stone deep in her heart no one else in the land could contend with.

To see Rhoswen was to see a woman possessed, each breath swelling her chest for but one purpose.

To once again take the Throne.

"In the spirit of competition," Rhoswen said as she spun around to the group. Most all of her two-thousand followers were at the training ground just a mile away from the loch. Those who hadn't eaten were about to, but some had to work nearly all day long. "I'm going to bring back the Circle."

A small murmur grew to cheers and claps and whistles. Rhoswen held her hands up to still the crowd again, and the noonday sun flared the shine of her steel breastplate as she spun to call for quiet.

"What's the Circle?" Finleigh whispered.

Aerlyn shrugged, staring at her leader as if the hero of an epic saga had come to life before her eyes.

Rhoswen looked downright resplendent in the sun, her hair a curly mass of dark brown cascading over her chest and shoulders, and those multicolored eyes of hers were alive with the hope of what was unfolding before her, as her green cloak trimmed with a silver thread of endless knots and whorls, captured all the colors of her irises in shape-shifting portions.

"As you know, the rules of the Circle are sovereign," Rhoswen continued. "One may enter at their own risk, but one can only enter when challenged." A hand moved to the sword hilt in a leather scabbard at her waist. "And while those who risk the Circle have seen their fair share of injuries…I see no other way to keep us strong than to fight one another. For the time is coming when we will stand as one against our enemies, against the enemies of freedom."

Though Rhoswen offered no stimulus in her voice, the crowd roared a cheer as if she had been shouting herself.

Chills rippled through Aerlyn's bare arms to hear the unbroken oneness of the voice, as if they'd planned it all.

But it'd been too spontaneous.

It was the sound of unity.

The cheer continued as Rhoswen unsheathed her sword and drew the shape in the soft grass and marked it with four stones.

Aerlyn found herself clapping along with the crowd and looked to Finleigh, whose teeth flashed bright against her caramel skin to see even more displays of blade and bravery on just her first day in the camp.

To Finleigh, Aerlyn assumed, that meant more shirtless men.

Aerlyn rolled her eyes at her new friend but found a grin warming her own traditionally grim and shadow-smothered features.

"And who shall begin?" Rhoswen asked, a thin smile lining her lips. The resounding cheer died as soon as it had left the group's mouth because the realization of *who* was standing in the Circle.

"Whoever is called does not have to come. This is the way of the Circle. It's a challenge only you can accept or deny, but no one will judge another for his or her choice concerning the matter. And…" Rhoswen's left eyebrow tipped above the right in a wry gesture, Aerlyn assumed of the sarcastic nature. "As your leader, I will be the first to demonstrate what I hope this exercise will achieve. For this time, next year, I will sit the Throne of Albanland or have died trying."

Rhoswen's sword sucked up all the light of the sun, glinting like a hot star fallen from heaven as she pointed the sharp tip into the crowd.

"I call our Master Archer to the Circle."

Ooh's and *Aah*'s made their way through the group, hovering above the anticipation and trepidation of the coming cycle. A winner could call as many as he or she wanted if they kept on winning, and retire at any moment. Traditions of the Circle stated that whoever held the longest streak of victories by the sunset would receive a double portion of food until their record was broken.

Finleigh clapped extra fast and squeezed Aerlyn's left arm, barely able to contain herself. Aeryn's neck snapped to the left at the lingering pain from her bruise, but Finleigh pointed to the tall woman emerging from the crowd.

Her hair was blonde and a braid ran around her head like a crown, to allow the rest to fall across her shoulders like a horse's mane.

Her footsteps were light and tender on the ground, much like Aerlyn's herself, obviously one used to hunting and stalking skittish game. Aerlyn squinted to see the lack of fear in her blue eyes. She, too, was quite young, but then again, Rhoswen couldn't afford to have that much age on her side. Too many of the older generations had either been bought off or broken to the will of the Angles or killed fighting Nørds.

No, it was her own brothers and sisters that would seize the Throne with her. Rhoswen's own peers, as a family of one heart.

The Master Archer lingered by a pile of weapons and selected a short-handled axe, set with two gruesome spikes opposite the blade end, flipping it around in a series of flourishes with broad and graceful hands, whopping the air with silver slices.

A cheer bubbled through the crowd as the Master Archer stepped into the Circle, face free of emotion.

And like the moment before a bird takes flight, the ground was still and silent.

Then broken by steel.

Aeryln's jaw slacked at the wizarding display of weaponry, but she, too, felt the same comfort in her dagger. It'd been with her for nearly eight years. Eight years of relying on its double-edged blade, and its ability to fly into her empty hand like magic when she needed it most.

But the whirl and twist of Rhoswen's green and silver cloak, sun slashing its own razors into the fight, flaring stars upon the silver steel, spoke to Aerlyn in some odd poetic beauty, stirring her blood deep within, like a dance of death.

And like Quill's peaceful presence and Finleigh's wide-eyed lust for life, Aerlyn was realizing the seed of something she'd never seen before grow in her mind.

War.

Of pain and suffering, yes, she'd seen her share, but war? War was something she'd avoided like Plague. Something of a distant black cloud of the Four Storms raining blood and howling daemon screams on the horizon, the same she'd run away to take shelter from in the unbroken hills of the highlands, counting her precious rubies.

But to watch the Crown Heir match her Master Archer blow for scintillating blow, whizzing sharp steel through the sunny air, it nearly brought her to tears.

And in it all, Rhoswen's promise kindled her own tri-colored eyes with blazing embers.

For this time, next year, I will sit the Throne of Albanland or have died trying...

And though the Master Archer was good, she could not best Rhoswen, a dainty damsel of death and determination.

She was one with her blade, a dark swirl of arms and artistry, impossible for the reed-like and slender Master Archer to contend with.

And after nearly four minutes of intense combat, Rhoswen feinted, catching the Master Archer off balanced, leapt and somersaulted, and landed on her knee with the tip of her sword gently touching Master Archer's spine.

A raucous cheer rocked the easily excitable crowd, and Rhoswen saluted them all with her sword and a wizened smile, giving her Master Archer a fierce embrace as they both stepped from the Circle.

"As I have more to attend to, I bequeath my spot in the Circle to Sir Craig of MacLellan. Choose wisely, Sir Craig, there's some hungry young men out there with a heart for glory."

The clapping caused Aerlyn to hug her knees to her chest as a man who could've been an advisor to Rhoswen's departed father, King Brom the Chosen, took the Circle with nothing more than a wooden staff. He was a big man, well into his years, with a limp nagging his inwardly twisted left foot, but a broad chin that promised to take any fist thrown its way, and a twinkle in his wink to the Crown Heir guaranteed he used the staff for more than just walking.

Aerlyn fell into study as several more matches caught her interest. Most of Rhoswen's army was her age, both men and women, and they fought together, sometimes in mixed matches. Keeping in line with her notion of angles and opportunities, each warrior held an advantage over the one they fought in some small way, but many failed to exploit them. It took Aerlyn a moment to realize that Rhoswen was not teaching them to pick a pocket or a lock, things of extreme focus and a delicate touch, but to fight. To overpower. To be bold and brave and stare another man or woman in the eye and strike them down without feeling a thing.

To war.

The thought stilled her and a morose calm fell upon her. Whatever Rhoswen's beautiful blade-wielding had inspired suddenly slipped away, reminding her of the dagger the slave had buried in the governor of Brachin.

"What do you think of the Circle?"

Aerlyn looked up to see Quill, the sun shining through his light brown hair. It was thin and widow-peaked, wavy and bunching beneath his ears, which Aerlyn saw were not straight along the frame of the skull like most, but angled like a legendary elf. He smiled and sat down next to her. He was missing two teeth, both on the top of his mouth, one on the right side, the other on the left, but all of these things suited him in the manner the wet and the cold suited Albanland and made the emerald green of the highlands look that much more surreal as they seemed to stretch out forever.

In a way, he didn't seem conscious of them.

Maybe that's what set him apart amongst a horde of puffed up young warriors. He lacked vanity. Was it wisdom? Or did he just not give a damn?

Either way, it was refreshing, and Aerlyn breathed in the welcome tonic of his presence in the storm of testosterone that'd gripped the training ground.

"I don't know." Aerlyn said as she squinted across a line of heads and shoulders to watch the combat. It was only then she noticed Finleigh had departed, probably capturing the eyes of just about every man in Rhoswen's army along with her.

"It's not for everyone, you know." Quill said, softly.

"Yes." Aerlyn nodded, and then frowned. "So where've you been all day?"

"Oh, you know. Here and there."

"No, I don't know." Aerlyn dipped her chin. "That's why I'm asking."

"Well," Quill tipped his blue eyes to her hands, a smile tugging at the corner of his mouth. "Maybe you'd like to come and see?"

Aerlyn gazed into his eyes for a moment, just a moment, before he looked back to the Circle, soaked in sunlight.

"Yes." Aerlyn nodded. "Maybe I would."

CHAPTER 34

Quill lead her through the woods on a small trail, darkened by the dense undergrowth and cut off from the hoots and howls of the sweat-stained Circle. Aerlyn noticed, as they walked single-file, the many bushes lining the path looked as if they'd been trampled by horses, though it was far too narrow to lead a horse down the trail. Blackberry vines reached out to grab her, but they'd been stripped of their berries. Pinkberries, too. Several times Quill had to walk sideways, pulling back the thorns and ferns to make sure they did not snag the bare alabaster skin of one of Aerlyn's lithe arms.

Anticipation fluttered in her stomach and she tried to bat it down before it rose up into her mind. Where was he taking her? Was he like every other man? Had she been wrong about him? Did he know a quiet spot where he...

No. Aerlyn thought. *You're not The Thistle anymore. Don't judge this man just for being a man. And if you've already judged him, you've told yourself he's not like the others and there's a reason for that.*

Don't doubt yourself now.

And just when she was about to ask where he was taking her, the darkness of the limbs and leaves broke to reveal a small meadow streaked by several long huts, covered in animal skins, built more in the Nørd style, complete with fenced areas abutting each other to house dubiously-gazing goats, gnawing on grass as if they were thinking upon the deepest mysteries life had to offer.

Quill only stood aside the trailhead and watched her face as Aerlyn could barely contain the emotion of seeing such a precious display stretch before her.

Children.

There must've been twenty of them, boys and girls both, some barely able to totter and stumble forward in the soft grass, grasping at dandelions and grasshoppers flitting from blade to blade, others purple-faced with blackberry juice. Even the oldest, still not more than nine or ten, huddled around a young woman with golden hair and radiant blue eyes.

Quill only jerked his head to the left for Aerlyn to follow.

The woman, who Aerlyn determined was teaching them languages, had the mellifluous voice of a highly educated Angle, but she didn't look like one. Neither Nørd nor Alban. Or even an Eire. Where was she from? Aerlyn assumed from somewhere off the eastern sea, from a land she'd never seen or even heard of.

The woman smiled at Quill and Aerlyn both, and Aerlyn stood like a statue as two tiny little girls with hair so red it was nearly orange, like hers had been at their age, ran up to her.

One spoke gibberish, the other hugged her knee.

Aerlyn pressed a hand to her heart, lips sagging at the corners. Blush kissed her cheeks and Quill laughed his meadow-filling guffaw.

"Now you know why Rhoswen fights." Quill said, retrieving his mandolin from a pile where the teacher had several sticks and colored shells stashed for counting games. "And none of us are that old, but we're older than them by a lifetime." He crossed his arms as a little boy with dark brown hair and eyes to match came up to him with hands bared like claws and roared. Quill simply put a hand to his forehead and pushed him into the grass. The child rolled and sprawled spread eagle, his body caught in fits of laughter. "We're their elders." Quill smiled, his blue eyes bottomless with emotion.

Aerlyn took in the scene again, the noises of the goats bringing her sharp eye back to their faces as they sat behind their pens and gnawed on grass, mulling the same old thought over and over again. Gnawing and thinking.

The memory of her elders as a child in the fishing village of Nochgull had been just like them, goats with vacant stares, forever contemplating and never doing.

But a man like Quill, to look up to? To love like an older brother, or an uncle, or whatever a child made up in their mind, without law or rule or inquisition, well, that would've changed a few things. If a man like Quill had been there to see her through the hard times, well, things would've been different.

For the better? The worse?

Different. Certainly no Thistle would've risen from the Four Storms to scourge the rich.

Quill spoke softly as he came to stand next to her.

"I'll bring you supper." He said, and she caught his arm as he turned to leave.

He stared at the strong grip of her lithe fingers for a moment and then gave her an appraising glance.

"Is it…is it this or the Circle?" Aerlyn asked, as children buzzed around her, oblivious. "Is there nothing else?"

Quill's lips flattened and he scratched the short red beard that covered his chin. It was nearly the same color as her hair, and for a second, some childish thought flashed a smile across her face to think of him with a beard as long and flowy as her own hair.

"No." Quill said. "Not now, anyway. But, Rhoswen has just as much hope in this as she does that. There's no point in winning a Crown by blood and war if the next generation is just going to lose it again in the same manner to someone else." Quill squinted up to the sun. For a second, Aerlyn thought she saw disgust creep across his face. "The whole thing's like a snake eating its own tail. And I'm damn sick of it."

Aerlyn swallowed the blunt statement with a nod and watched Quill walk off through the forest with his mandolin.

A tiny hand tugged at the hem of her sleeveless shirt, and Aerlyn couldn't fight a tear popping from her left eye at the precious little face of angel's cheeks and mossy eyes too big for the face the hand belonged to, bent under the weight of her light brown curls.

And with one hand, Aerlyn took the little blossom and hefted her up to her arms, using the other hand to wipe her eyes.

It was then, Aerlyn wondered, as Rhoswen's words rolled around her mind, mixing with Quill's, if drawing blood on behalf of an innocent little life was such a bad thing.

It was then she couldn't stop the tears.

In twelve years, the sweet little girl could've been the same helpless slave chained up in the governor's bedroom, or another forgotten face beheaded by Nørds in a midnight raid.

Aerlyn O'Rye would *not* let that happen.

At whatever price.

Whether the jeweled blood of rich Angle bird's heart rubies, or the crimson river of her own bones.

Aerlyn O'Rye would fight.

Or die trying.

CHAPTER 35

Three days after Rhoswen had drawn the Circle in the dirt and grass, Niles got called out by a scruffy young man with arms like tree limbs and dim-witted reactions to match. Sir Craig was keen to oversee the matches to insure against unnecessary injury or even death, and restricted the young men to sticks or bare hands. Niles was quick to catch the gaze of Finleigh after a win that surprised her just as much as it did him.

"Lucky knock on the chin." Aerlyn muttered, standing near the back of the crowd. It seemed after her taking leave of a spot with the teacher and the children, attending the matches in the Circle, she'd caught the brown eyes of the blonde known as Niles more than once. In fact, she could feel them look her up and down from nearly a mile away, as if just to watch her walk across the small creek that divided the camps was to see something beautiful, like a horse running wild in a field, or rain and sun casting a bow of colors across the sea. The sixteen year old's teeth were crooked, his smile nearly impish, and he walked with a fractured strut that made Aerlyn smirk.

But he sure did like himself, and he bloomed with every eye on him, the center of attention.

Fit and fancy, posh and prancy, the lowland Lord of the rogues gallery romancing the highland girl of his dreams with nothing more than what he thinks himself to be. Aerlyn mused, crossing her arms.

Back in the long sleeves, tight breeches and willowy brown cloak of The Thistle, despite the heat, Aerlyn produced her dagger and carved up an apple to enjoy as Niles, all puffed up, found himself badly beaten two matches later by a young man who looked no older than twelve, and fought as if he knew nothing other than the way of the Circle.

Aerlyn squinted to see the tattoo around the youngster's arm, chewing thoughtfully as she read into its meaning. The youngster went on to beat ten in a row, until a streak of pride made him call out the Master Archer, and she sent him packing with one thwack of the stick.

Aerlyn had just finished her apple and was reloading her knife in her spring-release harness when the young boy walked past, dripping sweat, headed off for the loch. The tattoo, on his right bicep, consisted of two blocks of ancient knots, split in the middle by a circle, wrapped with a trio of spirals and whorls.

Wonder what it means…

Voices clamored around her and she thought nothing of it as the tattoo consumed her thoughts. She'd seen them on several of the young men and a few women, but hadn't made sense of why. It was as if they belonged *to* something. There was something the bearers of the tattoos carried inside, as if they walked differently or looked at the world around them differently. Not a strong sense of division with the rest of Rhoswen's army, but it was as if there was a group *within* the group.

Aerlyn decided to chew on it.

It was then she looked back to the Circle and the chatter of voices to see the Master Archer pointing the length of the yew staff.

At her.

Aerlyn swallowed, a jump of tension punching her in the stomach before she advanced, bloodless and silent, her cloak covering her footfall to make her hover across the thinning grass. Part of her fought a grin as Niles' sightline fell heavy upon her, mouth slightly agape, cutting off Finleigh's singsong praises of how good he'd done in the Circle and how if she had any copper pennies left she would've bet the Eire who did most of the cooking, Fiona was her name, a day's rations that next time in the Circle Niles could get five wins in a row.

Seeing as Fiona had already wanted to give Niles more than an extra serving of venison, and Finleigh was there to see that didn't happen.

But somehow Niles was oblivious to that, since Aerlyn had caught *his* attention, the thorny queen of all highland roses. Sometime she'd try to tell Finleigh Niles didn't have a fishes' chance in the desert with The Thistle, as there was no room in The Thistle's heart for anything but the cover of night and the rich colors of bird's heart rubies and seer's eyes sapphires. Out of the corner of her razor-sharp sight, she spotted Finleigh's countenance fall as Niles ignored her.

One way to fix that, I think. Aerlyn chuckled to herself. *If I can beat the Master Archer, first.*

Cheer up, Finleigh, I'll teach Niles a lesson.

That's if the Master Archer doesn't teach me one I'll never forget.

Aerlyn approached the Circle slowly, trying to ignore the whispers and murmurs drifting through the crowd. If none had known The Thistle was among them, they knew now. Even in the full light of the sun, she seemed to disappear; a slender silhouette of brown. Pulling up her hood, she shadowed her midnight blue eyes so that nothing but the alabaster skin of her chin and the garnet slash of her lips could be seen.

Nothing for the Master Archer, or the crowd for that matter, to read.

She was, after all, the stuff of folklore and nightmares.

Best act like it, right?

Aerlyn stood just outside the edge of the Circle and raised her left hand up, holding the crowd in the empty palm of her hand, and with a twitch and a softened click, produced the dagger that'd become an extension of her body.

The trick whipped no small tempest of excitement throughout the younger men, minds still crawling with the stories of the hero sagas and cycles Quill told nearly every night around the campfire in the men's camp, and the hundreds of young eyes spread around her were ready to stick The Thistle just under the Crown Heir as *their* living, breathing, follow-to-the-depths-of-hell heroes.

They were eyes hungry for glory, hearts ready for legends.

The Master Archer tipped her gaze to Sir Craig, who reluctantly nodded, and the Master Archer snorted fresh air through flared nostrils and tossed the stick to the ground, reaching behind her back to produce a stiletto dagger from a slice in her belt; a slim and reed-like blade, a weaponized version of herself, obviously something that never left her person.

Aerlyn stepped inside the Circle.

"Begin." Sir Craig said, with a dull voice. She knew he was fatigued by overseeing the battles day in day and day out, but they could *all* feel the anticipation of the match tense the air around them and sear the grass with lightning.

And so it began.

The Master Archer feinted, as Aerlyn had seen her do with Rhoswen, and Aerlyn nudged her knee forward to plant the seed of a block in the Archer's mind. So, the next time that swipe wasn't a feint, but a finishing stroke, Aerlyn would use it to her advantage, knowing she'd seen the woman fight, but the same could not be said in reverse.

In actuality, as they traded loose swipes and near-missing kicks, *no one* knew a thing about The Thistle, other than what they'd heard and what they'd told each other. What they'd conjured up in their minds as Luna took to the sky and painted the lush and leafy treetops with their dreams. The thought sent itchy daggers up Aerlyn's spine, and she felt sweat glaze her hands within half a minute of combat.

If she dropped her knife, she'd be disqualified.

That wouldn't be too impressive. Aerlyn thought. *And if I am going to be a scourge of the enemies of freedom, I'd better show Rhoswen's Chosen, tattooed or not, that I can't be beaten.*

By man, by woman, by daylight, or even the fall of night.
The Thistle knows no master and The Thistle is here to stay.

Aerlyn caught the Master Archer's focused blue gaze and twitched her shoulders, slapping the Archer's drag of the knife across her body with her free hand and twisting her own knife to bring it precariously close to the Archer's throat.

A *woah* rushed through the crowd and Sir Craig flinched, as if he was responsible to stop the fight, but chewed on his lip instead.

The Master Archer bent awkwardly at the spine as Aerlyn committed herself, and fell to her left hand, kicking her foot into the soft space behind Aerlyn's knee. Aerlyn watched the horizon angle before her and poured into an acrobatic handstand and flip, feeling more alive than she'd ever felt since stealing something for the first time.

And that was a *long* time ago.

The world spun right way round again and Aerlyn fought a flinch for the stiletto spike flying toward her. Low and stretched. Too desperate for a quick win after so much posturing.

Aerlyn wheeled her leg in a high arc and slapped the Archer's lunge downward, whizzing her knife over the Archer's head, just barely missing a lock of blonde.

The second *woah* whooshed from the crowd and Sir Craig danced a conflicted two step, debating between coming and going, between stopping the fight and feeling every move as if he were in the mix with them.

Some of those seated took to standing, and in the periphery, Aerlyn swore she could've seen bets being cast.

But the stiletto jabbed her way twice again and she responded with a whip of her own blade. Her belly was harder than stone and her teeth clenched twice as tight as the Archer slashed and swiped deft and nuanced strokes, flipping her grip, and jabbing desperate lunges.

Hell on fire, Aerlyn thought. *If you're so good with a sword and a dagger, what on earth can you do with a bow and arrow?*

The Archer's gaze was cool and cold in response, speaking to her in a language beyond words.

You're good, Thistle, but this is no place for you.

Aerlyn dodged a quick jab, and put her weight in her shoulder. The Master Archer flew to the ground with an exhale of labored breath, but pounced up as if she'd never fell.

I've never killed a man or woman, but plenty a wild beast in the highlands. Aerlyn thought back. *Sometimes, I wonder if there's a difference between them.*

The Archer danced forward with her dagger but had no intention of using it. It was merely a distraction to pop Aerlyn in the chin with a fist, which she nearly dodged at the last minute, leaving the encounter with nothing more than a sting, even though it could've been a debilitating blow to shoot black spots of nausea through her hooded gaze.

I've killed men. The Archer's blue eyes declared. *Dozens of them. Killed them without knowing the arrow was coming for them. Killed them without them seeing who did it, or hearing the arrow whistle the air for their heart till it was too late.*

Aerlyn swallowed. The Master Archer was a weapon of war, just like Rhoswen. Someone born with battle in their blood, never known a peaceful day, or the quiet way.

You think I'm weak, don't you?

No.

Squeamish?

Certainly not.

You think you're better than me, then? Is that it?

A smile glinted across the stiletto and echoed through the Master Archer's face.

I don't ponder that which already is.

Aerlyn let a snarl twist her garnet lips and dashed forward to provoke the Master Archer who dived to her left, but misjudged The Thistle's speed or the length of her steps. Aerlyn mounted the Master Archer's bent knee with a vault and somersaulted over her shoulder, slipping a kiss of steel across the Archer's head just before Aerlyn found the ground in a roll.

Her momentum took her out of the Circle, causing Sir Craig to run into it, awkwardly, with his limp, to declare the match over.

The Master Archer rose with a smile on her face until Aerlyn simply held up the lock of blonde hair she'd taken from the warrior to an eruption of cheers and whistles behind her.

The smile stayed on the Master Archer's pretty face, and she bowed, tightly, her shoulders heaving in the slightest as her blue eyes promised *next time, Thistle. Next time.*

But the damage was done. Rhoswen's Chosen had seen The Thistle and she'd lived up to her legend. A chorus of praise showered her way like a summer wind pushing the scent of wildflowers around a glen.

And for someone as lonely as she, who lived in a land she never felt loved her, and never saw a purpose to serve with the fullness of her many skills, the warmth of every gleaming eye and gap-toothed smile slipped inside of her heart like a key fashioned for an unbreakable lock.

And Aerlyn pulled back her hood, feeling sunlight on her face.

Until her gaze fell to Quill, tucked in the back of the crowd near a broad spread of limbs and leaves, his features forever shadowed in sadness.

RHOSWEN

CHAPTER 36

A knock on the scant timber frame preceded the tall man's ducking through the deerskin coverings of Rhoswen's tent where she sat on her blankets, eyes closed in thought. The Crown Heir's eyes fluttered open, familiar colors bleeding through what she told herself had been a dream, too loose and vaporous to capture. It was dusk, and dusk always begged her to close her eyes, as if dreams themselves were simply waiting to take her by the hand until the rise of the sun the next day.

If only sleep could be so simple, with the weight of the yet to be claimed Crown suffocating her.

How would she sleep once, if in some grand miracle, she actually secured it by blood? How many would die before she saw the kind of unity she had in the forest stretch out over all of Albanland?

If ever?

"I thought you might be hungry."

Rhoswen looked over to see Quill bunch himself up in the corner of her small tent and pass her a plank of seared venison, black and crusted on the outside, fading to a tender core of nearly ruby in the center, drizzled with fireweed honey.

"Ooh! Strawberries!" Rhoswen chirped, popping one in her mouth. There had only been four on the plank, and they were small, but sweeter than a true love's kiss, warmed by the sun. "You're too good to me, Quill."

"You're my Queen." He said, watching her eat as if he were eating himself, until a growl gnawed through his stomach, and he looked off toward the flap in the tent, like a wild wolf was loose in the camp.

"And when are you going to eat something?"

"Hmm?"

The gaze of brown, green, and gray shot him a stern reprimand.

"I see everything that goes on here, Quill. *Everything.*" Rhoswen reached for a thick slice of venison and passed it to him, which he gracefully accepted. "I noticed you stopped eating when Aerlyn took the Circle."

"You mean The Thistle?" There a sharpness in his voice. Frustration, keener than an axe-blade. A pain Rhoswen hadn't heard since they'd met nearly three years ago, when he was nothing more than a baird apprentice travelling the world to find the meaning of life.

"Yes. Aerlyn O'Rye." Rhoswen corrected. "When was that? Two days ago?" Another strawberry popped in her mouth and Rhoswen clenched a fist to her forehead as her mouth watered with the freshness, the purity.

Just like her and Ultan had picked as children, running wild in the fields south of Ullraye, promising each other the world without knowing a damn thing about the way it spun.

To taste the fresh strawberry was to embrace a memory shoved so far down in her heart she nearly forgot it'd even been there.

"Three." Quill's gaze dropped to the venison and he bit a piece of it, chewing thoughtfully. "I'm sorry. You know how melancholy I can be."

"I rely on it." Rhoswen passed him a wizened wink. "All those stories of yours have to come from somewhere."

"The stories? Oh, they're nothing."

"That's easy for you to say!"

Quill chuckled, hollow and weak. Gray circles slept beneath puffy eyelids, making him look nearly sick.

"I just tell the same story over and over again and change a few names and places. A few small details. In the end, the good guys always win."

"Well now you ruined it for me." The Crown Heir mock pouted and nibbled some venison. "And how much have you slept?"

"Not much."

"You've been going out to the loch again?"

"I always go out to the loch."

Rhoswen passed him another piece of venison and her mouth ached for a strawberry but she only licked her lips, pursed them, and dropped her chin.

"Going out to the loch to strum your mandolin under Luna's gaze is different than going out to the loch to flood the shores with your tears and pine for a heart of stone."

Quill's blue eyes snapped up to meet her and his mouth stretched to say something, but Rhoswen's quicksilver reflexes caught his wrist and put the venison to his lips, the reaction of which caused him to shut his mouth and bite down on it.

Satisfied, Rhoswen ate her third strawberry, watching the last roll in a semi-circle as if tottering between factions as she set the plank down before them both.

"You were in a state when you came to me."

"I was."

"You wanted something."

"Yes, and I still do."

"Do you know what it is?"

Quill wiped his fingers clean on the billowy elbow fabric of his tunic. Being a mandolin player and writer he despised sticky and dirty fingers with a passion.

"I know now more than I knew then."

"But do you *know*?" Rhoswen folded her hands in her lap, watching his eyes fall to the venison. "Do you really *know* what it is that gives you hope to see a new dawn?"

Quill scrunched his eyes shut, pawing at them as they burned.

"My head hurts sooooo bad."

There was a pleading in his voice, a distinct weakness and vulnerability she'd heard a thousand times if she'd heard it once.

But she'd been the only one to hear it. His only confidant as he traveled the rocky road of trying to be that which others needed even when they didn't appear to give a damn.

They just expected him to be there. With a song, with a story, with a smile, with everything they needed, like a lake that never ran out of fresh water or fish.

A one-way trading post of soulish nourishment.

Rhoswen's hand gripped his shoulder and pressed strength and comfort through his body with slow squeezes.

She said nothing as he cried, silently. And he cried often. Mostly alone, but she would never turn away his tears.

She, too, had cried.

But when she realized no tears would bring her finger back, and no sorrow or lament would raise her beautiful mother and saintly father from the grave of Plague, the tears left her eyes and their swirl of colors, freezing silver streaks down her cheeks like polished sword blades.

"Talk to me, Uilleam."

He sighed again, eyes red as Aerlyn's hair.

"It's just the whole thing." He said, shaking his head as if every thought had come to the same solution.

And he was losing his hope because of it.

"What does that mean?"

"It means thousands of people are going to run off to die and for some reason I don't want it to be her."

Rhoswen waited for a moment. That last strawberry was calling her name, but she sat patiently with him.

"Why?"

"…Because…" Quill sighed and burrowed his head into his hands again. Hands as skilled as anyone's she'd ever met.

Just not with a bow, blade, or knife.

"Heavens, my head hurts like hell on fire." He looked up to her from his sobs with a gleam in his eye. "Would you knock me out tonight?"

"No." Rhoswen chuckled.

"One good punch right between the eyes."

She nibbled at a piece of venison as he rolled his broad shoulders and adjusted his seat so he was hugging his knees to his chest. Without even realizing, he was sitting just like Aerlyn had on the rock near the loch that first night they'd spoken together.

Rhoswen knew this because she'd been there, watching from the tree line.

She, too, had high hopes for Aerlyn O'Rye.

But not the same wishes as he, her loyal baird and chronicler.

"Uilleam, you have to realize that what you're hoping for isn't here yet, and it won't come unless something ugly happens first."

"I know."

"Well then I have to remind you." Rhoswen nicked a fingernail against her teeth and found a tiny strawberry seed stuck to the end of it. "It's just like this seed, Uilleam. Everything needed to grow a harvest of strawberries is in this *one* little seed. But until the seed splits open and dies to its sealed-up shape as a seed, all of that can't come out. Even then, it's a process. So much has to happen before we get to see a beautiful strawberry and taste the fruit of our labor. You have to realize," Rhoswen picked up the last strawberry and held it out to him in her dainty hands, hands that no man, unless he knew better, would think were so deadly wielding a blade. "That the day of Albanland at peace is a long ways off. But like the changing of the seasons and the turning of the earth, *it will come*. I draw breath to see this day. I dream about it. I am consumed by it."

Rhoswen squinted at the strawberry as Quill took it, whispers of her memories with Ultan departing as if simply touching the fruit brought them back, and to hold it no longer was to let them go.

To forget.

"I understand." Quill said.

Rhoswen pointed at him.

"Hope is like a sea. Sometimes you have so much of it you can drown in it. You need something firm to hold on to." Rhoswen dipped her forehead toward the strawberry, eyebrows nearly touching. "You need something to believe in. Not hope. Believe."

Quill wiped each eye with the same hand and smiled, offering her the strawberry.

"No, please. Enjoy it. Or better yet, go plant it somewhere. Come back when you're an old man and see what's grown from it."

Quill nodded and departed with silent gratitude and left Rhoswen to stare at the perfectly cooked venison, her face a sour storm of emotion.

For she though ached to take the Throne, she *needed* to see Ultan's face again.

He'd been but a boy when she'd run off, shamed and disgraced by haughty Morgance. And now he was Champion.

"Ultan..." She whispered, falling back on her bed, hiding behind a dark mess of curls.

Ultan I love you. Don't you know I love you? Have you felt me wait for you all these years? Can you hear my hunger stretch across the highlands?

Just to see your face! Just to hold you and be held by you!

Please, Ultan! Never forget me. If you fall in battle before I meet you again, remember me to your last breath.

Believe in me, Ultan.

I believe in you.

And for the first time in as many seasons as she'd taken up the sword as her only hope, Rhoswen cried.

But as Rhoswen cried herself to sleep in stifled sobs, she tossed and turned two simple thoughts over and over in her mind. Fighting and dueling like warriors stuck in the endless knot of the Swordsman's Circle.

Hope and faith. The rock and the sea.

The Crown and the love of a man she'd only known as a boy; a man who remembered her only as a girl, and not the swift steel retribution of King Brom the Chosen, only daughter of the

Lady of a Thousand Lochs, come to seize that which was rightfully hers.

And with the investment so precious, Rhoswen could only *believe* in one, committing the whole of her being to seeing it come to pass and hoping for the other, in the case of a miracle, that it too would come true.

And though she put on a brave face and knew her day with the sword would come, she'd be a fool a thousand ways from sunset if she could ever convince her own heart she wanted the Crown of a cloven Throne *more* than the strong arms of the land's sworn Champion and protector, wrapped around her body, crushing her in the consuming passion of his fierce embrace.

CHAPTER 37

The next day, Rhoswen found Quill sitting cross-legged on the grass, as he did when crafting one of the many intricate drawings of their life in the forest, an inkwell between his feet and a spare hawk's feather tucked behind his ear.

He nodded a greeting to Rhoswen and returned to his drawing with the strain of heavy concentration framing his face, as he was the kind of man that tended to pour himself into a moment without thinking much of anything else. Rhoswen squinted at the shafts of sunlight slicing dusky razors through the tangled greenery and smiled at the detail and perspective of what little secret was unfolding before them on the once blank page of vellum Quill had fashioned into a crude book.

The Master Archer oversaw the progress of Rhoswen's Bowgirls in their makeshift range like the eagle-eyed huntress that she was. Nothing escaped her view, and she was quick to raise elbows, tilt shoulders, set feet and legs at the correct angles, and offer kind words of encouragement to those who tired from draw after draw of their yew bows. She reminded them of their brothers, their sisters, even their parents, many of whom they'd left, in squalor and ruin in the southern border towns, eagerly awaiting the day of reckoning when Rhoswen could right the wrongs of a great many sins. Their range was little more than an overstretched hollow slipping through the forest with a leftward hook at the end of it,

and Rhoswen had given strict orders for those that weren't in the
Master Archer's Bowgirl company to steer clear of the hidden
archer's range, to save themselves from a stray arrow.

That, and…something about a girl with a bow, their hair
half-braided and falling free like the enigmatic Master Archer
herself, well, that made Rhoswen's Bowgirl company the stuff of
idle chatter and hopeful fancies amongst the stout woodcutters and
spearmen, eager to be free of the forest and speak their mind to
those who'd caught their eye, only to be whisked away for more
secretive training under the Master Archer's cool blue gaze.

Especially since Rhoswen had divided her forces primarily
by gender, with the quick-footed and agile young women suited to
the hit and run tactics of the bow rather than standing toe to toe
with armored Angles; some twice their height, age, and weight,
lifetimes of experience under their belts. Maneuvers with the
dagger, running ceaseless circuits around the loch, and
accompanying the blue-eyed eagle on her forest hunts rounded out
their intense training, and Rhoswen would count on them to be a
secret weapon when the time for a pitched battle came. After all,
what good was a horse and the man on top of it, armored to the
teeth and charging bloody thunder down on her line of spearmen if
one of her twelve year old girls could stick an arrow through the
horse's eye and throw the man to the ground?

And her Bowgirls, too, had not forgotten their share of
woodcutters and hunters alike, whispering to each other as night fell
across the gender-separated camps whom would be best suited for
whom.

Rhoswen knew this dream.

She knew it *very* well.

To kill it would be to die to something holy and as constant
as the sunrise itself, as all consuming as the sound of the Four
Storms drenching the glens and lochs lush with flood.

But the time for love was not yet.

If love was to be seen in Albanland, it was a love *for*
Albanland, or a love *of* it.

A love to shed blood to free *it* of its bonds and heavy
chains.

Or die trying.

Rhoswen nodded her approval to the Master Archer as a spindly girl, not much older than thirteen or fourteen, stuck an arrow in the eye of the furthest scarecrow, downrange.

The once homeless orphan looked back to her teacher in surprise and saw Rhoswen's approval on top of the rare praise of the Master Archer. Needless to say she would sleep the night through with stars sparkling her dreams.

The Master Archer ambled over, flipping her gray cloak back so it swooped around her wide belt and the sagging quiver at her side. Unlike the plain ash training arrows, hers were heart maple, tipped with steel bodkins, little fishhooks able to pierce armor and capable of latching on to bone.

"It won't be long now." Rhoswen said, her voice muted, and the Master Archer peered up past the razor shafts of light to the clouded sky hidden somewhere behind the interwoven laces of leafy green and twisted brown.

"These are ancient trees." She said cryptically.

"Older than all of us put together." Quill drew, dragging his hawk-feather pen with a scrape across his rudimentary book of vellum pages.

"I'm going to miss them..." The Archer crossed her arms and Rhoswen pointed downrange as the same girl put an arrow just below her first shot.

"That one doesn't seem to miss."

"Right..." The Archer flared her nostrils, something of disgust on her face. Not for the girl, but rather, who she'd be shooting at. "And can she do that with ten thousand Angles stomping like thunder across a sea of grass? Can she stick an arrow in a man's heart and watch him bleed out and not think about the man's wife and children? Is she ready for the screams of the battlefield, or the sound of the buzzards circling above?"

Quill looked up from his drawing, thinking of the number she'd thrown out.

"That many?"

Rhoswen nodded with pursed lips.

"The King of Angle can raise an army of ten *times* ten thousand if he wanted to wipe this place clean, but the thing is, he couldn't if his *nobles* didn't want to. I haven't heard from my agents in quite some time and paid them too much of what little gold we have as it is to get what I know, but it looks to me that only a few of the Lords and Barons want to march up to Ullraye and have it out, once and for all. Now, given the amount of professional soldiers your run-of-the-mill Angle Lord has in his employ, fleshed out with a rabble of weathered peasants and some very capable and experienced young men, you're looking at about ten thousand under the summer sun. Maybe half that by winter."

"By winter?" Quill frowned.

"Most of the Lords mercenary their troops across the sea where the weather's warmer. There's always a skirmish somewhere. I hear across the ocean, where there are too many kingdoms and rulerships to count, the fighting never stops. The beauty is a harsh and arid one, but there's a mystery among the people and their culture. Strange and magnificent beasts roam the earth. People dress in wind-whipped robes of vibrant colors."

"Stop." Quill waved his hand. "You're stealing all my best stuff."

"Lands of snakes and swarthy horse-thieves." The Master Archer nearly spat.

"But yet you've never been there!" Quill nearly laughed.

"I have." The Archer contended with a squiggly smile breaking her tough mask. "In your stories."

Quill all but blushed and kept drawing, scribbling down the details of the picture in an elegant script he'd adopted from one he'd learned from his time in an Eire monastery.

He had traveled across the sea, once, but'd been too young to remember it. Instead, his imagination had painted in the hollows where his memory fell short.

Rhoswen studied the display for a few more breaths before sighing so heavily her shoulders sagged, and she stared down the length of her green cloak as if the silver that edged it in the knots and whorls, the same as the tattoos certain of her army wore, was a tarnished and faded promise and would never shine like it did in her dreams.

"There's just not enough time." She said.

"Perhaps…" The Master Archer spoke quietly, her eyebrows hinting at the man writing intently next to them.

Quill stopped, his eyes tracking up slowly. He was too smart for them to conspire.

"You're thinking of using The Thistle?"

"Using is a terrible word." Rhoswen chided.

"Using is what it is for sure." Quill stood up, knocking over his inkwell, staring as it seeped into the soft grass like sticky black blood. Unable to fight the horror, he met Rhoswen's gaze, his mouth fell open, and his eyes blinked several times before his argument returned. "You know there's a price on her head for murder. You can't just have her out there, running around on her own."

"That's what she's best at." The Master Archer said, flatly, and Quill shot her a look that said *Shut up! I don't care if you are my second cousin! Shut up!*

Quill frowned at her, which Rhoswen interpreted as Quill *misinterpreting* the situation, but he did that frequently, quick to take responsibility for failures that were not his, and so ready to believe his devotions, affections, hopes, and aspirations were of little value to those around him.

So damn quick to give up.

It was as if Rhoswen was becoming sad in his presence, because he had the innate ability to affect the atmosphere around him.

She's seen it, like magic, how he could put people to sleep with his mandolin, or stoke them up to a roaring fire with a story and a hearty song that brought tears to her eyes to hear sung as one voice.

"Uilleam, she doesn't want to get rid of Aerlyn because Aerlyn beat her in the Circle, and as your second cousin, she certainly wants to see you with someone more…stable." Quill protested but Rhoswen held up her hand to continue. "Maybe you'd be interested to know I had her call Aerlyn *to* the Circle to prove something to Aerlyn herself. Maybe all two thousand of us need Aerlyn to be the very something she's always been, the very something she's better at than anyone else."

Quill's blue eyes were bloodshot with crying and the pain of his many headaches. Even though he was a strong, broad-shouldered man, his posture was hunched and bent.

Defeated.

"A thief."

"That's right." Rhoswen kneeled, pulling Quill's chin up with her three-fingered hand. "Aerlyn is something none of us are."

"Disposable." Quill muttered darkly.

"Feared."

Quill peered deep into her regal gaze, obvious tremors of pain pulsing through the squiggly veins near his hairline. He cast his own strained gaze quickly to his second cousin, and her blue eyes promised him it would all work out.

A gleam kissed Rhoswen's three-toned eyes just to think of it, and her fingertips trembled in anticipation.

"When I ride into Ullraye, it won't matter how many Angles are waiting across the plains below."

"Why?"

"Because I'll have all of Ullraye under *my* command."

"How the bloody hell you going to do that?"

Rhoswen stood, fingers idly tapping the hilt of her sword, lips curling with delight bordering upon insanity.

"Morgance, Faer Princess of the Night, once stole the Ring of Rule from me. And now, Aerlyn O'Rye, The Thistle of High Inverloch, is going to steal it back."

FINLEIGH

CHAPTER 38

With the cute lilt of her voice and the fact that she was the *only* gypsy in Rhoswen's army, Finleigh got to know just about everyone, free to roam around the camps, helping out where she saw fit. She never stayed in one place too long, and most enjoyed bringing the men their lunches, countenance brighter than the sun. But, as the days stretched along to weeks, she seldom strayed from the training ground where Nevan and Niles were committed to breaking each other's records in the Circle, making the best of friends with their peers, and growing increasingly better at combat and arms.

But, feeling the eyes of the Crown Heir watching her through the trees, as if every leaf and limb mirrored her sightline itself, Finleigh was beginning to feel Rhoswen wanted her for something special.

Something different.

She just didn't know what, yet, and had rightly been avoiding the Crown Heir and her intense aura.

Not that any of the men had a problem with her traipsing all over the place, quick with a word of humor cast over her shoulder or a practiced shrug as if, since she was supposedly from another land, she had no idea what they were talking about.

Even though she'd been born and raised and spent all of her days in the south.

Finleigh wondered a great many times if Rhoswen *knew* that she could see the future, even if it was something of a mystery when she did see it, but told herself she was letting her imaginative young mind run to conclusions, as she had as a young girl, cooped up in Baraburr and Nairnsmoor before that, where she'd been kicked out by her own people.

For being a liar.

Funny. They're the ones who lie, reading palms and leaves and telling fortunes for a shiny coin. Everybody knows it. They even seek it out when they feel like it. It's a service, like buying meat at the market. Everyone knows it's a farce. But for me to say I really can see the future, well, that makes me the liar, the outcast. Finleigh thought, taking a dagger to a whetstone as the sun danced along its afternoon arc for the trees. Before her, the sounds of staffs thwapping each other worked with the rhythmic motion of the whetstone to put her in something of a trance.

I don't think I'm better than anyone else!

But I know I'm different.

How can someone not know when they're different?

Niles was pouring sweat as he flopped down beside her and kicked back, seemingly exhausted. But Niles was never exhausted. And something about competition always brought out the best in him. It sharpened him to a fine point, like the tip of spear. He'd won seven matches in a row, and lost his last to a much younger man by simple fatigue.

Even then, it'd been a glancing blow, and Sir Craig had shot his arm out to stop the fight.

And though Niles protested, there was no arguing with Sir Craig. Especially if Niles had hopes of being tattooed to become one of Rhoswen's Chosen, as she'd overheard him say more than once.

But with Niles it was always talk. Like far off clouds. Nothing ever came of it. Just talk.

"This beats the tar out darts!" He exclaimed, still panting, even though he was loving every second of this new life. He'd never said it to her, Finleigh knew he was silently grateful she had led them into the forest, saying her dream had taken them there.

Even though it hadn't. She'd simply felt drawn to the trees. No pictures, no thoughts. Just a pulling, like a fish in a current.

"*Beats* is right, Niles. That scrawny little merchant's son made you look foolish a minute ago."

Niles shrugged it off, as if the sea tide was his way of life. Easy in, easy out; everything just an ebb and flow. And so the sea would sway this way and that, nothing ever changing its ability to do so and wash on past everything solid and stoic in its foamy wake.

His lust for life, like hers, was just too big.

So big he sometimes failed to notice her anymore, washing right on past to whatever caught his eye next. Maybe Aerlyn, maybe the meek young woman who collected all the men's cloaks to wash them in the loch. Maybe over to his mates to win a fist of money playing Rook's Table after supper only to loose it the very next day at lunch.

*Wonder what it's like not to care about anything...*Finleigh mused, testing the edge of the small blade she'd been sharpening on a piece of cloth. *I'm still waiting for the right moment to tell Rhoswen my dream of the future. It might help if I wasn't scared to death of her. But you just keep on living in that Circle like I'm not here, Niles.*

The carefree sixteen year old sat up straight and watched her drag the knife on the whetstone. While he was the kind of man that always offered "a better way" to do something, as if he'd invented whatever it was someone was doing, he silently studied her technique, failing to realize she'd been sharpening knives since she was five years old.

"You know..." Niles sighed. "I never got that kiss you promised me."

"Hmm?"

"For wrestling the Larlaith."

Finleigh took the dagger from the whetstone, lips pressed in a firm line.

Surprised it's taken you this long to remember! Maybe it'd help if you weren't so eager to get your arms around The Thistle!

"Well maybe later." She said.

"Later, like, in two minutes or later...tonight?"

Finleigh stared him down, him *and* his crooked smile and warm brown eyes, his blonde hair a ruffled mess.

The same thing that made him irresistible made him insufferable. And like the sea, there was a mystery about him that attracted some and repelled others, but in the end, no one could deny their watching him from a far as both the sunrise and the sunset cast its glow across his face.

"I am holding a dagger, you know." Finleigh said, trying to sound tough, but couldn't hide the gleam in her dark eyes.

"So?"

"So...to make sure a kiss is just a kiss."

Niles laughed one short honk and stared at her, his eyebrows munching together.

"If you really can read minds you'd know you wouldn't need it." He gently took it from her to inspect the keen edge she'd put on it. For a moment, their skin touched, and she quickly wiped her hands on the cloth in her lap, as his skin was wet with perspiration.

But she frowned at him. It was a knife. It was sharp. There was nothing more to it.

"There *are* wolves in the forest, Niles." She crossed her arms. "A young gypsy has to protect herself."

"And bears too. Big ones."

"Yes. Black as night."

"And claws that'll rip a man's heart out with one swipe."

"Yes, the very same."

"I haven't seen any yet. Have you?"

"No."

Niles chuckled.

"Well, if I do I'll make sure to ask if I can borrow your dagger."

He handed it back and pushed himself up, grabbing a discarded staff along the way back to the ready throng of young hopefuls before turning to her. The sun flashed in his blonde hair and dance across his glistening skin.

"Although between you, me, and the bear, I'd rather have the kiss."

Finleigh sighed as he ran back to the huddle and somehow the volume increased just by his presence, but she couldn't hear his voice in the chatter, as if it'd been lost in the sea.

It was then the gypsy moped back to the smith's hut, the old man's heavy moustache covering a smile over her expert work, but she didn't see. Her eyes on anything but where she was going.

She replaced the knife soundlessly and stared at the many instruments of war blunted by training, wishing one of them could cure Niles of his insufferable charm, especially since Finleigh knew him to flirt with every woman save those old enough to be his mother, and of them, there were so few, but the rouge had somehow made them all think they *were* his mother and slipped him extra portions of bread and cheese.

Maybe that's why he was doing better in the Circle.

"I've been looking for you." Finleigh heard to her right, nearly jumping at the sound as it ripped her from thought.

Startled, Finleigh turned to see the Crown Heir, staring a hole through her fine-featured body as only Rhoswen could. She had the stern gaze of a woman unafraid of death, smoldering hot and capable of setting fire to tinder.

"…Hi?" Finleigh peeped.

Rhoswen grabbed her by the arm and pulled her close, walking her past the cooking huts and leading her off behind the wood storage mounds to a dark trail, twisted with brambles and thorns, nearly impossible to access.

Finleigh had walked by it a hundred times without even seeing it.

"It's about time we had a talk, you and I."

"About what?" Finleigh's eyes were wide.

Rhoswen patted her on the shoulder with her three-fingered hand.

"Calm down, my little gypsy."

"…Sorry…it's just…"

"I know. I'm afraid of myself, sometimes."

"You are?" Finleigh squeaked and squinted again as the derelict path snaked into the dense cool of the forest, till no sound could be heard from the remainder of the camp. "What's this about?"

Rhoswen's smile was all her own, gently curving the edges of her mouth.

"About what you can do to help me get my Throne back."

Finleigh nearly fainted.

"Me! *Me???*"

Rhoswen laughed quietly.

"If you only knew, my little gypsy."

Finleigh swallowed and found herself tangled in the weeds between feeling very special about the whole thing, and being just about scared out of her skirts. She'd seen Rhoswen with the sword, and the hardened look in her eye promising *nothing*, animal nor human nor the savage onslaught of the Four Storms themselves would get between her and her Throne. She was a fearsome little woman. The ember that'd caught the forest on fire with revolution. The blade that would never lose her edge. But the dynamic power of Rhoswen's nearness made Finleigh all but forget how her own people had disowned her and kicked her out of their tight-knit community, the bitter words they'd said to her, and how they told her she *couldn't see*, that she was a liar, nothing more than a fool for dreaming up such ridiculous things and calling them truth.

And to have the woman, nearly eight years older than her, raised in the Court as the only daughter of the King and tempered to the sharpest steel by the loneliness of the forest itself take her by the hand…well, it was too much.

And in the stilled and cool hush of the forest, Finleigh felt her heart swell with love.

Rhoswen was her Queen. Rhoswen was her ruler, and her word was like stone and steel. And feeling Rhoswen's strength slide through her skin in the tender grip only a mother could have, Finleigh fought the urge to cry, and remained silent on their walk through the dark and twisted trail.

But the promise was already alive in her heart.

I love this land with everything I am, my Queen, and I'll do whatever you want me to in order to save it.

NEVAN & FINLEIGH

CHAPTER 39

Nearly a week of the usual routine had passed since Rhoswen had whisked Finleigh away to the deepest, darkest cool of the forest. There, they'd spoken for hours, just the two of them, perched on a fallen tree. The week had worked a spell over her, both Nevan and Niles had noticed, since she'd been at Rhoswen's side nearly every waking breath following that very conversation. And since that turn of events, her bright presence had been stolen from the Circle, and that bruising week of combat had unraveled itself into a long and arduous chore as the whooshing leaves of the trees began to show the very first hints of their turning, the north wind threatening to tear them from the limb before their time came to fall.

And since the brothers were convinced she'd told Rhoswen her dream of the future, Finleigh was ready to do her part to win back the Crown.

But neither knew that meant *leaving* Rhoswen's army.

That was until she'd told them both, after yesterday's dinner, speaking nothing more than a few words in passing and doing her best to avoid them the following day.

Nevan found her sitting in the Circle as dusk slowly draped its soul across the jagged teeth of the horizon, soaking lush green leaves and blue-black needles with tints of peach and hazy violet.

Strange to think the area that'd once been so thick with bodies from sun up till sun down since Rhoswen had scratched its round shape in the ground with the tip of her own sword was now empty and soundless, void of humanity, save that of the sixteen-year old España gypsy known to make every color pale in comparison wherever she walked.

But now, alone, in the Circle, Finleigh looked wilted and overwhelmed, as Nevan himself had been the first time he stepped inside its fearful confines.

"I've been looking for you." He said, which made Finleigh smile hollowly, to think Rhoswen had once said the same thing and now here she was, about to be an agent of the Crown Heir some thought had been killed, others wished to be killed, and others still who would gladly kill in the name of to restore the Throne to the memory of her father.

Sore, Nevan groaned as he sat down next to her, soaking up the sunset. A distinct chill snaked through the air and he rubbed the back of his neck, squinting across the grass.

"And here I am." Finleigh said, flatly, her bubbliness subdued and hushed by the emptiness around her. Nearly a mile away, the camp was feasting in preparation of their leaving of the forest, finally ready to head north and exact Rhoswen's revenge upon Faer Morgance.

"What do you have there?" Nevan asked.

Finleigh's delicate hands cupped a butterfly with jewel blue wings and two white spots, centered with pinpricks of black and nicked with flecks of green and gold to look like eyes. In *her* hand it didn't move, but its wings flinched as Nevan leaned over to admire it, and shadowed it.

"It's still alive." He said, surprised, yet keeping his voice quiet, not to spook it.

Niles would've tried to take if from her and made a joke about being too charming for it to handle as it flew off.

"For now." Finleigh sighed, and Nevan was taken aback by the reservation in her voice and the stillness of her body.

"You mean with the changing of the seasons?"

Finleigh nodded and held the butterfly up to the colors of dusk. Nevan marveled at the prismatic effect. Soft hues nearly glowed in vivid membranes as the creature gently twitched its wings.

"Butterflies are seers of the future." Finleigh smiled imperceptibly. "Did you know?" Nevan shook his head, eager to hear more on the subject, but still not wanting to disturb the beautiful creature in its repose. It was as if beauty was something he could only ever admire from afar, though he wanted to know it, face to face, to see it and touch it with his *own* two hands. But with Niles crashing and storming from town to town, grappling with his many adventures, Nevan had to be there to catch him when he fell, regardless of what *he* wanted to do.

Finleigh swallowed, her lips nearly puckered to smile at the lovely creature. "But you can only see the future if you can catch one. Even then, it can only tell if you don't smother it. You have to be sensitive. You have to let the truth unfold before you, like a pair of wings."

"How do you know what it says?" Nevan found himself whispering.

"The colors."

Finleigh brought the creature back down to her lap and a sigh of wind crept through the trees, rustling and shaking the interwoven chains of foliage from a great distance away before it reached them with its invisible fingers and raked across them both, tousling the jet black gloss of Finleigh's hair and lifting the butterfly up from the heat of her cupped hands to dance its departure across the green grass.

"And what did it say?"

"That I will marry soon and have two children."

Somewhere deep inside Nevan's stomach something tightened up and fell, as if clattering clumsily from a series of shelves, knocking everything on them over in the process.

Yet the wind was the only sound he heard, and the light was too poor to see his skin become ruddy and hot.

It was the way she said the truth, just as it was, just as a butterfly was.

"How do you know?" Nevan asked.

"I told you." Finleigh twisted to take him in with an odd gleam in her eye, her hair whipping and brushing the skin on the back of his arm as she did. "The colors."

"So..." Nevan struggled for something to say, anything other than the heavy weight he felt toppled over in his belly.

"The two eyes." Finleigh said. "Two children."

"And the blue wings?" Nevan rubbed his arm as if he were chilled by the wind, but he was rubbing away the burn where Finleigh's jet black hair had graced his skin.

Finleigh only stared back to the rough edge of the trees, scratching at what was left of the sun as if holding on for dear life.

"Did he do it?" She asked, her thoughts buried somewhere in the future.

"What?"

"Niles. Did he do it?"

Nevan gnawed on the uneasiness of being so close to her and wanting to say something else, or *do* something else, but failing to grasp just *what* that something was, even though the desire of it banged a heavy drum in his heart, like an innocent man locked inside a prison cell begging to be released.

"Oh, the tattoo..." Nevan rubbed the back of his neck again, ruffling his brown hair, which, like the color of his eyes, was nondescriptly Alban in the way that he could get lost in a crowd. All his life he'd been marked as something other than what he was, if he even knew *what it was* that he was, soaking up the skipped-over judgments and believing in their lies.

Forgotten.

"He is very good at the Circle." Finleigh added, her eyes climbing up Nevan's knees from his feet. "And he's been accepted by Rhoswen's Chosen. Maybe he'll be a spearman, or he could be lucky enough to get a sword and some good armor. Either way, when the time comes, he'll fight with her best, and he'll do it with the same flamboyance he seems to do everything else. It makes sense to me."

Nevan grimaced and squinted to see the butterfly finally leave the training ground, headed for the loch.

"Well, he hasn't done it yet. Tonight, though, with the mead flowing, he's not the only one who'll take the mark of Rhoswen's Chosen. It's a rite of honor, I know, but...since he's *always* been in the middle of chaos I don't think he knows another way."

Finleigh combed her hair behind her ears.

Nevan sat up and continued, his grimace stretching as the lingering colors of sunset died before them both.

"If he does take that mark, he'll be the first to die." Nevan shrugged. "Sure, he'll be remembered forever or whatever the hell those crazies think'll happen, but the thing is, for once, I can actually see the difference between us."

"What do you mean?" Finleigh asked. Though she'd spent so much time with the brothers, their differences always balanced each other out and she saw them as one *whole* complete team. And it occurred to her, just as she'd been cast out of her own community and forced to live in a form of isolation in the confines of the small and sleepy village that sat in the shadow of Brachin, Nevan and Niles had always been together, there for each other, taking their lumps as a team.

Until today.

"He's always sought it out, you know, and the harder something is the better he seems to be at it." Nevan scoffed to remember Brachin. "You saw him with the Larlaith. Bloody damn thing scared the hell out of me."

Finleigh laughed, her head tipping back as night stretched its wings upon them.

She sidled closer.

"It's okay, you know."

"What?"

"To watch someone take another path."

"I know." Nevan said, quickly, but continued nodding as if to convince himself. "It's just that..."

"You're going to miss him?"

"No." Nevan pressed his lips together, desperately trying to avert the dark sparkles in her eyes, and what she'd said about watching someone take a different path. "I knew this day would come a long time ago. I was just hoping to keep him safe till he found where he belonged. And I've done that. Heaven help me, I've actually done it. It's *your* leaving that I'm having a hard time with."

Finleigh's nostrils flared and the corners of her eyes tightened as Nevan drug his gaze up to meet hers.

The gypsy licked her lips and awaited her kiss. The distant butterfly's wings whirled a storm wind inside her lungs and the scent of a coming rain sent a shiver up her spine.

Yet she would not look away from him.

But unlike Niles, Nevan never could dive in the water. He couldn't toss darts or wrestle giant eels. He couldn't guzzle ale and stand tall while larger men fell down to the floor like trees. He couldn't win twenty-three matches straight and earn not just the tattoo of Rhoswen's Chosen, but the respect of its fierce brethren.

His brown eyes fell to her chest, staring at the rise and fall of her lungs. His fingertips burned to reach out and touch the caramel hues of her neck and trace the lines of her collarbones, just above the crisscrossed leather drawstrings of her white blouse.

An eternity stretched before him, darkening and slipping from his grip as the stone inside his soul pulled him further and further from the truth he longed to realize.

The truth she'd spoken as she'd seen it written on the wings of the butterfly.

And within the space of three heartbeats, Finleigh pressed herself up and ran off, with nothing but the cold north wind to wipe away the tears that fell from her eyes like the first fat drops of harvest season rain.

NEVAN & NILES

CHAPTER 40

Nevan found his brother slumped amidst the muscle-knotted arms of his *new* brothers inside the butchering hut. They were all shirtless and passing around a bottle of highly fermented apple cider so strong Nevan nearly fainted just to smell it. The joy of feasting and merrymaking tore through the no-longer separated camps around them, swaying on the backs of a hundred whispered promises and a thousand heart-swelling songs.

The heat of the cook fires, their hazy wheezes wafting the smell of smoked salmon and fatty bacon, rippled through the sharp bite of the breeze and made Niles think he might actually be able to forget the unease he'd felt only minutes ago with Finleigh.

If ever.

It'd gripped him, like an unseen hand, sickening him with paralysis. Just the thought of the dark sparkle in her eyes and to realize it was only for him made him want to pass out as if *he* was the one who had been drinking.

Why do you have to go, Finleigh? There's so much I could've said...I don't know why I didn't.

Nevan rubbed his eyes to try and rid his mind of regret and stepped closer to the shirtless men surrounding his brother.

The intricate processes of crafting the double block of knots and the circle of twisted whorls on the right bicep of the newest members of Rhoswen's Chosen had taken most of the day, and

Nevan tensed as Sir Craig limped up to the rowdy group. Though it was a time for celebration, since the day of leaving the forest had finally come, his presence sharpened their focus as if he was about to bark out an order to arms. He held a small torch high in greeting, the light of it bathing the eager young warriors with warm hues.

"Ready for your shares of the feast, yet, lads?" Sir Craig asked the group, who resounded with a *no*, dedicated to finish Niles' tattoo before they could all eat.

For when they did, it would be together.

The tattooist, none other than Quill, dabbed the blood that pooled on Niles skin with a washcloth, retrieving the iron chisel and a hammer to dip the sharp tip of the angled chisel in a cup of blue dye, made from the crushed petals of the glastrum flower.

Sir Craig grunted something of approval to hear their unity.

"Well, son," He said, his grizzled features grinning at Niles. "Don't drink too much of that apple rot, even though it looks like you've already drowned yourself in it. I'm here to tell you you've been selected for Rhoswen's *personal* guard. You'll be riding with her tomorrow, so stay sharp."

Nevan smiled and wanted to congratulate his brother, naturally, caught between wondering if that put him in *more* danger or less, but either way, he couldn't even get close to Niles as his tattooed brothers-in-arms saluted him and slapped their hands on his back, echoing proud congratulations that somehow belonged to all of them, sharing his quick ascent up the ranks as their own victory.

It wasn't until ten minutes later when Quill finished up that Nevan dared approach, watching the other members of Rhoswen's Chosen leave to feed their aching bellies in anticipation of tomorrow's long march north.

Nevan nearly ran into Quill in the darkness and excused himself, seeing how weary and run down the chronicler looked.

It was as if he had the Plague.

Niles tipped the bottle back, wincing as trickles of the sweet and sour alcohol trickled down his chin.

"Hey Nev, wassup?"

"I heard."

"You did?" He tottered on the creaky wooden bench where countless guinea fowl, rabbits, venison had been slaughtered.

But now, just like the Circle, it was empty.

"Yeah."

Niles looked down to his fresh tattoo, the alcohol freeing him of the pain of the procedure. The vivid blue ink still looked wet.

"And here I thought Quill worked in silence."

"Not your tattoo, Ni, your promotion."

Niles winked at him, the same winks he passed all the highland girls he came across. It was a cheap and easy gesture, more of a reaction he couldn't help.

"I know. I know…I wazzjuss being fun-funny."

Nevan took the bottle. Niles didn't fight him.

"You don't need this stuff to be funny, Ni."

Niles shrugged, his brown eyes caught for a moment on a distant pass of dancers, timbrels in their hands, skirts of Clan colors catching the orange wash of the fire. Whether it was fear or wonder to watch as they twisted and turned to the beat, Nevan couldn't tell, but the look in Niles' eye was a strange one.

He turned back to Nevan, giving him a *shove off* gesture.

"Try some."

"No thanks, Ni."

Niles pushed the bottle up to his brother's lips.

"Cummawn, bro…give us a tipple."

"No."

"You'll like it."

"I won't."

"Cummawn…"

"No!"

Niles sighed, leaning back to curl up in a ball on the table, his eyes slowly succumbing to the gooey warmth he felt inside, staring at the fire pits across the camp where the dancers twirled and kicked.

"Suit your-yourself." Niles mumbled, making a pillow of his hands. "It might help…"

Nevan squinted, thinking he could pick out that look that so often drifted across Niles face, but the flickering firelight often played tricks.

"Help me what?"

"With Fins."

Nevan's skin flushed bright red and Niles didn't seem to notice.

"Help me *what* with *Fins?*" Nevan enunciated slowly as to quell his anger. With Niles it was a scant look at a pretty young barmaid across a packed common house, hinting at a tumble in the stable but moving on to forget the fact that it never happened. Even so, the thought was stuck, in his dreams, and there the thought stayed. Replaying itself over and over like a fish swimming circles in a lake.

With Niles it was never something as holy as what Nevan had experienced with the sunset and the butterfly, something that felt so vast and endless, as if his heart had exploded without his knowing it could even *do* that, leaving him to shudder under the shower of emotion such an act lanced within.

Niles sat up and stared at his brother as if Nevan was the one who'd been tattooed, and it had been across his forehead.

"Don't be daft, Nev. Play at bucks and does, what the hell do you think?"

"Niles." Nevan nearly growled a warning.

"What? I've seen the way she looks at you. I know what she wants. If you weren't such a coward, you'd g-give it to her."

Nevan ground his teeth together as his brother winced to stand up straight and snatch the bottle of sour apple liquor from him, like a weapon. Never had he wanted to smack Niles across the chin so bad, and never had he proffered himself as such an easy target.

"Ni…"

"No, no," Niles' hands danced mockingly. "Don't upset the thinker, having a moment. Well, when are you gonna live life? When are you gonna go pick an apple off a tree instead of waiting f-for it to fall on your thick head? When are you going to pick up a s-sword and cut the enemy's arms off before you're holding what's left of y-your belly in your hands?"

Nevan bit his finger, but the cider had loosened Niles' tongue.

"You coulda had that girl, Nev, you coulda had her seven ways from Sixday and she woulda loved every second of it. But now, someone else'll get her because you're too much of a bleeding wazzock to be a real man." Niles staggered, eyes nearly crossed as he thought aloud. "Crows pick my bones clean, my own flesh and blood's a ruddy damn coward with a gypsy."

Was it the defense of her tenderness and the intimacy of their nearness he hated Niles sullying with the animal nature he'd absorbed from Rhoswen's macho Chosen?

Or was it a lifetime of looking after a spring storm of a brother whose final thank you for Nevan's faithfulness was no thank you at all but the dagger to the heart.

Or maybe even the way *gypsy* sounded derogatory when Nevan could imagine nothing more mysterious and exotic in the whole wide world.

Whatever it was, Nevan sucker punched Niles square in the chin.

Hatred fizzled through his body, leaving him flushed and sick, trembling and standing unevenly like a tree fighting the weight of snow. His hand stung, and his breathing was a harsh saw in his nostrils as his brother slipped and staggered and spun around with a limber twist.

Regaining his balance, Niles tipped the bottle to his lips, coolly, and bowed low at the waist before standing up, hooking a hand in his belt and spitting the alcohol in a thick stream across Nevan's waist.

"Oops..." Niles frowned. "Looks like someone had an accident. Better go get mom to clean it up for you."

Nevan took another swing but Niles only stepped aside and hooked his foot against Nevan's, tripping him.

Rage burned, pride flaming white hot as dancers danced kicking circles in the distance and feast food flowed with a free hand. Nevan bounced up.

"Come on, Nev," Niles opened his arms wide, as if for a hug, his breath reeking of apple liquor. "You don't wanna f-fight me? I'm one of the Chosen."

"Chosen your larded backside!" Nevan shoved him, and Niles took it in stride, tipping more alcohol down his throat, as his brother railed. "You're no saga hero yet! The only thing you've been chosen for is death! What good'll that damned tattoo do you when your body gets dumped in a mass grave a month from now?"

"Better to die a man than live to be a crippled old coward. Like dad." Nevan sneered. "You wanna be like dad? Do you? You always did have his eyes."

"And you got mom's? Right. They're both the same."

"Doesn't matter." Niles wiped his fist across his mouth. "You remember how he just sat there and watched while that Angle Lord took mom away to be *personal* servant for nine years? M-member that? Geezer didn't do a damn thing. He just watched, like someone'd taken a scoop too much grain in their sack." Niles chugged and wheezed and dropped the empty bottle. "And now the cutest España gypsy the world's ever seen is going off on her own and you couldn't even find the strength to kiss her goodbye? You're a sad little man Nevan Rodgers. Next time you see her she'll be in Angle chains."

Something of a muffled trumpeting noise steamed from Nevan's mouth as he charged forward, swinging wildly. Niles dodged the blows in the near dark with ease, despite his obvious intoxication. He'd spent twice the time in the Circle Nevan had and Sir Craig had overseen a portion of Niles' training personally.

Nothing in the way of words came from Nevan's mouth, but small peeps and grunts exhaled with his swings, like an old house under the buffeting of the Four Storms.

"Cummawn you soft old pumpkin." Niles goaded, giving Nevan a push. "Why do you always leave the f-fighting to me?"

Nevan stopped, nearly breathless.

"I protect you!"

"The hell you do! *I* protect *you*!"

"What?"

"Why do you think I was always the center of attention? Why do you think I stepped up to do everything you never would? Don't you think *I* wanted to ta-take a rest for once? Don't you think *I* like it quiet? That *I* want to kick back and say forget it, just leave me alone? Hell no! I'm the one who always has to play Rook's Table with guys that look like they want to slit my throat while you sit in the back corner and talk…weather patterns or some rubbish with some old geezer who's probably m-making it all up just to feel important!"

Nevan squinted as Niles fought the urge to fall face first in the grass. An aching sorrow was worming its way up his throat. So many things had been misunderstood, so many hard times that could've been avoided but were set so hard beneath them like the stones of a paved road.

"I was protecting you by always saying the right thing when you got too full of yourself."

Niles shook his head and jabbed back.

"If you were protecting me, how come I was always running for my life?"

"Cuz of your big mouth!"

"But I'm not the one who'd talk to a water barrel just because it would listen!" Niles twisted his lip in disgust. "Chew the fat. Chew the fat. Chew the fat like a couple of stale old codgers who've never seen the world but act like they have. If you want that, you can go on back to Crefton and rot. I'm gonna go out and fight. I'm gonna go be a hero and win all the glory this scrawny body of mine can handle and when we've won back our Kingdom, Rhoswen will make me a Lord and Finleigh will be my lady. You can muck out the stables, but you'll have to eat with the servants."

Nevan seethed but he said nothing, his mind still reeling over the countless hours they'd spent together, thinking the opposite of what'd been true.

And now they'd been ripped apart, savagely, like an iron split in between a stump of oak.

"You think she's too good for me?" Niles straightened and squinted as his perspective swayed like a ship at sea. "At least I would've bloody well given her a night to remember before she ran off to do Rhoswen's special secret mission. But you? She'll forget you like oatmeal passing through her stomach."

Nevan didn't even think, blinded by the frenzy of wanting to beat every single one of Niles' teeth out one at a time. He leapt with swift precision and tackled his brother, causing the taller and younger Niles to roll awkwardly on the ground to toss him off.

Nevan didn't even see the pain in Niles' gaze, launching himself again and their frustrations of what felt like a thousand years speaking through their fists where words failed.

And it was on the ground, in the dark, while dancers danced and sober men drank themselves to sleep to face the long march to death that would begin with the rise of the sun, Nevan and Niles beat each other within an inch of their lives.

AERLYN

CHAPTER 41

Silence stretched itself across the earth, a perfectly deep and brooding calm cradling the hearts and minds of those scattered upon the forest floor, sunken in the arms of sleep as if they would never rise again. Low clouds scraped the jagged treetops and dripped warm wet rain from the violet sky.

A world still and static.

Waiting.

And in this permanent hush, Aerlyn O'Rye drifted through the camps like a night spirit.

She *was* the silence, in no small way, relishing the tangible feeling of her senses attuned to the finest point like the twin edges of the dagger packed down in her spring-loaded holster.

Her shape was nothing more than a blur, dancing through smoke and dreams.

Able to go for hours without sleep, and sometimes just a minute or two of rest at that, Aerlyn bided the time before her scheduled departure down at the loch. There, she held herself in her own arms, watching tears fall from the sky and kiss the flat skin of the water with dark drops of sorrow and color.

Staring into the water, into the night, peering up at the bruised violet sky and its thin veil of clouds, she did nothing, and thought nothing, letting the silence speak to a soul that'd finally grown accustomed to the many sounds of Rhoswen's Army, only to leave them once again, as if she'd never been a part of them.

Always on the outside, looking in. Always someone nobody could truly understand.

Again, the silence of the night was with her, like an old friend.

Like a father.

"Beautiful, isn't it?" A voice called out beside her.

A knot in Aerlyn's throat tightened and burned fire down her spine. Like the heat and light of a campfire beckoning her closer to its warmth, its shine, Quill was behind her. She'd felt him approach two minutes ago, taking his time, keeping quiet. Watching, studying, as only he could do.

It was so like him just to let her be.

"Aye." She said, as Quill stepped from the shadows of the tall forest trees to stand next to her. He didn't look at her, hidden in her hood, a dark silhouette of nothing next to the shore.

Instead he cast his attention across the loch, as if his imagination was soaking up the somber beauty like a sponge, storing it all in a special place no one could get to. If Aerlyn lived for bird's heart rubies and the rush of stealing them, then Quill lived for the peace of the world asleep, exhausted by the waiting necessary to see it finally come to pass.

"How do you do it?" Quill asked.

"Do what?"

"Become The Thistle."

The look in his eye added, *when I know you're not just a thief. You're a lot more than that, Aerlyn O'Rye.*

A lot more.

Your eyes tell me things, Aerlyn, and I can't deny them any longer. Even when you avoid me.

I know who you are. And you're not just a thief.

You're so much more, Aerlyn O'Rye, so much more.

"I don't know." Aerlyn shook her head, squinting. "I don't think about it. It all just…happens. It's always happened. It's my life."

"Don't you ever want to stop?"

"It's what I'm good at."

"It's what you *know.*"

Aerlyn tilted her gaze toward him, toward the subtle way he was prying a crowbar into her mask of darkness.

"What are you saying?"

"I've seen a lot in my years, Aerlyn. And when I look at you, I see a rose, not a thistle."

Her heart caught in her throat and she nearly snorted.

"You see what you want to see."

Quill chuckled to himself. At the thorns in her voice.

"As do you, Thistle. Can you tell me what I can see anymore than I can tell you what you see?"

"No."

"Then let me see what I *want* to see." He said, turning to face her, and she jabbed her midnight gaze at him before twisting her head to see the many sorrows sleeping beneath his own lake blue eyes. "Because I see what no one else sees."

The garnet slash of Aerlyn's lips sagged to read the pain written across his own face. How many days had he gone without sleep and she hadn't showed? How many hurts did her avoiding him cause? How many songs had he written hoping she would hear them drift across the skin of the loch and beckon her close?

But she'd been in Rhoswen's grip, sharpened sharpened sharpened to slash and sting the one who'd stolen the Ring of Rule so long ago.

And in this, The Thistle was the very thing that Quill craved with all of his heart.

Stillness. Silence. A creature of the quiet sighs of the night.

"Don't deceive yourself, Uilleam. You're the nicest man I've ever met. In fact, you're the *only* man I've ever met that I would say that much of."

"Then tell me I'm wrong." A rough edge slipped into his singer's voice. "Tell me there's nothing soft inside of you. Tell me your heart is nothing but soot and ash. Tell me to go."

"I…can't do that."

"Why?"

"Because *I'm* the one who has to go."

"I know. I know all about it." Quill turned away, leaning on a tree as if he was about to fall over. "I fought for you like a fool. I want you to be something you don't even want to be yourself."

Aerlyn winced, and her hands nearly flinched to reach out to him.

Uilleam, please! That's not true!

So Quill sighed.

"I guess it's destiny, then."

"You believe in destiny, Uilleam?"

"Are you kidding?" Quill scoffed and stared back across the loch and pushed himself from the tree to walk toward her. "I *am* destiny." She could feel the heat of his body as each and every plink and ploink of rain echoed a chill within her belly. "I should be dead a thousand ways from sixday but I'm still here. Because of destiny. Heavens above, Thistle, I've got a long life ahead of me." There was a nearly mischievous gleam in his eye. "You think I made *all* those stories up? No, there's a lot of first hand experience there. That's why I'm sick of the fighting. I've seen too much of it already. So now it stays in my stories. Everyone else seems so damn thirsty for it, anyway. I carry the souls of a thousand ghosts within me. No wonder I'm going blind."

Aerlyn's shoulders sagged and she clasped her hands together. The rain began to pick up, and she sighed, the sound of it numbing her.

"I still would...love to hear one of your stories, someday."

"That's right. You've never heard me tell a story."

Aerlyn's chin dropped as she stared at the rocks beneath them.

It's not like I didn't want to.

But some people have to deny what they want for the betterment of others. Isn't that what you said, in so many words or less, the first time we met?

Isn't that a part of destiny?

"I haven't had time." Aerlyn muttered.

"Time..." Quill spat, as if it was a curse.

And it occurred to her it *was* a curse.

Time, the infinite enemy of all, unforgiveness and irreversibility weapons borne in each of its hands, crushing hills and quenching rivers like a giant fist crashing upon the land.

A shackle, a bond, a yoke of the unexplainable everlasting, time was so much bigger than her, forever ticking on and on and on and not giving a damn.

A giant noose constantly tightening around her long and pale neck till all the colors of the night no longer spoke to her in shadow and shade.

Just black.

The purest black of death.

But destiny? Destiny was like a dimly lit path through it all. Sometimes it didn't make sense.

Sometimes it did.

And in this quiet moment with Quill, only one thing made sense to her as destiny carved the faintest glow in the dark unknown stretching before her.

A pang stung her deep within and her gaze snapped to meet Quill, who took his time looking into her eyes.

Blue met blue, like rain upon the loch, the differences of sky and sea swelling with silent promises.

The sour garnet slash of her lips parted as Aerlyn fanned her graceful fingers across Quill's face, framing his lips for a kiss.

In her touch was sweetness, long buried, like honey, never ruined, just hardened.

Crystallized.

She kissed him again and again, slower and softer than the rain upon the water, dripping and trickling down the treetops and the unbound expanse of limbs and leaves. She kissed him as Luna broke silver light through the milky screen of the clouds and tickled the slick shine of the loch rocks and reeds with sparkles of starlight. She kissed him until the rain whipped up torrents so strong so she could barely hear her heart beat faster than any chase and she kissed him as if time had turned its back on them both.

"Aerlyn..."

"Shh…" She murmured, kissing him again, before dragging her gaze up his features to meet his bloodshot blue eyes. "I'm a thief. I take what I want."

She kissed him once more, pressing closer to the heat of his body as rain danced a hot sizzle across the woods.

"And I only take what is valuable to me."

Quill studied her as she drew a finger across the edge of his red beard and traced the shape of his lips. She inhaled deeply and grazed a hand through his hair to feel its thinness, its softness.

"But I never take what is given."

As soon as she said it, Quill straightened, and clarity broke through the immense pain shooting his eyes with squiggles of blood.

But she was already drawing away, into the shadows.

Into the snaking folds of darkness that had made her who she was.

"Aerlyn…" Quill reached out as shoulders slipped to elbows in his hands, and elbows to fingertips.

"Aerlyn…"

Longing hollowed out his voice. His eyes fluttered in rapid blinks not to cry.

But her smile was a whisper, just a faint ghost of moonlight illuminating alabaster skin.

ULTAN

CHAPTER 42

Sea salt and the spray of swollen wave caps always made Ultan feel alive and had a way of filling him with more gratitude than regret on the count of his departed mother. So many mothers had been lost to Plague or war, so many children carrying holes in their hearts forever unfilled.

But to see the sunrise unfurl ribbons of gold across the gray-blue sea was to remind him of the odd light of his mother's eyes, like shades of sky and light and water mingled together, swirled and sloshed with love. Some cursed their humble fishing villages, never content with the hard work and hearthfire such had to offer, but she never forgot where she came from, and brought its heart-felt goodness with her wherever she went.

Perhaps that's what'd won her to the regal and somewhat disenchanted Lord of Skyeshire. That feeling of honest blood running hot just beneath her skin, and the look in her eye that promised not only complete devotion but the fiery passion of a thousand sunsets spilled upon the gentle waves of the endless sea. And now that he was a man and had seen what the Chamber of Lords had to offer; their blockheaded sense of logic, their time-wasting chatter, their stony adherence to tradition, he could only imagine the purity of her pragmatic charm, cutting through their reasoning and rhetoric like a fillet knife.

"It seems you are the man I thought you weren't but hoped you were." Eyvind Frey said, striding up to Ultan. The Champion regarded his new ally and nodded, sea breeze whipping both their strawberry blonde curls across their faces as the mainsail creaked and groaned to harness the power of the north.

"I am my mother's son." Ultan smiled.

Behind them, fifteen dragon-boats, packed to the gunwales with men and supplies, sailed in formation for Curran Firth and the Mull of Montree like a flight of arrows. Heavy fog and rain clouds hid the black Tower of Ullraye from them, and the sea was violent, but Ultan was confident they'd reach the shore before the sun rose again.

A night in such seas could be terrifying, even for the most seasoned of sailors.

"How does it feel?" Ultan asked.

"To be King?" Eyvind Frey rubbed his blunt chin and shrugged, the wise and dark blue pools of his eyes drifting back toward his homeland. He looked even more powerful than before in the bristly black fur of his bear pelt, intricate silver clasps and amber broaches proclaiming his royalty. "It is too new to know. My wife is with child, though."

Ultan reached out his hand for a shake. Their clasp was firm.

"So I didn't hit you *that* hard."

Frey's grin was sheepish. He was a quick learner and even quicker to heal.

"I have you to thank, actually. If you had not beaten me so severely, my wife would've not taken such…*care* in seeing me recover. We have not spent very much time together with my father's bloodlust draining our coffers and stealing our young men to the cold arms of death. I told her how sorry I was that I had forgotten about her in trying to save the Kingdom from falling apart the very moment it'd come together. We were in love once, you know. She is…"

"She's lovely."

"Yes…like a diamond. Lovely but very hard. She is a complicated woman in some ways, but very simple in others. She wants what she wants and goes colder than ice when she doesn't get it." Frey rolled his eyes, a secret congratulations to Ultan that he did not know such troubles.

Frey had no knowledge of Ultan's delicate relationship with Faer Morgance.

And just to *think* about seeing Faer Morgance again released a cage of butterflies in his chest. Fluttering around, they were impossible to ignore. Impossible to catch.

"I can imagine." Ultan muttered, staring at the haze and fog. Frey continued.

"She was angry at me for not disagreeing with my father. She said I was a coward and did not deserve the crown if I couldn't make him see what was best for our people. She feels *she* has no power in our monarchy, and once my father united the country, she wished him to stop his fighting. After all, we were in love and just married. It seemed ideal. A united country, a young couple ready to take over for a warrior too old to fight anymore. But no. The Wolf couldn't stop himself. Spilling blood had driven him insane. He wanted Albanland, too, and to be honest, I was afraid he'd strike me down if I stood up to him."

Ultan only nodded. He wouldn't offer any condolences for the King's death, and Frey wouldn't accept any. Shortly after the duel, Father of The Wolf breathed his last, and Ultan had stayed for nearly two months with the Nørd, establishing a great many things in their new alliance.

Evidence of such new-found brotherhood rested in the shiny helms and knotted beards of an expeditionary force of six-hundred Nørd warriors eager to serve under Frey himself as the freshly coroneted King of his people buried the axe and joined arms *with* Albanland, instead of *against* them, pledging never to raise a finger against Skölhammer's own.

Though Ultan didn't want to agree to it, Frey had told him privately that every Nørd warrior who'd witnessed the duel was still afraid of him and thought he was a descendant of the gods. For in their mind, only a god, whether properly appeased or by rights of their own divinity, could offer forgiveness. It was not something the Nørd believed mere man was capable of.

To the Nørd, there was strength and weakness. Even the sea took what it wanted from the land, forever buffeting the shore with ten thousand frozen wet knives. If a man could not catch a fish he would starve. If a man could not start a fire he would freeze. If his enemy was faster with the axe or the bow he would die.

But to best a man in the bloodlust of combat and *spare him*? To secure the rights and entitlements to an *entire* Kingdom and give them back to the man he'd beaten? Give a Kingdom to a man who'd earned his own death with his failure to achieve victory?

What man would do such a thing?

Surely no man at all.

"I look forward to meeting the mysterious Morgance." Eyvind Frey admitted after some silence. Ultan raked a hard glare across the water as Frey continued. "We have only heard stories of her beauty, and of course, that she has magical powers."

Ultan chuckled hollowly to himself. The King was waiting for an answer, either a denial or a confirmation.

He would get none.

"They say the Faer, amongst other things, can speak the Haunted Tongue and sing songs to the wind. That they speak to others in their dreams and control the weather."

Ultan grit his teeth together.

"If anything she worships Solara. Sometimes the sun itself shines from her body."

Frey laughed.

"Tried to tempt you with a blanket on the grass, has she?"

Ultan couldn't fight a smirk, even though thoughts of Morgance being able to control the weather made him sick. Frey had a way about him, something of charm gone to hell. He was walking death but he seemed reluctant to embrace it. And his mind was constantly consumed with women though he seemed somewhat scared of his wife.

"It takes more than a blanket to get me."

"Oh…" Frey chuckled, letting his eyes drift up the sail as it flapped and smacked the wind. "Yes, you're a pillar of virtue."

Ultan sighed, gaze drifting. Inside of him, there was a *need* to see her. He couldn't fight it. It sat there like a stone. It'd been two months. Two months and he'd thought about her nearly every day.

But the thought of her was wrapped in some strange blanket, like the Tower of Ullraye, lost behind the mist and fog.

Because he couldn't *feel* her.

And most of all he couldn't understand why he couldn't *feel* her like he always did.

Like he wanted to.

"You'll have to wait it out in Montree." Ultan's smile was a grimace. "She might not be too happy to see me."

"Why not? You're her Champion. What could make a Princess happier than to grab ahold of those golden torcs around your arms?"

"Exactly. I've been out of contact for two months now."

Frey's dark blue eyes bulged in their sockets and he coughed in a fist.

"You didn't send her a message?"

"No."

Frey winced.

"My bride would kill me. I've sent a dispatch horse or two to the grave in hasting a message to her."

"Morgance is *not* my bride." Ultan said all too quickly.

"True." Frey smirked, his experience leaking through his gaze as it dug into Ultan's thoughts to assume the depths of his struggle.

And his commitment to resistance.

"But, my wife has no magical powers." He then snapped his fingers. "Save this one cake she makes. It's the food of angels!"

Ultan crossed his arms, eager to see the black Tower of Ullraye, and with it, once again feel the intense focus of Faer Morgance awaiting his arrival.

But it was as if the connection he always felt to her was blocked. Not just by the mist and the fog, not just tossed and tumbled by the heavy waves and the cold knives of the wind, but covered in a thick and murky haze he couldn't reach through if he wanted to.

Maybe she does have magical powers. Maybe she has kept me alive all this time. She's always singing over me, covering me with her beautiful voice like a cloak.

That night she spent at Hafnröth...perhaps she'd been...

No. It's impossible. The legends of old are merely stories for children. There is no such thing as magic.

But if there was...

Could it be true?

"You still should've sent her a message saying you were alive." Frey nearly whispered, standing shoulder to shoulder with Ultan.

"I couldn't." Ultan remained tense, heather-green gaze probing through the coughing congestion of wind and fog for those eyes he felt follow his every step, like an unseen shadow, following him everywhere since he'd been anointed Champion of Albanland.

But now he felt naked and alone, without that heat on the back of his neck.

Without that tangible taste her of desire to be with him, hovering like a night spirit.

"Well, if she is cross with you, we'll know soon enough. I'll sit it out just off the coast. I can't wait to fight the Angle barons and their giant horses but I shudder to think of fighting them when there's an angry Princess on the loose!"

Eyvind Frey, King of Nørd, laughed hilariously at his own humor, bringing upon him a fit of coughing.

Ultan smiled to see the young King in such levity, the threat of another hundred years of bloodshed with those of his mother's blood now averted.

But the silent gray darkness consuming the far off shores of his true home had already released the sick vapors of uncertainty within. For some reason, the very *idea* of Morgance being responsible for his still being alive chilled him to the very base of his spine and curled ice around his abdomen and his hips, reaching down through his legs to fasten his feet to the slick deck of the dragon-boat.

The thought of being ungrateful to her devotion, devotion that had been poured like molten alloys into a weapon maker's cast, drenched and soaked in ancient magic, devotion that refused to let him die as he stood alone to save his land.

Her land.

Devotion that fasted food, paced halls, fretted and worried and rushed his side the moment steel pierced his skin and threatened to mock her entire existence.

Devotion that meditated upon the chance of his touch, the whisper of his lips in her ear.

Ultan fought the thoughts but could not. *Was* Morgance actually a *real* Faer? Was there ever any such thing? Wasn't it just an epithet she'd been given as a child? Or a compliment to her beauty? Or an indulgence to her unpredictable nature?

Or had she deceived them *all*, acting so weak, when she could not only control the weather but *save* Ultan from death?

A million small moments flashed before his eyes. Ten thousand sword swipes inches from his neck. A hundred thousand arrows whistling so fast past his ear the cartilage burned red.

Too many eyes to count, mystified *why* on earth the damned Champion of Albanland just wouldn't *die*.

The dull gnaw of such understandings chewed at Ultan's neck, and he rubbed and rubbed but could not free himself of the tension twisting his muscles, the sounds of his plight echoing through the knots of rope and rigging, moaning and creaking under the splashing sea.

And as that cold *cold* ice of a life-altering realization spiraled up Ultan's core and wrapped around his chest like the searching fingers of her embrace, he all but heard a prayer, a plea, drifting upon breathy gust of salt and frost.

Come to me, Ultan. Come to me.

Whispers on the wind.

Come to me.

Come be my King.

The frozen cold of being wrong, so painfully cold it began to burn, possessed Ultan as he stood alone, fastened to the prow as if his life depended upon his holding on to the railing.

He felt faint.

Weak.

If only you could speak to me, Rhoswen. If only you could show your face. If only you could forgive me and take your place upon the Throne.

But the sighs faded to echo, lost in the lap and crash of the wet and the waves, and with them, the fog that'd obscured the shore.

Ultan looked up, squinting.

The sun was rising behind the black Tower of Ullraye, crowning the pinnacle where Faer Morgance awaited his return like a blinding golden-white halo of lover's passion.

Ultan paled in the sight, washed sick with guilt.

Ashamed. Scared. Afraid.

All these years, he'd been wrong.

Morgance held the knowledge that framed the stars and spun Luna and Solara around the horizon like weaver's fine thread. She held it dear to her heart as it wrecked her very own soul like merchant ships on the sea floor, pouring herself out for him and him alone.

Morgance was magic. Her magic was for him. Her magic was love. Her magic was truth.

Rhoswen was a lie.

Rhoswen was dead.

CHAPTER 43

Footsteps heavy on the rocky shoreline, Ultan walked as if in a daze. He was tired, the day-long sea-voyage hard and fast, and he'd relied on every bit of his half-Nørd blood not to vomit over the side of the boat. So tired was he that he didn't see the glorious sunset bending along the curve of the horizon, its colors splashed like the many juices of imported fruits.

Ultan had barely crested the low slope of the hill when he saw the shapes of several men approach him, and he stopped to rest his legs. Not so long ago, he told himself, he'd cleaved the Nørds their last pitched battle on the very same soil. So many screams and shouts silenced. The land vacant and hollow. Empty. And not so long ago Faer Morgance had pulled him from the pit of death with the airy rope of her song, wrapped around his body like silk.

Ultan squinted in waiting, his vision adjusting quickly in the falling dark. The trees, far beyond the sloped plain, did they look any different? No.

And Montree, on its jutting rocky fist, nearly a mile away, swarmed with dragon-boats, did it look any different?

No.

Then why did it all...*feel* so different?

Ultan cast a glower up to the black Tower of Ullraye, its ugly shape a shadow-casting scepter. Somewhere, up there, he knew Morgance was waiting for him.

Or did she think him dead? Was that the reason for the muddled block between them?

"My Champion." Bandon of Tavish rushed up to Ultan, five swordsmen and one of his hunting dogs at heel. Bandon bowed tightly, as he always did, with the stilted grace of someone who never fully learned the fineries of Court, though something stronger than fear was curled within his clan-patterned cloak of red, white, blue, and green.

"Bandon."

"We didn't know." Was all he said.

Ultan sighed. The man was not incompetent, but he was slow at times, and of a different mindset than men Ultan liked to surround himself with. His dogs were very good hunters, remarkably well-behaved, healthy and strong, and Ultan couldn't help but wonder if an administrative position such as Master Breeder would better suit him than to be so active...or *inactive* in the Chamber of Lords.

"I must speak to the Princess at once. Where is she?"

"Th-that's it." Bandon stumbled, and Ultan gazed past him at the Fortress guardsmen, slouching on the parapet walls as if drunk. If his sharp eyes weren't deceiving him, they were the same men who'd been posted when he left two months ago.

"Slow down." Ultan said as they began to walk. Bandon's nervous gaze travelled back to the dragon-boats, looking even more ominous and menacing in the spilt colors of Solara's escape.

They certainly weren't going anywhere. And every eye of their carved wooden faces seemed to be trained on the black Tower of Ullraye.

Watching?

Waiting.

"It's the Princess." Bandon's youngish voice was strained, features that many young Ladies found dashing looking worn thin, exasperated. Patchy stubble scratched at his cheeks and chin. "She shut herself up in the top of the Tower when no news of you came by the third day. She hasn't given a single order...nobody's spoken to her...the place is falling apart! Nobody knows what to do."

"What about the Lords?" Ultan nearly roared, his anger lost in a snatch of wind. Ultan looked painfully to the sky, rolling darkness across them like a hand passing over a flame.

"Most of them have gone to their own estates."

Gone to their own estates???

The pit of pain in his guts strengthened, like the gears of a war machine ready to snap its strings.

"Most?"

Bandon nodded and Ultan all but ran to the thickened arms of the Fortress, stopping just before the Tower's entrance.

"Tell all these men to rest." Ultan said, grabbing Bandon by the shoulder. "Every last one of them. You too."

"But...the guard?"

"No guard is needed." Ultan sighed. "Not tonight. The traitors have already made their play for the Throne and they won't be taking it tonight."

Bandon's uncleverly handsome face fell at the thought.

"Arturo?" He said, quietly, betrayed deep inside.

"He's not the only one." Ultan squinted off to Montree. To think that six hundred Nørd warriors and their new King would be his only ally against those he'd grown up with, and those who'd known his father to be a just and moral man, save the ignominious thought that he actually *loved* a Nørd and loved her so much he didn't rightly give a damn when they expelled him from the Chamber and increased his tribute by half.

Ultan shook his head.

Hollow rat bastards. Clansmen of hell's own hand.

Betrayed a dozen ways from sixday by his own blood.

Even then, there was always a chance Eyvind Frey could say, *nope! Sorry!* And take what his father never could.

The Tower. The Throne.

Ultan's life.

Ultan looked up again to the sky. Death was in it. Heavy and languid. Luna would not show her silver gaze tonight. No loch would favor her shine.

It would be a night of darkness. Full and endless darkness.

"Sleep, Bandon." Ultan turned, his white fox cloak flourishing in the breeze. "Heaven knows once the swords are drawn the only sleep I can promise you is death itself."

And with that, Ultan pressed himself into the smoke black Tower of Ullraye, anything but forgiveness for these runaway traitors on his mind.

CHAPTER 44

He found the Princess at the dining table, and entered the long room of cut stone and curtain-covered windows carefully. Pale light flickered in candelabras lining the length of the oaken table, some of them nearly burned to the wick, their wax spilling down the iron flutes like frozen waterfalls.

Like tears of milky stone.

Her posture slumped, Morgance' hand drew circles in the air over a crystal goblet of cherry liqueur, her head tipping to the left or the right as her lungs breathed ever so slowly.

In…and out. In…and out.

Silence burned in Ultan's ears. After two months with the Nørd and the entire day spent fighting a roiling sea, the last thing he expected to hear was…

Nothing.

Morgance lifted her head as he walked, causing him to stop. Her lids fluttered open and her eyes seemed to roll down from the top of her skull to stare at him, their light yellowy-green hue not brilliant, but eerie, like light lost in the forest.

"So…you're alive."

Ultan said nothing as she blinked wearily and let her gaze fall again to her goblet.

In the shimmering crystal, it looked like blood.

"Yes, Morgance." He crossed the distance till he reached the chair where he always sat, at her right hand. "And you're drunk."

Her laugh was the slightest of coughs, her shoulders slumped and she leaned on her left arm, pushing the goblet closer into a dark crook of black lace as Ultan took his seat, his body tender and tired.

"What do you expect with the man I love presumed dead?"

"Mor…"

"Oh, come on, Ultan." She straightened and took the goblet with both hands, the Ring of Rule heavy on her right hand, its matchless knots of gold catching all the light of the candles. "I know you don't give a damn about me. If I didn't know before I certainly do now."

"That's *not* true."

"Yesssit isss!" Morgance slurred, her soft and airy voice a snake-like hiss. Her head tottered on her shoulders and she pressed a hand to her forehead, sneering, and adding softly. "Yes it is."

Ultan couldn't help himself. The hand that hefted the Blade of the Champion reached across the table and grabbed her wrist.

"Listen to me Morgance." Ultan applied the slightest pressure. Her pulse was little more than a tip tap. "That's *not* true."

Though his voice a whisper, it echoed through her ears like the Four Storms.

Her eyes peeled wide as she beheld him, so close, with candlelight touching his face as she longed to since she was seven years old.

Her nostrils flared.

"It's just you and me now." Wet shine glazed her eyes. "You may've saved the Throne but *I've* lost it."

"No." Ultan hushed, giving her wrist a tug.

Morgance only nodded, her eyebrows an apologetic shrug as tears flowed free.

"Twenty-some Clans in the end. Every lowland family but two. They've all gone to meet Arturo and whatever Angle Barons he struck a deal with. I can't believe I was so foolish."

"No." Ultan leaned closer, his other hand resting on the back of her chair. "I'm the one who's to blame."

Morgance' gaze flicked over him twice and then a hushed laugh puffed from her mouth.

"Why? What makes you so sure you've done me wrong, Mr. Perfect?" Ultan pulled back, his lips a firm line. "Why are you always the one responsible? Why are you the only man who takes the fall? You're not even a Lord! You're nothing but the sword! You wouldn't even have a voice in the Chamber if they weren't afraid of you, the damned cowards."

Ultan winced as Morgance swiped up the goblet and guzzled half of it, sighing as she set it down with a snarl.

"And yet they follow *you* as if you were King."

Ultan stared at her as her chin pressed ever closer to his, her posture nearly bent in half, the oaken table knifing into the black lace tight around her bosom.

"But you're *nothing* to them. They turned their back on you as if you'd never been born. After all you've given."

"I haven't given it for them." Ultan said.

"For Albanland?" Morgance snickered, her goblet raised in a mock toast. "Well then, may the land receive your corpse with grace, noble Champion." She drained the cherry liqueur. "Because when Arturo comes riding up here with ten thousand spears and a half-dozen war machines, the only head he'll be after is *yours*."

Morgance stretched her hands across the table, staring at them.

"Heaven knows it's not *my* head he wants…no no…just the rest of my body. Every waking hour of the day."

Morgance shot upright, knocking her chair to the ground, her hand slapping the crystal goblet and shattering it on the stone wall.

"Am I to be a traitor's slave? Am I to bear a child of treason? ME? I AM DOMINAE TENEBRIS! Arturo, you bloody son of perdition! Curse the Clan of Pallantyne! Curse the blood in your bones, you wretched dog! Curse the day of your birth! Curse the…"

Ultan wrapped Morgance in his arms as sobs overtook her. The warrior's face was awash with horror to feel her shudder and rock in his embrace, her desolation vibrating throughout the taut muscles of his body.

She felt so light, so weak, so vulnerable.

So needy.

And Ultan sighed as he held her. So many times she had been the one to coax him from darkness and despair, from the cold grip of the grave.

He lifted her chin, meeting a gaze of fractured light and shadow, buried in the slick shine of sorrow.

"You don't need anyone else when you have me." Ultan said, tendrils of strawberry blonde framing a face that'd wrought pure and unfiltered fear in the hearts of many an enemy. "I am *your* Champion."

Morgance' nostrils flared and her chest swelled. She licked ruby lips and stared at him, slipping deep into his hurt.

"Leave me." Her soft voice was but a squeak, the plea of a little girl. The request of someone buried deep inside her soul, locked away. Prisoner. "Please, Ultan. Leave me now."

"I can't leave you."

Her beauty stretched and simmered with pain. Her chin nipped right and left, tightly and she tried to push herself from him.

"Please! Don't do this to me! Please…DON'T!"

Ultan wouldn't let her go. She was a feather in his arms. Arms that made the nearly four-foot long Blade look like a hollow reed.

"Morgance I know. I know how you've saved me."

"No no no…" The little girl's voice whimpered, the tiny hands pressing against his chest harmlessly, though sapping what little strength her inebriated body possessed.

"I don't understand your knowledge of the Faer, but I know how you've protected me at the cost of your own life. And before tomorrow comes, I wanted to say thank you."

Ultan took her chin in his hand. Her mouth parted and no sound came out. He looked hard into her yellow-green eyes and searched for the lost soul the liquor had stolen.

.

For in his own shame, inherited from his father, Ultan knew how alcohol could steal one's spirit and replace it with another.

But because of his own experience with it, he was reading the signs wrong.

Terribly wrong.

Morgance blinked twice and swallowed, her body becoming perfectly still, like a small bird in the hand of a young boy.

Ultan held her in his calming grip and felt her heart nearly beat itself out of her chest, her pulse ever increasing as if doubling itself in speed again and again.

Outside, a bright spit of white fire snaked across the sea, lighting up the curtains and the dinner room that'd all but lost its candle flicker. Thunder clapped in the distance and echoed across the water just seconds behind.

Caught by the voice of the storm, Ultan turned away, but when he looked again to fair Morgance something very different glazed her face.

Lust.

Ruby lips found his, her hands warm and sticky like candle wax as one slipped to the small of his back, the other grabbing his skull to press her desire deep into his mouth.

Ultan could barely breath as Morgance forced him back, back, back to the stone wall, where they hit its hardness with a thud.

Again, lighting zipped across the sea and thunder followed it, the two forces of nature caught in a race, a duel.

The Champion tried to pry himself from her, breathless, suffocated by the storm of her affection.

But he was weak and weary, and the unbridled passion of her touch washed his body with flame.

It was Morgance who broke free of him, doubling over, the tiniest whimper of a sob shaking her just before she straightened and laughed a low and rich gurgle.

Ultan stared at her, frozen against the cold wall, her touch igniting a bonfire within.

"The Champion of Albanland, afraid of a little girl." Morgance said, just as she had in the stone circle of *Hafnröth*, in a low and menacing voice.

Ultan's gaze swelled as her neck twitched and her whole body was wracked with shivers.

"Please please please…" The little girls voice begged, as the right hand that wore the Ring of Rule twisted and curled.

"Noooope." The low voice replied, Morgance eyes closing as she inhaled deep. "He's all mine now."

The eerie yellow green eyes fixed their paralyzing gaze on Ultan and as Morgance took a step forward, Ultan flinched to run for the door.

"You really are afraid of me." A twisted smile snaked through ruby lips, lips the warrior still tasted the sweetness of on his tongue, burning with the sour warmth of cherries.

Morgance held out her hand and he stayed put as she advanced.

"And now you see me, as I am," Her low voice swished with the sway of her hips, her body swathed in black lace. "Lady Darkness."

Lightning cut a jagged vein above and thunder followed so close Ultan felt the Tower would come down around them.

But he was stuck.

Stuck in her web.

"This is how you want to see me, isn't it? This is what you *really* want. Like thunder and lightning, our love is a storm that will ruin us."

Morgance stood before him, her right hand tracing the lines of his face, yellow-green eyes remembering every space she'd wished she could kiss. Her touch was warm and real.

Ultan swallowed, staring back at eyes that failed to blink.

"So you believe in my magic?"

The dry swallow attacked him again. Did he? Was he wrong about everything he'd thought on the voyage? Was it just…his own romantic longing, all twisted and jumbled? He did love Morgance, didn't he? In some way…maybe just the thought of her love…maybe that was all the magic was. A tangible sensation he knew nobody else in the world gave him but her.

Then why couldn't he take her? Why couldn't he reciprocate?

Why did he still hold onto Rhoswen when the enthralling taste of Faer Morgance' affection still lingered upon his tongue? Had she projected it all upon him, this unfulfilled craving, rushing like melt waters from the mountains?

He just needed a rest. He was so tired. But there was no time. No time anymore, forever. The Kingdom was going to hell, like Solara itself, never to rise again on the land, a land of nothing but blood and betrayal.

A frown crossed her eyebrows.

"You *don't* believe? You just said you do. Do you or don't you?"

Rain splattered the ground outside, slapping sea and stone with squelching tears. The sound of it made him realize he'd forgotten to drink all day.

"Do you...or don't you?"

Ultan only stared back, wondering why he felt so weak, so exhausted, so completely drained of everything that made him who he was.

So gutted by the treachery of his brothers.

Morgance walked to one of the windows and peeled back the curtain. She seemed to gain strength to see the storm, to smell its wet fury, to feel its electricity.

"You really are a coward, you know that? Why didn't you stop me when I cut off Rhoswen's finger? If you loved her so much why didn't you do something about it back then?" Lady Darkness threw the curtain back to its place and twisted to glare at him. "You don't see it, do you?"

"See what?" He managed to croak.

"You ARE the bloody King. Rhoswen and I are just women." Morgance' feet struck the ground as she rushed over to him, her teeth clenched. "Albanland doesn't follow women, they follow *MEN*, men who can kill and maim and destroy. Men who do whatever the hell they want and take other men to hell with them. Don't you see?" Her right hand jabbed an accusatory finger in his chest. "Everyone that stayed behind only did so because they *believe* in you, more than they believe in the stone beneath their feet. And if you want to stand in some glorious final battle against heaven knows how many thousand come to take the Throne, then they'll all die with you because they love you! WELL WHAT ABOUT ME???" Morgance roared, her body shaking, beautiful face torn with rage. "WHAT ABOUT WHAT I WANT?"

Sinking inside, sick and sore, Ultan reached a hand of comfort toward her and she slapped it away.

"They'll follow you to the grave, Ultan. But you don't have to lead them there."

"Morgance."

"NO!" She glared at him, yellow-green eyes sucking up the last of the candlelight before each and every one of them was burned to the wick. "No no no you weak little man. You couldn't do the right thing as a little boy and you still can't stand here and tell me whether you believe in magic or not. You choose right now," she drew out the words, each one a threat on her lips, "what you're going to do. No more sitting on the fence. Either you take them all to fight and die or you run away with me and no one will die."

"How do you know that?"

Morgance only shook her head, staring at him as if he had a hole in his.

"How can I love such a stupid man? Who did Father of the Wolf want to see *become* Son of Fenrir?"

Ultan cowered in the corner, eyes wide as she nodded.

"Yes, you handsome idiot, the wind tells me everything. Well? Did he want to see Arturo or Bandon? Or a dozen other Lords? No! He wanted you! And Arturo," Morgance pressed herself to him, her right hand reaching back as if holding a knife. "He wants you on your knees, begging for mercy as he *plunges* the knife straight through your heart!" She said, mimicking the motion, her fist against his chest. "And I..." She sighed. "I who loves you forever and ever. I want you. I want you and I need you. I *crave* you like a wild wolf craves the deer that runs through the forest. I love you, Ultan. I love you like I can't understand." Her touch was soft and sweet, simple and gentle.

"I love you." She said, kissing him delicately on the lips. Kissing him on the chin. Pulling back to run her hands across the breadth of his shoulders, inhaling his nearness as the storm tore at the curtains, slapping wind and wet across the Tower.

And as the candles lost their light, bathing the room in darkness, Ultan gave into Morgance, Faer Princess of the Night, his body but a flicker of consciousness, emptied out to serve a Throne that didn't give a damn about him.

And in the darkness, Ultan found himself wrapped in the blazing heat of black lace and yearning.

The oaken table was hard on his back, subduing his bruises. Candelabras clattered hollowly to the ground, wax splashed and spilled. Like the furious dance of the Blade, motion was taking him over, Morgance pressing across him like the flame of war.

But something inside of him revolted. Something harder than steel, a hate more destructive than fire.

The scream of young Rhoswen, holding her cloven hand as her royal blood poured into the soil. The howl of horror, torn from her lips, swallowed up by the forest never to be seen again.

And in that split second, as Morgance lifted up the black lace of her skirts, Ultan summoned every drop of strength within him to push her off, throwing her feather-light body against the wall.

A shriek ripped through the fathomless night, lost in the rage of the tempest, along with the scatter of footsteps scuffing stone, rushing to descend down the Tower.

Leaving nothing, save the howling voice of the storm and its hand of darkness, gashed by the sound of a little girl weeping herself to sleep.

AERLYN

CHAPTER 45

The rain came down in rippling sheets, gushing glittering rivers down the veins of mud and muck Brachin called streets, battering the soggy shoulders of its spiky timber walls like some cursed siege of wind and wet.

In the torrid fury of the storm, no one stood guard, and no one dared to watch their windows, or else they might've seen the scant shadow of a woman slipping into the city that'd declared her a murderer nearly two months ago.

The heat of Solstice was long lost, forgotten across the backs of a broken people, shivering in their hovels with the hope of a good harvest somehow as futile as wishing deepsea pearls to drop down from the night sky, along with the rain, or better yet, bodkin arrows to pierce the dark hearts of their Angle overlords, or those Albans who had allied with Angles, or worse, become them.

Such was soon to be rectified by the woman who stalked the darkness, gliding up and over half-constructed walls with movements too fluid to be human, cutting a swathe to the stables of *The King's Cloud* without so much as leaving a footprint in the gooey mud.

Ewan Ust sat at the long bar of *The King's Cloud* with a dram of whiskey left in his glass, his small mouth agape as he sighed away the sorrows of his bad chance in gambling. The other card sharks had since left, and the barman, having failed to take what little money the bountyman had held onto to support his drunken stupor, had since retired for the night, knowing Ewan Ust would waddle up to his room whenever he damn well felt like it.

After all, it'd been nothing more than a holler and a threat that'd poured the bountyman's last drink, the one he'd been nursing, tenderly, as if it knew his secrets, since he hadn't paid the barman for any of the whiskey he'd consumed within the last hour. Something to do with the fact that Ewan Ust took whatever he wanted from Brachin's own, with a smarmy smile, claiming he could shed doubt on them for the murder of the governor if they didn't give into his demands.

And the shape-shifting blur of brown cloth and silence was to be his reward.

The bountyman was about to finish the last of his liquor when a canvas bag clinked on the bar top next to him, the near whisper of a rough voice stirring behind his ear.

"Miss me?"

Ust's falcon-eyes darted around the dead space just before the crook of his nose, drowned in a dozen thumbs of drink.

Then a surge of blood shot up his neck.

That voice. He remembered it. And to remember was to feel anger. Seething, like a marsh snake slithering around in his belly.

And the canvas bag…yes, to remember the voice was to remember the last time he'd seen his precious bag of gold.

The bountyman twisted and reached for his knife but the plaster walls of *The King's Cloud*, splattered with sweat and ale stains in wan candle light, spun on end as a hand mashed his head into the hard wood of the bar top.

Then there was a scraping, a scuffling, and the bar was torn from his view, drowned in blackness, as his head hit the much harder wood of the floor.

The bountyman squealed, his protest a hoarse thing, caught in a dehydrated throat covered by weeks of patchy growth. Falcon eyes strained to climb up the lithe limbs of the dark figure who stood above him, legs splayed so that one foot clamped his knife to the floor, the other gently applying pressure on his neck.

The Thistle had returned to Brachin.

Covered in a loose hood, the brown cloak made her all but disappear in the poor candlelight, and Ewan Ust squirmed under her shadowed gaze, his own benumbed legs tangled up in the crashed barstool, his squints able to grab nothing more than the pale crescent of her alabaster chin and the sour slash of her garnet lips.

"I asked you a question." She snarled.

With a swipe, she drug the heavy pouch from the bar top and the bountyman squirmed as it fell toward his eyes like a giant boulder, thunking off his head to spread a dull and echoing sort of pain through his inebriated body, causing his heart to race as the sound of his precious coins spilling all across the floor filled his ears.

When Ust didn't answer, he found her foot curl and clamp down tighter and tighter on a throat as dry as the sands of the many Kingdoms beyond the Greener Sea.

"Thistle…"

It was then Aerlyn pulled back her hood and stared coldly, eyes of midnight full of the kind of hatred that sat just short of murder. Garnet lips stretched, with teeth bared.

"I've come to collect, *bountyman*."

Ewan Ust squealed again, a near pig-like noise as Aerlyn removed her right foot from his throat and drug it across the hand holding the knife. Harmlessly, the knife clattered across the floor, as if seeking out a dark corner, never to be found again.

Aerlyn drew back, in a soundless sway, as he shot up and staggered back, twitchy falcon eyes bulging as he collared his own throat with his hand.

His small mouth opened and closed as he worked his jaw around.

"Well, pick it up." Aerlyn said, thrusting her chin to the gold. "It's yours, isn't it?"

That curved nose of his scrunched as he squinted.

Aerlyn stared him down, hard.

You damn fool. I'd gut you if I had it in me to kill.

But since I don't you're just going to have to deal with my benign sense of generosity.

Or rather, that of Crown Heir Rhoswen, the righteous one who's going to turn this land upside down and drive every snake like you back into the bloody sea.

Swallowing, Ewan Ust stepped forward unevenly and reached for his gold, only to find a swishing noise precede a kick as Aerlyn's foot rammed against his neck.

The bountyman spun to the ground, like a cow sliding across an icy pond, until equilibrium failed him.

"Go ahead." Aerlyn crossed her arms. "Pick it up."

Ewan Ust glared up at her, his hatred thinking a thousand thoughts, each one pounded into submission by the sizzle of the rain outside, and the fact that The Thistle stood perfectly still, her stony features an impassible mask.

Drained of color.

Drained of emotion.

Ust stood up, straightening out his jerkin and his belt, eyeing her carefully as he strode proudly to the gold and, kneeling down slowly, reached around for the bag without taking his eyes off of her. Once he found it, fingertips greedily grabbing for the shiny hardness of the gold, Ust rushed to scrape it into the canvas bag, his fingernails making the skittering noises of a rat running through a hole in the wall.

When all that was near to him had been corralled, the bountyman slapped the floor and pawed around, scraping to get what he could without breaking eye contact.

Until his greed got the better of him.

Once again the dim interior of *The King's Cloud* seemed to invert with a quick slap of pain, an upheaval rivaling the storm-tossing of a merchant ship as the world spun.

And deep within the bountyman's body, the lurching had taken its toll, and hugging the sagging bag of gold to his belly, the bountyman vomited.

Aerlyn rolled her eyes.

This is going to be a long night.

Avoiding the contents of his stomach, Aerlyn grabbed the bountyman by the collar and drug him across the floor like a sack of potatoes, kicking the front door wide. Ust recoiled at the howl of the wind, but Aerlyn, with a grunt, wrangled him up and over to the edge of the covered deck, where gutter runoff gushed down into a dark alley. Shoving his head in the waterfall, Aerlyn counted ten seconds before bringing him back inside, his recoils cut with half mumbles and curses.

Again, Ewan Ust was tossed to the ground. But now, his gold wasn't the only thing consuming him.

Or so Aerlyn gambled.

"What do you want?" He tried to sound tough, but couldn't, too weakened with whiskey to be anything other than pathetic.

"Right now, an apple." Aerlyn said, reaching into her cloak for a Shiny Green, her favorite. They only grew in the south. Ust gave her a dark look as she held her left arm straight out at her side and her twin-edge knife flicked into her palm as if by magic.

"So what's up your sleeve this time, Thistle?" Ust rubbed his stomach, the back of his neck burning in shame.

Aerlyn sliced herself a piece of her beloved fruit and chewed thoughtfully, her smattering of freckles catching what was left of the candles.

"A little deal."

"What sort of deal."

"The kind that keeps you alive."

"Me?" Ust scoffed. "People *fear* me."

"No, people fear *me*."

"I don't." He said, unevenly, still rubbing his stomach.

"And you," Aerlyn sliced herself another piece, tart droplets of juice beading on her shiny knife. "Who do you fear?"

"Not you!" Ust was too quick to say, though there was a twitch in his eye when he did.

"Oh no, certainly not me." Aerlyn shook her head, a mocking pout hiding a smile. "Well then, what about the ghost of Kingdoms past?"

The bountyman frowned, looking tired and wet and drunk and sick all at the same time.

Perfect time to reason with an irrational man.

When he doesn't know what end is up. Give him the top and tell him it's the bottom and he'll knock it all sideways eventually.

But through it all you'll have slipped the noose around his neck.

"What *are* you talking about?"

Aerlyn shaved herself another thin and refreshing slice of apple, pointing the shiny knife at her enemy.

"I'm talking about the one bounty that'll make you the richest and most famous man in the whole wide world, if not, just our broken-down little corner of it."

Ust pressed himself up, wiping the gutter runoff from his face with a sleeve that wasn't exactly dry. Aerlyn watched him carefully as he moped to a corner table, avoiding his own vomit as he walked.

"I'm listening."

"Good." Aerlyn chucked the apple core out the door and wiped her knife on her sleeve. "Because I'm talking about you riding up to Ullraye with news on the whereabouts of someone our Faer Princess would pay you handsomely to hear…and maybe even conscript a man of your services to hunt and capture."

The beady falcon eyes probed, but Aerlyn's alabaster face was unreadable, her midnight gaze soaked in mystery like the edge of the sea.

"You wouldn't be speaking of yourself?" The bountyman chided, his sarcasm weak against the rampant slaps of wind and rain.

"No." Aerlyn shook her head, stuffing the knife down her sleeve as she turned for the door. "Rhoswen of Kathron Caelie."

Ust shot up, wincing and reaching out for the edge of the table.

"Wait…she's alive?" Aerlyn was nearly out the door, gone again to the torrent. "Wait…okay, fine, what do I do?"

"Just what I said…" Aerlyn peered at him over her shoulder. "Go up to Faer Morgance and tell her you've seen Rhoswen and you know where to find her."

"That's it?"

"Yes…as soon as possible. As in, if you don't leave now, you won't be paid."

At the sound of the four letters *p-a-i-d*, Ewan Ust seemed to straighten and swallow his self-loathing and inebriation.

"Paid…what?"

"Your life, of course." Aerlyn turned from the door and watched his ugly face pale. No gold for the bountyman, just a chance to save his own damnable slaver's skin. "Oh, and Her Highness will ask you how you know it's her. She *is* Dominae Tenebris. Do be convincing, or it's your head in a basket. If you don't believe what you're saying, there's no way she will. She'll see right through you like a peddler's scarf. Tell her Rhoswen only has three fingers on her right hand." Aerlyn held up her own lithe and nimble hand and bent her ring finger down to her palm. "Cut off at the joint. Tell her that and watch her reaction. Tell her you've seen her in the pasture lands southwest of High Inverloch." Aerlyn peered out into the muddle of darkness. "If you ride like the wind and give her this message *exactly* as I have given it to you, you just *might* earn the right to live. Understand?"

Ewan Ust nodded once and then again, and grabbed his pouch of gold on the way out the door, pausing to stare at her once, for an interminably long second.

If it was to say sorry, or to promise revenge, Aerlyn could not tell.

But it took everything within her not to move, watching him like a cold and impassible statue as he ran, out into the night, to fetch his gray and white stallion and ride north to Ullraye like hell was on his heels.

Even though hell was not on his heels.

Just a woman, named The Thistle.

Robed in darkness, clothed in wind and rain.

RHOSWEN

CHAPTER 46

The spot was nothing irregular. Just a tuft of grass in and amongst the hill heather, swaying in the sighs of the wind like the lace of a woman's skirts. In fact, so simple and unimpressive was it that Rhoswen had to stare and the spot long and hard before finally giving the order to dig.

There was only so much time.

Sir Craig was at her side, Niles next to him, some forty other of her Chosen nearby on their horses. Niles complained about having to ride a horse in confidence to his mates but Rhoswen knew a proper cavalier attitude when she saw one, and with the scrawny black stallion beneath him, he looked every bit one of her Chosen.

Though she'd been wondering about that black eye that'd taken so long to heal.

Rhoswen squinted up at the low sun, scattering a harsh shine across the smothering blankets of the gray-white clouds, scratching at the rich hues of the highland hills like ill-spun wool.

The Army trickled and trudged to keep pace behind them, strung out along the valley that carved an invisible river through the massive fists of emerald. Around them, the shoulders and knees of the highlands buckled and twisted as if the earth itself was frozen in a struggle for redemption. Soon they'd be free of it all, this raw and

unexposed labyrinth of nature, this mindless maze of green without
a tree in sight.

How on earth Aerlyn O'Rye ever lasted out here by herself
was beyond Rhoswen. The forest? Yes, well, the forest was home to
plenty of dangers; wolves chief among them. Still, one could hide in
the forest.

But in the highlands? There was nowhere to hide, nowhere
to run to when the skies opened up and unleashed the wild fury of
the Four Storms. Nothing to save one from the tearing down of the
soul, from the brutal weathering of the mind, from the hopeless
isolation of being lost in a grandeur older than the language one
spoke, forged in mystery the common man would never unravel.

Rhoswen shivered to think of Aerlyn's darkest days,
bouncing gazes between the sun and the small tuft of grass stranded
amidst a sea of purple heather. Next to her, Sir Craig poured over a
map.

Rhoswen checked on the Army behind and the position of
the sun, guessing, since she couldn't see it, buried behind the
clouds, and looked over to Niles.

"You." She said, tersely. He snapped upright, fixing her
with his crooked smile.

"Yes, Your Highness?"

"Come here. I want to ask you something."

Niles wheeled his horse over. There were some one
hundred and fifty marked with the tattoo, only one hundred and
fifty out of two-thousand. But of them all, Niles Rodgers had
caught her eye and she kept him close at all times.

Close enough to hear his off-color jokes to the lads, close
enough to see him stare off into the sunset, some kind of longing
stuffed deep down in his heart.

"Where'd you get your black eye?" Rhoswen asked.

"It's not still there, is it?" Niles touched his cheek, half-
wincing.

Rhoswen smiled, thinly. His wince was not in pain, no, but
to think that his dashing young face had been ruined by something
as ugly.

"No, it's not. But don't think I didn't notice it for the week after we left the forest."

"So all those new followers?" He tipped his chin to the snaking line of humanity, nearly three-hundred of them added to their ranks, now, all trudging through the wet grass behind them. "They saw it too?"

Rhoswen shook her head at his vanity, running a hand through her mass of dark brown curls. He was speaking of the able bodied they'd met, passing by farms and small villages. Her name was all but dead in their hearts but to see her, ambling along upon a white horse with a brown star on its forehead, the sun straining through the gray haze to kiss the shine of her polished silver armor, well, that was reason enough to leave everything behind and follow her to brighter days.

Especially with winter falling upon them with the changing of the seasons.

In Albanland, especially travelling north, there were but two seasons, summer and winter. And harvest connected them. Spring was merely a prelude to the stifling heat, but winter, well, winter was longer than the other three seasons combined. Harsher than a cruel taskmaster with a bitter whip.

"There was hardly a young lass amongst our newest arrivals to care about your face as much as you do." Rhoswen smirked.

He took it in stride, sitting tall with a hand on the hilt of his sword. Hard to think he was sixteen, with the sort of confidence he had, and the daring attitude. Definitely the kind of man she wanted *after* the fight, the kind that would help rebuild a land that'd been torn apart. She would hate herself if he died in it, just before the victory had been won for the next generation. But his kind, the sort that couldn't say no to the impossible, how could she keep such a daredevil *from* the battlefield?

The poor bastard probably dreamed about it.

That's when he wasn't dreaming about whomever it was he'd taken a black eye for.

And she'd seen him fight in the Circle. Watched him chalk up twenty-seven duels straight. So who was good enough to give him such a nasty blow?

"Her Highness' concern for my face is noted." Niles bowed.

Rhoswen laughed quietly to herself, and watched four of her Chosen hoist a big, heavy oaken chest out of the earth.

Niles scratched his right ear, it seemed to poke out more than the left. A fly buzzed around the mane of his horse and he watched it carefully for a second and snatched it out of the air before rubbing the squish of it on his trousers, just below the knee.

"Must you know?" Niles asked, softly.

"I must."

Niles shrugged.

"It was my brother, Nevan."

"Your elder?"

"Yes, Your Highness."

"And were either of you drunk at the time?"

"Umm…one of us was."

Rhoswen could bet which.

"And you were fighting over a girl?"

"…Yes, Your Highness."

"Does she have a name?"

Niles stared at the dirty chest, hoping its discovery would distract Rhoswen.

But *nothing* distracted the Crown Heir. Her senses were attuned in the extreme, her ability to *focus* chief among them.

And those eyes of hers, they were hard for him to look at directly. It was as if he felt himself shrink in her gaze, though he was so much taller than her.

"I would rather not shame her with our foolishness."

Rhoswen clucked her tongue, her beautiful horse perking up from searching for clover. She wheeled him around, guiding him toward the spread of heather.

"Quite the opposite, Niles, she should be so happy that two fine young lads would have her affection."

Niles urged his own scrawny black stallion to follow.

"Well then…it was the gypsy, Miss Finleigh of Baraburr."

Rhoswen laughed, the kind of laugh that all but filled the scooped out hollows of the highlands, bouncing off the low swirl of the clouds as she tipped her chin back.

"Ah, yes, such beguiling eyes, my little España wildflower." Rhoswen tipped her shoulder, flashing her own almond-shaped colors across the folds of her mossy green cloak just like Finleigh would've in a perfect impression, making Niles turn away with a flash of blush. "And the way she rolls her shoulders when she gets excited…" Rhoswen laughed again, a smaller bubble, trailing off like a brook, losing its way in the forest. "Yes, she is a delightful young woman. I am quite fond of her myself. That's why I sent her away, you know. She is a special girl, and she deserves a special task."

Rhoswen shook her head, thinking of how big those dark eyes could swell, and how warm her caramel colored hands were to grip. What it was like to be so free, so full of Solara's shining rays? Never in her life had she known the levity young Finleigh walked the earth with. Even as a child, her eye for Ultan had been that of partnership, their wishes to one day rule Albanland interspersed with chasing glittering butterflies, tickling loch trout till their fingers froze in the ice blue water, or playing hide-and-go seek in the weeping wings of the forest.

But always coming again to the knowledge, just as Solara shined upon the day and Luna glowed across the night, they would one day sit the High Throne of Albanland and rule, hand in hand.

"Finleigh's the kind of girl worth fighting over." Niles admitted as they drew near the buried chest.

"Worth fighting *for*." Rhoswen corrected. "There's a difference."

One of her Chosen mopped his brow and the other swiped at the thick lock clamping the chest shut. Three good hacks and he split the lock. Rhoswen dismounted as they opened the chest and a brief inhale of surprise caught her.

The riches. Even in the arms of Ullraye, growing up in the court, she had not seen such beauty. Gems of every shape and size, rings and bangles of gold and hammered silver pendants.

Either my parents were modest, or they were poor…or are these all Angle treasures?

"All this was stolen…by one woman?" Sir Craig called out, behind her, his eyes darting back to the map that stated there were four more chests of equal wealth scattered around the highlands.

Rhoswen reached down to select a bird's heart ruby the size of her own tiny palm. Cabochon cut, simply exquisite. Nearly irrational. What would one do with a ruby so large?

It seemed to glow, resonating in the heat of her hand, colored with a dream of its own, speaking to her a great many promises.

If she could just make it to the battlefield.

And win.

"Yes, she did." Rhoswen held the ruby tight before slipping it into a saddle bag. "One piece at a time. And with all of this wealth we're going to steal the hearts and minds of our people back by making sure everyone gets a fair share. Everything we take from those who will not follow us, we pay for, but heaven help them if they won't swear fealty to me once the crown is on my head. But until this land belongs to me, and I to it, before I sit on the Stone of Destiny and take the sacred oath, I'll walk this land a saint paying for the atonement of a great many sins."

And with that, Rhoswen ordered the Chosen to dole out the treasures quietly as they made camp in the rifted valley of the highland's bitter embrace.

Hoping to heaven, as she did, that riches would not ruin her people as it had the Angles and those of the south, who, unless pledging fealty and making restitution for their crimes of slavery and treason, would all perish by the sword of Albanland's own Crown Heir one by one by one.

FINLEIGH

CHAPTER 47

Above and beyond, spread across the flat farmlands squished in between the highlands and the sea, the sky was a dream of clotted cream and drizzled brandy, brightly burning amber in the dusk as Solara sought refuge behind the massive hills.

Finleigh looked to the sea, smelling it, though it was distant. Her dark and sparkly eyes were all but glazed over to sit sit sit in the rickety wagon day after day, manned as it were by a thin-lipped olive-eyed man with a salt-and pepper beard and camel teeth, as the wagon squeaked and trundled up the winding road to Ullraye. Her thoughts, on these long days bound to the hard wagon bench, were spent on those she'd come to love being around so much as they marched their way to an empty battlefield some hundreds of miles away.

To their deaths.

Yes, she'd seen the future, or part of it...a version of it.

And Rhoswen knew it.

But it was the gamble, Rhoswen had said, the fact that the future Finleigh had seen could be *a* future, not necessarily *the* future, set in stone, like the eerie white markers circling *Hafnröth*, and Rhoswen would meet that battlefield, the sword she was, to write the future Albanland needed.

Or die trying.

Next to her, Quill walked a kind-eyed donkey with long lashes, happy to carry all of his belongings, his books and such, until it was time to sleep. The donkey, named Fane, then found a suitable spot to doze, and once the morning came, and with it the time for the journey to continue, Fane just about made herself a stone carving, refusing to leave camp.

That was until Quill started walking. Then she followed him as if he was responsible for Solara's light. No coercing needed. If he stopped, she stopped, making it for tough going, since Quill was in charge of the wagon and all it held, from Rhoswen's secret mission up to Ullraye involving the young gypsy and the elder next to her who could pass for one, given the right clothing, as well as all the supplies they carried and the children stuffed in the back with their blue-eyed teacher.

Finleigh found Quill to be nicer than a cool drink on a hot day, but she didn't get to speak with him much. Quill's attention was oft given to the children, sometimes as loud and as hard to pen in as a pack of wild sheep in the back of wagon. So many times he'd paused their conversation with an apology, left for ten or twenty minutes, the span of which Finleigh spent staring at the sky, only to return and pick up the exact place he'd left off, even though Finleigh had forgotten what they'd been talking about. Other times, when Finleigh wished to talk with him, bored by the travelling, she could see him talking with the teacher, the blonde's luminous blue eyes heavy as spending all day with the children had taken its toll. Recently the teacher had been having dreams about a raven and wanted to talk to Quill about what those dreams meant.

And after a long day of wrangling the kids and finally putting them to rest in the wagon with a quick and extra sleepy tune, Quill wearily drank the enchanting dance of sun and sky as dusk lazily swept across the earth.

"Quill." Finleigh said. "Do you mind if I ask you about Faer Morgance?"

"No," He said, always having time for everyone, even if he could barely keep himself upright. "What would you like to know?"

"Well...first off, is the Faer real? I mean..."

"Rhoswen told me."

Finleigh turned to him so quickly her hair whipped the wagon driver, slapping jet black strands across his cheek, to which he said nothing and simply scooted his bony frame further away, manning the reins with the focus of a fisherman waiting for a bite on the line.

"About…"

"About you being able to see the future. She believes it, and I do too. That's one of the reasons why we have to take you to *Hafnröth*."

"What's that mean?"

Quill inhaled deeply and sighed it out, the dusk coloring his skin with an autumnal glaze.

"You in for a bit of a history lesson?"

"Will it be told with as much flair as your stories?"

Quill stroked his short red beard.

"…Nnnno."

"Okay." Finleigh shrugged. "Forget it, then. Tell me about a bastard prince who gets defeated in a duel by the long-lost brother of the prince's betrothed."

"I…"

"Or…like something with fantastic beasts that fly and breath fire and a little gypsy with black eyes who fights them all off with a cast-iron skillet!"

Quill laughed, loudly as usual, only cupping a hand over his mouth as to not wake the children. Finleigh frowned at him as he pulled his hand back, caught in a memory, somehow, as if the action of cupping his mouth had unnerved him.

He stared at his own hand, mystified.

"The history." She said, and when he didn't seem to hear, she leaned over, nearly falling out of the wagon to tap him on one of his broad shoulders.

"Quill! Hey! I want my history."

"Oh, yes…well." Quill swallowed and shook his hand out, as if it'd fallen asleep. His voice deepened, and his eyes found a spot on the horizon, glowing beautiful and warm. "All that is and was and will be was once nothing-nothing but the silence of an unborn night. Silence of death, silence darkness, silence everywhere and the endlessness thereof. Across this hush stretched the wind, and in it the whisper of a voice, like a seed in the soil, that of the Word That Knows No End, spoken by Life Everlasting, The Great Fountain of Fire, The Unnamed Heart, The Blood of the Ages, and on and on, as the names go."

Finleigh's shiny eyes stretched wide and her hands were buried in her lap. She all but forgot about the wagon driver next to her, and how he smelled strongly of pungent garlic and Angle blue rot cheese.

"And there are those that believe that we, so far down the line from our ancestors, can still reach out to that spark of…indefinable material that lives in all of nature. Well, all that which does not have a mind of its own, I should say. All that we can see, brimming with that spark which refuses to die, in the beauty of life as it struggles with death. So…in the days long before Albanland *was* Albanland, there were a people who made it their life's work to know *how* to do just that, for the sake of others. Or so they say. They were known as the Faer."

Finleigh swallowed gently, feeling a chill as he spoke. Yet there was no wind.

"Were they beautiful?" Her voice was quiet, though her eyes couldn't have been larger.

"That's one mark *for* Morgance." Quill stared into the amber sea of the sky, clouds breaking like cold waves of darkness. "She certainly *looks* like a Faer." He continued before Finleigh could ask. "Yes, so beautiful they were there was much division between them and everybody else." Quill coughed into his hand, no longer staring at the horizon, but the ground. "Anyway, I could tell you this story all the way to Ullraye and wouldn't hit the half of it." A small sourness seemed to seep in, as if he'd said something he didn't want to remember. "What you have to know is that a true Faer can control forces of nature, all that contains that undying spark of creation. Like…the weather. They can also…*manipulate* certain things."

"Control and manipulate? There's a difference?"

"Oh yes, very much so."

"What kinds of things?"

"Well, more things in nature. A Faer could walk through a forest and keep the fruit from falling in harvest. Or turn all the flowers of a meadow white. Faer are so fond of the color. But also, umm…human things. You know, thoughts and whatnot. Strangely, just like the weather. They can turn someone's thoughts to storm. Or freeze them. Or make them so hot one would feel like they're on fire."

"Is that where her other names come in?"

Quill smiled, showing one of his missing teeth as he combed his light brown hair to tuck it behind his slanted, nearly elfin ears.

"You know much of her, don't you?"

"Only what I've heard!" Finleigh pulled back, defensively, adding. "And young gypsies don't have much to talk about, sometimes."

Quill waved his hand.

"You can do no harm talking about her. She *is* the ruler of this land. I just didn't know you were so interested in her. Most everyone is scared of her. Which name would you be thinking of?"

Finleigh bit her lip, but something about Quill's easy nature made her feel less of a shiver when she spoke the name she'd always wondered about, as if there was a jolt that ran through her just to think about it.

"Dominae Tenebris."

Quill nodded, stroking his beard. Perhaps wondering where she'd heard the name. But, like anyone who heard, it had a pull over her, one she couldn't fight thinking about.

"It means Lady Darkness."

"Sinister." Finleigh mocked, though she scooted closer to Quill. With his height, they were nearly eye to eye, though she still looked down upon him.

Quill laughed quietly.

"As sinister as a shadow puppet. You know the tongue?"

"No. It's not common."

"Correct. It's the Haunted Tongue. The original spoken language of this land. It's not a written language, though, so it died quickly. To speak certain words in it can bring about powerful curses. Or so they say."

"Do you know it?"

"Yes, of course."

Finleigh flashed him her cunning smile, the kind that could open a locked door with one glance.

"Do you know everything?"

"Only when speaking to inquisitive gypsies."

Finleigh rolled her eyes.

"And *Hafnröth*, you were going to tell me of how it ties in to all this and why I need to go there with my…abilities."

Quill scratched Fane behind one of her ears and the donkey leaned into him, to which he wrapped his arm around her neck for a patting hug.

"Let's just say the early inhabitants of this land, those *before* the Faer, knew of the laws and rules of nature in a way we can only imagine. Of the stars and the sea and the sun and the sky…and all things beneath…they knew these things like we know how to eat, drink and sleep. And *Hafnröth* was a connecting point between two worlds. Not a physical place, like a door, but more or less a vessel of something intransigent."

Finleigh frowned as if inhaling a bad smell.

"Inawhat?"

"Obdurate."

She shook her head, again whipping the wagon driver with her long black hair. He scooted over, practically falling off the wagon with a sigh.

"I still don't know what you mean."

"Stubborn." Quill chuckled. "Like Fane the donkey."

"Oh, gotcha!"

"Yeah, so imagine *Hafnröth* is actually like a lake of something invisible that won't come into this realm we live in unless someone can…more or less, translate it. It's like a color, up here in this sky, but we can't see it. It's there, it's always been there, and it will always be there. But right now, we just can't *see* it. *Hafnröth* is the place where these two worlds mesh and mingle. It's the place where, if you're able, you *can* see it. You can see so much it makes your eyes hurt."

"But what *is* it?"

Quill coughed into his hand again, and Finleigh noticed the dark circles under his eyes. How long had it been since he last slept a night through?

"It's a mound of grass that never dies covering a small, empty cave. Surrounding the mound are stones, white magnus stones, balanced in push and pull so that if you were to stand next to one and toss a coin in the air, you'd watch it fly to the center of two stones and hover there, as if by magic, when in truth it's just a physical rule of the earth. A natural phenomenon of perfect balance the original constructors knew was necessary to connect the two worlds. But what are they connecting? What is this vessel holding? Well, the answer's in the name." Quill coughed again, so much talking making his voice tremble with weakness, but he continued. "Translated from the Haunted Tongue, *Hafnröth* means *Vault of Dreams.*"

It made sense. Finleigh let her gaze drift to the sky where the last remnants of light were holding on to the spread of the steely clouds, as if drowning in darkness. To hear all this scared Finleigh, deep within. Her thoughts turned to Morgance, as if Morgance was responsible for the coming of darkness, even though it happened every day.

The mound, she'd seen it, in her dream, the one that wouldn't leave her alone each and every Solstice. The mound and the white stones. And those people, three of them, two women and a man.

One of them was Morgance, wasn't it? It had to be, ruling the skies and the sea with her ancient powers.

If she even had any. But they were real, weren't they?

And the dread. That's what told her they *had* to be real. Dread soaking her skin like rainwater.

And the wind? She'd dreamed it'd been so windy, the scene buried in the blackest depths of night, lost in the funnel of a storm for the ages.

Finleigh spoke, her nerves tightening her throat. Regardless, Quill would know. She felt that, of anyone, he could help. Everything he said she took to be true. And even if it wasn't, there was something about him she knew she could trust. Even though she was a loyal, trusting person by nature, her trust had been forever abused by her own people.

"And so...I can see into *Hafnröth*? That's how I know?"

"I would think so." He nodded, gravely. "But we'll see. It's very close to Ullraye. I'll take you there after we're in place to assist The Thistle."

Finleigh hunched in the seat, combing her hair behind her ears.

"I'm scared, Quill."

"Why?"

"I'm scared of Morgance and this ancient... hafnerooth thing. I don't want to see the future!"

"Morgance is nothing to be afraid of."

"How do you know? Do you know her personally? Do you know what she might do to me if she finds out?"

Quill didn't answer directly, but instead, reached up to place a hand on her shoulder.

"What you're seeing is like the sky, Finleigh. It's just so big and dark and overwhelming. And Solara, all that hope, all that brightness, all that joy that you are, you're just letting that slide away. I'll be there with you. I'll hold your hand if you need me to. But don't for one second regret that you are something special. Don't fight being different. For whatever reason, there's a connection between you and this ancient place. Whether people believe you or not doesn't matter as long as *you* believe. After all, you're here, aren't you? And we'll be there soon. Just hold onto that."

Finleigh pushed out an exasperated sigh and stared at the man, a thought falling from her mouth.

"And you, what do you hold onto? Seeing Aerlyn again?"

Quill paled.

"Am I that transparent?"

"I *can* see the future."

"You can also take a damn good guess, along with the rest of us."

Finleigh curled a lock of silky black hair in her finger. "...Well?"

Quill straightened and rolled his neck, his blue eyes small in his face. He looked so tired, as if any moment he would just pull off the road and fall over like a thick tree trunk in a strong breeze.

When he did speak, his voice was soft, barely audible over the squeak of the wagon axels and the clip clop of horses hooves in the squelching mud.

"Yes, Finleigh, with all my heart I want to see Aerlyn again, and I know that she's giving up all of her stolen treasure to fund Rhoswen's uprising. But every woman has a treasure buried deep within their heart...even a woman who's had as hard of a life as The Thistle...who's been hurt the way she has. And just before she left, she let me know it wasn't all tarnished, trampled, and ruined, that it was still pure and perfect." Quill wiped an eye and sniffed, peering to the last of the sunset. "I got the feeling that *I* was the one responsible for bringing that out of her. But it was just a flash, you know? Just a moment. I guess that's all it takes sometimes. And you know me, with the way I take care of these kids, and the way I look after young women like you and our esteemed teacher...well...let's just say I'm not so quick to love someone that way because I love everyone around me so much the other way."

Finleigh felt a gnawing ache down in her belly as he looked her in the eyes, a glossy shine making them out to be small blue pools of loch water.

"I'm your brother, Finleigh, I'm brother to every woman who needs me to be. To those children I'm father but when they grow up I'll be brother to them too. That's what Albanland is...or what it should be, maybe what it used to be, when the Clans were rich in story and song, hearthfires towering higher than the highlands themselves, harvests reaping in excess so that no man could starve. Freely given, freely received. That's...my dream, you know. That's why Rhoswen takes such good care of me. She knows when the fighting's over the healing times will come. The rebuilding. And that's where I come in. Uilleam of Blackmoor, brother to the brotherless." Finliegh watched as Quill squinted in pain, perhaps equal parts of the strain of his own eyes, mixed to think about those of whom he spoke. "How many young southern women, slaves to Angle masters, will want to ever see another man's face again? Perhaps they could take comfort in mine, knowing all I can give them is an honest song and a promise that I'll be there for them. I'll be there if they need someone to shout at. I'll be there if they need someone to hug. Someone to make them forget the way they were with nothing more than a smile that says *you are who you are and who you are is not broken but beautiful and rebuilt to be stronger than the steel that won your freedom in blood.* And let's not forget the mothers who've lost their sons. *You remind me of him,* they'll say. *My young lad had blue eyes like yours.* Or, *he played the mandolin, too. Heavens do I miss the boy. He was my sunshine.*" Quill rubbed the back of his neck. "Don't you see, Finliegh? If anything I'm afraid of Aerlyn and everything she stirred within me. Even though it wasn't more than a month, I could scarely think about anything else *but* her. Just the two of us, out on the shore of the hidden loch. Time slowed when I was with her, as if, for once, everything else in my mind vanished. It felt so amazing. Like I lost weight. But when she left, the weight fell back on me. A yoke of it, tightened around my neck." Quill shrugged. "I may be wrong but I feel like there's a love you can give everyone else. But then there's a love you can only give one person. It's like the dance of the fire or the foam of a rushing river. It's a power beyond you, all consuming. It's that...*magic* they call the Faer. But then, it's not that at all. It's something much simpler. Something that you...can't really analyze because it just makes sense."

It was then Finliegh hopped down from the wagon to walk with him, standing close enough to see the stain of tears streak his cheeks. Shoulder to shoulder, she could see the sickly shine of his skin, the bloody veins shooting his eyes with pain.

"I have a duty to my people, Finliegh. My love is to be all things to them, but namely, a brother to those who have none. I've even drafted a document I hope Rhoswen will pass once the Crown is actually hers, even if all in the land will not honor her rule straightaway. It's like the hills and the sea. It's just something that needs to be, something right and true. If anything happens to me, you won't forget, will you?"

Finleigh sucked in a sharp breath of chilly air. Around her, darkness reigned, like Solara had been stolen from them by the deft hand of Faer Morgance.

Finleigh shivered.

At the thought of Morgance' power, at the thought of something bad happening to Quill. At the realization of how small she felt, *not special*, but tiny and insignificant next to the sea and the hills and the looming dread of her dreams.

But young Finleigh smiled and stood on her tiptoes to give Quill a peck on the cheek.

"No my brother, I will *never* forget."

ULTAN

CHAPTER 48

It was the evening of Ultan's third day with the Nørd warriors, hidden in the cleft of a cave on the shores just south of Ullraye, when Eyvind Frey finally approached the sullen Champion, still afraid of his battle rage.

Even though Ultan looked whittled down, like a tree stripped by the wilds of winter; green eyes dark and morose, hulking shoulders sunken and hollow to bear the snow white fox cape that was his mark of honor as if it were sewn in stone. The swollen muscles of his bare arms were flushed red against the cold of the sea, all heat gone so quickly with the passing of Solstice.

Three days with the Nørd. Three days and not a bite of food.

Smoky cook fires spread a haze across the rocky shore. Talk and laughter died against the lap and slosh of the waves. Stuck in the cave, their dragon-boats gone back to Nørd, the six hundred warriors patiently awaited orders from their King.

Even when their King was biding his time in issuing them due to the silence of his fractured new alliance.

"Here." The King of Nørd handed Ultan a plank of salmon. The Champion eyed the wholesome meal, as if it were poison, though the rich smell of its healthy fats made his stomach growl. And the fish itself, yes, it was a good memory, always. Capable of making him feel whole and complete, strong and clear-minded, like a tonic.

But Ultan shook his head and returned again to his melancholy gazing upon the sea.

"Okay then, more for me."

Frey sat down next to his very distant relative and sighed, picking into the freshly cooked salmon, steam still rising from its charred skin. Strange they shared so many features yet still appeared so different. Like walking gait, for instance. Ultan carried himself with a springy lightness for his size, and the earth seemed to creak and groan, cowering wherever Frey chose to tread.

But it was their eyes, mainly. Ultan's hues of highland hills still held some semblance of innocence, despite the blood they'd seen run like rivers to the sea; whereas Eyvind Frey's dark blue colors always slid in his sockets with a crafty glaze, as if soundlessly seeking some foothold on the land his father never could win by strength, the need to possess it rippling through him like the surface of a loch guarding a deadly beast from long ago.

"What are we going to do now?" The King asked plainly.

Ultan's gaze fell to his hands, hands that could cleave a line of men with one swipe, severing flesh and bone in the blink of an eye.

Why then did they burn to never pick up a sword again, let alone the giant Blade of the Champion? Why did they seem to be too heavy to lift, the kiss of Faer Morgance' ruby lips still fizzling his spine with a gooey warmth that made him feel anything *but* a man that other men feared.

"You know..." Frey said quietly amidst thoughtful chews, "We can't go on like this. This has to end."

Ultan snapped his neck to glare at the man.

As if that was all there was to it.

Frey continued chewing slowly, feeling the intensity of Ultan's gaze nearly cook his own skin like the salmon's.

Charred.

Black.

"We all die sometime." The King said, as if it didn't really matter how or when, because it was merely the way of things, unchangeable and constant, like Solara and Luna chasing each other's presence.

Picking a tender piece near the spine, Eyvind Frey held it out for Ultan.

"And if you leave this land with that pretty little deceiver you'll leave a coward. It's no choice to me. I don't care how beautiful she is. When you won our duel you did so because you're the only man who can win the Crown. To leave now would be to make a mockery of yourself and everything you've done for the past four years."

Ultan stared at the pink flesh, its juicy flakes, dusted with salt. The words ringing true. Truer that her words.

When Ultan finally spoke, his mouth was dry, but it watered for the nourishment of the fish.

If he was ever going to yield to Morgance' desires, it should've been long ago, and whatever promises her touch sparked within would've been his. But the road he was on, dark as it was, was the only path he'd ever taken, the only one he'd ever *wanted* to take. It was too late to change. Even though the heat of her nearness still lingered like the strongest whiskey, her yearning an indelible print in his mind, echoing throughout his skin and bones.

And his diet for the past three days had been her kisses.

Rushing through his soul like rainwater upon a dry riverbed.

There was no going to her now. To go to her was to leave his kin, even though most of the Clans had been the ones to abandon *him*, and those who hadn't still didn't acknowledge his place in Lordship, faulting his mixed heritage.

Nevertheless the words fell from his mouth.

"You're right, King of Nørd. You know what it's like to watch your Kingdom fall apart. Whatever it takes, I refuse to do the same. Even though it might be the death of me."

Frey hid a smile as Ultan took the salmon and stretched back across the rocks, groaning as he did.

It'd been a long fight. Four years of never staying in one place. And when he finally did, it was Ullraye, with Morgance panting for him like a hungry wolf walking in between the trees, her need for him as unquenchable as his own need for rest.

The kind of rest that he dreamed of.

And for the last year, he'd been stuck in Ullraye's confines as the Nørd sought to break him, only to find fire could not be broken.

Burned out? Washed away? Yes.

But never broken.

"Thank you for this." Ultan said, tasting every bite as if eating salmon for the first time.

After all, if it could be done, the time of peace would finally be upon them all.

Peace or death.

Up above, somewhere beyond the haze, the stars were all shining, as they did, unconsciously bright and brilliant and perfect. They did not care for the lowly plans of men, either haughty or humble, but impartially scattered their light to be seen by all.

"My pleasure, Skölhammer. I just don't want to see you do the same when peace is so close at hand for *both* of us. I know you're as tired of burying bodies as I am. The only reason I'm here with you now is to secure my *own* borders from Angle lust. Today, Albanland. Tomorrow, the world. My spies have seen their shipwright guilds and tell me unspeakable things of what they build there. Ships that could squash our own dragon-boats like spiders. Concepts of floating palaces built to sail to the edge of the horizon and back." Frey's eyes darkened as he reached for a skin of water. "Trust me, Skölhammer. If you don't fight now, you won't last the winter, and neither will we. And if our end is not this year, then it sure as hell will be the next."

"Then what do I do?" Ultan sat up, snorting in clean sea air. "I can't wait for them to come to me, and I can't go back to Morgance. Bandon's assumed captaincy of the guard, like her little pet on a leash. Most all those men would fight for me, but a few would remain with him. If I get them a message, and tell them where we'll be, we could add maybe another two hundred experienced men."

"Sounds promising." Frey took more salmon for himself, segmenting a chunk for Ultan. "But these rogue Clans of yours, how many are we talking about?"

Ultan ate silently, making calculations.

"Anywhere from…four to five thousand."

"Oh boy…" Frey took a squeeze of the water bag and passed it to Ultan, who did the same. "Well then, it was nice knowing you."

Ultan frowned but caught the humor wrinkling Frey's much older looking eyes.

His words joggled an idea in Ultan's mind.

"That's it. That's the answer."

"What?"

"A duel."

"Against whom?"

"Lord Arturo of Pallantyne, the Wolf of Westwood Hollow, Overseer of the Midland Townships…mind you, not the kind of *wolf* you Nørds perceive me to be…the other kind."

"A lech? A rake?"

"Incurably."

"Sounds like a well-bred bastard." Frey occupied himself with some of the crispy skin, crunching it as he talked. "Perhaps good-looking, too. Not a hair out of place. He may have distant Fränk blood. Is he any good?"

"He certainly has spent a great deal of his time in the Swordsman's Circle."

"Oh really? How's the rest of his time spent?"

"Trying to get into Morgance' bed."

"Ah yes…my kind of soul. Well, then he won't back down to a challenge from his rival."

Ultan reached over and picked out a tender portion of fish near the gills.

"I know just the place. And if we leave tonight, I'm sure we can make it right about the time he shows up with another five to ten thousand Angles and their mounts and war machines."

The way he said it made it seem so obviously laughable, yet the slightest bit *possible*. As if embracing the ridiculous and extreme was the only way out of the corner they were in.

It was then Frey smiled at Ultan in a way that made Ultan nervous.

The bear, again, was returning to his hulking form. Something about the impossible appealed to him, as if he was addicted to the challenge.

"Well then, Skölhammer." The King's smile was wide and slightly insane in the colors of evening. "I'll see you in Valhöll."

MORGANCE

CHAPTER 49

The wind tousled the curtains hanging heavy along the stone walls, whistling through her ears with a hollow, piercing quality, wrapping chilling fingers around her body as she bathed.

The water, far from hot, was scented with the last of the imported jasmine, and Morgance relished the chance to soak in its scented embrace as the cold breath of the wind stirred and wafted its beauty throughout the drafty room.

In the end, all she could do was sit in the tub, near comatose, staring at the rafters of her chambers. Drifting, drifting, drifting into thought so blank, in the end, she was thinking nothing at all.

Because, what did the Rook's Table deal to those who lost?

The door. Empty pockets. See you later. Bad chance. So sorry. Maybe next time.

Part of her wanted to sing, even just a sad melody to herself for what semblance of comfort it might've held, but she couldn't bring herself to. Even in dragging Ultan back from death's doorstep, her songs had been more for her *own* comfort than his. Just a tonic so that she wouldn't fall apart at the seams, to see his dark blood, spilling into the soil, his skin all scraped and scared, bones broken…to keep herself together, a young woman who'd never known the love of a man, let alone the one she craved.

Unreasonably beautiful, and yet, still, *so* alone.

There was a knock on her door, and without thinking, Morgance called out *enter*, thinking it was one of the chamber maids to bring a hot pitcher of water from the kitchen.

It wasn't.

It was Lord Bandon of Tavish.

He nearly stumbled in the low-lit room, exhausted and worn ragged, failing to notice she was actually *in* the tub till he was halfway in the room, as if driven blind by sleeplessness.

The small mouth of his long face sagged, eyes blinking rapidly, burning beneath disheveled brown hair.

"Yes?" Morgance asked, failing to move, or be stirred in any way, though there was the hint of a thought beckoning her a curling finger, like the first ghost of smoke from a freshly lit fire.

"Um...Your Highness." Bandon remembered manners and bowed with a snap of his heels, eyes fixed on the floor, skin flushing.

Manners never *were* his forte.

"Speak."

"There's some...umm...gypsies in the compound. Singing and dancing. Lots of kids with them...should I feed them or send them away?"

Morgance arched an eyebrow and brought her hands together, clasped over her chest, sinking down in the tub so her knees poked out. Clarity spread across what ethereally elegant features despair and despondency had tried to make ashen and weak, but in the end, just waxed mysterious and distant, and Morgance sifted through several thoughts before speaking, quite aware of the voice tugging at Bandon, standing there, forcing himself not to stare.

Really Bandon, what's the harm? You raise dogs, don't you? You know how it all works.

But you're afraid of me. You're afraid of Ultan and Arturo and every single old and crusted-over Lord in the Chamber who's left you for dead in this empty Fortress for a brighter future with a new deck of traitors.

Hell, you're afraid of your own bloody shadow.

Fifty thousand men in on this cursed rock and I have to be surrounded by a pack of mewling whelps.

You couldn't take me to my bed if someone paid you all the gold in the world. Your heart would beat itself to death by the time you reached this tub.

But I wouldn't stop you now if you tried.

It was then Morgance said nothing, but stared at young and ruggedly handsome Bandon, with the fixation of a sunbeam, until he met her eyes.

And then looked away, backing up a step, half-out the door.

Too bad you don't have the guts to take what you want. Does anybody but me? ANYBODY? Am I the only one that can stare the Storm in the eye and wrestle it to the ground and make it my own weapon?

After all, this bloody Crown wasn't given to me.

I stole it.

Morgance scoffed, rubbing her forehead.

"No, let them stay. I'm sure the guards are enjoying hearing their fortunes and watching...charades of giraffes and lions from the desert Kingdoms, guessing at animals they know nothing of."

Morgance shook her head to herself.

Pansy.

But yet, he stayed.

She eyed him expectantly, white-gold hair darkened with jasmine water, clinging to her forehead, begging to be swept aside by a man's touch.

"There's one more thing." His voice trembled.

Morgance let her eyebrows slide higher. The man was simply infuriating.

"Aaaaand?"

"There's a...um...a bountyman here to see you."

"What's his name?"

Bandon frowned.

"How did you know it was a he?"

"You said bounty *man*, didn't you? Now get on with it."

Bandon stammered, rubbing his chin. He was highly distracted and doing a poor job of hiding it. Apparently he'd never seen a woman without yards of fabric before...even though he couldn't see much of Faer Morgance. Perhaps it was merely the thought that was turning his mind to squash.

"Right, yes…a boutyman by the name of er…Ewan Ust. He caught a thief accused of murder."

"Does the thief have a name?"

"Oh…I'm not sure, Your Highness, but she *is* the one that goes by *The Thistle*."

Morgance sat up, exposing more of herself than Bandon could handle, and he coughed in his hand, as it stabbed by lightning.

"The Thistle is here? Finally caught?"

"Yes, Your Majestic, I mean, Your…"

"In the dungeon?"

"Yes, but…"

Morgance threw herself from the bath with a splash, rushing to gather her clothes. Not the most ornate of dresses, but something warm and comfortable, of the highest quality. Something soft and durable…Morgance thrashed through her wardrobe, bare skin dripping pearl beads of liquid.

She nearly forgot Bandon standing there. No longer flushed, he now looked sick, as if he was going to fall face first on the stone floor.

"That will be all, Bandon, thank you for telling me."

"There's one more thing." He said, watching her pull on her boots, wondering why she did before she…

And then she strode the distance to stand before him with her back to him, flicking her wet hair aside in a practiced gesture.

"Button me up, please."

Bandon's fingers trembled at first but he focused on what he'd come to say, never the best speaker in the Chamber of Lords as it were, always getting stomped on by the deep velveteen tones of Lord Arturo of Pallantyne. So much like the dress Morgance had chosen, dark and soft and brown but rich, so unattainably fine. Everything Bandon was not, forever in the shadow of Arturo and the wolfish smile that made every Lady in sight weak-kneed and restless.

"The bountyman…" Bandon fumbled a button.

"Ewan Ust."

"Yes, Ewan Ust has information he says you'll be dying to hear. He requests a private audience."

Morgance twitched a blink as she cast a look over her shoulder at him.

"Really?"

"Yes."

The buttoning was finished but his hand lingered on the last one. Bandon's nostrils flared to inhale the jasmine. He'd never smelt it before. It had a paralyzing effect, like a sunset of every color imaginable, particularly the dusky fruits of near midnight, as if the color of the sky had been powdered to cling to her luminous skin.

"Did he say what *kind* of information?" Morgance gathered her hair in both hands, over her right shoulder, pursing ruby lips to think.

"No...just...well, you know, for your ears only."

She turned to him, hands on her hips, biting back a snarl. There would be no reason to ask for his opinion. He was clearly still a child captured inside of a lean and athletic body. Immature to the ways of the world, to the veins of the Crown and the shadows it cast upon the land. She wanted desperately to see The Thistle, having heard so much about her *on top of* what'd happened in Brachin, to see what kind of woman could stir up enough legends to rival her own, but, if the information had anything to do with the sudden disappearance of Ultan, well then, she was all ears.

And Bandon? Well...he was like the dogs he raised.

Neutered.

"Okay." She sighed, patting him on the cheek twice. "Thanks. See what you can do about getting some dinner sent to the Chamber of Lords? I'll be in there. Some leek and potato soup and milkbread would be nice. Oh, and some blackberry jam, if we still have any."

And with that, Faer Morgance whisked away through the door, leaving Bandon stunned in a wash of jasmine and images that would plague his dreams for the rest of his life.

Least of all the imprint of her hand, burning on his skin.

CHAPTER 50

    The wind, agitated and turbulent, raging another uneventful evening to a close, tugged at the hem of her brown velvet dress as she walked the exposed causeway to the Chamber of Lords, and she pulled at cuffs of her black sleeves and adjusted the white lace of her bodice to compensate for the harsh bite of the salty sea.

    But in truth, she loved the wind.

    It made her feel alive.

    And before rushing into the relative warmth of the maple-paneled Chamber of Lords for the breadth of its oaken tables and cushioned chairs, its wealth of pewter sconces and memories, Morgance stopped for a quiet moment to survey the courtyard below.

    A tall man in the flowy, nearly feminine white tunic of a minstrel strummed a lively melody on a mandolin, while an exotic young gypsy, España, by the look of her rich skin and captivating eyes that twinkled with each and every twist and turn, danced a quick series of steps, every kick of her leg accented with a clap, a clap, and then a double clap.

    Morgance' yellow-green gaze drifted across the fire barrels to the rickety wagon they'd come in, surprised it didn't crash to the mud, sagging on rotting axels and wobbly wheels. Near the wagon a scruffy donkey hung its head, dozy-eyed and lethargic, staring at the two entertainers, as if either patiently waiting for its turn of attention, or trying to figure out in its donkey mind what the humans were up to, and why they were enjoying their apparent foolery with such gusto, while a gristly man with a graying beard doled out bread from a long and chewy loaf to a collection of dirty-faced children, sitting in a semi-circle to the left of the man and woman entertainers.

What a simple life those poor folks have. Morgance thought. *Not a bad life. Just a simple one.*

My life hasn't been simple since heaven knows when.

If ever.

Actually, no…never.

The life of the Faer is not simple. It comes at a great cost.

Her thoughts suddenly turned sour as the wind seemed eager to puff her skirts and toss her over the wall. Simple was what she wanted, once, before the thought of being a royal princess became too irresistible to dream about.

And destiny, well, it was a strange thing sometimes.

She was enjoying her soup and bread when Ewan Ust entered the Chamber of Lords with a stilted cadence, as if he had a limp. Morgance squinted at him, an ugly man to say the least, in that his features were hawkish and hooked. Certainly no man she wished to be chasing her.

"Do come in and sit." Morgance said, softly, as the man seemed to be spooked by something.

And as he walked, she could see he did, in fact, have a limp.

"Your Highness." He bowed.

"Did The Thistle give you that limp?" She asked.

He only nodded, skin splotchy from hard travel. When was the last time he slept?

"Well, she's safe in the dungeon now."

"No dungeon can hold her." He said, darkly, and she disregarded him, spreading sticky blackberry jam on a crust of bread. The sound of the bountyman swallowing his own hunger at the sight of food seemed to echo around the wood-paneled chamber, candlelight glowing the walls and floor with an amber glaze.

"We'll see about that." Morgance said before taking a bite and chewed, staring at the man, his purple jacket crusted with splatters of mud and streaks of rain, black boots looking as if they'd been chewed by a pack of stray dogs. "So, what would you like to tell me?"

Ewan Ust inhaled sharply as if he were about to speak and closed his mouth again. Morgance ceased eating and shoved the food aside.

"You have my *full* attention, now please, out with it."

Still, Ust would not speak, his dark eyes blinking rapidly before he finally did, as if in a trance.

"I have seen...Rhoswen of Kathron Caelie."

Instantly, Morgance felt sick to her stomach.

Rhoswen? RHOSWEN???

She felt her chest flush, and she brought her hands together, steepled before her, the dazzling gold Ring of Rule heavy on her third finger, sucking up all the light in the room to glare at her and say *you are a usurper Faer Queen of Lies, a fraud and a fake, and your time has finally come to an end.*

But she said nothing, managing the roiling sea within her belly in silence and only nodded a tight jerk of her chin for the man to continue.

"I have seen Rhoswen of...Kathron Caelie." The man repeated, his trance less intense than before. It was obviously *some* burden to bear. "And I know where to find her."

"How do you know it was her?" Morgance asked, ruby lips curving in a gentle smile.

Yes, the very name buckles my knees with fear, even me, Faer Princess of the Night, that cursed name of Rhoswen, the ghost forever haunting me. But a name is not a real thing. A name is not flesh and blood. More of an idea. Just a scatter of words burnt to the wick. Granted, a name can start a war or bring a person to forsake their homeland, but you'll have to do better than that, bountyman.

And still Ewan Ust stood. Transfixed by her beauty? Worn out from travel? Still in pain from wrangling The Thistle?

Stunned from seeing the truth with his own eyes?

Who cares? Talk. Talk now. Talk and I will know all your secrets. I will see into your mind. I will know the darkness that lies within.

"How do you know it was her?" Morgance asked, sternly, feeling her chest and back stiffen.

And as if her very ghost was in the room, Ewan Ust held up his right hand and bent his third finger to touch his palm.

"Her finger…cut off at the joint."

Morgance shot up from her seat, the plush chair in which she'd lounged to eat clattering to the floor, spreading a resounding *smack* throughout the hollows of the resonant Chamber. Her skin tingled, drowning in the memory, drenched in hatred and blood, and Morgance stared at the man in choked horror before slowly twisting to see the chair on the ground, her chair, the sound of its fall ringing through her ears as if she didn't know how it'd happened, caught in a surreal moment too profound to remove herself from.

Deliberately, she gathered herself within, lids gently lowering to shield the half-glance of her eyes, and she bent at the knees to daintily pick up the chair, standing behind it with a sigh, as if it were some sort of defense.

Morgance thought for a second, glaring a hole in the table.

"….And…where did you see her?"

"So it is true." The bountyman said.

Morgance raised her yellow-green gaze to him, catching a peep in his throat. Her eyes were dead, rock hard and sharp as glass.

Her voice was low.

It was her Faer voice. A breathy and drawn-out cadence, as intoxicating as it was intimidating.

Paralyzing, with her eyes. Like sunlight through grass.

"*Where…did…you…see…her?*"

"Pasture lands southwest of High Inverloch."

"HA!" Morgance threw back her head, the laughter one single punch of air echoing through the empty Chamber. "There *is* *no* pasture land southwest of High Inverloch!"

"But…"

Morgance was on him, having divined his weakness. In a flash she vaulted herself upon the table, slick velvet sliding her across its breadth and down to her feet to stand before the bountyman with two steps.

"Speak." She growled.

"I…"

"SSSSPEEEAAAK!"

"That's what I was told to say."

Morgance whirled around, hands tensing like claws, her mind a flurry of thoughts and emotions.

Rage, queen among them.

The equations were quick, the calculations instant.

Like jagged lightning splattered upon the sky, she spun, reached out, and grabbed Ewan Ust by the neck, squeezing him as she whispered through grit teeth.

"Who told you to say that?"

The bountyman's hooded eyes bulged. He was bigger than her, *stronger* than her, but her grip forced him lower and lower till his knees thudded the floor, and his hands weakly latched onto her black sleeves.

"Tell me the truth, bountyman," Her eyes flashed fire. "Or you will *not* like the consequences."

AERLYN

CHAPTER 51

The picking of the dungeon lock a distant memory lost in the swish of her earthy brown cloak and the bounding of steps up to the perilous width of the courtyard, Aerlyn felt her heart race like hoofbeats thundering the ground though she hadn't even seen the half of it yet.

Yes, the plan was a wild one, but in the moment it made more sense...something about the peace of the forest, and Rhoswen's childhood memory of a place she said she learned every nook and crook of by the time she was five.

But the hatching of the plan seemed so long ago and, well, Aerlyn had never seen the Fortress of Ullraye before, and that big black Tower some three hundred feet straight up in the air just about made her feel woozy.

It wasn't that she was afraid of heights, just that she'd never in her life been able to scale something that high and at the same time so precariously small.

To climb a mountain was to cling to a razorback spine of the earth's crust, resonating with life. To climb a tower was like scaling a fat and slick rope made of stone as dead as fish bones.

It just didn't make sense.

Mountains were for climbing. Towers were for watching.

But Aerlyn snorted the fresh air up her nostrils with as much force as she could, cracking her knuckles one at a time.

After all, High Inverloch wasn't far away.

It was nearly like being home again.

If she even wanted to remember what'd happened to her there. Just being so close to the blasted place was making it hard to forget.

Aerlyn darted, her thinness a blurry shadow dancing in the wind and darkness of the vicious night. No rain fell from the sky, but the smoky char of the clouds rushed along the horizon as if driven by a whip, and Aerlyn stowed thoughts of Faer Morgance and what intercession she may or may not've been responsible for. But to be under it was to feel the heaviness of something stirring from far beyond the bend of the sea, something dark and terrible and ancient and hungry.

Aerlyn shivered and dashed along the grass next to the inner wall.

The Fortress was a simple thing if one's mind was made up of mazes, and Aerlyn found Rhoswen's directions to be excellent, seeing as the nature of her duties forced her to avoid the light. And with her own abilities, highly attuned by years of experience though dulled by the overpowering whoosh of the wind and the weight of the atmosphere, Aerlyn was able to avoid the roving pattern of the guardsmen and their pikes and halfblades, no sort of protectorate she'd encountered in her adventures to date. Hardened soldiers, cycled in and out of combat with the Nørd, not hesitating to run her through with the sharps of their swords and shrug and blame the darkness if pressed by a higher power as to what'd happened.

But it was only Morgance Aerlyn knew to watch out for, stuck up in the blackness of the Tower skimming the belly of the clouds. So many had left, abandoning her *and* the Throne.

It was as if there was no one home.

Even the dungeon. Hollowed rats without enough energy to loaf around the store rooms and sniff through dismally thin sacks of grain.

It was as if Ullraye was the husk of an insect, sucked clean by a spider of winds and shadows.

It made Aerlyn's dizzying journey through anterooms and side passages easy, and her crossing of the courtyard after navigating a confusing string of defensive causeways and elbow joints a breeze.

But just to be safe, she cast one last gaze around the intimidating spread of the inner and outer walls, looping around her like a massive black stone basket sitting on the edge of a cliff, before sneaking to the gypsy wagon and knocking thrice on the running board.

Finleigh's eyes were shiny despite the lack of light, and she stood impossibly close to The Thistle as Quill retrieved what equipment they'd snuck into the Fortress.

In the end, Finleigh ended up passing the scant few minutes in a silent side embrace for what Aerlyn assumed to be warmth *and* well-wishing, and when Quill had finally fished out the last of equipment, he held out the compact redwood bow the Master Archer had crafted especially for her.

His face was sullen, his eyes cold.

Aerlyn swallowed, her garnet lips parting, but her words caught in her throat, torn away by the wind.

Quill nodded once, his eyes downcast, and Aerlyn ducked off toward the stairs to the parapet without looking back.

How could she?

The sky above was nothing compared to how she felt inside, weighed against how she hated the cruel stroke of destiny to see him again when the hardest job of her life was at hand, demanding every part and portion of her soul.

So much so that she couldn't spare Quill even a drop of it, though what drop she longed to give would wet her soul like rain in the desert. Even a kiss on the cheek, or a squeeze of the shoulder.

And she hated herself for it.

But to think, if she could steal the Ring of Rule, then the whole of Albanland would be made right again! Damn her feelings! Rhoswen, only daughter of beloved King Brom the Chosen, still mourned by his faithful subjects, back from the dead, *with* the Ring of Rule around her...

Aerlyn stopped and kneeled as if she'd been punched. Ahead, near a fire kettle, running along the wall that guarded the sea and the access to Montree and the ghost town it'd become, two guardsmen chatted in low voices. Sparks of fire flashed and lingered on the hilts of their halfblades and patterns of Clan Cavan colors and tickled dancing light up the length of their sharp pikes.

But it wasn't for them the fear had caught her like an ill-timed sickness. It was Rhoswen, thoughts of her. Maybe it *wouldn't* all be made right with the stealing of the Ring. Maybe it would become far worse than it was already, like the skies above, sliding and sliding across the horizon darker and darker till no one could see their own hand in front of their face.

To see the shackles that bound them, to see the gauntness of famine, to see the wormy white scars of fighting a losing battle stretch across their skin.

The Thistle's nostrils flared and she kicked over the wall with a swoosh, lithe fingers grabbing the uneven teeth of the parapet to shimmy along the length of the wall, past the soldiers, shoving Rhoswen out of her mind while she did.

It was damning work, and she smashed her teeth together to muffle the sounds of exertion, blazing pain snaking through her arms and gritty stone biting into her fingertips. The men's conversation grew louder and louder, cut by the wash of the tide crashing and falling far below her feet as she shimmied and gripped and slid along the wall, struggling against gravity, re-gripping to shimmy again and again until she could hear the men no more. It was then she hung, on the wall, with the sea and the shore a ten-second drop below, bowing her head to the cold stone for a sigh before flipping herself back over the teeth of the parapet to run off into the darkness.

The black Tower of Ullraye stood before Aerlyn like a challenge as she removed the satchel and the short redwood bow from her back. Neatly tucked in a corner crook of the wall, she worked quickly as rain began to spit down upon her, puffed up by the wind to slash across the open gap of the courtyard. Ever so often, she would flick her eyes across the parapet walkways behind her, scanning the damning breadth of it all, thanking the heavens for the muddle of darkness above.

Tying a thin rope to a metal arrow with a small hole set just behind the fletching, Aerlyn stretched the bow a few times and stood up, standing clear of the lines of rope she'd laid out before her. The work leading up to the moment of finally being able to shoot her arrow had been a furious blizzard of sweat and madness, overwhelmed by gratitude that the Fortress was so empty, and the patrols so lethargic with no one in sight.

Neither Nørds, nor Angles.

Not even Albans.

Aerlyn notched the specially made arrow in the specially made bow and sighed, stilling herself within to try and forget just how much was weighing on her when she was supposed to be as light as a feather, as harmless as a gentle breeze, as swift as a shadow...

The arrow whistled from the bow with a squishy snap Aerlyn felt reverberate through her body, and she squinted to watch the arrow sail for the teeth of the Tower, bending in the wind as it climbed and sailed and then fell, dragging the line of rope with it. Somewhere, on the back of the wind, she heard a tinny *plink*, like a coin had struck the bottom of a dry well.

A smile snuck across garnet lips. She was a better shot than she remembered. But the Master Archer sure knew her craft, having taken great care in making sure Aerlyn had the tools she needed to get the job done.

And once she'd tested the metal arrow, snagged in the crenellated teeth of the top, she began to scale the sheer vertical tube of the Tower, its rounded black face slicker than ice in the cold howl of the wind and its slapping of spittle across the ever so slowly shrinking landscape of Ullraye.

It was surprisingly simple. Too simple, considering how hard the journey had been to reach the empty space Aerlyn found herself occupying like the thief that she was. Alone, a stoic shadow of fabric, sneaking into that which she was forbidden to see.

The Princess' bedchambers.

But it was one of those moments, one of those splashes of the surreal, swaddled in an odd and disconcerting silence, and Aerlyn sighed to herself as she stared at the Ring of Rule and its golden signet of an endless clover knot sitting heavily on top of a wardrobe, scattered with clothes as if Faer Morgance had left in a hurry.

If there was but any magic in the land, it was that damnable object, somehow having molded itself to the third finger of royalty over the years as if it had a malleable mind of its own.

Still, it felt all wrong.

Staged.

The room smelled strongly of jasmine, and Aerlyn fought a dizzy wobble, nearly intoxicated. Jasmine alone wasn't in the air. There was something else, something hidden behind the floral notes that still lingered in the cold liquid of the tub.

Smelling the air did no good, and whatever was in the air was not only silent, but invisible. Fighting the night and the wind near the crash of the salty sea had ruined her nose, and her entire body felt rubbery from the travel, the crowning achievement of it all being the fact that she actually *made* it up the Tower and wasn't a heap of bones thrashing around where the rocks met the sea.

But her ears were pricked, as if she was being watched, though she couldn't see anyone else in the near perfect dark of the room she knew to be Morgance' for the fact that it dominated the top of the Tower.

Her knife ached to cut the silence and challenge the ghosts she felt creeping upon her.

But she stayed still.

Watching.

Thinking.

And feeling her skin crawl, just to stand feet from where Dominae Tenebris slept, dreaming her dark dreams, Aerlyn grabbed the Ring of Rule, shoved it on her pinkie, and ran for the winding staircase that would take her to the bottom of the Tower.

CHAPTER 52

No one had to tell The Thistle who was responsible for the presence she felt, instantly shrinking the half-dark hall around them both. So Aerlyn simply stepped from the alcove of the Tower door, knowing there was no way out for her now.

Down the hall, waiting beneath one of the structure's many arches as if she were a timeless sculpture no eye could refuse to linger upon, stood Morgance, Faer Princess of the Night.

And here they both were, together, finally, legendary entities of the land's many barren darknesses, surging together like two storm fronts or wave caps ready to shatter the sky and the sea with a scatter of lightning and a splash of foam.

Aerlyn stilled herself with a single breath, moving to the center of the hall. Of course her knife ached to be drawn, as if it had a mind of its own, a voice she had to deny cutting through the tension that was clamping itself about her shoulders and lower back.

Yes, show her some of your own magic! Show her a trick or two and scare the stuffing out of her.

Morgance stood but three paces from her, arms crossed, leaning against the wall.

She was holding an apple in her hand.

"You like these, don't you?" She said, a challenge in her voice.

I know everything about you, yet you know nothing about me, the high and breathy voice argued. The lining of wall sconces, flickering a sickly flame down the dank tube of the hall, cast a haughty ripple across the most beautiful face Aerlyn had ever seen.

Yes, Thistle. I know why you're here and what you want.

And you shant have it.

Aerlyn curled her right hand to form a fist, the Ring heavy on her pinkie; no doubt, sucking up all the light in the room as her own face was shrouded in her hood.

Morgance inhaled slowly, appearing too tired to stand anymore, such being the cause for her leaning. Something about the way she stood nearly reminded Aerlyn of Quill and their quiet moment at the hidden loch, with the way Quill could barely keep himself upright anymore and leaned on that tree for support as the rain came down. Was it his complete dedication to service sucking him dry in the same manner Morgance' lust for control of powers beyond humanity…

No. It couldn't be. How could the two desires, the two *devotions*, even be compared? One sought to give, the other to take take take and then take again.

And why was it, in her time of confrontation, she was reaching out to him?

Certainly he wasn't so far away. But in Morgance' presence, everything was gone in a puff of dust and smoke, like a dream forgotten the moment of waking, so that *nothing* save her piercing and unblinking stare remained, matched only by her immortal beauty.

Yes, she was the kind of face artists dreamed of carving in clay, cursing themselves for failing to capture the softness of her skin, or the enchantment of the appraisal she ran up and down Aerlyn's tall and spindly frame.

I know. Aerlyn read in the eerie dance of light and shadow, the interplay of thoughts and gestures, kissing the Princess' eyes. *I know everything. I know you're afraid of me but you want to hear what I have to say. People fear what they do not understand and you're too proud to believe you can be afraid of anything, even being alone. So you think if you could understand me you wouldn't be afraid of me. Well? Walk out that door, escaped murderer, notorious thief. See how far you get knowing that I've seen your face and control the night you love so much like a farmer controls the seed which he plants or a fisherman the net that he casts.*

Yes, Thistle. I own you. I own you because I own your choice, right now, in this moment. I own your fate and I love it.

Morgance eyed her once more and cocked her chin to the left, inquisitively.

"Shall I tell you a story and then ask you a question, O rarest Thistle, Master of Thieves?"

Aerlyn couldn't fight the tensing of her jaw. She hated being mocked. Being called out, being selected, being the object of attention.

Hated it.

And, unable to move, and unable to think about Quill any longer or the way her stomach grumbled to see the delicious apple in Morgance' hand, Aerlyn said nothing, and stood stone still.

Morgance stared at the apple and removed a bejeweled dagger from behind her back, and, pressing the blade to the green skin, began to speak in the beguiling voice of a born storyteller.

"There once was a girl, second-born of a noble family, who loved life for the mysteries it held. Her family was close to the royal family, and she played with all the noble children of her age as if they would all live forever in a magical world of summer wind and wildflowers."

Morgance dug the blade into the skin and twisted the apple, just beginning to shave the peel.

"But the girl's entire family was killed in a voyage to Eire, across the usually placid Sunset Sea, a voyage which she was spared from by a simple twist of fate."

The shaving continued, now a full circle of unbroken green peel.

"A sniffle. A cough. Nothing more. But with all of her family dead, the royal family, bless their soft hearts, took pity upon the little girl, adopting her as their own."

The knife slid down as Aerlyn's heart beat faster. The peel was getting longer, dangling from the apple like snakeskin, and she was beginning to feel she knew this girl of whom Morgance spoke.

"But soon after, as if the shipwreck was a harbinger of the darkness that was to beset this young girl's life like a birthmark, the royal family fell victim to Plague, as did the land itself."

A dark smile wormed across Morgance' ruby lips, as if to laugh at it all, like a great big joke.

"It was around this time the royal family's own chosen Heir ran off, never to be seen again. Good riddance. As it would stand, the little girl was then the only one of the royal family to survive Plague, and rose from the ashes as Morgance, Faer Princess of the Night."

The smile spread, nearly devilish as the light hooded her eyes in shadows with her gaze dipping to behold the fruit, now half skinned and naked of its shiny snake-like peel.

"You see, some claimed she orchestrated the whole thing, the death of her family, the coming of Plague, all of it, seeing as she was found to be immune to Plauge, and had risen to take the Crown with the passing of her new family. And at such a young age, too, so impressionable. She had to be strong. But to be Faer? Beautiful, yes, every eye was instantly captured by her loveliness…but Faer, well…that's like saying she descended from the sun itself in a dewdrop."

A small laugh rippled through her chest and shoulders, dainty grip still twisting, knife-hand strong with the steady practice of a hunter.

"Is she Faer or is she not? That's the question on your mind. Well, I say, do you believe in the Faer or don't you? Don't you know? Don't you know what you believe? Maybe at times you can hear the earth groan, or taste sorrow in the wind. The seed of life wars with the Four Storms for supremacy and lightning strikes the forest to burn it down with fire, but the sea washes the fire out, taking away bits of the land as it does. All things are connected, you see, life an equal partner with death. But can one claim the knowledge to control them? Influence them? Manipulate them?"

It was then the peel fell to the ground with a bounce, and Aerlyn tensed inside, for some reason thinking it actually *was* a snake and was going to start slithering toward her. Aerlyn shivered. It was just a jump of the light, a flash of candle flame twisting in a draft. She looked again to Morgance and she hadn't moved, yet, though Aerlyn felt she had. Aerlyn swore she was closer, like the walls were shrinking and the space narrowing.

"Some call her *Illumanser Adept*...nothing more than an illusionist, a bender of light able to make people believe what she wants them to. Like a disappearing gypsy who drops from the Solstice stage to pick pockets in the crowd and give them back their money with a smile, keeping exactly one copper penny to himself for every pocket because no man could remember in the excitement of the trick how many pennies he had in his pocket in the first place. Acutely aware of other's perceptions, she is but a hand on the till, trimming the sails."

Morgance spun the apple, its juices dripping down her hand. The knife gleamed cold and thin, a blade for carving fish from the bones. Why would such be bejeweled? Why would it be made of woven silver and gold, its bands bearing the knots and whorls she'd seen tattooed onto the arms of Rhoswen's Chosen?

"Can she call storms? Can she start wars? Can she raise the dead and remember what it means to be a little girl with nothing but the sun in her eyes and the wind in her hair?"

Morgance tipped her gaze, pride glazing her Faer cheeks and chin, hair of light cascading down her head like a crown of ethereally silken fabric.

"I ask you, Master of Thieves, what is Faer Morgance? Is she the truth or the lie?"

Aerlyn found her mouth sagging open but her throat was stricken with drought.

The woman before her was anything but a lie.

She was a nightmare.

Aerlyn turned to run, taking two steps before slipping on the slick and polished stone, her boots still damp from the damned three hundred feet of wet Tower stone and storm. Her breath left her lungs, binding her to the hard floor to stare off into the darkness with wide eyes. A swish of fabric rippled in her ears and as she pressed herself up, an arm snaked around her neck, and a knee jabbed in her back. Aerlyn's lips stretched wide with a shout of pain and Morgance shoved the apple in her mouth as if she were a pig for the spit.

The bejeweled fish-boning knife went to her throat.

"I believe you have something that belongs to me." Aerlyn *mmphed*, her words of no effect, just a desperate vibration. "Oh, no, don't bother, I'll get it myself."

Morgance shifted with jagged speed, stamping her boot to Aerlyn's face, grinding it into the marble floor. Stretching out the thief's right arm, she bent down to cut the Ring from her finger.

Aerlyn tried to wiggle herself free, whimpering. Her left arm was buried under her body. To twitch her knife free would be to stick it in her own belly.

"You want to share so much with her?" Morgance frowned. "You want to be like her so badly? What does she have that is so desirable? What was she that her parents *still* mourned her and ignored me, letting me drift off to *Hafnröth* to pledge my heart and soul to whoever would listen, to whomever was out there. Whomever or whatever. It didn't matter."

The knife leapt to Aerlyn's alabaster skin, as if Morgance wanted to carve off her freckles one at a time.

"You see, there's nothing that hurts worse than *not* being loved." Aerlyn eyed her, watching the perfect pucker of her ruby lips twist and invert, the graceful streaks of her eyebrows wrinkle and bunch. Her soft whisper was barely audible. "Nothing."

Morgance stood up and took a step away, standing with her back to the thief.

To tempt her?

Aerlyn felt drained, and swore it took all her strength to lean on her side and remove the sour apple from her mouth, spitting blood and saliva across the floor.

"Give me the Ring of Rule and leave this place." Morgance said, solemly. "But first, tell me where she is. I must know.

"Why, so you can kill her?"

"Tell me where she is or you will die."

"I'm not afraid of death."

The punch of Morgance' single *HA!* echoed throughout the chamber like a rolling fog. She spun slowly, firelight glazing her Faerness with madness.

"No?"

Aerlyn found her teeth grinding together in defiance. Somehow, she'd bit her own tongue in the attempted escape, and its sting was hot and wet in her mouth.

"*No.*"

"Well, there *are* worse things than death. I'm sure it wouldn't be that hard to find a man or two around here who'd like a moment with you."

"Why? Are they bored with you already?"

"Cute, Thistle. Such a sailor's mouth you have. I had so hoped you'd work with me but you'd only come here to steal the Ring of Rule." A strange smile snuck across Morgance' lips. There and gone. But Aerlyn saw it.

And it scared her.

"Yes, I know all about you. I know what happened to you that made you who you are."

"You don't know anything!" Aerlyn tried to press herself up but she was too tired, too spent. "Nobody knows and nobody ever will know!"

"Like me and Rhoswen, then? Our little secret? No secret stays safe forever. Someone has to tell."

"I don't believe you." Aerlyn spat. "I don't believe in *anything* you say. You kill me and it won't matter. Rhoswen is coming here, Ring or not. She's the Queen, we both know it. She always has been and always will be. The Ring just gives her more sway over the weak. But you know all about that, don't you? You're the strongest of the weak, but just enough. The fattest rat in the barrel. You're so addicted to the attention, so hungry for the whispers of your legend, you've forgotten to love your loyal subjects. The slaves, the starving...you don't give a damn about them because you can't see past your own nose."

The soft line of her chin jutting, as if she didn't know what to do with what lie before her, Morgance shook her head.

"Who can love those that don't love them?"

Aerlyn stopped, thinking of Quill.

In many ways, their relationship was something of the proof of it, but yet, the very opposite. It was as if they were both putting a love of something greater above what they both ached to realize, in many ways, *because* of the idea of what could be, what they knew in their hearts to be their secret hope, and how much it meant to them.

With an earth-rending groan, Aerlyn pushed herself up, standing tall, even though the weight of the Ring of Rule on her finger made her want to fall back down to the marble and sleep forever.

Her voice was her thiefly growl, the vicious snarl of the dark story The Thistle had become.

"They should burn you at the stake just to hear you scream."

Morgance rolled her eyes.

"Charming."

A smirk worked its way to the slash of Aerlyn's garnet lips, and she reached down to retrieve the apple, wiping her mouth with the sleeve of her cloak, streaking it with blood.

"But I bet you my life, given the chance, Rhoswen would look you in the eye and say to you, after all you've done to her...*I forgive you.*"

It was then Morgance snapped, as if thunder had finally rolled its cackling explosion through her soul and lightning was but the only blood in her veins.

Her footfall skittered across the distance, her Faer voice low and wolfish.

"Don't you ever say that again, you hear me!" She leaned into Aerlyn and pressed the knife to her throat. Aerlyn felt her flesh bend, the sharp and silvery point but a hair's breadth from piercing alabaster skin. "Don't you dare even think it! I can *feel* it! I will gut you like a brook trout if you so much as whisper that word, you understand? Now tell me where Rhoswen is and what she plans to do or you will die right here, right now! I will slice your neck *wiiiiiide* open and hang you from the top of the Tower by your feet like a harvest goose."

But Aerlyn said nothing, eyes of midnight staring back into the yellow-green gaze of Faer madness.

And with her heart beating out of her chest, The Thistle played it as if she couldn't be bothered, bringing the apple to her mouth to take a bite.

ULTAN

CHAPTER 53

The highlands that had once spread before Ultan like two giant hands promising the magic and mystery of childhood adventure had since closed the infinite hardness of their emerald fingers and knuckle joints around him as he stood alone on the crest of the valley, staring at that which curdled his stomach rancid with fear.

Solara had not shined upon him since Luna had retreated to her dark grave beyond the horizon. And in anticipation of midday, Solara hid her radiant face behind a flat wall of wet and sleepy slate, sick of the violence and death Albanland's verdant valleys had been forced to witness, bound to embrace, as seasons turned and blood mixed with soil. Even the tops of the rolling hills were lost in mist and fog, as if the Angle Army had brought some ancient magic with them, or the vaporous presence of another realm had come to observe just who would emerge victorious this day.

Ultan stayed still as they arranged themselves, rank and file, with the massive breadth of the highlands all but shrinking around him, making him feel larger and larger and larger.

Though I walk the death god's trail, he remembered, *I will not be afraid. Though I hear the fallen wail, I will not be afraid.*

But there was no wailing, no drums. Not even the dull munch of footsteps in this apocalyptic gathering of man and beast.

Just him, here.

And them, there.

I will climb the hills, I will cross the sea, I will face my fear and I will be set free.

But the words of his old oath were hollow in his ears as a lone figure strode from the line of footmen broad enough to stretch the curved edges of the valley, the sharp tips of their spears catching the palest glimmer of light hiding behind the slate curtain of the sky, as if Solara favored them and not him. Behind the woven barrier of spearman horses waited, the shape of a fingernail in the distance, and bore men so heavily armored they could scarely move. Lords of Angle, they were, rich Barons eager to seize battlefield glory as if it were real estate. And behind the horses, wooden war machines capable of launching giant wall-wrecking boulders as if they were the simple river rocks of a young boy's sling, stood like the ruins of small villages.

Yet there was no army for the assembly to fight.

Only Ultan.

And he stood, thick and resolute, his feet swathed in Nørd fur boots, his own black Skyeshire kilt about his waist. Bare-chested in the clinging cold, the golden torcs around his arms squashed red rings against the inflation of his muscles, rippling with the hot blood of war. The fox cape of his oath and office had been replaced by that of the white winter wolf, clasped about his neck with a thick silver chain. A sacred animal to the Nørd seers, it had been one of Eyvind Frey's final gifts to Ultan, the other being the black blowing horn that dangled at the Champion's waist.

After the week of hard travel and the desperation of what his destiny had become, Ultan looked every bit of what he was, a feral hybrid of his two bloods, a tall and weathered stone with wind-swept strawberry blonde curls, rooted in the crossroads of unity to say *pass me all who dare.*

And near the staggering of weapons too numerous to count, stuffed behind footmen so dense it made Ultan's stomach sour even further to try and count their number, a collection of cowards awaited no sword *but* his own, each one of their ugly faces a shame to their Clan's proud history of service to the Throne.

The lone figure drew closer, his steps purposeful; not as one possessed by duty, but as one who was being watched.

Yet Ultan did not move.

He *would not* move.

He was the rock, the last stone to stand before the sea swallowed him alive, and if he was going to drown in this new Albanland, this land of imbalance and slavery, this land of strife and division, of riches staring down their noses upon poverty, then he was going to drown in his own blood and the blood of everyone he could take with him before Solara shined upon him no more.

Beginning with Arturo of Pallantyne.

The man stopped, some ten feet from Ultan, and removed the boxy helm known to Angle Barons, as if they even *had* faces worth saving from a stray swipe of the sword.

Dark brown hair seeming to gleam with morning dew, perfectly trimmed beard a frame of velvet to compliment his sunny coloring, Arturo of Pallantyne let the boxy helm drop to the ground, where it clattered, rolled, and sunk in the soft earth as if destined to be a relic, a witness of what was about to take place, the helm's eye slits but pools of an empty void.

Shadows.

"The time has come, my friend." He said, his rich voice stretching across the space like a spiteful handshake.

"You are no friend of mine."

"It's merely an expression."

"I'll give you an expression." Ultan said, and then stared death, silently, deep into Arturo's brown eyes.

"You don't scare me."

"I don't give a damn."

Arturo's hard chin tipped up, gesturing behind him.

"And my true *friends*," Arturo's lids wizened at his own humor, brown eyes flickering with greed under brows that may or may not've been plucked and shaped by a woman's hand. "My new friends. They don't scare you? They belong to me, you know. As long as we're in this land, they're under *my* thumb."

Ultan's nostrils flared as he inhaled and in a flash, he spit a thick wad of phlegm upon Arturo's forehead, offering his rival a faint smile as the nasty gesture slid down Arturo's nose like a cracked egg.

The future Angle Lord only shook his head and slowly drew his sword, letting it gnaw from the scabbard with long-buried angst. It was a thin thing, seemingly brand new, perfectly shiny, but nimble and strong.

He wiped his face in an elbow crook of fine cloth, black leather gauntlets croaking to flex his grip around the hilt of his weapon.

"All the patience I have in my body waits for Faer Morgance, you Nørd-loving bastard." He nearly whispered. "So I'll make this quick."

Ultan drew his own weapon and just about licked his chapped lips over the thought of shattering Arturo's dainty sword and watching the milk white Blade of the Champion, that ancient tool of chaos and carnage, keep on falling till it hit him right between the eyes.

"Well now's your chance, Wolf of Westwood Hollow. But to be the wolf you have to *beat* the wolf."

Arturo frowned, removing his cloak, something that no longer bore the Pallantyne colors but was merely a rich and shimmery shade of purple.

The color of a Prince.

"What the hell does that mean? Some Nørd gibberish you learned from mommy?"

"At least she was a faithful woman. Can't say the same for the strumpet that birthed you."

"Ooh…" Arturo chuckled, beginning to pace. Ultan could sense the bubbles of adrenaline began to simmer up his rival's spine, like the gasses of a mountain hot spring. "My skin's thicker than that. And *my* blood is *pure*."

"So pure, cutting you open will rust my blade."

"Cutting *you* open will dull mine. When was the last time you bathed?"

"This morning."

Arturo scoffed, his paces tightening, his athletic frame gaining a bounce as he worked himself into a lather.

"In what? Cattle piss? What did Morgance see in you, anyway? Reeking of fish, like your mother, disowned by the Lords Chamber like your narrow-minded father. You *disgust* me. I lower my fine self to slay you, you ditch-water half-breed."

"I'm proud of what I am." Ultan growled, letting the rage of knowing that the division he now found himself in the middle of had begun *long* before his birth, when the Lord of Skyeshire so loved a simple young fisherman's daughter, a Nørd in thought and deed, in blood and body; a woman in whom the Lord of Skyeshire delighted so fondly the exile of the Clans meant nothing to him.

And now his son would make it right.

"Well, then you're the only one." Arturo's smile was a broad snarl, white teeth gleaming.

Silence consumed the highland valley for the space of three heartbeats.

It was then Arturo leapt.

He was a big man, just a bit smaller than Ultan, and Ultan found himself fighting the shock of just how quickly he moved. The first three strikes of his thin and nimble blade were blocked merely on instinct, a tingle flushing Ultan's arms as Arturo nearly gashed him deeply with a *woosh*.

"Just look at you, you bloody damn Nørd lover," Arturo hissed, whipping his sword to a high and fancy arc, parallel to the ground as he paced a half circle, his artful sword form as Angle as Ultan's was brutal and Nørd. "Even now your mother rules you from the grave."

Arturo dashed forward, his lunge a slice of lightning. Ultan countered with a grunt and twisted away as Arturo nearly drug the whistling tip of his sword across Ultan's neck. Ultan blinked the splashes of sap from his eyes, slowed by the stress of Faer Morgance and the treachery of his brethren, worn thin and sleepless by anger's rancid diet.

The Lord of Pallantyne moved with cleanliness, his statuesque frame that of a male dancer, nearly beautiful as his long arms cut exaggerated swathes Ultan could only throw the weight of his overly heavy sword to block.

Desperation was his shield. Hopelessness his defender.

Suddenly, Ultan was conscious of those behind him. He'd been turned around, and his back steps were broad as Arturo drove into him with wheeling strikes and fluid swirls of sliver.

The spearmen cheered and clapped as seven clashes and clinks ended with Arturo rising in a leaping twirl to strike his finishing blow, which Ultan blocked, poorly, stumbling upon the soft ground and rolling over on his back, his legs flying in the air.

The line of spearmen laughed as Ultan's kilt flew up and he couldn't bear to think about anything other than Arturo's laughter, bubbling through the green valley like wind through tree leaves.

"Running away from Faer Morgance like the coward you are has made you *so* terribly slow." He said, whipping his sword in a fanciful flourish before settling to a stronger two-handed guard as Ultan pressed himself up with far more focus, as if fury was a blade white hot in the blacksmith's forge, and only hammering it to shape would yield victory. Behind him the spearmen laughed, like a wall of derision, shoving him back toward the gleaming greed of the future Prince of Albanland.

Control yourself, just like you did with Frey, something in his mind told him. *CONTROL!!!*

But he couldn't. He couldn't forgive Arturo. In the savage squish of his heart he wanted him dead, realizing in the wheezing fog of the moment he'd never actually *wanted* to kill anyone before. He'd only done so to save a land that didn't give a damn about him anymore.

But Arturo, hell on fire, he wanted to wipe the smirk off his handsome face with the breadth of his Blade.

By any means necessary.

"Morgance is dead!" Ultan lied with a shout, and caught his rival in a split-second of paralysis, driving toward him with a feint to rip his weapon across his rival's waist in a storm-wind *swoosh*.

Arturo flew back, his skin hot, barely avoiding being eviscerated, and Ultan was upon him without mercy, hacking down the heavy Blade of the Champion as if it were an axe to finally remove the bitter roots of an ancient tree.

But Arturo knew this, his time practicing in the Circle too deft for Ultan's half-Nørd fury.

He simply somersaulted away, rolling over his back and up to his feet as Ultan's weapon cleaved the soft earth and stuck, buried nearly to the hilt.

Foolishly, Ultan tried to remove the sword from the ground but it would not budge, and Ultan melted away from the whistle aimed his direction, the hot sting of steel biting into the bare skin of his arm and squirting blood upon the white wolf cloak.

Arturo's laugh was louder than before and he advanced slowly, Ultan staggering back to hiss his pain in control.

"First thing I'm going to do concerns the woman you weren't man enough to take." He said, his eyes wide with his dream of glory materializing before his eyes. "Second thing I'm going to do is dig up your mother's bones and burn them."

Who's the Champion now? The taunts burned in Arturo's gaze, swift sword shifting hands as he sought to corner Ultan in the breadth of the valley, sluggish steps cursing him as whistles mixed with a slow-building chant.

Ar-tu-ro. Ar-tu-ro. Ar-tu-ro.

Ultan grimaced as the man's name rolled off the tongue. Some he may've bought, others he charmed, beguiled with the grand inspiration of leadership, but him, this handsome mass of jealously and bigotry, *he* was the man they wanted to be the new King of whatever new Albanland they sought to make, raping and pillaging their way up the valley as the highlands ended and the Fortress of Ullraye and all the coastal towns it guarded began.

Was it so easy? Ultan thought, wondering why the back of his arm was bleeding so furiously, like a stream of melt water in spring, only to look down and see the pure sharpness of Arturo's blade and the clarity of his stroke had almost cut to the bone.

Ultan bit back bile to see the goo of flesh.

Was it so easy to conquer this land? Is there any fight left in us? Who is us, anyway? Am I the only one?

And whether he was or not, Ultan charged with a howl.

CHAPTER 54

The Champion flew through the air. Muscle and bone collided before Arturo could raise his nifty blade to run Ultan through. Ultan roared as they rolled across the soft grass, and somewhere along the way Arturo lost his weapon in the fight for his life.

It was then Ultan was sure he had the bastard dead to rights.

The bigger and more experienced fist-fighter, Ultan let the fancy Prince-to-be taste the tang of his own blood and see how he liked the stuff empires were forged in, as one blunt fist across the nose woke the young man up with a blur of pain right about the same time another fist flying the opposite direction split his lip.

But worming beneath Ultan's strength the scheming Arturo seemed to coil and slither. Just before Ultan could land another punch, a blow he leaned back to put everything he had into, one of Arturo's highly polished boots thumped the Champion's solar plexus.

The highlands spun with a gust of wind. Slate sky and emerald hills dimmed as his breath escaped him, replaced by the wheezing fire of suffocating within his own skin.

It took everything he had to stand tall, whirling to regain his balance, only to fall again as Arturo snagged the gift of Eyvind Frey's winter wolf cape and yanked and twisted so savagely that a tremor of lifelessness squished through Ultan's body. Ultan's left leg shook under an involuntary spasm. His soft green eyes nearly popped out of his skull.

The chain, the silver chain clasp, so well made, so strong, like the bond of friendship that'd been forged by forgiveness' hand…well, it was damning him now, dimming the sky and darkening the curve of the hills around him.

They were sinking inward, shrinking, melting into one blurry color. The highlands became a muted storm upon a pond, caught in the perfect lightlessness of dusk despite the brightness of midday. Blood, boiling in the depths of the sea, buried in his bones, damned him for all he'd done as tremors shook his chest.

Arturo's fine leather gauntlets croaked, his face red as he squeezed. Air hissed across his teeth, whiter than the cape itself.

Ultan flailed to connect to something, anything, if even a fingernail to the eye. But it was as if Arturo wasn't even there, so perfectly angled behind him, the speed and strength of his weight so well balanced that there was *nothing* Ultan could do but die.

Gurgles escaped his gaping throat as the sky burned with fire blacker than night, rimmed with a mist of blood. In his ears, ringing through the tunnel that stood between the living and the dead, he heard a foaming roar of thunder.

The thunder of Valhöll, ready to welcome him home.

Because, dammit, they sure didn't want him in Albanland any more.

He felt it. He could taste it rising up from the ground, rolling like a thousand stray stones down a sky-scarring mountain.

The thunder shook his bones.

But he couldn't let go. He couldn't fight back, but he couldn't just *give up* and let that darkness so close to consuming his aching joints and weary limbs invade his every part and portion.

Though it came for him, sweeping from around the highlands, the death of the light in his green eyes, the death of the light itself.

Still he growled against it, dancing the dizzying sway of a man whose life was but seconds away from leaving his body. The sleek-boned and fine-figured animal that was Arturo of Pallantyne twisted again with the last of his own strength, so eager to rip and tear into Faer Morgance and Albanland both, as if they were pieces of meat fresh from the roasting fire. Arturo screamed, his hands now rocking their own earthquake as the greed to end Ultan's reign possessed him. Choked and breathless, hot tears were forced from Ultan's eyes, mixed with sweat, running rivers down the weathered lines of his cheeks.

It was over.

He could do nothing about it now, nothing about his guilt, his regret, his wondering if the love of the most beautiful woman he'd ever seen would've eaten him alive like he always thought or if it actually would've made sense the morning after, realizing that he'd misinterpreted the whole damn thing, just a man who could never see straight because he'd grown under the shadow of half-blood and self-hate, tempered with an inherited addiction to large quantities of whiskey, deep-rooted in the pain of killing his own Nørd brothers because the Crown gave him no other choice.

Had it made him blind to everything else?

What was there in a man's life, but what he saw and what he could not?

So in his final moments, he released it all, the tears of losing and letting go flowing fast and free, wrecked, ruined, and broken, and he focused, with everything in him, on death, on its blackness and its hunger.

On the great big all-encompassing cloud of its thunder.

It came for him. It rolled. It surged, surrounding him.

Like the endless sea, his mind echoed the same thought though with a tidal wash, drifting back to the stories he'd heard in the arms of his mother. The birth of the Nørd under a dark sky and a roiling cauldron fire, the splash of the shore and the howl of a white wolf in the forest. Hunting, alone, searching for that which would make itself clear when it was finally found. A place, where...where...

Ultan felt himself fall free, staggering on limbs working without the knowledge of his mind. The chain no longer wrapped around his neck, and he didn't know how. The thunder was so loud he couldn't think. His breath was a choke, a cough, a spasm, and he whirled around as the sky flickered with the harsh light he'd never tire of seeing, though so many hated the flat glare that hid Solara's warmth from the land for so many days of the year.

Ultan loved it. How could he not? It was his home.

The thunder deafened and he wondered why he wasn't dead as he staggered, twisting and turning to make sense of it all. Was he leaving his body? Was this how it went?

No, he realized, as his eyes found Arturo, running away from him like someone who'd seen an evil creature from myth and lore in the flesh.

Ultan grabbed his neck and felt the grooves of the chain as his vision cleared. With each blink, Arturo moved further from him. One pace became two. But the thunder grew louder.

And in a flash of white, the thunder took form, beautiful and furious form, riding with the Four Storms beneath its feet.

Ultan staggered as the rider produced a slender wick of silver, its slim shape divining a scatter of brilliant light.

A sword.

And he watched as the silver thread slashed and struck, slicing Aturo's head clean from his body with a splash of rich red blood as if he were a garden vegetable.

But it was not the way his head harmlessly rolled from his shoulders that found Ultan once again breathless and flushed with the freezing fire of death's doorstep. No, it was the rider, turning to behold him, her features framed in a mass of dark curls.

Her summoned thunder consumed the highland valley with the righteous fury of being risen from the dead. The deafening roar of hooves was not from her horse alone, or even from a band of horses, but from an Army of One, the anointed Chosen of King Brom's legacy.

And before the wind stole her away from him and his staggering shock, as she charged for the line of spearmen stretching endlessly before her, Ultan locked eyes with the woman on the horse. They were the exotic almond-shaped eyes of a childhood promise, the eyes of his dreams, and he let himself fall deep into their gaze of ruddy brown, marbled with segments of green and gray.

They were the eyes of Rhoswen of Kathron Caelie, and they burned with something so fierce, Ultan told himself it could only be love.

RHOSWEN

CHAPTER 55

Battle was a savage thing, a passion far beyond the mind, something feral and untamed, like the swell of the sea's deepest currents rising up from within.

Yet victory was only given to those who could take it by the scruff of the neck and tame it.

For some reason Rhoswen remembered her father's rhetoric as the line of spearman grew and grew, beckoning her close, before she whipped her horse around and ran back the other direction.

It was a swirl of madness, and she loved it.

Some idiot Angle gave the order for the spearman to advance, and they did so unevenly. Like a ripple of water, her cavalry flowed behind her at full gallop, following her every move like a formation of shoals darting through a reef.

"Archers!" Her voice sounded quiet in her ears, barely audible above the pulse of blood and war, and out of the corner of her eye she saw a formless mass of green cloaks, blending in with the crest of the valley hill, twitching once or twice before a haze of black streaked the sky.

Hundreds of spearmen fell, their ranks too thick. Even the most novice arrow hit its mark.

"Chosen!" She bellowed, "Split Two!"

Watching carefully, her head on a swivel, she sought to balance the chaotic living organism that brought the primal fear of every soul caught within its grip to light with the madness that would shun that fear and do such brave things in spite of its shackles.

For Albanland.

For her.

Many would die today, she knew that, and she would take their souls upon her own, never forgetting their sacrifice.

But she would be damned if she wasted one single life like a drunken chancer blowing his father's inheritance in a game of Rook's Table.

War was no game.

At the head of its V-shaped formation, Rhoswen rolled the cavalry up the hill as her own spearmen waited behind the archers. Most were levy, those not suited for combat but damn sick enough of the oppression that they would die for a shot at what freedom Rhoswen had promised to give them. The Bowgirls released another hail, every arrow thumping true as her Chosen, armed with their choice of brutal two-handed axes or dull swords and thin wooden shields, advanced in two columns with the dread purpose of those who were not afraid of death, the blue knot tattoos on their bare arms a vivid reminder of the promises they'd made in the depths of the forest.

"Come on, come on…" Rhoswen said, teeth clenched as she slowed her horse next to the Master Archer, the young woman's graceful form bearing an oddly serene expression as her Bowgirls loaded another hail.

"Hold." The Master Archer said, and quickly lowered her gaze. "We need to draw out the cavalry before we engage. There must be eight-hundred armed knights to our forty or so."

"They're not coming." Rhoswen tried to still her restless horse, but her own breath came in rushes beneath the stiff plate armor that covered her body from the neck to the waist. "They're guarding those war machines."

"You know why?" The Master Archer smirked, her long blonde hair woven into a braid running down her back.

Rhoswen swallowed as the Angle spearmen spread. There were enough of them to swallow her Chosen, her best foot soldiers, like a rock in the sea.

"Let them." She grunted, whipping her horse into a run. The Master Archer followed, her tall black Friesian eating up the ground with the ease in which she drew her antler bow, the rich and vivid shade of the horse's perfect blackness kissed by wings about her hoofs and the glossy shine of her eyes.

And upon the black horse, The Master Archer was death herself.

Her bow was nearly five feet of elk antlers, joined together by a rod of silver in which she notched one of her bodkin arrows. Rhoswen watched as she peeled her giant horse from Rhoswen's pack, riding into the fray. Rhoswen fought a pang to see her leave, but thought to herself that if the Master Archer died, they would all die.

The Crown Heir sat up in the saddle and wheeled the thunder of her cavalry around to the precarious edge of the valley as her Chosen ran with a roar of One to engage the endless sea of spearman. The clash of flesh and bone, wood and steel rocked the earth, peppered with sickening snaps and the crisp clang of weapons. The Bowgirls wisely rained death over the heads of their own swordbrothers as the Angle spearmen fought in a congested tangle of glory-seeking, as if trying to push through a door too small for them all to fit.

"Charge!" Rhoswen shouted, whipping her horse down the curved edge of the valley, watching as the endless line of Angles grew and grew and grew till they were right before her, unaware that they'd been outflanked because their generals were arrogant men unaccustomed to bravery bristle the battlefield before them like a forest fire.

Rhoswen steeled herself to poorly commanded Angle's screams, and the savagery of killing them lost in blurs and flashes, the slender steel of her sword gleaming and gashing as if it had a mind of its own.

Perhaps it did.

It belonged to her father.

The Chosen fought the urge to crumble and shifted to the left, tightening around each other as Rhoswen and her small band of horses cut a swath to meet them, trampling all in their way to mulch. She could see their eyes, hear their shouts as they fought for their lives, and felt their pain as they bled for her.

"Retreat!" She cried as the Angle spearman found themselves stuck between lines, another wave of arrows whistling for their heads, and Rhoswen curled her horses around the remaining body of the Chosen, some eighty or so left alive and ready for more, the Angles unwilling to pursue.

A whistle shrieked from her lips and her own spearman, far too many of them old farmers and scrawny youths with willing hearts, stamped their weapons to the ground and began to march forward.

Somewhere, in the storm of it all, the single blast of a horn filled the valley, as if the misty green spread of earth amplified the purity of that one long and beautiful note, and Rhoswen snapped her head to the left and right till she found the source.

Ultan.

He looked dead, his skin stripped of the color that always felt so hot in her hand when she touched his cheek, thinking thoughts not fit for a child in their summers together, shrinking away from the fact that she had somehow, strangely, dreamed the moment they now found themselves in.

And she swallowed.

If she didn't know him, she would've thought he was a Nørd. Dressed like one, blowing the horn of one.

Distracted, Rhoswen looked back as her retreat ended, cavalry and Chosen both catching their breath.

Her eyes swelled in their sockets as if she'd angered gods she didn't knew existed.

For there were stones in the sky. Giant stones.

And they were flying toward her and her pitiful little army of misfits.

NEVAN & NILES

CHAPTER 56

In the horrid riptide of chaos, Niles Rodgers somehow grew taller and more slender and athletic, rising to the occasion as he nudged his horse closer to the Crown Heir and shoved a defiant gesture toward the sky as a deadly smoke gray quarry stone flew over his head and thudded to the earth, biting a clod of dirt and grass from the ground the size of a small house before skidding to a halt.

"Form up!" Rhoswen shouted to the levies, the old men, the young boys, their long spears but sharp shafts of wood with no steel to tip them. Niles felt better about his sword and shield, his skill meriting that each be made of good heavy steel.

Not the same for Nevan, clutching his paltry weapon some sixty feet away, ill-fitting helm cocked unevenly on his head. Niles caught his eye and Nevan looked away.

Sir Craig was next to Niles, managing the Chosen on foot. Even with his limp, he was surprisingly fast when he needed to be. Those of their numbers still left alive were strong and ready for more, too filled with adrenaline to think about their fallen comrades, chopped up and gutted, not that far away.

Niles threw his glance to Rhoswen, who juggled her agitated horse and her thoughts, her heart rattling off the cage of polished silver that was her form-fitting plate armor.

No arrow could pierce her, no sword could slice her through. But a boulder, larger than a horse, thrown from a weight and balance catapult the size of a small tower?

Even Niles was a bit scared of the thought.

To be squashed, like a bug.

Skin, bones, guts, everything.

Splat.

Out of the swirling chaos the tall black Friesian of the Master Archer materialized, her face flat and free of emotion, though her skin was pale.

"Rhoswen!" She snapped, and Rhoswen eyed her as if she were a ghost.

But the ghost was not the Master Archer, it was the hulking strawberry-haired Nørd warrior that'd blown that Nørd horn and filled the valley with its strange and mournful note. It'd done something to Rhoswen, Niles thought, feeling weak and vulnerable on his scrawny black stallion next to the Master Archer and her magnificently powerful creature.

"Shall we engage or hold our position?" Sir Craig piped in. What was left of Rhoswen's four thousand and some odd soldiers, most of them not really soldiers at all, just the rabble of revolution, held fast for the time being.

Till more boulders took to the sky.

Damn, it stole the breath, to see something so big so carelessly launched into the air. The sheer marvel of the mechanics of the giant war machines promised that no matter *what* Rhoswen did, some day, they would come again, with more, bigger and better, hungrier and stronger.

Niles swallowed as four giant stones tumbled through the smoky sea above them all, their unevenness tearing vaporous trails as they flew. Rhoswen stared at them, transfixed, watching in silence as they shadowed her face and landed harmlessly behind the Bowgirls with ground-shaking thuds.

"It won't take them long to calibrate the distance." The Master Archer said, a scientist of such things herself. "We *must* move. We must try to flank them and destroy those machines!"

"We move, we die!" Sir Craig said, feeling vulnerable in his old age with a scatter of semi-crazed young men under his command, their weapons not sharp enough to make up for their lack of battlefield experience. "The Angles haven't even let loose their cavalry! They want us to close the distance so they can chop us down like harvest wheat. We hold the high ground and we should keep it."

The Master Archer bit her lip. He was right about their horses. The Angle cavalry were like little fortresses, and fear was their greatest weapon. What was a simple farmer with a long wooden spear to do against the earth-rending rush of eight hundred rumbling beasts, sharp lances staring down spit-flecked muzzles and galloping hooves.

"We must do *something*." The Master Archer's whisper was harsh, like the gnaw of a bowstring pulling taut.

And she was right. The army was one stone splat away from snapping and running every direction like madmen.

It was then Niles felt his stomach lurch within, hearing a sound his ears had never heard before.

Something so devastatingly fierce, it must've been a sound shorn straight from an epic saga.

Voices. Tons of them, hundreds upon hundreds.

Niles watched Rhoswen's almond eyes narrow and then stretch wide only to narrow again as she threw her gaze to the mist-covered hills and back to the strawberry-haired man who staggered, dazed and confused, alone, in the middle of the battlefield, as if trying to walk to her but his feet were stuck in the mud and muck.

They were Nørd voices.

Rhoswen sat tall in her saddle, her small frame fierce and wild as the voices spilled from the fog and echoed throughout the valley.

"This day, my friends," She shouted, wheeling her horse around and trotting down the line of levies, Bowgirls behind them. "This day we bury the past and forge the future in our own blood, with our *own* hands." Her three-color eyes sought to touch each and every soul as the massive war machines readied another flight of stones. She would not be rushed, and scanned the faces set grim and cold before her.

"Today, there is no color. No creed. No race. No gender. No strife. No division. Nothing else but one mighty hand," Her sword flashed high, zinging the air, "One mighty body, made one by the hatred of oppression, the hatred of death and darkness and the evil shackles and chains that have stifled the growth of the generations. Only our love of freedom will make us whole again!"

Not one mouth cheered, but there was a pulse rippling along Niles' spine, bubbling like whitecaps along the rocks and he knew he wasn't the only one ready to run faster than his feet knew how, faster than the scrawny stallion upon which he sat, flying straight into the mouth of death on the wings of the wind.

"Fight and die for one another's dreams of a brighter day, and it shall come! Fight and die for one another's children, and they shall realize the truth of this precious promise!" Rhoswen shouted, running her horse along the line again as the voices roared through the hills, louder, and the war machines creaked and groaned, ready to launch.

"Fight for those who have already fallen in the darkness so that you may honor their legacy as you taste the light of a new dawn. Fight for yourself, fight for me, fight for my late father and my mother, and I will make you all peers of the Realm."

Rhoswen jerked her horse to a halt at the edge of the line, staring hot and defiant into the valley as the war machines flipped and flung their stones with savage jerks and slaps, great big *whooshes* and *whumps* scarring the air.

Her voice was hushed, as if coming from a place far across the sea.

"For we are One and the same. We are Albans, and we will not be denied our equal right to live in our land as we please. In the name of all that is sacred, we are the Chosen, and we will not be denied! Today is the day we seize the substance of that which we believe! Today is the Day of Destiny! WE WILL NOT BE DENIED!!!"

Whether it was a shout or a scream, Niles would never know. It was an incredible wall of sound, rising up like an invisible castle keep, up through the sky, establishing something holy between the heavens and the earth.

Niles lost himself in that tremendous rush of human emotion, torn from the throat to rage against the oppressive sky clinging lower and lower to the misty hills and the deadly stones tumbling down from its slate skin, and before he knew it, he was moving, tears streaming his eyes to whip his horse into full gallop, riding on a surge of voices rushing to close the distance between the living and the dead.

ULTAN

CHAPTER 57

It was instinct that had blown the horn, not really knowing what would happen once he did, but the moment Ultan heard the voices of Eyvind Frey's six hundred elite Nørd warriors, rocking the highland hills to shower down from the mist, it was like spitting whiskey on a fire.

Suddenly his senses burned from within, flared to life, caught in the middle of no man's land, while around him, madness reigned, vicious and insane. He ran to retrieve Arturo's nimble sword as Rhoswen's Army advanced, her cavalry rushing around the edge of the valley to provoke a reaction from the heavily armored Angles.

Ultan knew the tides of battle. In split seconds judgments were made, decisions sabotaged by jealousies and old wounds when so many men threw their fist in the air to say they were in command, so many ways to go wrong and spoil the victory.

The masses of spearmen threatened to break and bolt for their lives, their group leaders hollering for them to hold. The Lords and Barons argued amongst themselves over who to engage as Rhoswen rushed to outflank them, letting her some four-thousand strong levies, interspersed with her Bowgirls and her fierce Chosen, trudge faithfully up the field to nullify the distance of the stone-slinging war machines.

Ultan soured to see the war machines were operated by slaves.

He wanted to kill the lot of the Angles for it, one by one till there were no more of them, their slaver legacy erased from the land.

But there were just too damn many of them, scattered across the valley like weeds in spring. Embedding themselves, threatening to take root.

The ground-shaking Nørd holler spiraled down from the heights and told Ultan to run, feeling the rage of life awakened surge within. His green eyes jumped to the hills. Thick and fearless men, wrapped in the heavy pelts of black bears, wolves, badgers and deer to make them look even bigger than they were, spilled from the mist in a human landslide of hefty axes and round shields marked by colored dragons and three-headed dogs bearing fangs.

The Angle Barons were caught in their pandering, and one of them gave the order to divide the spearmen, shifting nearly half of them to cut off Rhoswen's effort to sweep around behind the mass of bodies. They replied with what haste and order they could manage.

But it was too late.

Nearly six hundred muscle-bound Nørds gushed down the hill and shoved their way deep into the spearmen, still too congested to use the length of their weapons to their full advantage, and the Nørds buried themselves deep in the heart of the pack, allowing themselves to be swallowed alive in the throng.

The Angle Barons quickly ordered the traitorous Albans to help shore up the holes the Nørd warriors had hacked through, the ill-prepared spearmen falling in fear, shocked at the speed and severity in which the Nørd skillfully sliced through their ranks, their weapons and experience giving them something of a ten to one advantage over the shocked quagmire of Angle levies.

Maybe the Angles were realizing in that fateful moment their numbers were nothing more than bodies, thrown like dice across the green felt of the valley.

But with the death of their future King, Arturo of Pallantyne, at the hand of the fierce and plate-armored woman charging straight for their blindside, the traitorous Albans that were supposed to turn the tide simply bolted and ran.

Ultan nearly leapt for joy as Rhoswen changed direction, not allowing the thirst for revenge to chase down the fleeing cowards and cut them down take her over.

She was in control.

In control like he *hadn't* been fighting Arturo.

Seamlessly, her cavalry followed as if connected to one another by an invisible thread, and they rode straight through a weakness in the divided forces to punch through the gap and leave a scatter of flattened and cleaved bodies in their wake.

"You!" Ultan heard behind him and nearly jumped out of his skin as a massive black Friesian pounded closer, nearly materializing out of the mist that the Nørds seemed to bring with them as they descended into the valley. The horses' eyes were somehow as just sweet as they were strong, and the blonde-haired woman on the horse leaned in the saddle to stretch her graceful grip toward him, her other hand on a bow fashioned from elk antlers.

"You're him, aren't you?" She said, more of a challenge than a question. He couldn't read the expression in her blue eyes, but it said a great deal.

Ultan's mind spun, his right arm still dripping blood from the near-bone gash of the swift blade.

But he knew what she meant.

"Ultan of Skyeshire is my name." He said. "And Rhoswen is *my* Queen and will be for as long as I live."

The faintest flash of a smile rippled across the Master Archer's face and she leapt off her horse and shoved him into the broad saddle.

He heard her hiss to see his wound, stowing the confiscated sword in a sheath buried in the saddle.

"You can handle her?" She asked.

"Rhoswen?"

"No, Eemkje."

Ultan assumed she meant the horse.

"Oh yes, absolutely."

"Alright then," The Master Archer vaulted up behind him, shoving him forward in the saddle and removing a small white surrender flag to tie up his wound. "Bring us around to the back of the cavalry, on the eastern edge of the valley. Time for a turkey shoot."

Ultan liked her tremendously, her confidence and her pragmatism. With all the strength he could muster, he obeyed her order to the fullest.

Eemkje rode tall and dignified, pounding across the field with ease. He arced their path around behind the Bowgirls just as they launched a hail into the divided group of spearman left facing the Nørd berserkers. There were hardly any of them left.

Ultan squinted, his eyes nearly tearing up. His body felt so weak, each thud of the horse's hooves echoing through his body, the clangor and mayhem of war some dark and distant smudge, like rain smeared upon the sea, muted and dying in his ears as the world darkened around him.

"Don't you dare die on me, Skölhammer." The Master Archer said, tightening the white surrender flag around his arm to staunch the bleeding. His body rocked as she jerked the bandage tight. "You just hold on. Eemkje knows what to do."

And she was right.

The massive horse skirted the edge of conflict, and the Master Archer notched a bodkin arrow in her bow.

Ultan barely heard the whistle, but he twitched his eyes across the field and saw one of the Angle Barons fall from his horse, a wooden shaft protruding from the soft space between the bottom of his shiny helm and the collar of his expensive chainmail.

"How many of those do you have?" Ultan asked, his eye catching Rhoswen's second charge of the dislocated spearmen, ending in a tangle with a counter-attack of the bolder Barons. Upon their horses, pennants flapping house colors in the wind their gallops made, they were like self-contained empires, each heavily armored horse a name, an estate, a legacy of greed and courrpution.

"Not enough." She nearly growled through grit teeth as Eemkje rushed toward the knot of cavalry, Rhoswen's Chosen now locked in horse to horse combat with the ravenous Lords of Angle.

He felt every one of their clatters and smacks, wincing at the weight of the Angle maces, the spiked balls and chains whipped and whacked in survivalist frenzy, the light of midday seeming to dim the nearer he drew to the rhythmic calamity of death.

The Master Archer's breath was hot on his neck as she leaned behind him and *pliffed* another arrow across the mayhem, striking a heavyset slaver in the leg. He fell from the saddle, just as he was about to stab Niles in the back, the sixteen year old as white as the bandage around Ultan's arm to realize he'd almost died without even knowing it.

Without seeing it coming.

Without having the time to make it right in the storm of his soul.

Ultan stretched his gaze past the combat before it enveloped them, and his flexed the fingers of his arm to see if they still worked, if he could draw a sword.

The Nørd berserkers had devastated the spearmen that once surrounded them. Howling like wild hounds, loosed to the night of a full moon, they broke through and were now rushing the second mass of spearmen, their numbers hardly dwindled.

Leading from the back was a man with strawberry blonde hair and devious blue eyes, his long sword stained red, his skin splattered with mud.

Ultan caught his eye and smiled.

Eyvind Frey winked at him and picked up the pace to jog after his men, shouting orders in the lilting language Ultan knew he'd be speaking a lot of in the future.

If he lived to see another day.

The remaining spearmen, nearly five thousand to their number, took it upon themselves to stuff their weapons tight under their armpits and shout their own charge, though no one was leading them. A scatter of arrows pierced them from the side as they ran wildly into the teeth of the Nørd, and Rhoswen's some four thousand broken-down revolutionaries released their own war cries as they lowered their sharpened wooden sticks and crushed into the fray.

Crying for their mothers and fathers, brothers and sisters, sons and daughters.

Even for their cattle, for the ground itself.

Crying for freedom.

It was then Ultan felt his body melt like animal fat on the roasting spit, a hot and sizzling goo squeezed from the inside out, spinning spinning spinning away from the tangle of his mind. The sky above him hung heavy and low, darker than the memories of his mother's arms.

Arms.

Yes, arms did wrap around him and hold him tight, the violence of the battle but the bubble of a pot boiling over, cut with the scattered slashes and smacks of tiny silver trinkets like pots and pans and knives and spoons in the kitchen.

For some reason, the scent of a rose was strong in his untethered mind before the world around him bled crimson, coughing up sour bile darker than the night sea, black as the beautiful horse that carried his corpse straight into Valhöll upon the swiftest wings, his head slumping against his chest to remember no more.

NEVAN & NILES

CHAPTER 58

Niles shuddered to think of what he'd become, what war had done to him within a fraction of a second.

If he could even spare a second to think.

In that tender, fractious space of time, worlds had been cleaved, minds cracked open, spilt upon the soil, arms tossed and tangled, hopes and fears chomping and chewing the chains of chaos.

Thinking? It was the furthest thing from him, pushed back by the wind of the Four Storms. No, he had *become* war, become a man possessed by the foaming fury running through his body, controlling him with a white-hot desire that stretched far beyond the moment, as if he were but a sickle of retribution ready for harvest, drawing upon every breath of the nine years his mother had been the slave of an Angle Baron.

The din clattered around him, munching through his muscles and bones, tempting to bury him alive in the roiling sea noise and confusion, trying to strip him of the razor-like focus he'd always held onto as his secret weapon to avoid the irresistible feeling of drowning in the overwhelming wash of it all.

But this was not cards or darts.

This was war.

Fighting just to stay in the saddle of his scrawny black stallion, scrapping and jostling just to resist the screams and the stray spear points, Niles ducked and dived, urging his horse to stray pockets of space for safety, as if he were caught in a living puzzle of horrors.

But those spaces would close as soon as they opened up, splashed with the blood of the fallen, thrown from the saddle or trampled under hooves, their cries muffled by clods of mud and swathes of cloth, death and the defiance of it echoing around the tinny smack of weapons and armor.

Niles ignored the chopping breath in his throat turning his lungs to sticky porridge and drove his stallion forward.

He had to find his Queen.

But Rhoswen was lost in his sight behind two brick-like Angle Lords, wildly flinging their spiked maces at her slight form.

He wanted to help her, but he couldn't.

He had his own problems.

Niles twisted away from the sword slashed his way at the very last moment and reached out with his own weapon, squeezing the hilt tight as it jerked so violently in his grip he nearly dropped it.

His eyes all but glazed over. The Angle Baron that'd tried to end his life grabbed the stump of his arm where Niles had severed it from the joint. The man was silent and sick behind the blocky silver helmet, eyes cast in shadow as he fell from the saddle in slow motion.

A cry slashed through his ear, distinguished through the swirling storm of all the others by the tang of its desperation, the utter despair of its plea.

It was Nevan's voice.

Niles whipped his gaze back to Rhoswen, lost in the muddle of no longer two armored knights but four, collapsing about her like points of the compass. Closing in, greedy for the glory that came from sticking the head of the long-lost Crown Heir on a spike. A whip of curly brown hair twisted to mingle with a fluid spire of silver, sucking up all the light in the sky. Something wild framed her body, something so beautiful and painfully out of place, as if she shouldn't even be here, in the thick of it, but rather, royal and regal on the Throne, even though everything in her life had gone so terribly wrong.

But here she was, the woman she was *because* of it, hacking and chopping her way back to her inheritance with every fiber of her being.

Queen of War, Queen of Rage, Queen of the New Dawn of the New Day.

If death and darkness didn't gut her like loch trout first.

Niles had to bite down on his tongue to avoid rushing to her aid.

Still horribly outnumbered, she didn't need it.

But his brother did.

Nevan ran, scared out of his shoes with the dark swathes of Nørds, their tree-splitting axes cracking limbs and spears, roaring and rushing around him to charge the Angle footmen, running over the lifeless bodies of those poor souls Nevan had come to know as friends and near family over the past few months, marching and marching and marching to finally meet this moment.

As if it was all worth it.

Their blood was on his hands, falling from once being shoulder to shoulder, leaning against his elbows and knees as the order came to press on, though his body was limper than a carrot that'd sat too long in the broth. His fallen friends squelched his steps in the mud, making it hard to move as he ran toward the wall of spears, his own voice lost in the mingle of others, but his legs refused to respond, as if bravery held no home in his bones.

Nothing more than an empty holler foreign to his ears.

Chaos splattered and streaked around him and he felt fire gush free from his belly in the moment of the clash, casting him down, unevenly, to the mud. Momentum carried him in a tumble, stripping him of his spear, as if he could even hold onto it anyway, weak hands unfit for war.

And though he fell, the battle raged on, its savage nature seizing the valley like a freshly bloomed flower in a fist, squeezing and squeezing and squeezing till the tender and beautiful young petals had been turned to dust, their vibrant colors the painful stain of a memory.

Still, he had charged, he had not given up, he had not broken or turned his back to run the other direction, despite every rational thought in his mind telling him to do so.

And now, as his reward, the ground welcomed him with its coolness, pulling him close with a soft and squishy embrace.

He rolled on his back.

Grubby hands shook as they touched the liquid flame eating up his belly. Pulling them back, he stared at them. Crimson dripped from his fingertips as they trembled, odd glare of the sky stabbing at his brown eyes through the spread of his fingers.

And that was when he cried.

He emptied every regret in his soul to the sky, pushing the jumble of his misunderstandings through the mesh of blood and broken flesh, his face a twisted grimace of pain and sorrow.

He didn't get it. He would never get it.

He did not belong here. He did not want to die here.

Please, he begged the obstinate gray sky, as if it gave a damn, since it'd seen him rise to a moment of self-sacrifice only to have it take a horrible turn for the worst.

Please, don't let me die. I don't want to die. Please, don't let me...

A cough sputtered through his throat, wracking his body as he twisted in the mud to spit out something hot and sticky, squishing more life from his skin, feeling light-headed and weak as the cool ground beckoned him close, again.

Just stay here awhile, the soft valley grass said, giant emerald hills bending around him, mist and clouds wispy about their shoulders like blankets, or cottonseed blossoms, tangled in the refreshing wind that brushed a finger across his dark hair, cooling the sticky sweat clinging to his forehead.

Nevan took a breath to still himself, letting his arms fall to his side. Pain flooded him with a numbing burn, slowing his breath, emptying him of the burden of life, and he relaxed to the notion that battle wasn't for him, and he was going to die, staring at the sky and the matchless beauty of the unbroken hills just at the edge of his dimming vision.

It was okay with him.

A clod of hooves drew near and he heard a smooth swish just over the rattle of swords. Grunting, a squelch of mud. Silver spiked and spoke up for him with brutality, with efficiency, but he didn't hear it.

He didn't think about it.

He couldn't.

Somewhere near, a dull sword worked its magic through a duo of Angles, staggering and tripping but failing to give up, thrusting through the fray with one single purpose shining brighter than the sun. Just kids, most of them, scruffy little dreamers with their entire lives ahead of them, paths twisted and ruined by the stony greed of a hundred Lords and Barons as if they were gods among men.

And where were they now?

Nevan blinked and blinked.

Please...

It was okay, it was okay to die alone, peacefully alone, not even knowing who had stabbed him, not seeing the Angle face at the end of that terribly ugly spear in that mad dash to try and be brave, failing so miserably.

It was okay...

"Nev!" Niles splashed down in the smear of mud and blood, his face red with exertion. "Nev!" He shook his brother again, Nevan's head lolling loosely as if his bones were no longer stiff and strong.

"Ni..." Was the lonely muffle in his throat.

"Hell on fire, Nev, don't you dare leave me."

Nevan felt his younger brother hoist him upright, sitting next to him, a shelter in the storm.

"Ni...I'm s-sorry."

His eyes were too blurry to see what Nevan was talking about. Niles scraped a sleeve across his face, tears mixing with dust and dirt.

"About what?" He shook his brother gently, not allowing himself to admit it.

There was no light in those brown eyes.

"About Fins…tell her I'm sorry."

"*You* tell her." Niles said, looking around desperately for something, someone, realizing, in that moment, it was the way of war.

People got hurt and died.

In the time it took someone to cough, a life was snuffed, a candle robbed of its light, a soul bound to a wisp of dissipating smoke, never to return.

"N-no…" Nevan eyes rolled back in his skull and he turned to Niles, somehow grabbing a spark of consciousness from the murk he'd fallen into. Niles' hand was pressed to his stomach, but it was too late.

"Nev, don't leave me. I don't want to be alone."

"You won't be." He said, lucidly, as if that made up for his dying. "You have her."

Niles frowned.

"Don't be stupid. She loves you, man. Don't you know that? Don't hang on for me…I know I've been an ass. But hang on for her, okay? She deserves it."

Nevan nearly drowned in his own skin again and Niles shook him.

"No no no…" Nevan said, trailing off. At least it was the only word Niles could make sense of, some cold delirium stretching its fingers across his brother.

Niles cringed, feeling helpless, his muscles suddenly weary, pulled from the blaze of the fighting, where the madness somehow made sense, as if he were the eye of the storm, made brave by speed and confusion, like it was all a race and death couldn't catch him.

But holding his smaller, weaker, soft-spoken brother, he felt so vulnerable and helpless himself, not so majestic and fierce, like the right hand of Rhoswen.

And there wasn't a damn thing he could do about it.

Niles shivered.

Death was in the air, stalking whom it willed, whom it pleased. The silent executioner, the thief of a single moment in time, slicing the spine of those who had their back turned, stopping the pulse of them who dared take a moment to catch their breath.

Niles grabbed his brother's face in both hands.

"Listen to me, you bastard! There's no point without you!" Tears dripped upon his brothers chest like drops of rain on a loch. "We're brothers! Please forgive me for everything I said…for the way I've been, I just…it's…"

Eloquent words evaded him.

And he kept on repeating *we're brothers we're brothers we're brothers*, weeping and shaking his brother's body as the last of Nevan's life sat bunched up deep inside a dark corner of his soul like a young boy that never wanted to leave his home or the comfort of his mother's arms, wishing to hear her stories and songs over a simmering pot of stew, but had no choice in the matter when destiny had, that awful day, so many years ago, reached its poisoned claws down into his little world and snatched it all away.

And the last thing Nevan heard was his brothers words, begging him not to go, though the rotten stench of mud and sweat and death had somehow been replaced in his delirious mind by the savory smell of stew, spicy and warm with his mother's laughter.

RHOSWEN

CHAPTER 59

Tearing at the clinging fog with skeletal claws, the death of midday saw the silence of the fallen mix and mingle with eerie curls and coils of mist, hushed and chilling.

To Rhoswen, the brutality of the battle's inevitable end had been lost in the bewildering realization that she'd survived its horror. Stunned, as if frozen and numb to it all, she let the warrior's fire slide away, sheathing it once again, only to fear the moment of its summons in the coming future.

For it was *complete* possession, war and battle. Nothing could be held back.

Rhoswen surveyed the stoic tableau of madness through a beleaguered squint and sighed. Breathlessly she set about picking up the broken pieces of her ravaged Army.

They had won.

They had *actually* won.

But there was no cheer to shake the foundations of the earth, no rousing war song to fill the hearts and minds with the stuff of legends.

Just silence.

That strange sound of nothing.

The coming of the fog was a bad omen, she noted, for those who believed in them, and she nearly shivered in the subtle fall of darkness and the cold that would come with it. What had become of summer? Gone, so soon? Yes, gone, like the many youths who'd died that day her revolutionary campaign.

Above, Solara's light was still scattered throughout the thickness of the clouds, but that light was being pulled away, slowly, as if by a cord, just like so many poor souls scattered across the valley.

Valley of the Brave? Valley of the Damned?

Valley of the Chosen.

Rhoswen drifted through the scattered remains of what was left, not surprised to see familiar faces, and saddened to see the smudges and stains of those who hadn't made it, their injuries too great to bear, or their lives ended in but an instant. Though her legs were leaden and heavy, she roamed the field as Sir Craig organized the retreat with some rich Angle Barons in tow as prisoners, and, the best bounty of all, their war machines, now her prize.

Hopefully she'd never need to use them.

Rhoswen stood stone still as she watched the tall young blonde, Niles Rodgers was his name, of Clan Ross, distantly, a Southern youth whose mother had been enslaved by lowland Angle for nine years. He'd fought with the heart of two lions and had become a blubbering mess when his brother fell to the crush of the charge that'd broken the battle in half. Rhoswen watched as Niles attended to his brother Nevan's body with two older women, what little life remained in the boy holding on by the tenderest of threads.

So much ran through her mind as she walked the field, her heart breaking a thousand times like the endless sea upon the shore, as if it did nothing *but* break, again and again and again and again, only to spot the look of freedom in someone's eye, that undeniable ember aching set the soul ablaze.

Somehow it made it all worth it.

Or did it?

And even now, her new Army of One had but one battle under their belt, *one* small battle in a battle-life…could they bring themselves to do it again? Or would the seizing of peace, that elusive treasure, make them again soft and weak, unwilling to stand up for themselves when oppression once again stretched its hand across their families and their farms?

Rhoswen spat and cursed, walking and walking, thinking and thinking. Each thought was a knife to her tenderness, beaten back by the shield that made her tough and fierce, the mechanisms that made her Queen, though she hated having to be so, wanting so desperately to run away and cry over the waste of life and wealth scarring the field with blood and corpses.

It would forever be gambler's chance. Some would die, some would live. Some would find peace, but only if they were prepared for war.

And she would be responsible for all of it.

And so Rhoswen walked, wondering what to do.

Was there, in heaven and hell, a way to stop it all from ever happening again, a way to somehow save the land from the curse of such a terrible duel?

If only she knew.

And she didn't care about it anymore, because out of the swirling mist, leaning on the slender and reed-like Master Archer for stability, strode Ultan of Skyeshire.

Alive and well.

Rhoswen rushed to meet him, her feet freed of the glue that'd bound her to the ground when she'd been thrown from her horse to fight for her life. The sunlight of spring splashed beneath her, and the Master Archer whispered up into the mass of bare-chested muscle, Ultan's strawberry blonde hair swaying with labored steps, his white wolf cloak streaked by dried crimson.

Green eyes rose to meet her gaze, melting with sorrow, tasting her urgency as she sprinted to meet him.

Heir to the Wind, Champion of Nothing, he was Lord of No One, save the heart of a little girl who would never forget the calloused palms of her first love, or the sound of his voice.

The glorious hue of those heather green eyes, somehow humble and hard in the same measure.

So human.

In those eyes slept every desire of her royal heart, and to see them was to remember that she *hadn't* forgotten.

To finally feel the shards of heat and life rippling inside of them was to once again taste something so pure and so ancient, it seemed like it belonged to someone else, forever ago.

"Looks like I found something that belonged to you." The Master Archer nearly winked with a rare dose of humor, proud of herself that she'd all but saved Ultan from sure death.

Ultan's mouth opened to speak but Rhoswen didn't give him the chance. She planted her feet just inside the spread of his own and reached up to clasp her hands on the hard lines of his cheeks.

And kiss him.

If a kiss could span a wicked spell of darkness like a bridge of light and glass, Rhoswen built that bridge and ran across the depthless chasm of lies and despair howling beneath, spanning the hopelessness and the confusion that had split them apart so many years ago, sealing it all up in the space of that perfect kiss.

The days of shaking her fist at the sky, staring at the gap in her hand and its blatant emptiness, the chattering little thoughts and images of Ultan, *her* Ultan, in the arms of another, keeping her awake at night as she tossed and turned, so horribly alone. And Ultan, she could only *dream* of what he'd become, aching to realize that which a young boy had promised to her and *only* her, knowing what that oath would mean as he became a man.

How damn hard it would be to keep.

Rhoswen felt scarred hands draw her closer, swallowing up the small of her back to squeeze their forms together, and she poured every drop of life and energy she had into kissing him.

Beside them, the Master Archer cleared her throat, hands clasped behind her back.

Still Rhoswen and Ultan kissed, passionately, and when the Master Archer realized, now that the fruit of their patience had finally been manifested, not heaven or hell would separate them.

So she left with a scoff and a stray smile, scratching the back of her neck, just beneath the length of her blonde braid.

"I take no responsibility for whatever happens now…" She mumbled to herself, smirking and walking off into the fallen fog, where brilliant black Eemkje awaited with her elken bow and bodkin arrows, neither a scratch nor a scar on either of them.

Nearly breathless after their kiss, Ultan framed her face in his large fingers and stared deep into her eyes.

"They haven't changed at all…yet, so much." His voice cracked, emotion welling up from within. He loved her eyes, their triple-braided cord of colors, exemplifying the essence of who she was in a marbled mosaic.

"Yours look the *exact* same." Rhoswen said, a thin smile drifting across her face, as if the kiss she'd given him was nothing more than a snowflake on a mountain, and the falling of the first snow would soon trigger an avalanche. "Thank heavens, too," She laughed, her face reddened to stuff the moment of Arturo's beheading far from her. "I nearly thought you were a Nørd."

"I am." He said. She tipped her chin up in a silent question. "I am Nørd. I am Alban. Never again will I hate myself for being what I am." Ultan pulled her to his bare chest, squishing her against his strength. She could *hear* the blood beating through him, the breath in his lungs a resonant harmony of her own.

"Fine by me." She said, softly.

"And as long as I live," His voice rumbled, heather green eyes scanning the valley of death and destruction, the valley of *their* victory, "No one who dwells in my land will be ashamed of the blood in their veins."

Rhoswen tipped her gaze toward him, one eyebrow raised. "*My* land?"

"Yes, that's right." Ultan slid her to the cradle of his right arm, ushering them to walk. Away from the battle. "It's mine now as I am its. We have been made one in a trial of fire, never to be separated."

The Crown Heir pursed her lips.

"I'm not so sure you're talking about the land anymore."

"Aren't I?" Ultan surprised himself as a laugh fell unevenly from his mouth. Rhoswen nearly cringed in veiled sorrow to remember the gesture being so adorable when his ears were too big for his head and his eyes too big for his face, when his hair wasn't fully grown out, shaggy, like a ruddy sheep. How he would laugh out of the side of his mouth, as if hiding the joke from the rest of the world, sharing it only with her, how she loved it so.

How she had forgotten the little things and longed so desperately to remember them, in a rush, in a whirlwind, to wrap them all up in her forest green cloak and rush off into a quiet place to eat them up and never let them go.

Well now it was enough to squash her heart like a ripe piece of fruit, that stab of regret, just to think that those years had been squandered in the suffocation of survival's darkest depths. To live through the battle would've been something, but to know that Ultan, the purest promise of the Crown Heir's heart, would be waiting for her, well, it made up for the burden of loosing so many lives.

Rhoswen rested her head on his chest as they walked.

Dark was their past. Blinding would be their dawn.

She couldn't fight the single tear that came to her eye as he stopped and faced her and brought her right hand up to his chapped lips and tenderly kissed the nub of her knuckle where Morgance had removed her finger.

"I never forgot you." He said, his features grim.

"I never forgot *you*."

"You would've if you'd known." He winced, the guilt of a thousand year curse hanging over him like a sword.

Rhoswen shook her head silently, peering into his eyes for an explanation as they hardened.

"What do you mean?"

"I…" Ultan sighed, staring at the ugly gap between her fingers. "I followed you two into the forest that day. I knew you were fighting over me."

Rhoswen swallowed. The last thing she wanted to do was rake over the past and smell the ashes. Death reeked all around them, pushed away by a stagnant wind, choked in the fog. The *last* thing she needed was to recall that day in the woods with the vivid slash of memory she'd lived her life trying so hard to forget.

With all that'd happened, and Ultan *finally* being in her arms and well and alive, she just wanted to let it all…die.

Ancient history.

Die. Go away. Don't come near me! I don't belong to you anymore. I will not be made a prisoner by my memories.

I am a new woman, a life reborn, a destiny made right, that little girl is gone.

Lives lived by others. Not them. Others. People who no longer existed, people who had dissolved in the mists of time.

But she could nearly taste his heaviness, bitter in his voice and cording his muscles like shackles and chains.

"I saw what she did, Rhoswen," his voice fell to a moan. "...I watched it happen, and I..."

Rhoswen's own eyes misted as she watched the tall and broad-chested warrior redden and burn with sorrows so deep they reduced him to an incoherent babble.

He fell to his knees, burying tears of guilt and shame against the woolen fabric of her thighs, his back heaving with heavy sobs that nearly shook the ground beneath her feet.

Rhoswen swallowed her emotion, still so raw and enraged.

Not at him.

No, never at him.

At herself.

Why *had* she run? Why had she left her parents, the best parents a child could ever want, a wise warrior King and a beautiful and loving Queen? Why had she let Morgance win, taking her place? Why had the confusion of the wide open beckoned her when her father had never turned her away, for any reason, and had never said a cross word to her?

What was the matter with her? What had she been afraid of?

Why had she left it all to seek out the forest, only to find that her departure had set off a string of evils the land would never recover from?

Rhoswen stared for a painful moment at her right hand and the emptiness that reigned desolate where there should've been flesh and bone.

It wasn't coming back. And neither was that moment to know why. It'd happened, in another land, in another soul, and she couldn't even remember why, having run so far so fast with so much hatred for what Morgance had made her to be.

King Brom and The Lady of a Thousand Lochs were relics of a bygone era, distant dreams of the wishful, just as were the childhood promises passed between summer buttercups and splashes on the lochshore.

The Crown Heir's eyes fell to the powerfully-built man hugging her knees, his murmurs of grief lost in the turf.

And yet here he was.

Rhoswen knelt and took his face in her hands. His green eyes were rimmed with red, puffy and sleep-worn. Death had been his diet for so long now, dealing it and dodging it, and he nearly crumpled in the tenderness of her touch, like an empty paper sack. The masses of his muscles must've ached, his bones, too, but it was his soul that'd been run ragged a hundred ways from sixday.

Trampled. Broken. Left for dead.

She looked into his eyes for an eternal moment.

And when she spoke, her voice was as clear as the loch spring in which they'd caught their first trout, some eighteen years ago, Solara's light never brighter than that day when they'd shared that little fish over a small fire and knew, somewhere in the substance of secrets that slept deep within their bones, that they and they alone would share something beyond their comprehension for as long as time allowed.

"Ultan of Skyeshire, you are my first love. You are my only love. Whatever has happened will never un-happen, but what will happen from now on will be worth every evil thing that has befallen us both. As sure are there are stars in the sky and sand on the beach, we were meant to be together and I will never forget this moment, more than all that have been, more than all that will be. This is the moment, Ultan of Skyeshire, *this is the moment* that we promised each other we would taste, and no matter what, I will never *ever* forget it."

Calmed by her words, Ultan stilled himself with a heavy sigh, and smiled faintly as she wiped his eyes and kissed away his tears, her lips straying to his, sweetly. Urgently.

When they finally stood, and began to walk hand in hand towards the crown of the valley, leaving the dismay of death and destruction behind them, Ultan let the silence mend him, tempered by the warmth of her presence, inhaling the spice of her sweat and wondering a thousand thoughts about the future.

"Where *is* Morgance?" Rhoswen said, after the silence had wrought its perfect nature between them, and they ceased their walking to behold the coming of evening. Solara's departure mixed majestic threads of peach and gold throughout the thick slabs of pale blue, melting to violet upon wispy straw-like clouds.

"Last I saw her, the Tower of Ullraye."

Rhoswen peered into the darkening horizon, her nostrils flaring at the second coming of retribution and war.

"It doesn't matter to me." Rhoswen promised. "Because she's about to die."

Next to her, Ultan swallowed, hating the idea but being able to do nothing about it.

For Rhoswen could not be Queen with the Ring of Rule around *Morgance'* finger.

Even if it was a ghost of a Kingdom she ruled.

And now that the Angle invasion had been repelled for a season, Rhoswen would not sleep till Morgance, the usurper, drew breath no more.

Ultan could see it in her face.

And it scared him.

CHAPTER 60

The sky was a tortured thing of black and star-gem blue, streaked with the dark scars of storm clouds sliding behind the sulking Tower of Ullraye.

As if driven.

Luna was nowhere to be seen, hiding silver brilliance behind the unnerving power of the gathering gloom. Ice and water laced the sigh of the wind, promising the brooding and mystic doom reserved for nightmares.

"I don't remember it being so ugly up here." Rhoswen said, staring up the length of the Tower, shivering as she did. The shine of her armor had dulled from the week of travel, and she looked dead tired and worn down. Behind her, lugging torches and banners and weapons, snaked the entirety of her Army. Prisoners, war machines, and all those who'd joined the cause followed along, coming from far and wide after hearing of the Angle defeat in the highlands valley at the hands of Rhoswen the Resurrected, as they were now calling her.

But the fight was far from over.

"It wasn't ugly when you were here." Ultan offered a weak smile, though his features were grave, shielded behind her fierce form from those eyes he always felt watching him up in the Tower on a large gray mare. His thick shoulders were bowed and his gaze downcast, heavy with the knowledge, *the sense*, that Morgance was near.

Somewhere.

The Master Archer sat astride Eemkje at the Crown Heir's left hand, surveying the area with her keen eye. Quickly she jostled Rhoswen and pointed as a thin form moped through the gate.

Rhoswen craned her neck to stare into the darkness, her lips thinning at the despondency in which the wispy shape walked, buffeted by each random puff of wind, as if in dream, legs buried to the knee in water.

It was The Thistle.

Rhoswen leapt from her saddle, rushing to catch Aerlyn before she fell.

She felt as if she didn't weigh anything at all, just the palest shadow slipped into folds of cloth like paper in an envelope. Rhoswen jerked her eyes to The Master Archer as she knelt down with a skin of water. Someone brought a torch.

Rhoswen nearly hissed to see the faint green tinge to Aerlyn's alabaster skin, and the near pine-colored smudges under her eyes. Her skin was wet with the sweat of sickness.

"Poison." The Master Archer whispered.

Rhoswen nodded, gently cradling the length of Aerlyn's neck in the crook of her arm.

"What happened here?" She nearly whispered. "Where is everybody?"

"…" Aerlyn tried to speak but the eyes of midnight fluttered as her lips parted. There was a harsh raking in her throat and she arched her back in pain before burying her head in the welcome comfort of Rhoswen's armor and the billowing finery of her green cloak. The Crown Heir sighed as she felt thick tears, wrung from The Thistles' eyes, smear the silver knots woven into the hem of her garment.

Tears of regret, the sorrows of failure.

"Take some men with you and have a look around." Rhoswen ordered, her voice clipped, and The Master Archer was off with a squish of turf and a swish of dark fabric, but not before Rhoswen could add, "And set up your Bowgirls on the walls, just in case." Then she leaned back and ordered Sir Craig to set up camp on the sloped plateau near the trees. Ultan grimaced at the order, since it'd been where he'd broken the Nørd army, but they couldn't fill up the Fortress till it'd been checked to be safe.

Ultan knelt next to Rhoswen and the waif-like woman.

"So this is The Thistle." He said, having heard so much about her and then some throughout their week long journey, as well as the fortuitous story about Rhoswen stumbling upon the battle and figuring if she couldn't win by surprise, then she'd never win, even though it meant having no idea how many she'd be up against or how they'd be arrayed.

But more on The Thistle, he'd learned that her illegal bravery had stolen so much from the Angles over the years, and her gifting the booty to Rhoswen would mean the Crown Heir would be able to feed the thousands and thousands flocking to her and her promise of newness.

Not only that, they'd be able to rebuild that which had fallen to decay, and little by little, take back what'd been ravaged, ruined, or some sick display of both.

"She's quite the wonder." Rhoswen said with a faint smile, nearly parental and wise, but the look in her eyes was somewhat desperate. Echoing.

As if lost.

The Master Archer returned after ten minutes time with Quill and Finleigh, and Rhoswen passed Quill a beleaguered grimace as he fell to the turf next to her and took Aerlyn in his arms, running his hands gently across her brow and beneath her eyes. Rhoswen noticed Ultan squint at the man, just a bit shorter than he and built solidly despite the strangely feminine shirt no Alban man would be caught dead in. It was impossible to miss the small signs that spoke of starvation and imprisonment stretching across his body, from the cuts and bruises on his face and hands to the torn sleeves of the frilly white shirt, stained with soot and dried blood. Behind him, Finleigh looked okay, but desperately scared, her teeth chattering.

Rhoswen's nostrils flared with anger to look into those beguiling España eyes and see their sparkle was gone, stolen by the wicked night and the woman who'd summoned the spooky stain smeared across Ullraye.

She was about to ask a question but Quill spoke, Aerlyn murmuring something in his arms.

"It's a spell." He said. "I could break it but I…" He stopped, as if riding a horse in a race and had just come face to face with a wall that shouldn't be before him but was.

Like he'd said something aloud he didn't mean to, and the mistake of having done so burned through his bones.

Rhoswen read his face as such and her voice was laced with the authority he knew *not* to question.

"But *what?*"

Her stern gaze questioned so much more. Quill had never before expressed knowledge of the Faer to her. How could he tell poison from a spell?

Rhoswen didn't even believe in spells.

But it didn't really matter. She sure believed in Quill's desire for Aerlyn. She could see the way it took him over and flattened his mouth in strained silence as he held her thinness close.

Ultan was still beside her but she felt him tighten up and glance around, focused on several different spaces throughout the dark slurry of Ullraye. The gate. The walls. The twisted path to the sea. The sloping plain. The woods beyond them. And a spot over Rhoswen's shoulder. A dark spot. Darker than the darkness clamped around them.

She caught him looking and stood up.

"What?" She said, her voice harsh. Next to her, The Master Archer had her bow in hand, notching a steel-tipped bodkin arrow, and was casting sharp eyes up to the sky, reading the splashes of ice blue, cut by the razors of near black clouds.

Ultan stared at Quill for a moment.

"You came how long ago?" He asked.

"Nearly a week."

"And how many were here when you came?"

"Hardly any." Quill looked around. "That's before they went crazy."

"What?" Rhoswen crouched, too many thoughts rushing through her mind. Aerlyn seem to warm under Quill's touch, curling inward at the sound of his voice, as if there were embers in it, and the probing fingers of the wind were trying to dig secrets out of her skull. A soft moan fell in Quill's lap as he stood up, her body limp across his arms, and he hugged her tightly to him.

"I knew it didn't go well with Aerlyn when we were thrown in the dungeon," Quill said, quickly, his own light blue eyes jittery to scan the darkened smudge behind the Fortress. Away from the sea. Away from the slope of the field. Deep into the prickled edges of a scant copse of trees. And the skies above, well, they followed his focus, as if being herded toward that thorny embrace along the horizon.

"I did my best to protect Finleigh's honor but they were determined to have their way with her when they threw us in the dungeon. They knocked another one of my teeth out and nearly chopped off my right hand. And they would've had not the scream turned the place loose."

The way he said *the scream* plunged a knife in Rhoswen's back and twisted.

Hard.

And the sour splash of anguish that curdled her blood was that of a memory, soaked in hatred, a scream that had shattered her spirit before the knife took her finger.

Yes, Rhoswen knew *the scream*.

The scream that tore through the roots of the forest and shot those paralyzing green eyes with the odd yellow light she'd never forget. The scream that seared like steel, the scream that sheared flesh from bone, the scream that splashed blood.

Rhoswen flinched in the memory's stain and shook it off, hoping no one'd noticed.

"So what happened?" She steeled herself to say, drawing her cloak around her as Aerlyn took a normal sigh, nice and deep, though her eyes were slow to open.

"One of the guards was about to take an axe to my wrist but he froze as the scream ran through the stone. Everyone heard it. The guard who'd stretched his hand toward Finleigh to tear her shirt off pulled it back instantly and they all looked at each other for a moment and then they left. About an hour later, we heard six hells break loose. Every kind of noise under the sun. It was absolute chaos, like the Four Storms had been unleashed inside everyone's mind. They…they all just went crazy and ran off, leaving us for dead. This is the first time I've seen Aerlyn since that night she climbed up the Tower to steal the Ring."

Rhoswen's eyes drifted to Ultan, who stood, neck jutted, hands trembling at the hilt of his sword, the Blade of the Champion restored to him from the valley.

Not that it mattered. His fingers weren't steady on the hilt.

Trembling at the cold? Hell no, he was half Nørd.

Trembling in fear.

Rhoswen's thoughts were broken by Aerlyn sliding down Quill's grip to stand up straight. Though still syrupy and stuck in a stupor, leaning against him like a pillar, Rhoswen knew whatever had been wrong with her affected her no more and was about to ask Quill why when he pulled Aerlyn tight to him.

"She's waiting for *you*." He nearly whispered, as if not wanting the wind to carry his voice. "I *know* it."

Rhoswen's mouth fell open but she could say nothing.

She. Her.

Morgance.

"*She* sent them all away, whatever she unleashed with that hideous scream. Luckily the teacher and the children escaped out to Montree before Finleigh and I were taken. They'll be scared, hiding out there, but at least they didn't have to see the madness we felt being down in the dungeon. It was like being at the bottom of the ocean, knowing every ship in the water was sinking." Quill jerked his chin behind him, now warming Aerlyn by rubbing her back. "Look around. It's vacant. She put a spell on Aerlyn and locked us away to die. She knew you'd come, I don't know how, but she knew, and she'd wait as long as it took to see you again."

Rhoswen swallowed the stone in her throat and chanced a glance behind her.

The Master Archer stood tall, a sentinel, staring into the bandied black tangle of the trees guarding the way to the hidden glen.

Rhoswen's voice was a croak, weak in her throat.

"Where is she?"

It was Ultan who spoke, his voice clouded with emotion, a wan reflection of the tormented sky above.

"*Hafnröth.*" He said. "Vault of Dreams."

ULTAN

CHAPTER 61

Ultan didn't say a word leading the way to the hidden glen. Though he wished otherwise, the moment deciding the future of Albanland pressed upon him.

Crushing him.

Rampant slashes of wind howled a mourning song and scattered the remnants of rains past, caught up in the limbs and leaves of the beeches and elms stuck in the thorny copse. The random slaps of wet felt like some cold insult on the skin. Rhoswen was behind him, three-fingered hand resting on the hilt of her slim sword, eyes stretched and weary, steps light and guarded. She was tailed by one of her Chosen, a carelessly bold youth named Niles Rodgers. Ultan judged him to be a spindly athlete who would never back down from a challenge and seldom slept a whole night through. Ultan had seen him fight, a tenacious soul worthy to accompany the Crown Heir wherever she went.

Quill, Finleigh, and Aerlyn brought up the rear with their whispers since the Master Archer had stayed behind to protect Ullraye with her Bowgirls.

So many things rushed through Ultan, leading the way.

Strongest among them, the memories.

Rhoswen avoided *Hafnröth* because her parents forbade her from seeing its ancient white stones, fearing she, like so many other ladies of the nobility, would fall to the temptation of courting that vaporous magic and mystery that supposedly sat just beyond the world in which they lived and breathed.

There is no need to seek the mystic and the divine when you have mouths to feed, courts to judge, and lands to administrate. Her father had lectured, pacing in the courtyard as Ultan waited but a stone's throw away for the quick approval to run off and play like usual.

But not this time.

And wars, my dearest, even the talk of their coming sets the strongest man to worry! Yes, so much to keep you up at night, so…please, I beg of you, don't go thinking about the night itself, or any of its creatures, or the many legends thankfully lost in its colors. Only know that the stars and the sea and all the forces of nature live their own lives in the same way as we are to live ours. And you, young Rhoswen, my little flower, you are to be the star and the sea and all the forces of nature to those who swear fealty to you and live in the land of your rule. Yours is not to question or to seek, but to stand strong and proud. To be everything. To be Queen.

Ultan swore he'd never forget King Brom's words to his daughter or the sword-like look he'd jabbed toward young Ultan afterword, that day she'd wanted to visit *Hafnröth* with Ultan and play. It was the same day she decided not to play anymore, ever, and to become the Princess of pragmatism, to devote her life to the form and function that made a diplomatic warrior Queen a monarch of memory.

Two weeks later, she'd vanished.

But Ultan realized that was the day Rhoswen as he knew her now had been born, and that little girl, that free-spirited and capricious little butterfly he wanted so desperately to return to the sunshine of youth with, well, she was gone.

Forever.

Severed from the soul of the woman who now followed him through the trees like one of his own soldiers, hand on her sword hilt.

The woman who now stopped as he stopped, and stared, as he stared, in silence, to behold the swollen mound of *Hafnröth*, the stoic white stone markers of ages past, and the feminine form of her bitter rival kneeling in meditation between the gaping teeth of those tall white celestial markers.

Bejeweled dagger suspended in the dead space of air above her head.

Silence struck the party as they trickled into the hidden glen to stand, stunned and frozen. That horrid silence only the deepest depths of night could possess, where everything had been stripped away save the barely audible rumble of the earth as it toiled and spun.

For in that moment of perfect silence, Rhoswen's rival stretched her delicate hands to touch the stones and the wind died.

And in that moment of stillness, the poisoned black clouds parted their muddled veil, and Luna's silver gaze cut a brilliant sliver across the face of the mound, as if a door had been opened, slowly at first, before being flung wide to wash Vault of Dreams in the ethereal glaze of moonlight and shadow.

It was then Faer Morgance stood, every bit Dominae Tenebris in her suffocatingly tight and intricately woven black lace, nearly white-gold hair spilling wildly to frame her small doll's face.

Plucking the suspended dagger from the air with her left hand, she held it low at her side.

And opened her eyes.

In the deadly black and blue night, glazed in ghostly silver, they were the contentious orbs of a sick and morbid sun, the very illustration of Solara scorned and spurned, the kind of sun that slayed ill-fated travellers wandering the desert kingdoms.

Blazing in their bitterness, they scorched the base of Ultan's spine with living tongues of guilt, saying, *Have I not been faithful to you, Ultan? Will I not wait forever to prove my love?*

The fire spread up his back as she stared and stared and stared.

And yet, it is you who has left me. Whose love is pure, now?

But she didn't say that.

Instead, she stretched out the bejeweled dagger that'd once claimed the finger of the Crown Heir and said, her Faer voice low and urgent,

"Rhoswen of Kathron Caelie, I challenge you to a duel."

CHAPTER 62

Rhoswen took a step forward, standing next to Ultan.

"What are the terms?"

Morgance let her chin drift left and right.

"I've missed you, too, *Rhos*wen." She sneered. "How noble of you to return."

"I've waited long enough." She said, and Ultan could feel her bristle, discipline getting the better of her and keeping her feet planted firm when something feral wanted to run up the mound and gouge those dazzling eyes right out of Morgance' beautiful little skull.

"Well, we have that in common." Morgance proffered a conceited bow.

"The terms." Rhoswen said, and Ultan glanced behind him as Finleigh and Niles stared wide-eyed at the rare beauty up above them, the full figure of her Faer legend, standing statuesque beneath the light of a full moon.

But Quill was sullen, his gaze unblinking.

As if he was torn to shreds inside.

Morgance' Faer voice gathered depth, like water bound tightly, surging up the face of sea cliff.

"These are the terms of my duel, Crown Heir of Albanland, rightful Ruler and Regent, accept them if you dare. You will fight me with no weapons and no armor. You will fight me within the circle of these stones and will forfeit and lose if you leave them before the winner has been decided."

Rhoswen slouched casually and looped her hands in her swordbelt.

"And how is the winner to be decided?"

Morgance smiled a thin and serpentine thing.

"By death, of course."

Rhoswen let her eyes fall to the ground.

"And what does the winner stand to gain?"

Morgance raised her right hand in a loose salute. The Ring of Rule caught a glimmer of light before falling again to the darkness swathing her like a cloak, as if it had been nothing more than an illusion banded about her finger.

"The Throne and all that goes with it." Morgance said.

"That's it?"

"No." The smile spread, and the dagger's point slid to Ultan. "And *him*."

Ultan couldn't fight flushing. He felt his skin redden under frost and his insides turn to mush. He'd cut down a thousand Nørds and twice as many Angles in his years.

And never had he felt fear as he did now.

Rhoswen let her eyes travel up his body, her gaze pained and racked with doubt.

There was so much he wanted to say, but her plea had been to forget it all, to let it all break away and dissolve into the mists of time.

But Morgance was a dark resurrection of those mists, summoning every evil memory and every misunderstood twist of Destiny. She would forever be a challenge to all that which longed to forget and forge on unless she, herself, drew breath no more.

"What do you mean?"

"You know damn well what I mean." Morgance said. "If you accept the terms of this duel, then that means Ultan has to accept as well. Whoever wins, Ultan will pledge to marry or will be judged with an act of treason to the Crown and sentenced to death."

Ultan heard Finleigh gasp and Aerlyn, apparently healthy enough now, growl out a sailor's string of swear words.

Rhoswen's hand was on his shoulder and he turned to meet her gaze.

Her question was unspoken.

And he nodded his approval.

Rhoswen stepped to the side and shrugged off her cloak, eliciting a bubble of laughter from Faer Morgance.

"It takes so much to make a woman and so little to destroy her."

Rhoswen said nothing to the barb.

Her eyes of three colors said enough.

Her molded breastplate followed her swordbelt. Both were handed off to Niles and neatly arranged. In her thin white tunic and rough brown pants, she could've been a stable maid, or a farm hand, anybody. Nothing like the dark dewdrops and spider webs of the otherworld Morgance made herself out to be. Even now, the smell of myrrh stretched a beckoning finger to Ultan's nose, and he turned to stare up at her, burning his gaze into her own.

I love you, Ultan. He could nearly hear her say, her voice weaving through his head like a haunting pipe melody. *More than she ever could.* That enchanting voice, so beautiful and perfect, forever the rope to draw him up from death.

Don't you dare forget me. Even if I die tonight, my last thoughts will be of you. My soul will possess you when my body cannot. My heart will swallow yours and you will live inside my love. My memory will shadow your every waking breath and you will never, ever forget me as long as blood runs in your veins.

I am your destiny, Ultan, I am your Queen.

And like everything else in my life I will take what should've been given to me.

For whether I live or die, to not have what I want is agony and I have had my last of such emptiness, Ultan of Skyeshire.

Mark my words I shall never taste such bitter waters again.

This night, my dreams shall be realized.

Rhoswen took a step forward, breaking Ultan's focus upon Morgance and her gaze of yellow-green light.

"I accept the terms." She said, deathly tired and worn ragged without the fierce anointing that seemed to come with her plate armor and dashing cloak. She looked small and vulnerable.

She looked normal.

Ultan swallowed as the others joined about him, watching Morgance recede back into the circle of stones. Above, the sky was clear and cloudless, the moon a fat silver eye.

Aerlyn's voice was harsh and dry as Rhoswen slowly walked up the mound.

"What are you doing?"

Ultan turned, eyeing her in a haze.

"You're just going to let them go at each other? What the hell's wrong with you? That woman's a monster."

"I know what she is." Ultan said, split between Rhoswen and Morgance, Morgance and Rhoswen.

He scanned the faces. Finleigh looked sick, her caramel skin ashen beneath the moonlight.

And Quill, well, he looked sicker.

Niles stared Ultan down and swallowed as Ultan drew the milk white Blade of the Champion and stabbed it in the dirt between the spread of his feet.

His voice carried a severe promise to all who would listen.

"If I do not serve the Throne and whoever sits upon it, I am nothing, I am *less* than nothing, spitting upon the proud legacy of all those who have served before me."

Aerlyn strode up to him jabbing her chin in his face.

"To *hell* with your honor if you can't pick a side."

"Aerlyn…" Quill pulled her back, calming, though the eyes of midnight were clouded in storm.

She drifted from his grip but her voice was weak, soaked in sorrow.

"To hell with you if you don't even know who you love."

Ultan sighed and cast his attention upon the mound. Niles' mouth was slightly agape as he watched, and Ultan wondered how much time the youth had spent in the circle.

For *Hafnröth* was the Circle to end all Circles, and the rites and rituals of the duel were sovereign. It made sense that Aerlyn, despite her own code of morality, failed to see the hallowed method of conduct Morgance had evoked, just as deep as the ties that linked him to the Throne, no matter who it belonged to.

At least that's what he told himself.

Morgance, twelve paces away from Rhoswen, removed the Ring of Rule from her finger and tossed it to the turf in the middle of the circle of stones and flipped her dagger to hold it by the blade, her paralyzing gaze never moving from her rival.

Then, with a flick and a *pling*, the dagger was in the soft ground, all but nailing the Ring to the soil.

"Come and get it." Morgance sneered.

Rhoswen swallowed and rolled up her sleeves.

It was then Finleigh fainted, falling to the ground with a hollow thud.

Rhoswen's focus was torn away from Morgance for the one moment it took to track the sound and spot the precious gypsy crumpled up in a pile of flesh and fabric at Niles' feet.

When Rhoswen drew her eyes back to the circle, it was too late.

Morgance was upon her, bearing the knife.

MORGANCE

CHAPTER 63

The clatter of steel upon stone was a hideous thing that gnawed through the bones and sent shivers up the spine, but Morgance was so red hot with rage that she didn't feel a thing.

Her skin, though her eyes were alight with bitter embers, was freezing cold.

Rhoswen was slower than she thought she'd be, darting and ducking away from Morgance' vicious swipes.

She wanted her, anything she could get of her, just a piece to start with, a little tear in that clean white shirt, a little dewdrop of a red stain like the first taste of a rain sent to quench drought.

She would use the dagger as she should've that fateful day and *take take take* till there was nothing left of the little *chosen one* but a ruined heap.

Rhoswen flashed before her and Morgance swung the weapon wildly, her arm connecting with Rhoswen's shoulder near the elbow, splashing pain throughout her body.

Morgance hissed and recoiled, fighting to keep hold of the dagger.

But the ground smothered her, cold and wet and soft, and she rolled over on her back as the breeze of a flying boot heel narrowly missed her head.

Faer Morgance pressed herself up and jabbed, causing Rhoswen to launch herself backward and smack her head against a stone.

Even Morgance felt the knock, the hollowness of stone against bone, and watched with glee as Rhoswen's gaze dimmed and she winced to make herself right again, to pull herself from the sticky sap and the glue.

"Why do you fight that which you know to be true?" Morgance nearly laughed.

"I fight you." Rhoswen staggered, determined to stay in the circle of stones, though the chance of taking a step forward and slipping and falling was enough to keep her leaning against the stone.

"No no no, *Crown Heir.*" Morgance straightened and worked forward in a small, circular motion. "I mean the masquerade you've convinced yourself is a revolution. You play at leadership. That's all you do. You play. We both know it's a job for men, not women."

Something of an animal noise gurgled in Rhoswen's throat and she pressed herself forward with clenched fists.

"Authority knows no sex." She said, huffing her dizziness out with a sigh. "People follow me because I am born to lead them and I have paid the price to do so."

"Born?" Morgance scoffed, letting the knife hang near her waist, her movements jagged and treacherous as she advanced. "Leaders are not born, they are anointed by a gathering of fools, thrust out to a herd of sheep who know no better and given a golden staff and a fancy hat and a speech. That," Morgance glowered. "Is a job for men. It is a women's job to *control.* Whether glory comes of it or not makes no difference. It is history that we crave, molding it in our hands like clay."

"You're so wrong." Rhoswen said, steeling herself for another grapple with the woman. "I live my life to serve. Not to control, not to write history. I don't give a damn if no one remembers me, but they sure as hell know me now and believe in what I want to give them."

"Oh?" Morgance' ruby lips twisted. "And what's that?"

"Everything you let slip away." Rhoswen cracked her knuckles. "Freedom!"

Rhoswen ducked as the dagger clattered along the stone and Morgance felt herself lifted from the ground and driven through the air, the dagger loosed from her grip.

But Rhoswen misjudged her own strength, and barreled on through Morgance, slipping and sliding along the turf as Morgance barely landed on her feet in a haphazard somersault, and, eschewing the knife, ran across the space between them to mash her boot heel into Rhoswen's right hand before Rhoswen could press herself up.

On the joint of her missing finger.

Rhoswen screamed and shied away from the pain, rolling to expose her face, which Morgance flicked her foot across like a whip.

The Crown Heir's cry was lost in a gurgle of blood and saliva, and she threw herself to height as Morgance ran to her, clasped her in a rough embrace, and drove her into the nearest stone.

Again, Rhoswen's head smacked the hardness behind her, the sound of it seeming to echo throughout the dead night.

And, with blood dripping down her nose, Rhoswen slid down the stone, a muffled squeal her only companion.

Her was gaze hazy. Disconnected.

Drifting, reaching out and failing to grasp a lifeline of any kind as Morgance bent at the waist to grab the dagger.

AERLYN

CHAPTER 64

Aerlyn knew what it took to fight for one's survival and couldn't avoid the horrible feeling chewing through her guts as the duel began. Morgance had embraced a new level of madness, so old and rotten, festering and fermenting till its poison had taken her over, possessed her.

But Rhoswen didn't look so hot. No, she was stuck somewhere between sadness and exhaustion, forced to fight the foe of her every nightmare.

Finleigh was breathing fine, alive and well, but had fallen into some sort of unshakeable sleep fit, and Niles couldn't wake her from it, no matter what he did.

So he let her be.

Ultan just stood, holding onto his sword, planted in the turf like a legendary carving.

Unblinking, unflinching, unfeeling.

Could he not *taste* the madness in the air, crackling and buzzing with the greedy lightning of Morgance' hatred, leaping from her eyes, charging her limbs with hunger and fury as she brandished the dagger.

Rhoswen had already spent it all, saving the land from having to bow to Angle masters. What more did she have left to give?

Was Aerlyn the only one who could see the simplicity of it all? Cut the head off of the snake and throw the serpent into the sea. If she wasn't so wasted from whatever had been in that apple, thrown to that dark and cobwebbed corner of the Fortress to be locked away, she would've ran back to get The Master Archer and her bow and be done with it.

But it was too late for that. And she wondered if Ultan would cut her down for breaking the sovereign laws of the duel.

Next to her, Quill seemed to melt just to watch the duel, to feel the magnetism of the white stones, reeling with each swipe and swoosh as if he was in the fight himself, on both sides. His breathing increasing ever so rapidly until he finally took a step forward.

"This has gone on long enough."

It wasn't so much what he said as the *way* he said it.

Aerlyn turned.

"What?"

"No one has run more than I," His voice throbbed, "And no one has ruined more lives for a more selfish motive."

Aerlyn felt the world slow around her, dimming and blurring so only Quill remained, pale under the hushing wash of the full moon. Rhoswen was losing the duel, fighting a horrible knock to the head that slowed sagging limbs and tangled tired feet. Doing her best, though in such a state with no weapons she was no match for Morgance' long-tempered wrath.

But Quill, his words sliced across her throat like the very dagger in Morgance' hand. In the depthless chasm within, she felt the dry ache of the pain she'd learned to rely on, the pain that drove her to be brave, the stabbing hunger that told her something was wrong, terribly wrong, and would never be made right again unless she did something about it herself.

Why, then, why did his words hurt so?

It was the blizzard of emotions that came with those words, each sound lost in an ocean of memory she knew was still raw and wounded within him, so real and vivid she could taste it herself.

He was not a whole man. He was a cripple.

A prisoner caged in the jaws of time.

Aerlyn's rough voice was a jagged plea, her eyes suddenly wet, as if she was cut adrift from a ship, drowning.

Yes, drowning in the Greener Sea, like the night the men had thrown her overboard and laughed as she fought the waves and two of the Four Storms raging careless and wild above.

"Please…what are you saying?"

"Listen to me, Aerlyn," He shadowed her face and grabbed her by the shoulders. "Once I was not what I am now. If it could be possible for someone to have done a horrible thing for a good cause, then that is what I did, but this is what has come of it."

The Thistle felt herself float in his sea blue gaze, drifting further and further away from the warmth that held had her close, the voice that'd sung to her, driving away the poison as if there was magic in his touch and healing in his voice.

For certainly that's what she felt, *magic*, though she didn't believe in magic or any of its fireside stories, only in that she believed what could be explained and used to trick someone into thinking something other than the truth, *practical magic*, but that's the only way she could describe what she heard fizzle deep inside her spine every time he spoke, and whenever his hands came in contact with her body.

And then it dawned on her, the truth too painful for him to even speak, its revelation splashing across the dry bones of her soul like a mouthful of saltwater.

His voice was tender.

"You stole my heart before I could give it to you."

A tremor shivered across the slash of her lips.

Quill peered into her eyes of midnight, his own eyebrows twisted to fight the throbbing punch of his chronic headaches, the throes of his blindness.

"You…" He shook his head. "You…are…"

But words, *his magic*, evaded him. Aerlyn sniffled and felt light headed. He suddenly softened, with a sigh, as if giving up inside, no longer holding onto the struggle that made him speechless, while up in the Circle, Rhoswen smacked into the stone for a second time, blood pouring from her nose.

Love pooled in Quill's eyes.

"Aerlyn, my rose, Let it be said of us...*he drew the spark in her eye no one else could capture, her smile was warm yet hidden was the pain he saw could rupture at any moment, at any time her life could be but one more rhyme, but yet she saw the radiant light that he so brightly shined, and there the heavy chains collapsed from her clouded mind.*"

And then he turned from her presence to enter *Hafnröth* before it was too late.

But not before Aerlyn caught his arm, grasping on to him with all the strength she had, like a piece of driftwood in the froth and splash of the waves, just like that very same plank of providence that'd saved her life that night those men tossed her overboard.

Quill spun and threw his arms around her, squeezing the breath out of her lungs as he kissed her with the unending passion of the dream he dreamed every night, pouring his hopes of being in love deep into a soul that so desperately needed to be the mirror of the same.

And though it was but a heartbeat's length, Aerlyn tasted every color of that beautiful dream, before Quill all but threw himself from her and dashed from her embrace, sprinting up the curve of the mound, into the stone circle.

MORGANCE

CHAPTER 65

The scream shattered the stone-silent night before the dagger fell. But when it fell, it was driven in a blizzard of jealously, arcing through the blind tempest of every dark and foul thought that Morgance had ever cultivated in her soul toward *the precious chosen one*, diving and hacking and biting again and again and again and again.

Morgance felt the hottest fire of six hells sear her skin, consuming her from the inside out as if Solara's distant blaze was a liquid rope driving the knife down with power beyond humanity, lashing and whipping the gale force of her envy into the heart of her rival, the fullest vengeance of her hatred toward the girl who had anything and everything she wished she had.

Love.

She just wanted love.

Everyone loved Rhoswen, and followed her like her heart was made of glittering diamonds and her presence was the shade of a cool tree in the high noon of summer. Her parents had cooed and doted, lavishing everything within the Realm upon her, bending over backwards to give her the best and guide her and groom her and Ultan! He wasn't the only boy who'd wanted to be hers forever, hoping to one day stand by her side, just the only one brave enough to say so.

Everyone loved her.

And no one loved Morgance.

Blood splashed and spattered like pebbles thrown into a stagnant pond and Morgance could not stop herself. Not after the sticky crimson sap had soaked her black lace to the skin, not after the scream had finally squished the last breath of air from her lungs.

Not until the earthquake of being overcome by such hatred had left her trembling uncontrollably and feeling so terribly alone that she couldn't even hold the dagger anymore, and staggered backward, staring, as her focus slowly cleared to behold what just she'd done.

The man dropped to his knees, the thirty-odd pinpricks and jagged gashes stretched across the front of his frilly white shirt drooling blood.

Morgance covered her mouth, shock stealing a gasp from her as Rhoswen's face mirrored much of the same disbelief.

Both women were speechless, the storm of what'd happened breaking their volatile bond within the blink of an eye, changing the destiny of the duel forever.

In one moment the duel had been ruined, its rites and rituals shattered by the manifestation of a long-forgotten revelation.

And the horror of it all slept in the sorrow Morgance couldn't fight as it overcame her, splashing in an ever-swallowing tidal wave, deeper than a desert well as the man stood up with an earth-rending groan and placed a hand on her shoulder.

"It's me…Mor Mor." He coughed. "…it's *me*…"

Dominae Tenebris quivered, the odd light flickering in her eyes. She stepped back. His hand slipped off and he swayed, fighting for balance, as if standing on the rim of the Tower of Ullraye, the wild wind tearing at his arms and legs. But there was no wind, and the ground was flat, though he tottered and struggled to stand straight. His breath raked in his throat. Seeking equilibrium and leverage against the creeping throes of death, their bonds riddled across his chest, shoulders, and arms, his blue eyes swam around the white stones

Mor Mor…

The sound of his voice, the way he said it.

Mor Mor…

It could only mean…

"No…" The high and breathy pitch of a little girl escaped her throat, the deep darkness of Dominae Tenebris sucked away and exorcised by the presence of the man she could only taste in a memory as soft, sweet, and divine.

"No! It can't be!"

"It's me, Mor Mor. It's your brother Uilleam." Quill gurgled out a sigh and lurched toward her, his skin covered in sickly sweat.

"You…you died in the shipwreck!!!" Morgance peeped, ruby lips shivering, shoulders bunched as her hands squeezed together across her heart. "You died with Mom and Dad!!! You all died and left me to fend for myself in this rotten world!!!"

"No, Mor Mor." Quill snarled up the agony killing him and mashed his teeth together. "Mom and Dad died in the storm…I was rescued. M-merchants took me off to the desert Kingdoms…" Quill took a step with everything in him, his blue-eyes heavy with death. "I was raised by the Caliph of Aegyptus until-til he sent me to t-travel…to s-seek knowledge…to find the meaning of life. He knew I'd come back here, to be made com-complete." Quill's breath sucked in his throat, trying to leave for good and he captured it, like a bird snagged midair. His eyes darted around her face, body awash with ripples of sticky heat.

"He knew I'd need to ask you…to forgive me…for leaving you, for letting you down, for being s-such a horrible brother to you and letting you think I was d-dead."

Morgance drifted away from him, her beautiful features a frozen mask of shock, pure and uncontrollable astonishment and disbelief, flushed with the white hot fizzle of realizing that if she'd known her beloved brother was alive, she would've left Albanland and everything it was and had been to her to find him, to be by his side, forever.

Yes, *forever*, that's what Uilleam was to her, the endlessness of friendship and brotherhood, where she was forever looking up to him and his golden voice, the way his hands made her feel gooey and cherished and perfect when he used to hold her close to his heart as a tiny baby, his smile so broad and pure that it made her think of heaven and all of its dazzling lights.

Forever, the stories he used to tell her as he walked with her, hand in hand through the forest or along the sea shore, pointing up to the stars to plant the seeds of magic and mystery within, as if life was a big puzzle, and it wasn't worth solving unless you had someone there with you, walking side by side, hand in hand.

"Forgive me Morgance." Quill plead, voice broken between life and death. He fell to his knees as he took a step toward, twisting and landing unevenly in the grass. "Forgive me for leaving you! I hate myself f-for it but I couldn't come back to the little world our parents forced us to inherit, just to…maintain, like some rel-relic, to be slaves to their little castle and their land! I had to know what else was…was out there!" He hacked and spat blood, his shoulders rippling and straining as he clawed forward, stretching toward her as she backed away from the ghost that he was to her, the legend, the memory.

"Forgive me, my sister, my heartbeat!" His face was nearly purple with exertion, but dammit, he pushed himself to full height even if it would be the death of him "…it was *I* who ruined you! It was *I* made you what you are…*I* let you be taken, by bitterness and jealousy…*I* let the thoughts of rejection and ridicule destroy you…*I* left you alone in this wild cauldron…to fend for yourself against the wolves…*I* ruined the first precious little life I ever loved."

Deathly still, Morgance let him fall into her arms, tears hot and wet against her cheeks as whatever was left of what she used to be gushed, her every regret emptied in heaving sobs against his shoulder.

Her breath stuttered through her weeping in chops and slaps as his lungs worked, like a dimming day, to breath their last.

But before he breathed no more, she heard his golden voice, but a whisper on the wind, as his lips brushed her ear in a gentle kiss.

"I love you, Morgance, and I always will."

It was then the Faer Princess of the Night squeezed her older brother as hard as she could, letting the ugly ruin of her every choice be absolved and made absolute in his love.

And, her face a furious storm of pain and heartache, she buried herself in the breadth of his embrace, letting her soul drift into his arms as darkness reigned within and without, and her balance failed her to tumble with him, end over end, down the slope of the mound.

FINLEIGH

CHAPTER 66

Finleigh awoke in a world of green and gold, the sky above her a haze of pink streaked with lavender and the silver shadows of an age-old storm long since exhausted of its fury.

Where am I? She thought, instantly, but the thought was then dispelled.

Exhaled and gone.

I am here.

The ground beneath her was soft and squishy, and while she felt the cool of evening on her skin, she couldn't place the hour.

Was it dawn or dusk?

Or both at the same time?

The Española gypsy folded herself up, clutching her knees to her chest. Her head spun in the slightest, as if bigger or broader, *or emptier*, and her body was infused with lightness, that of high mountain air.

Free.

She let her gaze drift across a distant copse of trees gently swaying in the breeze. Rising up along the curve of the horizon, light seemed to emanate from somewhere beyond their reach.

Finleigh stood slowly.

She was barefoot and her sleeveless summer dress was a simple and seamless garment of white linen. It shimmered with a pearlescent glow as she beheld it, grabbing shafts of light in the dawn or dusk to shoot them across the folds of the fabric, where, if she squinted, she could spot the traces of each and every color up in the sky, as if the dress was *made* of the sky, or a single pearl alive enough to capture its lovely hues.

Her jet-black hair was longer, softer, and shinier than she remembered.

Where am I? I am here.

Where is here? Why am I here?

Again Finleigh peered across a flat expanse of green and gold to watch the trees guarding the curve of the horizon, studying their easy grace as they swayed and shook. She didn't feel the wind that tickled those trees at the edge of her vision, causing the flat palms and teardrops of the soft leaves stretching out from their broad trunks to clap and chatter in the whistling melodies of the wind.

It was then a refreshing cool and calm swallowed her, as if she was at the bottom of a great sea.

It was peace.

And it was *inside* of her, knit within the fabric of her skin and sewn throughout the marrow of her bones as if she was a vessel filled and overflowing with the steady stream of its constancy, its sense of completion.

Something hummed at the edge of silence, just like the trees nearly too fuzzy to see, and Finleigh squinted, trying to focus on that faint echo swirling around the rivers of the wind from somewhere far away.

It was music, lush and intoxicating, as if its many notes were the colors of earthen jewels, and only in the tender weaving of its many harmonies did it all make sense as *one* sound.

Were they voices? Instruments?

It doesn't matter. I love it. I want to stay here, wherever here is.

I feel at home here.

I never want to leave.

Finleigh sighed, as if she could finally rest, and inhaled a breath of music to feel the precious arms of a deep and endless sleep draw near.

Yet she felt *so* alive.

413

"Welcome to that which is, and was, and will be." She heard behind her.

It was a rich voice, one created to tell a story, to sing a song, to weave a tale that had no end.

It was Uilleam.

Finleigh turned and couldn't fight the gasp stolen from her lungs. She staggered back, a hand on her chest.

Standing beside Uilleam was the most beautiful woman she'd ever seen and could ever *even think* of seeing, as if the woman wasn't real, but merely the substance of an otherworldly dream.

A legend from another time.

It was Morgance.

"Peace be unto you." The Princess bowed, imbuing the young gypsy with a sense of grace, and Finleigh's spine tingled with the warmth that trailed through her words.

Finleigh squinted to look at her, a shine reflected across the stars in her own black eyes. Solara would dim in Morgance' sight, and Luna's gaze upon a thousand Lochs could not contend with the Princess' beauty.

In fact, Finleigh couldn't actually *see* the face she quickly remembered standing atop *Hafnröth*, so beautiful and at the same time so terribly frightening and filled with pain and hatred.

She had been the face of the Four Storms, aching to strip the land bare with the gale force of her wrath.

And now, Finleigh could only see light and love.

Her presence was overwhelming.

Uilleam stepped forward, his hand broad and strong. He seemed taller than she remembered, and thinner, the red of his beard and the blue of his eyes sharper and more vivid, not blood-shot and washed out and sickly and ready to keel over and die at any moment as he had been.

For a heartbeat his hand shadowed her eyes before resting atop her skull. Something like warm honey oozed through his touch and she swayed under his grasp.

"I give unto you, Finleigh De La Cruz of Baraburr, abandoned daughter of a wandering people, an understanding of the magic that lives inside us all. The sleeping seed of a giant tree, the faultless magic of storytelling."

Finleigh swooned but Morgance caught her in something of a firm and fierce embrace. The Princess smelled of a wildflower field in full bloom, stroked with sunlight.

"Tell the story." She said in a whisper. "Even if no one believes you."

"Yes." Uilleam smiled as Finleigh's eyes flickered open, her small chin tipping back and her gaze blinking rapidly to behold something that looked like a giant harp stretched up into the heavens, the strings of which ascended the glaze of colors spilled across the sky.

Finleigh stood still, rapt in silent awe as Morgance' hand slipped into Uilleam's and he pulled her away from Finleigh, who felt as if Morgance had given her a gift beyond comprehension in the lingering smile she cast over her shoulder.

"Dream a dream that will not die." Uilleam ordered, his tone firm with wisdom, realizing what it would take to do so, to dedicate herself to that which their spirits had imparted to her. "Let *this* world," He rolled his eyes around the endless spread of the landscape, "be your pallet and brush. Cast hope where the hopeless roam. Only forgiveness can cleanse the tainted soul. Dig a well in the mind of the seeker, and plant a tree in the spirits of the weak. Be bright and undying, be the light everlasting. Be the song. Be the breath. Be the story that never ends."

Finleigh found herself nodding ever so slowly as Uilleam took his sister, hand in hand, and walked her up that rainbow bridge of harp strings, their each and every step thrumming a synchronized melody of musical notes, steps that continued up and away, darkening the powerful purity of the world around her, silencing the music and stilling the wind as they walked and walked, higher and higher until Finleigh realized she was standing near the copse of trees that guarded the hidden glen of *Hafnröth* from the Fortress of Ullraye.

In Albanland.

Finleigh stared down at her arms and legs.

She was no longer barefoot, no longer clothed in simple linen that shimmered like white pearls. The dirty rags she'd been unable to change out of since her imprisonment clung to her skin like some sort of curse.

But she didn't care.

She had dreamed a dream that would not die, and the world she had seen would be her pallet and her brush.

The wind kissed her cheeks and mussed her hair and she ran, as fast as she could, toward Vault of Dreams where the two souls she'd met just across the veil of this life had left their bodies for dead.

Niles spotted her first, but she expected no less.

"Fins, you're okay!"

She disregarded him, drawing closer to the circle that'd formed at the base of the mound, tripping and falling to her knees.

She crawled the last three feet to them, nearly breathless.

Quill's body was a mess of crimson stains and his shirt a jagged tangle of ribbons and shreds. Faer Morgance, in her skin-tight black lace, was crushed in his embrace, a smudge of puce discoloring her skin where her neck was broken.

"What happened?" She gasped, torn between the two worlds, between that which she'd seen and had so quickly dissolved around her to leave her alone in the cold fangs of reality.

"They fell." Ultan said, flatly, but like the milk white Blade of the Champion he'd sheathed at his side, his words carried a razor-sharp edge. "It was an accident."

"No it *wasn't*." Aerlyn muttered. Finleigh looked up into the dark swathe of her hood and couldn't see her eyes, merely the streaks of tears that stained her alabaster skin and garnet lips that still longed for Quill's kiss. Moonlight hazed her thin body with melancholy and mourning. "*Quill* killed her."

The unspoken subtext of her words hung heavy in the air.

Quill killed her because Ultan couldn't. He did what he had to, what was right.

Niles ran a hand through the messy ruffle of his blonde hair, pinching one of his ears.

"No...guys." He winced to say it, as if he had no place to but couldn't stop himself. "Quill couldn't even stand up anymore. *She* pulled him. She jumped off...knowing...his weight would make her fall faster. She wanted them to die together."

Finleigh stood up and took a step back, unable to fight the warm fuzz of what she'd seen only moments ago creep back over her body.

It was far more powerful than the darkness, than death, far stronger than the varying shades that cast a haze across *Hafnröth*.

It's okay. They're not here anymore.

They're gone.

There was a groan from the top of the mound and Finleigh threw herself up the turf as Rhoswen drifted to the stability of a tall white stone and leaned, sighing away her aches and pains.

Finleigh slipped an arm around her shoulder and tried to spread the comfort she knew was alive within her to the Crown Heir.

That enduring light and heat, *the dream that would never die.*

And, as if by magic, Rhoswen lifted her chin up, passed Finleigh a pale but pure smile, and straightened herself to walk down the length of the mound.

Starry black eyes missed nothing. Rhoswen stood next to the intertwined bodies, offered a prayer of silent regret, stooped down, and slipped the Ring of Rule she'd retrieved from the stone Circle back on Morgance' third finger.

"You won the duel, Morgance." She whispered to the lifeless form of Dominae Tenebris. "And you will be forever remembered as the true Last Queen of Albanland. The monarchy shall die with you and your many tragedies. May heaven grace us to never see the likes of them again."

Then Rhoswen tipped her gaze back up to Finleigh and ushered her close, waiting to speak till Finleigh completed the circle of five encompassing Morgance and Quill.

"You are *all* witnesses of what has happened here." She said, hands on her hips. "And because of it you are all regents of a new dawn, and a new age, and a new Albanland."

Rhoswen's three-colored eyes touched each and every soul with confirmation, waiting for their nod before moving on to the next set of eyes.

"Let us all vow to make it right again."

Finally, the pact made, Rhoswen sighed.

It was then Finleigh smiled, starlight glittering her black eyes and tinting her coffee-colored skin with the glow of that which sat *just* beyond the veil.

Tell the story, Morgance had said, *even if no one believes you.*

"I will." She said aloud.

ULTAN

CHAPTER 67

The place felt empty.

Hollow.

Dead.

Perhaps, Ultan thought as he peered across the spread that used to be scattered with sheep and the shimmer of a thousand memories, *that's because it really did die the day I left it.*

Skyeshire's old holdings consisted of a stout and narrow-shouldered castle on the shores of Loch Darvin, wisely built to watch the eastern edge of the highlands and the parceled-out pastureland that ran unevenly along the Loch till they were lost in the smoky mist of the verdant hills responsible for the legends of seasons past. Ultan stood, arrayed in the finest of Skyeshire's black and gold, his tunic soft and white and clean and free from the threat of blood, dirt, and sweat ruining it all so quickly.

A hand slipped around his waist, a hand of three fingers, hugging a waist that held no sword, not even a pouch of gold.

Rhoswen burrowed herself between Ultan and the crenellated keep of the small castle and gazed across the water.

"Tell me, Lord of Skyeshire." She said with a smile. "What do you see?"

Ultan stood tall and shielded his eyes. The sun had only just risen behind them, and the wild scatter of land, the long sword of the ice-blue loch and the emerald sheath that hid its beauty from the rest of the world, still clung to the drowsy remnants of night.

"I see…" Ultan laughed at himself in disbelief. A shard of cruelty stabbed him within and pushed him from her. Even in such a perfect moment he could not escape what was, what would always stay there, within his mind, built of cut stones, smirking its dark and dirty stain. "I see too much."

Still he couldn't escape the curses seeping into his blood, framing the broad space that'd once been his home.

Rhoswen turned to him but did not pursue him as he strode to the furthest edge of the small keep. Her nostrils flared, and she still looked fierce as the day of battle.

"You see what has been, not what *will be*."

Arrayed in Kathron Caelie's rich velvets of violet and ivory, her dark mess of curls pinned up like a blooming flower, the warrior spirit still smoldered within.

But the sword of steel had been traded for a weapon of a different kind.

Words.

For the Kingdom was still a fractured and shattered vessel, its breathtaking beauty hanging on the precipice of the ugly fight for survival as winter drew near.

So much was to be done.

"I will not be your King." Ultan said, nearly in a whisper.

"And I will not be the Queen." Rhoswen clasped her hands together behind her, patiently. "The monarchy died with my parents…with Morgance. No more will Albanland be ruled by one, or two, but by a Council of *all*."

"You cannot do this." Ultan twisted. "You play with fire."

"I have to."

"And all those who abandoned the Crown, you cannot let them come back. They are traitors."

"They are cowards. There is a difference."

"But they took the field against you."

"And they fled. We killed none of them and they killed none of us." Rhoswen placed her three-fingered hand on Ultan's shoulder. "You are…so…"

"Stupid."

"No…" Rhoswen rolled her eyes. "So…*used.* You've been surviving this struggle so long, you can't see it any differently. It isn't us and them anymore. We are a tree. We have deep roots and strong limbs. But some are withered. Some of the fruit is rotten. But the tree hasn't died. And I'm not going to cut it down just because it's stuck in the middle of such a hard season." Rhoswen's hand slid to the breadth of his chest, her sunned skin vivid against the stark white of his tunic. "I'll have to prune it…but that tree won't make it through the winter without you."

It was then her eyes leapt up to meet his so quickly so that he could not look away without rejecting her.

Which he did.

Ultan rushed to the edge of the keep, his skin hot and flushed across his cheeks as tears welled in eyes the color of the hollow fields snaking away from the small gray castle.

"I can't, Rhoswen. I can't marry you. Don't ask me to…"

Her features frozen in pain, Rhoswen took a step forward and reached out to him and stopped herself.

Her eyes drifted down his form, falling to the hard stone underfoot.

And then she turned to go.

"Wait." Ultan said, tipping his gaze to the sky, letting his tears flow freely. "It's…" He sighed, and Rhoswen bit her lip to see how deeply wrought his pain was.

It was *a part* of him, like his hands, or his eyes.

Pain *was* Ultan. Ultan *was* pain.

"There was a battle once…I was just nineteen…and in this battle…I sustained an injury. A very *very* severe injury."

Rhoswen crept closer.

"I…" His mouth worked and nothing came out till she stood next to him along the jagged teeth of the keep's roof. Even then, his words were but a whisper, as if he didn't even want the clover and heather dotted across his family holdings to know his dark secret.

The truth he'd never told a single soul.

"You *cannot* choose me, Rhoswen. You must let whatever has been between us stay in the past where it belongs." He shook his head, wiping each eye with a white-knuckled fist. "Because of my injury…I am unable to have children."

Ultan beheld her as her mask of strength crumbled and she wept against his chest.

And in that moment, he knew. He *knew.*

But, when her tears dried, she said it anyway.

"I don't want a legacy." She laughed through a wrecked and weak smile, and he brushed back what curly coils of dark hair had fallen across her forehead. Her voice was husky and close. For his ears alone. "I don't want a dynasty. I don't want a castle. I don't want a kingdom. I don't want titles. I don't want treasures. Ultan of Skyeshire. I. Want. *You.*"

The warrior was overcome with emotion.

Broken in sorrow and shame, the gluey substance of each and every dark and horrid moment of self-loathing was smothered in the ache of her love as his mouth pressed to hers. Longing for wholeness welled deep within, and he felt himself dive down into that mystery as the Skyeshire family lands blurred around him and her touch carried him somewhere safe, where it was just the two of them.

Together.

Forever.

All that which he had held in his heart toward her as a simple and earnest little child was laced in his lips and reflected in the strength of her arms around his waist, her three-fingered hand cupping his chin and running through his strawberry blonde curls.

Every pure and perfect thought of life being some endless summer had been tempered by the cold years of hardened steel and silence since Rhoswen had vanished and he grew tall and strong in the begrudging shadows of bigotry and ridicule, the derision of the Chamber of Lords finally turning to fear as he let what howled in his half blood drive him to battle madness, and his battle madness push him to loneliness, knowing that if he ever *did* meet Rhoswen again, or if he ever *did* give into Morgance, they would realize that he was a man who'd been physically disabled by the very thing he'd been forced to embrace, and the depth of his hatred for himself because of it was a fathomless chasm of despair no kiss or kind word could ever pull him out of.

How wrong he was.

And with each touch of Rhoswen's lips against his own, Solara's gaze grew brighter and brighter across the quiet skin of Loch Darvin, pushing away the muddle of the mist that still clung to the emerald shoulders of magic and mystery and set Skyeshire castle like a secret sentinel on the edge of the untamed wilds.

Ultan squeezed Rhoswen against his chest. Fire burned in his veins, and, through the soft swathe of violet velvet trimmed in ivory, he could feel the gallop of Rhoswen's heart tremble against the steady thump of his own.

It was a new day in Albanland, and with it came the death of two memories too dark to bear against the bright and beautiful light and heat of the new dawn sun.

NEVAN & NILES

CHAPTER 68

Living in between the back alleys of common houses and the elbows of scratchy hay-filled stables since their escape from the tiny border village of Crefton, where Angle dominion was still a fist of iron and everything that drew breath was a slave to Angle will and whim, neither Nevan nor Niles had ever seen a construction as grand as the Fortress of Ullraye with their own eyes.

Sprawling strong and defiant against the sea cliffs and the late summer sunlight, it was an awe-inspiring image of all that was Alban.

And now it was a symbol of freedom the stories of which were spreading through the darkest and most isolated corners of the land. A pilgrimage to the oppressed. A source of justice that'd withstood the many storms of tyranny and war. And it would blaze hot against the coming threat of a cold and bitter winter, turning away none who would seek safety or asylum, pledging their heart to the newly christened Alban Empire.

Two weeks after the battle, Nevan and Niles had been separated in the organized chaos of restructuring the remnants of a nation, only to be united again by the Summons of the First Court, Rhoswen's first official act as Regent of the Empire.

Nevan had walked up to Ullraye from Montree, just two miles away, down on the Mull that jutted into the sea, where he had been recovering from his injuries on the battlefield. Little by little, he'd been helping out with the young children that Quill had so diligently taken care of with the golden-haired and radiant blue-eyed teacher from across the eastern sea. Though mathematics were not his strongest, he came alive when demonstrating reasoning skills and logics, telling the precious little lives the names of every plant they came across and all the different kinds of fish and birds that called the green shoals and rocky eddies along the eastern sea home. By night he pitched in with the mending of nets and the learning of the loom, weaving unique Clan patterns in celebration rather than strife.

He even began to learn Nørd.

And of course, a harmless game of darts now and then with the oldest of the boys from the makeshift school didn't hurt.

He'd even shown the golden-haired teacher how to toss them and now that she was pretty good, playing for copper pennies had made him a poor young man.

Montree, once emptied and vacated by the Nørd campaign, was now bristling with life and commerce, as Ultan's military alliance and trade agreements with King Eyvind Frey had quickly breathed new life into the charred husks of two dying nations, catching embers strong enough to last through the winter with the harsh conditions of both nations a pale shadow compared to the spurned giant sleeping just across the border.

Though the old wounds between the two were slow to heal, the sons of Kings would never be nobler than the need to eat, and the chance to leave the past *in the past* was something those who remained alive after the great ravaging were eager to embrace.

But as good as life in the north was shaping up to be, the south *still* awaited liberation, and lawlessness reigned. Souls were disappearing into night in hopes of escaping to a better life up north as the news of Rhoswen's return had become something of a holy wildfire amongst the poor and oppressed.

Their day would come.

Nevan spotted Niles in the rambling courtyard of Ullraye's impenetrable walls, the entire structure thrumming with life and hope. He was waiting with his scrawny black stallion amidst a host of others eager to meet their fate, and rumors of Lordships and estates were up in the air, as well as places of rank in Albanland's new army, since a campaign to free the south would more than likely consume the long winter nights with strategies and the dispatch of spies.

By spring, Niles hoped, the Alban Empire would be made complete, and the swill of southern oppression that'd raised him and his brother would swell and stretch in the freedom that'd so easily consumed the broad expanses of the north, its rugged beauty sharp and vivid against the brisk winds of the sea.

No doubt Niles would be a part of that daring campaign to free the south.

Military life was suiting the sixteen year old well. Niles looked wild and untamed, his blonde hair now nearly to his shoulders, and his sleeveless vest of doeskin and ermine showing off more defined musculature than Nevan remembered, not to mention the blue tattoo that looked nearly iridescent against his Alban skin. The shadow of a beard was beginning to chisel his cheeky face, setting those brown eyes of his in a brow hardened from its wayward nature by the hammer and anvil of war.

Nevan smiled at the fine pair of tawny breeches his brother was wearing, and an even finer pair of black boots. A satin blue cape embroidered with a pair of swords crossing a shield gave him reason to stand taller, his shoulder blades pinched and proud, though Nevan knew he'd grown in more ways than one. No doubt the clothes were the bounties of Rhoswen's prisoner exchange, rich Angle Barons traded for dissenters who had tried to raise revolution in the southern towns and had evoked the name of King Brom to do it, but Niles' bounty of experience couldn't be quantified.

Neither could the way he wore the sword on his hip.

Nevan walked as softly as he could, feeling some trepidation to approach. He hadn't seen Niles since the battle, and knew he'd been there in his darkest moment, though it was a blur. His life with the children and the busy bodies of Montree fulfilled him to no end, and his taste of war was something he could scarcely drum up any more, as if it'd been a smudge wiped clean from a garment.

"Hopefully she'll get you a better horse." Nevan said, causing Niles to turn and smile, quickly clasping him in a hug before registering the remark.

War had changed them both, and whatever had come between them in the fair form of Finleigh had split them cleanly, only to re-unite them stronger than ever before.

Because they were so different.

Nevan patted Niles' stallion on the neck and couldn't stop smiling at him.

"What?" Niles asked, sheepishly.

"You're going to get it. I know it."

Nevan didn't say what *it* was and Niles stared at the thinning waif of a steed, who stared back as if thinking the same thing.

"I don't want another horse." Sadness laced his words to think of it. Since having the leftover horse appointed to him when leaving Rhoswen's forest, he'd grown rather attached to it, and how ridiculous it looked next to the Master Archer's magnificent mount, even though he had yet to name his companion.

Niles passed Nevan a smirk about it, though. After all he'd said back in the forest, he still knew how wise his brother was. Nevan could always pick out which ruffian would be first to throw a punch or which merchant would give them a loaf of bread for free and tell them both to be on their way. Niles had always known which way to run, but Nevan had always known *where to go*.

Niles lived for chaos, because in the storm, life finally made sense to him, but it was *Nevan* who'd kept him on the straight and narrow in the long and arduous spaces of time between those moments of ferocious intensity, those moments where he felt perfect, like a sword red-hot in the smithy.

But, finally, standing together in the courtyard of the Fortress, they could stop running from being slaves in Crefton, rotting away their lives under the yoke and the whip.

"No, not your horse, dummy, a *Lordship*."

"What?" Niles jerked his head back and Nevan slapped his younger brother's tattooed bicep, wincing comically at the thick *thud* of muscle. Gone was the hollowed awkwardness of his youth.

"Look at you. Look what real food's doing to you! Soon you'll be Ultan-sized."

Niles laughed and Nevan thought he'd forgotten how much he loved to hear his brother laugh.

"Well, being with children seems to be shrinking you!"

"No, you're just growing."

"No I'm not!"

"Yes you are. I'll prove it. We'll take a measurement."

"How?"

"Back to back."

"Nah."

"Come on!"

"Oh, alright…"

And waiting for the time of their appointment with the First Court, they talked and talked and filled the courtyard with laughter and old stories until Nevan finally threw his arms around Niles and squeezed the stuffing out of him and thanked him with every word he had in his vocabulary for saving his life on the battlefield that day when the crows had been ready to pick his bones clean.

No matter what, Nevan thought, with Finleigh being the unspoken subtext, and his brother's possible elevation in status and what natural division and separation such would bring being the other, *no matter what I'll always love you and I'll never forget what you did for me that day on the battlefield. I don't belong out there, being a soldier, but you do. And I never knew that until I thought I had breathed my last and you came and saved me like some hero from an epic saga. Ultan didn't save me. You did. And only six bloody teen, too, your first battle. Hopefully it's your last. I know it won't be, but I know what it's like now, and I never want you to know what I felt lying out there, watching the sky go dark at high noon. You're a legend in the making, Ni, but I can't tell you that or your head won't fit through the bloody door when they call your name for the Summons of the First Court. Forgive me for not realizing that a long time ago, for not realizing how differently you see the world, how differently you comprehend life, and how different you are from me. I've always looked down upon you like that, I guess, thinking you're not as smart as I am because you can't remember the names of every common house we've ever raised hell in and every plant we've ever tripped across, or which star pattern sits in which quadrant of the sky at what time and season. I hope I've taught you a lot since we ran away from home, because I had a lot to make up for with dad being the way he was and mom being taken away from us…but, it is you who has taught me something I could never learn on my own. You taught me how to live. Just like you. Without fear.*

Niles heard his name, cleared his throat for no good reason, and began to walk forward. The Chamber of Lords was an arched octangle of oaken wood panels that glowed with a warm amber luminescence and gave each and every voice in the elevated and richly upholstered seats and tables surrounding the common floor a sense of power and dignity.

It was the austere and hallowed ground of the Throne.

But the Throne was gone. And the Crown. And the scepter.

Even the milk white Blade of the Champion.

The old had been abolished, cut down and cleared, and a new thought and idea had already taken root in the ground mulched by rage and ruin.

Niles' quick brown eyes jumped between the faces before seeing Rhoswen rise out of the corner of his eyes, an empty chair next to her.

Wrapped in snug violet and ivory, she was no longer the lioness of the battlefield he would follow straight into the fires of hell with his sword held high, yet the battlefield still slept in the swirl of her gaze.

Tempered by Highborn grace, it would never leave her.

Niles straightened, ignoring the burn of every eye in the prestigious room upon him, and placed his hand on the hilt of the sword that had been given to him *by* her when she had selected him as one of her Chosen back in the forest.

Even though it seemed like a lifetime ago, now.

"Niles Rodgers of Clan Ross of Crefton." She said, and he bowed. He had his summons when organizing work parties of soldiers with Sir Craig for what remained of the coming harvest only weeks away. He'd made good time from the east, though bets had been cast that his dismally muscled stallion wouldn't make it.

And now he was the richer for it.

"My Lady."

A smile nicked at Rhoswen's mouth and she folded her hands demurely before her, as if relishing each and every moment of what was about to unfold.

"When you walked into my camp in the forest, you came with two other precious souls, but had I known what rare gifts you carried with you, I would've taken you under my wing to train you personally that very day."

Niles fought a shiver. His feet were stone in the middle of the inlaid wood floor, its delicate pattern too intricate to see as a thousand thoughts drifted through his head like honeybees attacking the last of the clover.

"Such was only proven by what you did, at just sixteen years of age, in the Battle of Braddack Valley. And," the smile widened, "it is my pleasure, and the will of this Court, to commission you as the First Lord of Halliwick." Rhoswen placed her hands on the table before her, a table upon which parchments were arrayed like food at a wedding feast. "Do you accept the will of the Court?"

Niles did not hesitate.

"I do, your Highness."

Rhoswen sat down, hiding the coloring of her cheeks in a dip of a quill and a quick flourish.

"Well then you must forget *my* old title as well as your own, Lord Niles, as I am Lady Rhoswen of Kathron Caelie, First Regent of the Empire." She set the quill down and clasped her hands. "But you can call me Rhoswen. Your holdings will consist of a manor and thirty acres of hunting land north of the Skyeshire estate and east of the Tavish estate left vacated by the yet to be accounted for Lord Bandon. You will have a staff to assist you in your duties of providing suitable game for the Alban Empire, as well as a small retinue of man at arms to help you in your hunting and defend your lands, should the case arise that you ever have to do so. And...I...er..." Rhoswen's lips wriggled. "I shall advise you in privacy on the matter of noble Ladies and the temperamental disposition of their fathers, now that you are a Lord and are so obviously unmarried, though prudence would dictate that I advise what remains of our noble Ladies in privacy about the temperamental disposition of heroic young warriors that have just become Lords as well."

A small river of laughter bubbled throughout the room.

Rhoswen ran her quill through another flourish.

"Also, due to your actions in the Battle of Braddack Valley you will be henceforth known as Niles the Brave..." Rhoswen set the quill down and leaned forward over her desk. "For there is no greater love to be given from one man to another than to give up your life for your brother, and don't think for a moment I didn't see what happened out there. You should've died a hundred different times and didn't even think about it."

Niles sniffed quietly, fighting the sting in his eyes.

"Don't ever forget what happened in Braddack Valley, Niles the Brave, Lord of Halliwick. Don't forget what *you* did. I will not. This Court will not. And neither will the future sons and daughters of the Alban Empire. Long may heaven favor the truest heart of this Court's intent."

And with that, his judgment was pronounced.

Rhoswen nodded to seal the words in stone, her three-colored eyes studiously following the silhouette of the young man striding with unbroken purpose out into the welcome arms of the cold sunlight.

FINLEIGH

CHAPTER 69

Finleigh squinted away sleep as she combed her hair.
Candlelight flickered across the bleached pages of the miss-matched
parchments Quill had fashioned into rudimentary books. A pang of
sadness squeezed itself through her stomach and she set the comb
down, sighing to flip another page and remark at the detail in which
he had captured Rhoswen's ascendancy from the forest.

And he was gone.

But not forgotten. Never forgotten.

And though she wished to return to that wonderful vision
where she'd seen him so happy and healthy and strong with
Morgance, his sister, she knew she couldn't. She could only hold
onto it, and let it marinate in her soul as she let the story that
Morgance had instructed her to tell write itself.

As of now, Finleigh's pages were blank.

Quill had so many books, and they were strewn across the
room around Finleigh, but most of them were blank inside. Only
the barest details concerned his travels and his time in Aegyptus in
the house of the Caliph, and she now knew why his eyes were so
bloodshot.

He had nearly gone blind.

His journal said so and it broke her heart to read through
his deterioration as it became harder and harder for him to see, and

nearly impossible to read his writing as it rambled and jittered into strings of incoherent scribbles.

And then there were the songs and the poems.

Finleigh could only think he'd written most of them for Morgance, her spirit always a dark cloud above his head till that fateful night at Vault of Dreams. She had been a shadow buried deep within the Four Storms since the shipwreck that killed his parents had given him a choice no one should ever have to make.

Destiny had placed him on the altar of decision and raised the axe, letting the weight of life do the rest. His heart was to see the world, a deep compelling *need* to go out and touch and taste and feel and see, but he so dearly loved his sister.

In the end, the axe had fallen, and it had taken his last breath to bring him back home and make it all right again.

The path of absolution.

Finleigh sighed, still not over his death, even when she should be letting the vision of his spirit lift her up and inspire her to continue the work he had begun.

A knock on the door startled her.

"Yes?"

The door squeaked on its hinges and a shock of blonde hair poked through. Soft brown eyes below a stern brow.

"Can I come in?"

Finleigh hugged herself against the chill of night and smiled, dangling her feet off the edge of the bed.

"Sure."

Niles scratched his ear with a thumb as he entered. The candle he held in a pewter stick had nearly been burnt to the wick, obviously an indication of how long it'd taken him to find her.

"I didn't see you at the summons." He said, softly, staring at her as if he had never seen her before in his life.

"I wasn't summoned."

In the small room at the top of the Tower, the bedroom that'd belonged to Morgance and her sickening spell of melancholia, Finleigh looked different.

Older.

Finleigh knew Niles was running those brown eyes up and down her and let him.

She was barefoot, a sleeveless dress of pearlescent white making her coffee-colored skin and jet black hair look exotic and timeless under the steady flicker of amber candlelight.

"You look beautiful." Niles said, and Finleigh studied his face.

No flecks of red colored his cheeks, and his hands stayed stone still, one around the candlestick, the other steady on the hilt of his sword.

He wasn't embarrassed to tell her how he felt, or what he thought. Confidence oozed from his shoulders, sewn into the satin fabric of his new cloak.

"Can't say the same for you." She smiled, her dark eyes sparkling.

"Good." Niles scoffed and walked around the room, lifting his candle and peering as if searching for the fingernail marks of a madwoman, a prisoner. Or mystic symbols etched into the stones. "I can't afford to look beautiful. I've gotta be tough, you know."

"I heard." Finleigh smiled, feeling a bit embarrassed for no good reason.

Other than Niles was a Lord now. A real one.

And she, well, she hadn't been summoned. Commissioned by the spirits of the dead? Yes, and Rhoswen knew she would continue Quill's work, but she hadn't been involved in all the pageantry.

Left alone in the Tower.

And Finleigh, cast out from her blood to find a home amongst whoever would have her, loved the eye of the storm just as much as Niles. She dreamed about it, as if it would one day come and sweep her off her feet.

Finleigh twisted the hem of her dress in her hand, letting her legs dangle on the edge of the bed. The very bed where Morgance had slept and dreamed the dreams that'd driven her mad.

"Well..." Niles cleared his throat, determining the space was free of specters, even though, if there were such a thing, Finleigh would be the only one who could see them and the sword at his waist wouldn't do much good, though he'd be quick to draw it in Finleigh's honor. "If you heard then you'll know I'll be leaving tonight. There's a lot to do. The place's been abandoned for a season…and winter hunting is hard, but it's good."

"I would love to visit you." Finleigh said, letting the heat of her smile linger across his face.

Niles said nothing and stared at the books.

"Quill's?" She nodded, and he said, "I admire you for continuing his work. I'm going to miss the old man. He never did finish that one story about the España gypsy and the rogue who became a Lord."

Finleigh laughed, her shoulders bunching as her chin tipped back. Niles smiled a broad and charming grimace, shaking his head at his own humor.

"Oh Niles…"

"Forgive my being blunt, Fins." His smile wended its way toward a sigh, like a lost dog working its way home in the night. "But I'm going to miss you, you know. It seems whenever I catch a glimpse of you…just a glimpse, it's like tasting just a tiny drop of wine on my tongue."

Finleigh cocked her head and squinted.

"What do you mean?"

Mystery spread itself in the form of a grin across Niles' face.

"Goodnight, Miss Finleigh De La Cruz of Baraburr."

A frown fell across the sixteen year-old's features, her thoughts stolen by a flourish of blue satin, the last image, burned into her mind before the door croaked shut, that of two swords locked in a duel over an angular shield. Her starry black gaze drifted around the room, *Morgance'* room, the room no one would take, the place where she told Rhoswen she would write the story that would tell itself. But a butterfly was alive in her stomach, dancing through the still chill of the night.

Finleigh gathered her skirts and ran.

She spotted him on the causeway looping around the Fortress, his athletic form and stretched stride a swaggering silhouette under Luna's watchful gaze.

Her bare feet slapped cold stones as she ran, stinging with frozen fire.

She didn't care.

The sound of pearlescent fabric rustling through the empty night stopped the man in his tracks, and he became a statue in the hush as she drew near.

She couldn't read the expression written across his face when he turned to her and she didn't care.

She threw her arms around his neck and pulled her lips to his, kissing him.

And with her kiss, she told him she understood what he'd said.

For to Niles Rodgers, just sixteen and a newly minted Lord with heaven and earth stretching their arms before him, the very thought of her was like a drop of wine on his tongue, and to let himself fall in love with her would be like indulging in wine, slipping his soul into a drunken sea of sweet excess.

Niles licked dry lips as they parted.

She did owe him that kiss from wrestling the Larlaith.

"You didn't forget." He said, his smile faint.

"How could I?" Finleigh slipped her arms around his back and sighed as he wrapped the extra folds of his fabric around her to save her from shivers. "You said crows should pick your bones clean if a kiss from a pretty girl would ever fail to make you a hero." She nicked her chin up his chest to steal a crooked smirk. "And now you're a *Lord*."

His laugh was more of a sneeze and made her smile broader, her dark eyes capturing all the starlight in the sky.

"What are you saying?"

"I'm saying I earned some of that glory too." Niles scoffed and Finleigh pushed herself from him. "You don't mean wanting to kiss Rhoswen made you a hero! Oh no, you can't deny it now! You did everything for *me*. You're so conniving and sly. All those wins in the Circle, with me sitting there watching. Just the very thought of me and how much I like the dashing princes of Quill's sagas, well, you planned your every move from the moment we met, pretending not to like me. Every slash of the sword, every thrust of the spear. Even down to sitting yourself atop that ridiculously skinny horse to look stronger by comparison. Yes, it was all planned and I take the credit because I made you face the Larlaith and I made you wait for the kiss that I promised would come of it."

Niles squeezed her close, a lovely heat burning within.

"If only it were so simple, Fins."

Silence drifted through their ears, cut by the thump of their hearts.

"Why can't it be?" She nearly whispered.

And when the silence begged again for another kiss, he stared down at her slight and pearlescent form and the glitter alive in her eyes.

He had no answer for her.

And so he kissed her and tried to think of one.

And when no answer came he kissed her again and wondered how in the hell his waiflike horse was going to be able to haul *all* of Quill's books that rough two-day ride over to Halliwick when he'd nearly killed the horse just to answer the Summons.

But Finleigh was not thinking any more of Quill's books and the tremendous pressure she felt to finish them.

No, she was thinking of her last day in Rhoswen's forest, when a big blue-winged butterfly had drifted into her hands on a cool breeze and divined her future.

That day she had let the butterfly go, sadly watching as it took off and flew its own meandering course on the wings of the wind, trusting Destiny to make it all right again.

It was that butterfly that'd pulled her out of the heartache of being a castoff amongst her own people, and that butterfly that had come back to her after a battle that'd claimed tens of thousands.

"Finleigh?" Niles asked as their embrace wove its way through them. His voice softened and she nodded expectantly.

"We're going to liberate the south in the spring, I know it. Rhoswen's going to raise the greatest army this land has ever seen and I'm going to be proudly by her side."

Finleigh's glow began to dim just to think about him leaving again, though she knew he was right.

Soon, she would be alone again.

"But when we get to Brachin," Niles promised, "I'm going to see if the bloody Larlaith is still there and thank it from the bottom of my heart for giving me the second best day of my life."

The young gypsy smirked at him.

"*Second* best? Well then what's the best?"

Niles' eyes winked a roguish gleam.

"Ask me tomorrow."

AERLYN

CHAPTER 70

The reedy roll of pipes droned down throughout the glen, whistles of tin weaving in between thumps of drums, strums of lutes and thrums of mandolins.

It was harvest.

And as First Regent, Rhoswen made sure no stomach would leave Ullraye empty, and no mind would ever forget the day a new nation celebrated its birth with some strange mixture of fist-in-the-sky triumph and head-bowing gratitude, relief and rest and relaxation as sweet as fireweed honey on the tongue and as fulfilling as smoked salmon in the belly.

Rhowsen milled about the party, its living tapestry of flesh and blood woven from the broken spirits of her redeemed kin. Mirth glittered the brooms and heathers of the hidden glen of *Hafnröth* all the way up to the thick arms of Ullraye, where the stoic Tower didn't look so hideous anymore as pennants and ribbons dazzled from its heights under the last wheeze of the summer sun.

She walked amongst her people as their peer, and old women who remembered her father's reign would stop her, clasp her three-fingered hand, and bow repeatedly, with as much grace and dignity as their weak and weary frames would allow. Tears of joy streaked their faces to know they would be able to die in peace, because *restoration* had finally come to a once-beautiful land.

Cursed. Ravaged. Raided. Ruined.

Redeemed.

By Rhoswen, Rhoswen the Resurrected, and every single brave soul who had given their life, either in a heated moment of painful glory, or in the dark and bitter agony of silence, in the bowels of a prison cell, failing to relinquish the hope that had kept so many dreams alive.

To let that dream of freedom burn bright and hot through the nightmare, hoping that hope itself would someday still the storm.

Believing the day would come.

Rhoswen, arrayed in her richest violets, her dark curls unbound and fluffed by the sea breeze, passed the champion of her heart a sly wink as she walked close enough for him to smell the beguiling fragrance of lavender on her skin, and the Lord of Skyeshire returned her gesture with the heat of his green-eyed gaze, which she held, silently, until her form disappeared in a blur of sunlight and silk.

Secrets slept within that gaze, precious words of love and longing reserved for the perfect hush of the deepest night, as Luna spun its silver threads across Loch Darvin and the strong shadows of Skyeshire castle.

Lord Ultan of Skyeshire, Supreme Commander of the Alban Army, stood tall next to similarly black and gold-clad Eyvind Frey, King of Nørd, and his retinue near the roasting pits as they oversaw cookery of the meats like a highly strategized military operation, no doubt a precursor to the coming campaign to free the border towns of the south.

Sticks of whole squab and lamb shank stuffed with pears and walnuts, studded with cloves of garlic and sprigs of rosemary crisped over seas of angry coals. Whole pheasants and venison loins glazed with mop upon mop of sticky blackberry jam and red vinegar sizzled and dripped as men sharpened the carving knives.

Many of the unmarried men entertained themselves with games of strength and contests of balance, dexterity, and skill, though the good nature of sport and the freedom of the mead barrels loosened many a tongue, sabotaging the spirit of competition with riotous shocks of laughter and playful bouts of grappling, upon which bets were instantly set, only inciting further games of dice and cards.

Finleigh danced barefoot amongst the finest and fairest highlanders to the blazing melodies of days gone by, her own eclectic series of steps and twirls mixed and mingled with the fiery braids and colorful kilts of her adopted sisterhood. She was a rare jewel set in a crown of heavenly hues, Solara dimming in midday when the flash of her teeth flushed the most chiseled of young men's cheeks, and she traded off arm and arm with each and every eligible bachelor along the *Dance of the Sea-Wheels* until Niles looped his arm in hers and refused to let her go, till they danced off down the sloping field where Nørds had once been slain, picked pale yellow flowers and chased each other into a thinning forest of lazy green sunlight and feathery shadows.

Down in the moss-green sheath of the hidden glen, Nevan was telling stories to a host of children, berry-stained cheeks, wild curls and wide eyes spread around him like some small amphitheater, peppering his tales with the freshly-squeezed embellishment of whatever came to him in the moment. He reimagined Quill's sagas of heroes and dragons and castles and magics with his own taste of war and his many colorful exploits throughout the south, uglying the villains with comically gross faces, gnarled voices, and gimpy gaits to a chorus of laughter, wending his way through character after character as if each word gave him new life and he lost himself somewhere in the beginning and the ending of each tale.

But Aerlyn O'Rye, The Thistle of High Inverloch, *the hand without shadow in a land without sun*, partook of none of the harvest festivities, nor the celebration of the birth of a nation.

For she was on a mission.

And having selected the finest green apple she could get her lithe and nimble hands on without anyone noticing, Aerlyn faded away from the bubble and squeak of the crowd to the near silence of *Hafnröth* and its bleached white stones, where Morgance and Quill had been buried, side by side, and there, she dug a small hole with the sleek new dagger she'd been given, and planted the seeds of that beautifully crisp and sour apple and told them to grow.

And in leaving Vault of Dreams, Aerlyn walked north and west of the mound and the hidden glen to the rambling mess of grassy dunes that ran along the highshore of the Greener Sea to the small and rugged estate and holdings of the Master Archer. There, waiting for her by the gate, sitting atop the gorgeous Eemkje, she was equal measure grace and strength. The Master Archer's long blonde hair, plaited in a rope braid that lined her head like a crown, was a striking image in a tunic and breeches of white and gold with tawny sea-faring boots to the knee. A cape of scarlet stitched with the petals of roses in bloom was clasped about her shoulders with a hammered pewter broach of thorny roses, and her bow of elk antlers was safely strapped on Eemkje's back with her steel-tipped bodkin arrows and dozens of other leather pouches and fabric satchels.

Beside the Master Archer, a sorrel mare had been equally prepared, and Aerlyn wrapped and bound her plain brown thief's cloak around her thin body and kicked herself up in the saddle, her own clothing comfortable threads of black and gray, her soft boots silent on the grass.

"Ready?" The Master Archer asked, and Aerlyn only nodded, her alabaster skin shaded from the sun in the hood of her heavy cloak, the very same dull and drab mud-colored cloak that made her nothing more than a whisper in the night, a wicked barb in the neck of every Angle Baron from here to Kirkcade and Benyllyn and back as their riches dwindled and disappeared like the bejeweled colors of the dawn falling to the sad spell of gray morning clouds and fat drops of rain.

"You know…" Aerlyn said, her rough voice gravel in her throat as they trotted along the rocky path of the highshore, the foamy sea a gentle swoosh miles below the cliff face. "If we're going to be working together I should at least know your name."

"Why? You don't want to call me Master?"

"Not unless you want to call me Thistle."

The Master Archer only laughed, her vivid blue eyes looking, for just that one moment that Aerlyn stole a glance at them, a bit like her second-cousin Quill.

"Fair enough." The warrior said, and they talked and talked and talked, till they reached a small and sleepy fishing village where Aerlyn's riches in reward for her secret service to the Throne of Albanland and her pledge of future service awaited in the form of a swift two-masted clipper littered with the best of Rhoswen's Bowgirls. Ready to take them all to Eire as emissaries of a dark and sordid new source of employment, the ship held every promise of being a terror to tyranny and a scourge to slavery as long as The Thistle drew breath.

For The Thistle, once stolen from her home and abandoned to the howling duel of the Four Storms and the depths of despair and darkness on the bleakest edge of a black horizon, was finally returning to the sea that had once whispered a perfect promise to a little red-haired girl who had then dreamed a dream that would not die. That ache in her heart, stretching across her skin as her body grew and that golden dream took root, had offered her a world of opportunity if she would only step out from that ramshackle hut her family called a home and dive into the raging cauldron of Destiny, wherein slept the divine hues of every beauty, and the ugly scars of every pain.

And now, having been melted by that which tempered her heart into such a hard and brittle vessel, Aerlyn would use the embers of Quill's affection to fuel her fires, as they burned deep down within, and whipped her eyes of midnight and her ghostly shape straight into the heart of the Four Storms and the frothing rage of the sea, to seek and save the lost, to steal back the stolen, the homeless, the abused, the wayfaring, the wanderers, the slaves, the forgotten sisters and daughters of a ruined nation.

To hunt the horizon the world over to find the Thistles, that they may, some day, hopefully, become Roses.

ACKNOWLEDGEMENTS
AND THANKS

VoD is in no way a piece of historical fiction, merely a piece of entertainment, but most of it was written while watching Neil Oliver's *A History of Scotland*. Before I knew it, staring at the breathtaking scenery and hearing the true stories of such a mysterious and beautiful land found its way into my own dreams. I highly recommend the series if you want to know the incredible narrative of this special land and its people, or even just to see how poorly I described its truly fantastical landscape.

Rena Hoberman, I couldn't dream up a better cover. You are a true artist. I always judge a book by its cover and thank you for making every reader's first impression of VoD that of magic, mystery, and adventure.

Four albums were essential to the creation of VoD, those being Evanescence *The Open Door* (2006), Flyleaf *Beyond The Stars* (2014), and Trivium *Silence in the Snow* (2015). Everything that is Ultan is found in *Silence*, Aerlyn refused to come out of the shadows unless the angelic Amy Lee was singing, and it seemed Flyleaf fit everybody and everything else perfectly and "Set Me On Fire" as a writer. I've never had music be such an integral part of the writing process, and I am so thankful to have each of your perfect albums be *my* soundtrack for VoD. And of course, my favorite album of all time, Trivium *Shogun* (2007) was there for me like an old friend when conceptualizing, researching, and editing. Thank you all for the heartbeat, the thunder, the lightning, the dissonance, the harmonies, the sounds, and the stories for this adventure.

My family. I wouldn't be writing if it wasn't for you and may your eternal reward be rich for the blessings of this journey and your different parts in it. Thank you for loving me and listening to me go on and on and on. Thank you for being patient with the mathematical equation (idea) + computer + *time* = book. I love you very much and am so blessed to have seen this through with all of you.

Hannah, the poet responsible for Quill's song and poem. Thank you for being a shining golden thread woven in this beautiful tapestry. Thank you for watering such deep roots.

True gratitude goes out to certain distinguished members of the Goodreads community for all for your generous support, kind comments, thoughtful reviews, and unique perspectives. Thank you for encouraging me to bring this story to light. I so hope you have enjoyed this labor of love! Katerina, thank you for telling me I should write YA fantasy. I won't ever be the same now. Thank you for Rhoswen's eyes! Chelsea, mijn vriend, the teacher, thank you for being my friend and for letting me be yours. I can't thank you enough! Victoria, The Captain, my fearless guide throughout the endless sea of TBR. Vashe zdorov'e! Amber, let your light shine! Mia, may the sun shine on you! Christina, thank you for our talks and for finding those typos! Nastassja, Becky, Viktoria, Lashaan and Trang, Vera, Kainat, Steysha, Celine, Jasmine, Ash, Choko, Aubrey, Lonna, Kim, Kelley, Savannah, Amanda, Jackie, Lindsey Lynn, Alyssa, Laura, Christina, Bea, Anna Soliveres, Chenda, Cindy, Max, Gabby, Lexie…all of you have been there eagerly supporting me and this novel, full of kind words. Thank you so much. I hope you love it!

Julie Eshbaugh, for reaching out to me and blessing me with your friendship, your time and wisdom, and your incomparable masterpiece *Ivory and Bone*.

Rose Reid, for being a sister in arms and letting me be a part of your awesome debut *Crown of Crimson*, and its magnificent sequel, for spurring me on and writing with me and sharing the joy of this journey.

And finally, God and Jesus Christ, for the gracious gifts of life, love, forgiveness, and the breath in my lungs. Thank you for giving me the dream to write, and the faithfulness to see it through. All things work together!

Thank *you* for reading, and if you have a story to tell, then let the dream grow and the words will soon follow.

59136243R00270

Made in the USA
Charleston, SC
27 July 2016